Mila's Rescue

(Rotari Warriors Book 4)

Crystaverse Chronicles

Amanda LaBrooy

This is a work of fiction. Names, characters, businesses, places, events, locales, and incidents are either the products of the author's imagination or used in a fictitious manner. Any resemblance to actual persons, living or dead, or actual events is purely coincidental.

First Published 2026

ISBN: 978-0-6486346-9-0 (paperback)

ISBN: 978-1-7645362-0-2 (ebook)

MILA'S RESCUE (ROTARI WARRIORS BOOK 4)

First edition. March 2, 2026.

ISBN: 978-0648634690

Written by Amanda LaBrooy.

DEDICATION

To the characters who keep hijacking the plot.
And to the readers who think I'm in control.
Bless you all and thank you.

Amanda LaBrooy

Books in the Crystaverse Chronicles Series

Shadows Before the Flame (a short prequel)

Rorkk's Captive (Rotari Warriors Book 1)

Dane's Fugitive (Rotari Warriors Book 2)

Kei's Guardian and the Crystal Heist (Rotari Warriors Book 3)

Mila's Rescue (Rotari Warriors Book 4)

Alex's Salvation (Rotari Warriors Book 5)

CHAPTER 1

A wave of oppressive heat slammed into Mila as the ship's hatch hissed open, thrusting her instantly back into nightmares she'd fought to forget. Her stomach clenched into a tight knot, and her pulse pounded in her ears. Was she back on Krylan? She had barely escaped that hell once. Would she be forced to face punishment for daring to break free?

A hard shove between Mila's shoulder blades brought her back to the present. Loathing didn't begin to describe the beings who held her and her pilot, Rhen, prisoner after hijacking their ship two days ago.

Mila hesitated at the main hatch, and a familiar pressure urged her toward the rainforest just metres away. The shifting shadows at the canopy's edge suggested midday, though the thick cloud cover made certainty impossible.

Mila raised an eyebrow slightly, her eyes searching Rhen's with a question she dared not voice aloud. A faint shake of his head conveyed all she needed to know. He had no idea where they were, either. The landscape around them was alien, the flora unfamiliar.

Relief flooded Mila when she realised this wasn't Krylan, but it quickly dissolved into fresh anxiety. If this wasn't Krylan, then where were they? And more importantly, who had abducted them and why?

Despite her repeated attempts to communicate using Galactic Standard, their abductors remained stoically silent. Mila didn't need her extensive exobiology knowledge or medical degree to deduce they'd understood her perfectly well when it suited them.

In the stifling heat of the clearing, Mila and Rhen stood waiting under the unyielding gaze of a helmeted guard, while the other two moved away to conduct a heated discussion. Finally, some accord must have been reached because they saluted each other.

Mila braced herself as the helmets folded away with a hiss. The faces beneath were unmistakable. Ash-grey skin, thick and faintly ridged, caught the light like worn stone. Pale, slit-pupiled eyes swept the clearing, reflective and cold, weighing everything as though it were a threat. Heavy brow ridges threw their gaze into shadow, and when the nearest one's mouth twitched, she caught a glimpse of narrow, pointed teeth. Scars cut pale lines across their angular faces, making them appear even more menacing.

She cut a look at Rhen. "Zoldacks," she whispered. "Bottom-feeding skum." The shock in his eyes was a perfect mirror of her own. Mila quickly quelled the urge to run. But where would she run to? The only visible sign that someone had been here before was a dirt track into the rainforest. The last two years of living in the colder climate of Rotari meant she was no longer acclimatised to heat and humidity. And these Zoldacks looked fit. Very fit.

The sound of a ship landing snagged her attention. She breathed a sigh of relief when she recognised the Halo Insurgent III. At least the Zoldacks hadn't ditched their ship after the hijack and transfer.

How quickly Mila's fortunes had turned. Just two days ago, she'd been riding high, basking in praise from her speech at the Federation of Fair-Trade Conference and savouring glowing reviews. Next, every system shut down, and they were boarded, taken prisoner and transferred to another ship. She still had no idea why they had been targeted, but at least she'd gained one more piece of the puzzle.

Representing the Rotari President at the conference, she had condemned the Galactic Trading Academy (GTA) for its ruthless pursuit of economic dominance. Controlling most of the quadrant's trade meant controlling its people. And the GTA wasn't the only player. Its direct competitor, the League of Universal Trade (LOUT), was even worse, operating with fewer scruples. Both organisations exploited the less developed planets for profit. So, she couldn't rule out their involvement. While her current home planet of Rotari kept both organisations at arm's length, perhaps this was a play to change that. Or, the Krylans still had a bounty on her head, and the Zoldacks hadn't got the memo that the war was over.

A jab between her shoulder blades nudged her onto the trail in front of Rhen. Without glancing up, she put one foot in front of the other. Luckily, she'd traded her flashy heels for more comfortable walking shoes before their capture; otherwise, she would have been in trouble on the rough, damp ground.

After a few minutes, she found her stride. The trail had a certain peaceful ambience. The only sounds to be heard were the dead branches and leaf matter snapping underfoot and the occasional flutter and raucous bird call in the canopy above.

Small plants and a carpet of dead leaves littered the ground, indicating this wasn't a well-worn trail. She inwardly groaned as they came upon yet another fallen tree. As with the previous logs, a gloved hand gripped her upper arm, hauled her over, then released her. Mila's hands were riddled with splinters as she grasped the rough bark, desperately trying to slow her descent. She rubbed her stinging hands against her trousers in an unconscious but futile gesture, given it would take a jackhammer and a crowbar to dig out the splinters. She cursed as she hoisted herself upright, whacked the excess mud from her trousers and pushed her long brown hair out of her green eyes before being hauled forward. With a muttered curse, she wished she'd spent more time in the gym than in her laboratory. But that's what it took to be a leading scientist and medical geneticist. Her profession relied on mental stamina and not on building muscle.

Trailing behind her, Rhen had not been as lucky. With his hands tied behind his back, every climb and scramble became a negotiation with gravity, but his agility and stamina still caught her off guard. They should not have. He was tall, athletic, and not yet thirty, a full ten years her junior, and he carried the same quiet competence that seemed to run through the men in his family, technical wizards, every one of them. His sapphire-blue gaze was steady, his blond curls damp with sweat, and the sharp lines of his prominent cheekbones, aquiline nose, and chiselled jaw gave him a hard-edged handsomeness.

A sudden thud and a pained grunt made Mila spin around, her breath catching sharply at the sight of Rhen lying motionless on the ground. She dropped to her knees beside him, carefully rolling him onto his back. A lump the size of an egg was already forming on his forehead. He was out cold, but she exhaled in relief when she felt the steady beat of his pulse beneath her fingers. "He needs medical attention!" she cried, her voice pleading to an indifferent audience.

The Zoldacks grew agitated with the delay and nudged Rhen's unresponsive body with their weapons. Prompting the group leader to break his silence and speak to her in Galactic Standard. "Leave him. You are the one we are being paid to deliver."

"We can't leave him here," she cried, her voice edged with desperation. But before she could resist, a rough hand jerked her upright and forcefully dragged her away.

The track grew rougher, tangled with massive roots that snaked across the rainforest floor, slowing their progress. Scattered in their path were fresh droppings. Enormous mounds that hinted ominously at the size of the creatures lurking unseen within the dense foliage. She shivered at the thought of Rhen, vulnerable and defenceless.

After an hour of relentless walking, she paused briefly when the dense wall of trees finally began to thin, revealing mountains rising in the distance like slumbering giants.

"Keep going. We are nearly there," snapped one of the Zoldacks.

"I'm sure whoever's paying you wants me alive," she replied, her voice trembling with defiance. Her mind raced with possibilities. They said, paid to deliver, not paid to kill, which meant someone had put a price on her head, with a set of instructions that included delivery. The Zoldacks were only the middlemen. It appeared that the buyer had resources, reach, and patience. She replayed the leader's sentence, measuring every syllable for what it had accidentally given away. You are the one, not you are one of them. Not a hostage of convenience. A target. And Rhen. If they could abandon him without consequence, then he was not part of the contract, making him disposable. Her throat tightened as she forced herself to breathe through the panic, to think like a survivor, not a victim.

She lifted her chin, letting them see fear if it bought her seconds, letting them hear defiance if it bought her space. Whoever was paying wanted her alive. That was her one advantage.

Tired and thirsty, she let out a sigh of relief when they finally halted. Right now, she wanted water more than anything and the opportunity to remove her shoes to give her blistered feet the relief they demanded. As a breeze rippled over her damp shirt, she stretched her arms above her head. It was a relief after the stifling rainforest. At the sound of trickling water, Mila's parched throat tried to swallow. Not willing to suffer any longer, she demanded, "I need water." Several grumbles later, she was herded to the stream. Kneeling on the soft grass, she hungrily scooped up as much water as her hands would allow.

With her thirst quenched, her mind returned to Rhen. Scanning the horizon, her eyes traced the mountains in the distance before dipping to the vast valley below, where cropped fields surrounded a walled settlement with cylindrical dwellings. At least it didn't look like a military garrison. Perhaps, people who grew things weren't all bad?

Her thoughts barely had time to form before a hand clamped around her bicep, yanking her abruptly back to the waiting area. While the Zoldacks paced, Mila collapsed on the soft grass, unable to discern anything from her captors' closed expressions. Were they waiting for someone or something? Mila was usually good at reading what wasn't said, but she came up empty just when her life depended on it. Rolling her stiff shoulders, she wished mind-reading were one of her talents. Looking down, she had unconsciously plucked every reachable blade of grass.

As the sun lowered towards the horizon, a group of men strode into the clearing, carrying large crates, their lively banter starkly contrasting the Zoldacks' quiet solidarity. For the first time today, her captors were animated and alert. And while their weapons weren't pointed at the approaching men, they were subtly placed at the ready.

One of the men pinged her with a quick glance before approaching the Zoldacks to start what sounded like a heated negotiation process. And while they were using Galactic Standard, she was too far away to pick out more than a few words. She took in their pale green skin first, the colour so unfamiliar it surprised her. Then her gaze dropped to their homespun tunics and trousers, searching for some clue to who they were, but she came up empty. After a loud, lively exchange, an agreement was reached quickly. The Zoldacks took possession of the crated booty and disappeared down the trail without a backward glance.

If she read the signals correctly, she'd just been bartered. Why? Hopefully, she was about to find out. She'd noticed a few things in the last few minutes. It was clear who the leader was. He confidently directed others in the group, and his aqua stare oozed authority. She'd also noticed that he continually and unapologetically interrupted the Zoldacks during the negotiation process. And if anyone in his group made a statement, they deferred to him for approval. He exhibited no nervousness or wasted movement. In fact, every action was calculated and measured.

With the negotiations finally over, he strode toward her, and she hated that she couldn't tear her eyes away. It was as if the very forces of nature bent around him, clearing a path, bowing to his will. Authority clung to him like a second skin, radiating from every controlled movement. From the hard line of his chiselled jaw to the leashed power in his stride, he exuded that quiet, unshakable strength everyone seemed so eager to obey. Let them. He could command the whole damned universe for all she cared, but not her.

Now, standing directly before her, he extended a hand in silent invitation. She ignored it, snapping her gaze to his eyes instead.

He bowed slightly and waited for her to grasp his outstretched palm. "Doctor Doray, my name is Brom. It's a pleasure to finally meet you."

Mila ignored his gesture and pushed to her feet, brushing grass from her clothes in short, angry swipes. "Is that right?" she shot back. She slashed a hand toward the trail. "My pilot is injured and was left behind. We're going back for him. Now!"

Brom shook his head. "I'm sorry, but that's impossible. I apologise for bringing you here under these circumstances, but I need your counsel on a most important matter."

Her eyes narrowed. "Excuse me? Are you saying that our abduction was at your behest? Why didn't you ask for help?"

"The Rotari Government refused my request." His jaw tightened, and he crossed his arms. "I had no choice." Brom had used a purpose-built dead-drop beacon that was small, ugly, and expensive, designed to sleep in the dirt until a very specific signal passed overhead. He had used it once, timed to the Zoldacks' corridor cycle, and the message had made it to Rotari space. The answer had come back cold, not because the device failed, but because Rotari leadership wanted nothing to do with his war. So he kept it. When Mila became the leverage he could not ignore, Brom used the same beacon again, not to beg Rotari, but to hire the only people who could cross that perimeter cleanly. The moment the Zoldacks opened their corridor, the beacon heard their authentication tone, woke, dumped its packet, and died again. One message out, no channel left open for LOUT to trace. It was designed with a hard limit. Two bursts, then a self-termination routine. The moment that second packet left the planet, the beacon killed itself by design.

"Your so-called 'no choice' option may have cost my friend Rhen his life," Mila snapped. She jabbed her finger hard into Brom's chest. "You need to fix this. Now!"

Brom shrugged. "You need refreshment," he said, motioning for her to follow. "This way."

"No," she said, her chin held high, staring unflinchingly into his eyes with a courage and determination that could not be denied.

"As I said before, Doctor, it is impossible." He pointed to the settlement below. "We must return to Gromwell before the sun sets because snarks hunt at night."

"I refuse to leave without Rhen." She drew a deep breath, crossed her arms and stood her ground. "This is your fault, and you will fix it. And I am not going anywhere until you do."

Brom dragged a hand through his shoulder-length dark hair. "Look, even if I wanted to, I can't risk the lives of my men."

"So Rhen is collateral damage?" She planted her hands on her hips. "What sort of man are you?"

"For your information, I consider every life sacred. I'm sorry about your friend. I will send a search party at first light. Rest assured, there are several hunting lodges along the trail."

"He was unconscious with his hands tied behind his back." Although more angry words hovered on her tongue, she knew they wouldn't make a difference. This man wasn't going to budge. And until she knew more about the situation, she'd watch and wait. She closed her eyes and silently prayed that Rhen would awaken and find shelter.

"We must leave now. We're running out of daylight." Brom waited while she flicked an anxious glance back at the trail before bobbing her head in agreement.

CHAPTER 2

Arriving in Gromwell, ozone permeated the air and thunder and lightning illuminated the sky in a brilliant display. Brom scanned the settlement with pride as his team peeled away with quick farewells. Some might say it resembled a ship graveyard, but to his people, it was home.

Although he felt remorseful, at least the doctor wasn't harmed. And she wasn't bad on the eyes either. That bronzed skin was not so different from theirs, just a little more earthy. But right now, she looked exhausted. He should have given the Zoldacks more detailed instructions about their passengers' welfare, which they might or might not have followed. And while he felt guilty about leaving Rhen behind, he'd bet his last credit that Mila was planning to escape at the first opportunity, no matter how tired she was. "I know what you're thinking," he said as they strode past rows of old spaceships, now permanent dwellings. "I don't want your death on my conscience. The snarks will eat you alive."

Her eyes widened.

He realised his mistake immediately, especially with Rhen still out there. "The Zoldacks gave me new start-up codes for your ship," he added quickly. "Without them, you're not going anywhere."

"Wow," Mila said. "So you've got codes." She blinked, unimpressed. "Let me know when you have a pilot, because last I checked, he's tied up in the rainforest." Her smile didn't reach her eyes. "Where are you taking me?"

He stopped and flicked a hand toward a battered old spaceship squatting in front of them. "Home," he replied.

Mila raised an eyebrow.

He knew a furious woman when he saw one, and this one was a powder keg with the fuse already lit. He urged her up the stairs and into his battle-scarred abode. Glancing at the sky, he noted the bruised clouds piling on the horizon; tonight's storm would be fierce, but typical for this time of year.

Once he laid out his people's plight, Brom was sure he could convince Mila, and through her, the people of Rotari to help them. Their survival hinged on it, and he was counting on her. Counting on her far too damn much, but what choice did he have? He stifled a groan. The moment he'd heard a recording of her speech at the conference, he'd thought she was the answer to his prayers. He just hoped the universe agreed.

Sometimes, he made the mistake of expecting people to blindly follow his lead without explanation. He put it down to his time in the monastery, where questions and explanations were discouraged. And that hadn't bothered him. In fact, he missed the peace and quiet, which he didn't get while running this agricultural settlement.

The monastery shamans advocated that true peace and wisdom could only be achieved in quiet places. And until recently, he'd lived by that creed.

When his father handed him over to the monastery at eighteen, he'd thought he was being punished, so he ran away to Blackwell, a town known for its lawlessness and gritty streets, until his father found him a month later, worse for wear.

But in the long run, his father had been right. Monastery life suited him. And while he wasn't one to display his emotions, it didn't mean he didn't care deeply; it just meant he didn't spend time talking about his feelings. He was just single-minded and goal-oriented. None of his failings had been an issue until he'd been obligated to rejoin mainstream society and take over from his father.

Darkness had fallen, and the air was thick and charged, as if the sky was holding its breath. The first gusts pushed through the settlement like a warning, bending canvas, rattling sheet metal, sending grit skittering across the walkways. They arrived at his dwelling just as the storm broke. Rain came down in hard, snapping sheets, drumming on the structure, while thunder rolled so deep it felt embedded in the ground.

He followed Mila inside.

She paused at the threshold and silently examined his home.

He had to admit that, although it was sparse, it was functional and clean.

She dropped into a chair at his scarred table while Brom busied himself in the galley, reheating a batch of vegetable pastries delivered by the baker. A rich, savoury aroma soon filled the small space. When he set the steaming plate down between them, Mila was already reaching. She snatched up a pastry and bit into it, large and unrestrained, hunger sharpening every movement.

"They fed us very little," she said.

Her anger clearly simmered below the surface as she consumed another pastry in silence, which was fine by him.

Finished, she dusted the crumbs from her hands and then winced. "Damn, I forgot about the splinters."

Just then, an ear-splitting explosion rocked the dwelling and shattered kitchenware, which imploded upon impact with the metal floor. The lights flickered once, then died, plunging them into darkness. There was no time to think before another explosion shook the dwelling. At least everything that had fallen earlier was already on the floor.

Then came the screams, sharp, human, and close. Brom sprang from his chair, cursing as he stumbled over the scattered debris.

Seconds later, light flared from the small device in his palm, carving a narrow path through the dark. "I have to go. Stay here.

And remember what I said about the snarks." Brom yanked the hatch open and plunged into the wet, howling night, the light vanishing with him.

Moments later, footsteps pounded behind him. A quick glance confirmed that Mila had ignored his warning and slipped into the drenched crowd surging toward the towering fireball.

Reaching the site, the unmistakable sound of chaos surrounded him. Flames enshrouded much of the damage, which would only be revealed by daylight.

Witnesses reported that an explosion had preceded the ignition of the settlement's small methane gas plant, which processed food waste. This had been one of Brom's more recent innovations. Unfortunately, it was highly volatile if something went awry. But the question was, what had gone wrong?

Faces beaded with sweat worked feverishly to close the valves linking the gas pipes to the tanks. Satisfied the shutdown was under control, Brom dropped to his knees beside a prone man sprawled on the ground. Blood pooled beneath his shoulder and threaded in dark streaks across his chest.

Mila knelt opposite. She ran a quick, practised assessment, two fingers at his neck, eyes tracking the pattern of wounds, the slackness of his limbs. Then she looked up at Brom and gave a small, grim shake of her head. "Primary blast injury," she said."The shockwave likely caused massive internal damage." Mila's gaze swept the wreckage. "How many more are there?"

"I don't know, but I hope Maldron was the only casualty."

She rose to get a better view of the carnage.

With the fire reduced to a faint, smoking glow, shadows clung to the edges of the scene. Brom wiped his wet, sooty face and closed his eyes to pray over the body. When he felt Mila's gaze on him, he opened them again. Time seemed to stall in the silence as their eyes met, a brief, wordless acknowledgment of the cost still to come.

Breaking eye contact, Mila asked, "What happened, Brom? Was it a plant malfunction, or did you short-change the Zoldacks?"

"Neither. Our situation is a lot more serious, and the reason I brought you here."

"You still owe me an explanation."

He nodded.

With the rain reduced to a spit and several tripod lights in place, the extensive, targeted damage was evident. Someone had hit them where it hurt, sending a strong message.

Brom scrubbed a hand over his bristled jaw and glanced at Mila. "I must speak to Maldron's family and oversee repairs." He swung on his heels and approached the grieving family members. Grief, along with guilt, weighed heavily on his soul. If he'd just kept quiet and gone with the flow, Maldron might still be alive. He examined the devastation again, wondering how many others might die from his decisions. Was it worth it? Now, he would have to rethink everything. It was one thing to make a stand, but when lives were at stake, it was another matter.

AT FIRST, THE RAIN on Rhen's face had been a relief, proving he was not dead, even though the pain in his head made him wish he was. He vaguely recalled Mila pleading for help, but he couldn't remember anything after that. The question was, where was Mila? He had been tasked with her safety, and he'd failed. How had a successful trip taken such an unexpected and sinister turn?

The sound of howling in the distance and the sun sinking into the horizon brought him back to the present. His first thought was to find shelter. Attempting to stand with his hands secured behind his back was a struggle. With no way to use his arms, he rolled onto his side, then onto his knees. The effort was awkward and clumsy, each movement a battle against gravity, but finally, with a sharp intake of breath, he staggered upright.

Despite the rain, sweat trickled down his face and neck as he trudged through the undergrowth. With his hands secured behind his back, he couldn't shield himself from the stinging slap of wet foliage and rough vines scouring his face. Each step was a struggle. His eyes were constantly scanning for a safe haven until a nearby growl stopped him in his tracks. Unarmed and vulnerable, he spied a small side track snaking into the rainforest and, with nothing to lose, sprinted in that direction.

As the sinister howls grew closer and more menacing, his pace quickened, heartbeat pounding in his ears. He'd been in tight situations before, but he was a man of tech, not teeth and claws.

"Duck!" The shout tore through the air. He spun, searching the fading light, but saw no one. Instinct took over. He dropped flat. A heartbeat later, something sliced overhead with a vicious whoosh. A scream, cut off mid-howl, then a heavy thud. "Target down!" someone shouted.

The ground trembled with the thunder of running feet. Heart racing, he scrambled behind a thick tree trunk for cover. Moments later, shadows closed in around him, a ring of tall, powerful women. Even in the dim light, he could tell they looked like the women of Rotari, but he guessed they were not from his home planet.

One of the women stepped forward, weapon raised. A slim band of matte-black lenses hugged her eyes, projecting a faint green shimmer. He guessed they were military-grade multi-spectrum night optics, the kind that could pull heat signatures out of rain and smoke.

"You were lucky we didn't mistake you for the beast we have been tracking. And because of you, we nearly lost it," she barked. With a sharp flick of her fingers, she pushed the lenses up onto her forehead, and the words vanished from his mind as he caught sight of the golden-skinned Amazon with a heart-shaped face, sparkling green eyes, and a cascade of long dark hair. The woman was clothed in a rudimentary tube top and shorts, apparently fashioned from scraps of space-suit underarmour. A quick glance confirmed that her companions were similarly attired, night-vision rigs and all. In other circumstances, he would have thought he'd died and gone to heaven.

The woman shone a spotlight into Rhen's eyes, blinding him. "Who are you?" she asked. "You do not resemble the local people." She nudged him with her weapon. "Where are you from?"

"Off planet," he replied quickly. "Zoldacks boarded my ship, and I was dropped here with my colleague." He didn't want to admit where he was from or that his ship might still be accessible until he determined who they were.

"Astrea, we must butcher the beast and get home before full dark," one of the women cut in.

Relief washed through him; he was off the hook, at least for now.

"You're right, Dwolla," Astrea replied. "You," she said, pointing at Rhen. "Are coming with us." She glanced around. "Where's your colleague?"

"We got separated."

Astrea's eyes narrowed. "If you're lying, you'll end up like the beast. Understood?"

"Understood," Rhen confirmed, rolling his shoulders to take the pressure off his cuffed hands. "Could you untie me? My hands are numb."

Astrea stepped behind him. With one clean, practised motion, she slid a sharp knife under the cord. Then she frisked him methodically, stopping when her fingers closed around his sonic neutraliser wrist unit. "What is that?"

Rhen kept his face carefully schooled. It was just his luck that she was thorough, unlike the Zoldacks. Pasting a fake smile, he responded, "It's just a timekeeping device."

"Remove it," she demanded.

He reluctantly handed over his trusted multi-function diagnostic unit, capable of analysing, repairing, decrypting, or, when required, vaporising electronic components. It was a devastating loss, but he planned to get it back as soon as possible. He just had to work out how.

Slipping Rhen's wrist unit into her shoulder bag, Astrea beckoned to the other women, who quickly butchered the choice cuts before loading the meat onto a hover trolley.

The beast was formidable by the look of its jaw and sharp teeth. Without a high-powered weapon, he wouldn't have stood a chance. Moreover, its green skin was well-camouflaged and virtually invisible among the leaves. Its claws measured at least thirty centimetres from root to tip and looked sharper than a butcher's knife.

Astrea's brilliant green eyes narrowed on him like darts. "Despite being powerful animals, they are not fast runners. Instead, they ambush their prey, which is what it was doing to you."

Fantastic. He wasn't just in danger, he was the special of the day. Clueless, and apparently served with a side of bad luck.

Finished, the knot of four women watched him with suspicion as they cleaned their knives on the beast's hide and sheathed them, prompting Astrea to announce, "Let's go."

"You'll walk with me," she ordered.

"It's Rhen, by the way," he said, offering a hint of a smile.

She gave him a withering glance. "Noted. Move."

The walk totalled nearly two kilometres, a stitched route of rainforest trails and high-tech steel spans that skimmed the upper canopy. Ahead, the next crossing rose out of the mist, a cantilevered bridge arcing thirty metres above a canyon cut so deep the light seemed to vanish before it reached the bottom. Suspension cables, thick as Rhen's forearm, were anchored into weathered stone towers that looked older than the engineering they supported.

Under his boots, the grated steel walkway flexed just enough to remind him there was nothing but air and distance beneath. Waist-high cables ran along either side, the only thing between him and a fatal drop.

He was drenched, the breeze barely a rumour, the air heavy with moisture that clung to his skin and made every breath feel earned. The far end of the bridge resolved into something that did not belong to the jungle.

A tight cluster of huts crowded the cliff face, braced around the skeletal remains of a spacecraft. The wreck balanced on the canyon's lip, like it had hit, slid, and stopped one metre before the void took it. Its hull was split and scorched, ribs of twisted alloy exposed where plating had peeled back like torn skin. Vines had started to claim it, threading through seams and fractures.

On the canyon side, the void itself was their defence. On the far side, a fence had been improvised from the ship's own metal panels, bolted upright in a jagged line, a patchworked barricade made by people who expected pressure, not curiosity. It made Rhen's instincts tighten.

When they stepped off the swaying span onto solid ground, a larger group of women met them without ceremony. Their eyes tracked him in quick, assessing sweeps, cautious, unsmiling, then moved straight past him to the hover trolley. Hands closed on its handles with practised efficiency. Given their strict adherence to a chain of command and no-questions-asked attitude, he guessed they were soldiers.

"Rhen," Astrea called.

He turned.

"Sit. Don't move," she ordered, pointing to a log. "Dwolla, watch him. If he so much as twitches, lock him up."

"You can't be serious?" Rhen muttered.

Astrea lifted an eyebrow. "Keep talking, and you'll find out," she said before turning away to issue orders.

With nothing else to do, Rhen sat, and in his line of sight, a partial insignia showed through the grime on the fuselage. Unfortunately, it was the one he dreaded, Krylan, his planet's enemy. Then, it dawned on him that the women resembled his friend Gaia, who had been a Krylan soldier before the war ended. Now she was happily settled on Rotari with his half-brother, Dane. He remembered her mentioning that most of her squadron had been reported missing during the war, and he couldn't help wondering if these were the ones who'd never returned.

Erring on the side of caution, he would choose half-truths. Up close, he had no trouble imagining neural hardware buried behind their eyes, standard Krylan combat architecture, with the "behavioural compliance" hooks still active. If their chips were anything like Gaia's had been, orders could sit there for years, pulsing under conscious thought. And if that was true, then as far as these women knew, Krylan was still raging war on Rotari.

His mother had removed Gaia's damaged unit and replaced it with one of his father's designs. It was still an interface, but stripped of the control routines that ensured compliance and edited memories. The swap brought her nanites back online, driving a surge of strength through her muscles and restoring her body's rapid repair cycle. Only after that did Gaia start remembering who she'd been before she'd been programmed. He assumed Astrea would be no different. Until he gained her trust and found a way to shut down her neural unit, anything he told her might bounce off the walls of someone else's programming. Also, if their comms were operable, he would message Rotari for help, as they must be worried. As much as he didn't want to admit it, he probably needed help from Dane and Gaia to locate Mila. His mind swam with the tasks ahead, and everything hinged on gaining the Krylan women's cooperation.

He dragged a hand down his face, trying to figure out how to earn Astrea's trust. Then it hit him, and a grin spread across his face as he mentally awarded himself a gold star. Fortunately, Astrea approached with two bowls of steaming meat and handed him one.

"What are you smiling about?" she asked, eyeing him with suspicion.

"Nothing in particular."

She scoffed. "I can hear your brain overheating from here. Try again." She ripped off a piece of meat. "Where are you from?"

He sidestepped the question. "I'm a friend of Gaia's," he offered instead.

Her mouth dropped open. "Gaia Five?"

"Yes. But she dropped the 'Five' and goes by Gaia now." He swallowed a mouthful. "She never gave up hope that you were alive." It was a lie, and he knew it. But if it helped his case, he'd live with it. "She told me she was reassigned from the mission at the last minute."

The fire popped. Astrea's hand stopped halfway to her mouth. "That sounds correct," Astrea said, very softly.

Rhen nodded. "Why?"

For a heartbeat, her usual steel cracked. Something like guilt flickered across her face, then hardened into anger, not that he could tell whether it was aimed at him, at Gaia, or at the memory.

"Command ring-fenced her because she was walking around with half of Krylan's Military R&D in her skull and had no idea that she had black-budget augments, high-grade implants, and direct system hooks. The closest thing they'd built to a perfect soldier." Astrea's mouth twisted. "I only found out by accident through a misfiled clearance, wrong name on a med report. Too valuable to throw on a mission that might go bad, and far too dangerous to leave for an enemy to strip-mine if it did."

Rhen frowned. "Why did they think the mission might not succeed?"

"I filed a risk report," Astrea said. "Flagged the timings, the clearance gaps, the fact that our route cut straight through LOUT's interdiction corridor. It all stank. I said if they were going to fly a coffin into this system, they should use Nzumbes instead."

She leaned in. "The report made them question the risks. We were expendable, but not their golden girl. Internal Security reclassified my report, stamped it 'personnel suitability', and sent a sanitised version to the mission's commander. On paper, it looked like I was questioning Gaia Five's fitness for the mission, not the mission itself." Her mouth twisted. "That way, when they pulled her at the last minute, everyone could point to my complaint as the reason."

She tore off another strip of meat as though it had personally offended her. "They ordered her to stay and put me under a gag," Astrea said. "They called it operational secrecy and made it clear that if any leak were traced back to me, my career would be finished. Then they made sure I was the one who had to tell her she wasn't coming."

Rhen grimaced. "So she thinks you had her pulled."

That was the idea." Astrea's voice cooled. "You don't send a walking black box into a mission you're already planning to lie about." Astrea gave a short, humourless laugh. "Officially, it was called a cooperative agricultural delegation," she said. "In reality, we were told to grab as many seed specimens as possible, plus a handful of Kesk horticulturalists, and escort them to Krylan asap.

"Why the Kesk and seeds from this planet?"

"The Kesk are famous for growing rice in ocean water. Not by splicing in half the galaxy, either. They take the genes that handle salt excretion, cellular insulation, DNA protection, and crank their expression until the plants don't care if they're standing in a swamp or a bay." She looked into the distance. "It wasn't a military op. It was the Minister for Horticulture's pet project, and he had just enough pull to sign off on a ship and a squad."

Her gaze flicked back to him, flat and assessing. "Krylan's landmasses are going under. The public gets told it's 'coastal management' and 'periodic flooding.' The wild rice from the floating villages isn't enough to feed a drowning planet, so the Minister wanted Kesk seeds, Kesk methods, Kesk experts, quietly, before our people or our enemies realised how desperate we are."

She shrugged, the movement tight. "You send Gaia on a mission like that, and deniability evaporates. One crash, one sniffed transmission, and her implants dump an uneditable record into systems the military doesn't control. Then suddenly half the planet is panicking about a world that's already sinking." Her mouth twisted. "So they kept their perfect witness at home and sent us instead. A fanciful little 'not-a-military-mission' they could erase if it went wrong."

"But why hasn't anyone come looking for you?" Rhen asked.

Astrea cut him off with a sharp shake of her head. The anger in her eyes cooled into something colder. "It took months to cannibalise enough parts from the wreck to fix the comms. And then we realised we couldn't send a message without lighting ourselves up, so we disconnected it."

"Lighting yourselves up... to who?" Rhen asked.

"To LOUT." She spoke between mouthfuls now, forcing herself back into the practical. "They wrapped this planet in their own mesh. Since they haven't come looking for us, they must believe that after shooting us down, we perished in the crash. Given that they control all interplanetary movements and communications anywhere near this rock," Astrea said, "any rescue party would have to file a flight plan, request a corridor, and ping a relay. Pick your poison. LOUT would see it, connect the dots, and follow them straight here. It would be a death sentence for us and whoever came to the rescue."

She set her empty bowl on the ground and rose to her feet. "So as far as Krylan is concerned, we're dead," she said. "And if Gaia has any sense left, she'll keep believing that." Astrea paused, as if realising she'd said too much. "I will think about what you've said, and we will talk tomorrow." She turned away.

Rhen was elated that the comms might be operational, but disappointed that he couldn't transmit a message. Which meant he had to rely on the women's assistance. But first, LOUT's comms stranglehold on the planet needed to be addressed. And that would require a lot more thought. At any rate, any discussions with Astrea and her colleagues would not include Krylan losing the war. He would leave that discussion until later. Much later. For now, he needed to gain their trust to access what was left of the ship's tech.

After dinner, his optimism grew when Astrea returned to escort him to the damaged ship, but that quickly turned to disappointment when she secured his hands to a bulkhead with plascrete straps and then lay down a few metres away, weapon ready. Despite searching, he spied no sign of her shoulder bag containing his device.

RHEN WAS WOKEN BEFORE sunrise to break his fast with the others, who numbered about fifteen by his count. After a breakfast of cold meat from the night before, a handful of women scaled the rocky slopes to the creek below to catch salmog, whatever that was. They quickly disappeared amid a thick white mist rising from the canyon.

In stark contrast, some worked in silence, sharpening tools or repairing weapons, while others practised their combat skills in the open. The rainforest around them was alive with bird calls proudly announcing the dawn, mingling with the rhythmic movements of the women and the harsh, piercing shriek of metal being sharpened. The sounds of battle drills, grunts, thuds, and the clash of practice weapons added to the natural symphony. Rhen thought Gaia was intimidating. Now, it was multiplied by fifteen.

Speaking of intimidating, Astrea emerged from the ship. "Rhen, I want to talk to you."

Rhen was under no illusion that the said 'talk' would be more of an interrogation, and if she didn't like the answers, he might live to regret it. He wanted the meeting to be held on the ship as he hadn't been able to examine it in detail last night. Admittedly, he was anxious because his life depended on what he said and how it was received.

Astrea stood at the hatch and waved him toward what remained of the ship's bridge. From what he had observed, she was sharp, quick, and a natural-born leader. She pointed to a bench along the rear bulkhead while taking the captain's chair herself, laying her now unholstered weapon across her thighs. Beside her, another woman worked diligently at the console, eyes flicking between dead and half-dead displays.

"How do you know Gaia Five?" Astrea asked.

Rhen fidgeted, releasing a slow breath while he scrambled for an answer. Instead, he deflected. "Can you tell me the name of this planet?"

"Answer the question," she demanded.

"It's not that simple," Rhen replied.

Astrea studied him in silence, the failing-ship hum filling the gap. When she spoke again, her voice was cool. "I think it is. I've provided information about our mission. More than I'd usually give a stranger." Her gaze held his. "I don't know who you are, where you're from, or why Gaia Five trusted you. Start talking."

Rhen cleared his throat, buying himself a heartbeat. He'd stick to the truth where he could, and hope it was enough. "Gaia was sent on another mission," he said at last. "Her ship was attacked, and she crashed near our home."

Astrea's lips thinned. "No doubt the work of Rotari scum."

Rhen swallowed, every instinct urging him to veer away from the topic. But there was no way through this without putting something real on the table. "My half-brother, Dane, was the first on the scene," he said. "Gaia's neural link was blown, burnt pathways, corrupted signals and the control compounds were leaching into her brain. The headaches were... excruciating." He drew a breath. "My mother's a healer. She stabilised Gaia and removed the unit. Replaced it with a model my father designed." He hesitated. "I know you will find this difficult to believe, but once the military neural unit was gone, once the hooks weren't in her anymore, Gaia started seeing things differently. She didn't return to the military. She stayed planetside. With Dane."

Astrea's eyes flared.

He pushed on, lightly, as if that could soften it. "She's still the same feisty redhead who keeps my brother permanently off-balance. Just... without a rank attached to her name." He managed a small, hopeful smile.

"Now I know you are lying." Astrea's look could have stripped paint; her fingers tightened around the trigger. "Gaia Five would never walk away from the military. And if she tried, Command would have torn the system apart to retrieve her."

He was committed now; there was no way to reel it back. "Maybe, if there'd been anything left to retrieve," he said carefully. "If Gaia had the black-ops hardware you described, it would have been designed to keep screaming a signal into the net until there's literally nothing left to scream with. If she were out there with her head and that unit intact, Command wouldn't be guessing. They'd be drowning in her signal."

He forced himself to hold Astrea's gaze. "But her ship went in hard. Hull breakup, reactor spike, and every channel from her neural link flatlined in the same millisecond. One clean cut. No beacon, no recovery ping, just a smear of corrupted data and then nothing. From their side, it would have read like destruction. And you don't send another ship to chase a dead signal and advertise you had black-project hardware on board. Gaia had been lucky. To Command's diagnostics, that failure pattern would have looked exactly like obliteration. By the time my mother removed the damaged hardware, whatever was left of Krylan's network had already written Gaia off."

There was more he couldn't say, that by that time, Krylan's war was already sputtering out, fronts collapsing, priorities shifting to survival and damage control."

Steeling himself, he pushed the point he knew might cut deepest. "Do you remember your childhood?" he asked softly. "Your family?"

Astrea looked at him with narrowed eyes, but didn't speak.

He guessed it was because she couldn't answer. "Do you dream?"

This time, he was met with a look that said she was losing patience.

"Gaia recovered her memories after her old neural unit was removed. She also plans to look for her family and discover if she is an orphan, as she was told."

"I've interrogated better liars," Astrea snapped.

A rush of alarm swept over him.

She gave him a look that could slice through armour, cool, hard, and unreadable. Then, without breaking eye contact, she said, "The Gaia Five I know is not the one you describe." Astrea placed her hands on her hips. "Come to think of it, you haven't told me where you live on Krylan."

"Umm... you wouldn't know it. It's a remote village."

"Most villages stick to traditional practices, yet you seem to have superior technical skills, and your skin is lighter than usual. Why is that?" Her head tilted to the side, and her eyes narrowed. "You are hiding something. What is it?"

"My mother isn't from Krylan. Her people are called the Yetari, who are very tall, with white hair and skin like bleached bone." He knew he was safe mentioning the Yetari as she wouldn't know they were from Rotari.

Astrea's brows knit. "That's.... Krylan doesn't usually mix our genome with offworld stock. We prefer to manage the gen-rich and gen-poor pools, not dilute them with another planet's DNA." She planted her hands on her hips, jaw tight and eyes sharp.

"You may not have been told everything," he replied. What he didn't add was that Aurora, Rorkk's partner from Earth, was proof enough. Krylan had flagged her as a high-value outlier genotype, pulled full-sequence datasets, and filed her under "priority acquisition" for selective introgression into the core Krylan genome.

"Moving on from Gaia Five, you haven't explained how you and your colleague were separated."

"As far as I can guess, I fell and hit my head, and the Zoldacks took Mila. I hope she is still on this planet, which is called....?"

"Eania," she replied. "Why would they take her and leave you?"

"A good question and one that I have asked myself repeatedly. Mila is one of the most gifted doctors on Krylan." At least, that part was true before she defected to Rotari. "She would be an asset on any planet." Again, he chose a half-truth.

"Perhaps." Her lips narrowed to a fine line.

Just then, the woman working at the console made her presence known. "Excuse me, Commander, the perimeter security alarms have disappeared from the screen. I am unable to check their status, which might be dangerous if they have gone offline completely."

Rhen wasted no time jumping in, aware that this was his opportunity to avoid more awkward questions and show his usefulness. "I can fix it." A big statement he hoped to deliver.

Astrea lifted that eyebrow again as she weighed up her options, which, by his account, were few. After considering his statement, she nodded. "Orella, let Rhen examine the console. Stop him if he makes a move you don't like," she said, handing her weapon to the woman in question. "Our discussion is not over, Rhen, just delayed," she said.

Rhen smiled. "You won't regret this."

"For your sake, I hope not. You have more to lose than I do."

Rhen hesitated before making his next request. "If I fix the problem, will you return my wrist unit?"

"Perhaps. Now get to work."

Nervous and excited, Rhen slid into the chair Orella had vacated while Astrea watched from a distance. His fingers flew across the interface, chasing error codes and forcing a manual override. On any Krylan ship, even low-grade cranial links were usually routed through a neural sync node, a dedicated module that caught the implants' weak emissions, cleaned them, and handed a boosted signal to the main array. If Astrea's unit was running the inferior tech he suspected, there should have been a node buried somewhere in the bridge architecture.

He pulled up subsystem maps, drilled through diagnostic trees, hunting for the neural bus. Nothing. No sync node, no booster, just a scorched conduit feeding a half-starved transceiver.

That bothered him. Even a shoestring deployment rated a basic sync node; the hardware was cheap compared to the implants in their skulls. So why send a squad without one? Was the mission really so secret? Or had someone deliberately kept their neural links isolated, which meant no clean path to talk off-world, no easy way for a panicked soldier to scream the truth into the wider network?

Frustrated, he returned to the task at hand and rerouted around the dead pathways, spliced in a cleaner power rail from a quieter section of the console, and forced the array to accept a direct, low-level handshake. After several minutes of patchwork code and improvised wiring, he looked up with a grin. "It's fixed." He let out a breath, relieved.

"Let me see," Orella said, pushing Rhen out of her seat to test his handiwork. After several moments, she turned to Astrea with a crease between her eyebrows. "It's working, but I don't know how he did it."

Rhen smiled. "What can I say? "I'm told I'm very good with buttons. Occasionally even the right ones."

"Along with an overinflated ego and a penchant for avoiding answers," Astrea said, taking back her weapon and holstering it.

"May I have my wrist unit back?" Rhen asked.

Astrea reached into her pocket, produced the item and dropped it into his hand. "For now. I'm watching you closely. Make one wrong move, and you will be snark bait. And I want your full story, as soon as I have time."

Rhen nodded. "Of course." Just... not now. Maybe not ever, if he couldn't find a way to disable their neural units, starting with hers. Keeping his expression neutral, he asked, "Anything else technical you need help with?"

Astrea turned to go. "Orella will set you some tasks after you check each perimeter device to ensure they are working."

Rhen cleared his throat. "Could I ask a favour?"

Astrea rolled her eyes.

He knew he was pushing his luck, but he had to try. "Can you take me back to where I was found? The Zoldacks might have left tracks. And I know that you are talented trackers."

"I suspect that your colleague was taken to the nearest settlement called Gromwell."

"Can you take me there?"

"We're not on friendly terms with the plant-eaters. One of my soldiers accidentally clipped a Kesk man during a hunt. In our defence, the target was fully camouflaged. Since then, they've kept their distance. We also have reason to believe they're aligned with LOUT."

"Can you direct me to Gromwell so that I can speak with the locals?" Rhen asked.

Astrea crossed her arms. "Sure, if our goal is to be hunted, exposed, and imprisoned by LOUT. You're staying put. We're not exactly trying to make headlines."

Leaving that discussion for another time, Rhen tried another tack. "I am hoping that the Zoldacks left my ship behind after they departed. Is there any chance we can see if it is still there? It could be your ticket off this planet."

"Why is it that you keep questioning me and demanding favours, yet you avoid answering my questions?" One eyebrow lifted. "Anyway, we can't leave this planet until we complete our mission."

Astrea's programming was too ingrained, so decommissioning her neural link was Rhen's only option. And that was risky. Even if he programmed his wrist unit to the right frequency and placed it against her neural unit, there was no guarantee it would work or that she would survive unscathed. "Can you bring up a map of the planet and pinpoint where you found me?" He thought it might be the only way to get close enough to execute his plan.

Her eyes glinted with cold curiosity, and her gaze bore into him, challenging him to justify his request. "Why should I grant you another favour?" she asked. "What exactly do I stand to gain?" Astrea tilted her head slightly, a mocking smile curling the edges of her lips. "You know, Rhen," she said with biting sarcasm, "the flow of information seems to be a one-way street." Her voice was dangerously calm, a razor's edge beneath each word.

A confident smirk played on Rhen's lips. "Astrea, where else are you going to find someone with the skills, the wit, and the ship that could help you complete your mission and get us off this rock?" He raised an eyebrow, his tone teasing but with an edge of truth. "You might not like to admit it, but you need me."

"We don't need you, you arrogant, overinflated fool. We've managed just fine on our own."

Rhen laughed under his breath, the grin on his face pure provocation. "Really? And how's that working out?" He leaned in slightly. "You need a ship, and someone who can think beyond whatever corner you've backed yourself into." His eyes flicked over the place. "Unless you're planning to die here." He shrugged. "If that hits a nerve, that's on you."

Astrea stiffened slightly, and with an exasperated sigh, her eyes narrowed. "I suppose there's no chance of getting any peace until I indulge your ego, is there?"

Rhen winked. "Look on the bright side. There's a chance we might all leave this planet in one piece."

She reluctantly took the console and pulled up the map. The display's soft glow flickered across her face.

Rhen eased in, posture loose, harmless, under her companion's watch. He drifted closer as if reading over her shoulder, circling just enough to line up behind her. His wrist device sat primed beneath his jacket sleeve. He feigned a casual cuff adjustment, then stepped in as though to get a better look at the map Astrea was pulling up. In one smooth motion, he brought his wrist unit within centimetres of her neural implant at the base of her skull. A faint, near-inaudible pulse. Astrea stiffened, then went slack. Rhen caught her before she hit the floor.

Orella immediately called for reinforcement. Although he managed to procure Astrea's weapon, he was outnumbered and quickly taken into custody. His protestations that she simply collapsed were met with disbelief, and he was quickly locked in a storage hut while they held counsel regarding his fate. His only hope was that Astrea would quickly regain consciousness. Because if she didn't, his days were numbered.

Hours later, five women hauled him to the canyon's edge, without a word of explanation.

The suspension bridge was in clear view to his right while a turquoise stream below wound its way through the rainforest. Babbling and burbling, it leapt over boulders and rocks, whisking pebbles about in the underwash. Chords of soft light filtered through the trees and bathed the water's surface in gold. A flock of small bird-like creatures fluttered through the beams of light, wings glittering in the sun. Despite the beauty on display, the women were out for blood, and no amount of pleading or explanation swayed their determination. He hoped whatever they had in mind was quick and relatively painless.

Tightly held, he was secured to a cargo net face down and suspended high over the canyon like a wind chime. His heart lurched into his throat when another jolt plunged him deeper. Despite the mild morning, sweat broke out on his brow. He wondered what would kill him first, heat stroke, thirst or the snarks that roamed freely at night.

CHAPTER 3

By the time Mila stumbled back to Brom's home, soaked and dishevelled, daylight had broken. Every step throbbed through her aching limbs, and dread churned in her chest each time her thoughts turned to Rhen. What if he hadn't made it out? What have I gotten myself into? she wondered. More pressingly, daylight meant the mythical snarks wouldn't be stalking her. If they even existed.

A sharp knock at the hatch startled Mila, followed by the arrival of a short, round woman who bustled in without waiting for a reply, a woven basket cradled in her arms. "Brom asked me to deliver food," she announced briskly.

Mila rose to meet her and gently took the basket. "Thank you," she said warmly. "I'm Mila." She looked at the woman expectantly.

"Grettale, ma'am."

"Thank you, Grettale. I appreciate your kindness."

"I run the local bakehouse, so it was nothing to bring a few baked goods over," Grettale said with a smile. Then, with a knowing look, the woman added, "We know you're here to help us, and we're grateful."

Mila blinked. "Right. Good to know. I'm still short on details."

Grettale hesitated, her smile slipping as she searched Mila's face. "Well," she said lightly, "I suppose Brom hasn't filled you in yet." A soft chuckle, composure returning. "No matter. Eat first, talk later. That's how it should be."

Lured by the aroma, Mila pulled the wrapping aside to reveal a selection of buns, including a sizable round flatbread. "Is that truffles and garlic I smell?"

"Why, yes, it is. We add them to the flatbread. You have a good nose."

"Are truffles plentiful on this planet?"

"Yes, they are used in many dishes."

"They are rare on other planets and cost a fortune."

"I don't believe it."

"Believe it," Mila replied. "What is the situation out there?"

"After Brom inspected the temporary repair, he visited Maldron's family." Her voice broke at the mention of the man's name. "Brom's a good leader. Best we've had. Even better than his father."

Mila nodded, committing every detail to memory.

Grettale retrieved her now-empty basket. "Maldron was well-liked, always helping others. He took most of the night shifts at the plant because he and his partner have no children." Her eyes reddened, and she pulled a handkerchief from her apron pocket to wipe them dry. "I'm off, lots to do. I've left my eldest and the girls on the tonir clay ovens. When the power cuts, we fall back on those wood-fired beasts to bake Gromwell's bread. One wrong move and you're skin, I don't care how many times my son's done it, I still worry."

"What are tonir ovens and how do they work?"

"Old clay ovens our ancestors made and sunk into the ground, half above, half below. We only use them for flatbread when the power goes out. We preheat the tonir for six or seven hours until it's fierce enough, then brush the walls with a salty wash for flavour. The dough's white and unleavened, shaped over a dome mould. To get it close to the heat, my son grips the rim, leans in up to his waist, slaps the dough onto the wall, then hauls himself out and does the next. When it's golden, we fish the loaves out with a long hook."

"Mila nodded, unable to understand why they would put themselves in danger in pursuit of bread.

"You are most welcome to visit the bakery when you have time. Oh, before I forget, Brom said he would be sending out a search party." With that, she swept out with a wave.

Mila didn't need to be asked twice before she dug into the bread.

EXHAUSTION WEIGHED Brom down as he trudged home after spending time with the grieving family and checking the energy plant's rudimentary repair. Determined to grab a bite before sending his men out to search for Rhen, he was stopped in front of his home by Danelda. While she was the last person he wanted to see, his sense of duty prevailed.

"Brom, how are you? Is there anything I can do to help?"

He rubbed his tired eyes. "No, thank you. The best thing you can do is go home and help your elderly mother." He turned and put one foot on the stairs, but Danelda caught his arm, halting him.

"Who is she?" she snapped.

He swallowed the urge to say, 'none of your business'. "You mean our visitor?"

She gave a curt nod.

"She's here to help us," he said evenly.

"How can she? She doesn't know anything about us. She will ruin our future with LOUT. I can help you, Brom. We have a deep connection that can never be broken."

Her words hit him like a shockwave. Surely she didn't still have feelings for him. Danelda was promised to Flynn, his best friend. He needed to choose his words carefully, afraid he might say something he would regret. "Thanks, Danelda, but it might be better if you head home." They had been close when they were younger. A brief crush that had lasted a few months before he entered the monastery. At the time, he had been relieved when she'd announced that she would be relocating to Atmos, LOUT's centre of operations on the planet.

With a thunderous face, she swung on her heels and stormed off. The moment she was out of sight, his shoulders relaxed. Convinced she would be happy with Flynn even if she couldn't see it right now. She'd always been impulsive, immature, and quick to anger, traits he squarely blamed on her parents. They'd spoiled her, and when they couldn't provide the life she wanted, she left without a second thought, only to return much later without an explanation.

His mind turned to the woman inside. Now, she was a different matter. Truth be told, he was a little intimidated by her, but he refused to let that show. Dragging his aching legs up the stairs and into the living area, he was relieved to find Mila asleep on the couch, buying him precious time to freshen up and eat before their inevitable confrontation. He pressed a water bottle to his lips, causing a river of water to pour into his mouth and over his chin. Choking, Brom coughed and swiped his forearm across his mouth and headed for the shower.

Physically and emotionally tired, he longed for the time when dancing, laughter and long evenings of celebration were the norm because everyone needed that kind of medicine, even him. Hopefully, he could win the doctor over. Because she was his only hope, and delivering positive news on Rhen would help his cause. Hunger gnawed at Brom after his shower, but habit won out. He always began his day with meditation. It grounded him. And today, he needed that more than ever.

In his bedroom, he dropped to the floor, crossed his legs and closed his eyes. Breathing in, he exhaled slowly, focusing on his breath. As thoughts raced through his mind, he let them float by without attachment, which took willpower, given recent events. Despite distraction getting the better of him several times, he kept his focus on his breathing. Now sufficiently relaxed, his thoughts drifted to someone who made him happy. And to his surprise, Mila came to mind. Usually, his mind drifted to images of his family and happier times before LOUT's intrusion.

Unable to ignore footsteps in the adjoining room, he opened his eyes, aware that his meditation was over. Propelling himself upright, he plastered a smile on his face and entered the living area. In the dim light filtering through the small, dust-covered portholes, Mila sliced bread in his food prep area, and his heart warmed at the thought of this woman in his home.

From the corner of her eye, she caught his scrutiny. "Hi, Brom."

He felt an unrepentant grin widen his mouth. For him, dawn always brought a new perspective and a belief that today would be better than the one before. His family always said he was the ultimate optimist, which hadn't changed.

Mila halted her task and looked at him. "You look terrible. Sit down, and I'll make you something to eat."

Brom didn't argue. He needed his strength if he was going to find Rhen. He couldn't afford to collapse before the search even began.

Mila shot him a glance. "I hear you have organised a search."

Brom exhaled, running a hand through his hair. "Volunteers will be here at noon."

Mila exhaled sharply and dropped the knife onto the table with a decisive clack. "I'm running low on patience, and even lower on answers." She crossed her arms. "I get it. You've had a hell of a night. But so have Rhen and I." Her eyes narrowed. "Please find him, before I run out of the little goodwill I've got left." Leaning in slightly, her voice stayed firm, controlled. "I know you've got a town to save. But I've got one person, practically family, who is missing. And you'd better start explaining why I was brought here."

Too tired to argue, he sat at the table, slouched negligently in his chair and rested his chin on his hands. "Look, I'm sorry. Finding

Rhen is my priority. The search party will head out at noon. You will get your explanation."

Mila nodded.

Brom gestured toward the chiller unit. "There's some fruit and vegetables in there. The community keeps me well-stocked with food. They think that I can't look after myself."

After pulling a modest haul from the chiller, she glanced around at the sparse, well-worn furnishings. "Despite what you might think, I'm with them; you're clearly not one for creature comforts."

"I think it stems from my time in the monastery."

"You can't drop a truth bomb like that without elaborating," she said, dropping fruit onto the chopping board and picking up the knife again.

"I was sent to a monastery in the mountains at eighteen. At first, I thought it was a punishment, and I was resentful. But it didn't take me long to realise that I was well suited to monastic life. I spent another fifteen orbits there before being coerced into taking over from my father after he and my older brother died. I thought it would only be for a short time, but it's been two orbits, and no one else has offered to take my place."

Finished with her preparations, Mila brought his plate to the table and sat down across from him. Outside, the community was beginning to stir.

Brom took a quiet moment to savour the calm before heat, humidity, and responsibility set in. "I'm sorry," he said at last. "I should've handled things differently. All I can do now is try to fix the damage, starting with finding Rhen."

"And let's not forget," Mila added, meeting his eyes steadily, "a full explanation. And I'm coming with you. That's non-negotiable."

He nodded, and the tension between them eased, cooling into a tentative truce.

Brom nodded and stood, causing his chair to skitter backwards. "I should make preparations for the search party." He avoided her eyes and wondered how she would react to his plight and whether she would still be willing to help after her ordeal.

A few hours later, a handful of volunteers set out on foot. They cut across the lowlands, skirting crop fields laid out in rough, uneven strips, then began to climb. By the time they reached the rainforest boundary, sweat had soaked collars and backs. At the tree line, the world changed, light dimmed under the canopy, and the trees crowded together like a wall. Heat and humidity closed in at once, thick enough to breathe. Birds called overhead, and insects threaded through the scattered blooms in the undergrowth. Breathing hard from the climb, they stopped for water, then shouldered on into the green.

The rainforest flooded Brom's senses, sharp and clean in a way nothing else ever did. Out here, surrounded by living things, he felt most at home.

Finally, they arrived at the location where Mila had parted with Rhen, only to discover an area of trampled grass. This allowed everyone to stop and rehydrate again before moving on. Brom gestured towards a side track where the grass had been freshly trampled. "Let's see where it leads." After nods of agreement and a forced smile from Mila, Brom led the search party in single-file formation.

Brom wished his walk had been under better circumstances, but he still took in the rainforest, leaves and moss underfoot, sunlit webs, the sharp mix of scents, until a darker scent cut through it. He lifted his arm, halting them. Everyone recognised the all-too-familiar odour of dead flesh. With mounting dread, Brom pushed through the underbrush until he found the source of the smell. After a quick scan, he released a relieved breath. "It is a butchered snark, no doubt the work of the meat eaters that are as elusive as they are deadly."

Suddenly, Mila spotted something shiny and, without hesitation, sprinted forward to scoop it up. Dangling from her hand was a broken piece of cord that had secured Rhen's hands. As Brom and the others approached, she announced, "This was used to tie his hands."

The silence pressed in, heavy and unforgiving. Brom finally spoke, his voice a strained attempt at hope. "Maybe... maybe the hunters who killed the beast untied him. Took him with them."

In response, he was met with strained smiles. Everyone knew he was clinging to hope. "So far, the meat-eaters have stuck to hunting wild game. Only one of us has been harmed, and we don't believe it was intentional. We've kept our distance, stayed alert, and armed ourselves whenever we spotted signs of them nearby. But maybe it's time we changed that. Maybe it's time we approached them, on our terms."

This was met by a grunt from the men and a nod from Mila. Decision made, he approached her and placed a reassuring hand on her arm, only to have her flinch. Damn, he'd forgotten to mask his power before touching her, something he was always careful to do. She made him forget himself and drop his barriers. He wouldn't make that mistake again. With that, the group headed back home.

CHAPTER 4

Back in Gromwell, Brom and Mila peeled away from the search party and headed home. By the time they reached Brom's hatch, he knew his time was up and that Mila deserved the long-overdue answers he'd been putting off. She sat at the scarred table without a word, and he took the seat opposite, unsure where to even begin, wondering if his choices could be justified at all, especially if they led to the death of her pilot. It was a steep price to pay. Maybe too steep.

Brom cleared his throat. "We are known as the Kesk people. During an intergalactic war two hundred orbits ago, several hundred Kesk people were abducted from their home planet, Urlu, along with a seed bank. The ship also contained souls seized from other planets. En route, the ship was attacked and crash-landed on this planet. With war raging overhead, no one came to the rescue. Many survived, including the crew, passengers and a group of powerful Kesk shamans. We believe our people were taken because we have the power to help plants thrive even in the worst climates. Given this power, the Kesk abductees were fitted with Leadonium collars to neutralise their energy.

After freeing themselves from their collars and joining the other survivors, they stored the seeds in mountain caves while they analysed Eania's weather cycles. They quickly learned that dangerous predators roamed the forest at night, worked out what was safe to eat, and used their power to strengthen the local flora, ensuring the refugees did not go hungry that first season. The original Kesk had a deeper, more vivid green skin tone. Over generations, interbreeding with the other survivors diluted that colour, and with it, the strength of the gift. Those of us with a higher percentage of Kesk blood, like me, were trained at the monastery. We can touch the flora and exchange energy with it, and our skin can shift to match the living greens around us. In the rainforest, we are almost invisible.

Before the survivors had a chance to establish themselves in the lowlands, one of the intergalactic factions at war built a ground installation here to house their ships. It didn't last. It was discovered and swiftly obliterated. Their fleet never made it back into orbit. That's how the ship graveyard became our home, a monument to a war that touched even this forgotten world. For another two orbits, the Kesk people remained in the mountain caves as war raged overhead. Finally, quiet descended, and the inhabitants established a permanent settlement and planted the seeds.

Further exploration revealed the planet had once been a thriving Blackheart Crystal mining colony. The prevailing belief was that its former inhabitants abandoned it once the seams ran dry. In their wake, the lowlands had been stripped of native vegetation, leaving broad clearings that were already suited to cultivation.

The ship graveyard became the foundation of Gromwell. The residential zone was barricaded for safety, while the surrounding land was planted with crops. Over time, others established their own settlements. Since then, the people of Gromwell have continued to cultivate the land, using their unique gift to make things grow.

The Kesk shamans built their mountain monastery along one of the planet's energy lines and, as insurance, established a seed bank. As the years passed, the original Kesk intermingled with other survivors and ship crews, and the bloodline thinned, but the shamans endured, appointing successors, a chosen few among the Kesk descendants, to study the old ways, preserve the traditions, and maintain, update, and safeguard the technology and databanks salvaged from the ship graveyard. Everything remained stable until LOUT arrived about ten orbits ago. Despite strong objections from the Kesk Shamans, many settlements accepted the conglomerate's offer of advanced technology and formal education. In return, LOUT demanded access to the Kesk's power, especially what the shamans control, and they've refused. For years, LOUT has treaded carefully because it needs their cooperation, but that restraint is slipping, and recent moves suggest its patience is running out."

Brom drew a long breath. What came next was heavy. As the memory surged forward, it clenched into a burning knot in his chest. "My father and older brother held out against LOUT, refusing to send children from Gromwell to the LOUT boarding school and campaigning against involvement with the conglomerate.

Two orbits have passed since my father and brother boarded a shuttle for a LOUT meeting in Atmos, a city in the mountain range to the west. We were notified that the transport reportedly experienced mechanical difficulties en route and crashed, leaving no trace of the shuttle or its passengers. My sister disappeared shortly after the incident, and my mother died an orbit later. I believe from a broken heart. Since then, Gromwell has been plagued with unexplained deaths and accidents. LOUT's threats are escalating. The conglomerate doesn't want to live in harmony with us; it wants to dominate and subdue. We must learn to stand up for ourselves as Rotari has done."

With each statement, he heard his voice grow louder, so he pulled himself back to maintain an outward calm while a tsunami of emotion churned beneath the surface. "LOUT controls all interplanetary communications and travel and only allows outsiders like the Zoldacks free access to come and go."

Brom shifted in his chair. It was time to own his sin, apologise, and convey his willingness to make it right. "For a price, the Zoldacks ensured that your arrival would remain under the radar. Again, I am sorry." Guilt weighed heavily on him. Now he had to turn that into something positive and meaningful. He wanted forgiveness, but it had to be earned. Humility was a hard pill for him to swallow, but for this woman, he would learn.

Mila sat stiffly across from him, and her face revealed nothing about her thoughts. Her medical career had undoubtedly taught her to internalise her emotions.

Brom stood, shoved his hands into his pockets and looked out of a porthole, searching for the right words. "After learning that you represented the President of Rotari and hearing your speech about how Rotari thrived through self-reliance and trade, I realised your insight and Rotari's support would be invaluable. When your planet's president refused my request for assistance, I had to find another way to gain Rotari's help." Brom let out a deep breath and sat down again, wondering if it was enough. Enough for her to forgive his actions and possibly the loss of Rhen's life. He dropped his head into his hands, emotionally drained.

He glanced up as Mila stood, removed two glasses from the open shelving in the food prep area, filled them with water and returned to the table.

She placed one in front of Brom and took a sip from her glass. "That is quite a story, Brom. But I can't see how I can help your people. I am not a politician or diplomat, and I think that's what you need. Even I can see that removing LOUT's influence from this planet would be difficult given your limited resources." Mila shook her head. "I am a doctor first and foremost, not an activist. You're probably unaware that I was once a doctor on Krylan, Rotari's enemy. I barely escaped the horrors of that planet. But now, you've stripped away my freedom, cornered me with an ultimatum, and put Rhen in danger."

Put in those terms, Brom found it difficult to meet her eyes. She was correct; perhaps he should have planned this better and not put others in danger just because he was desperate. "Again, I regret my course of action."

Mila leaned forward. "We can't change what has happened. We can only move forward. My priority is to find Rhen, and then perhaps I can speak to the President of Rotari and arrange a meeting."

"That is more than I deserve, and I thank you."

Mila nodded. "I promised myself a long time ago to concentrate on the here and now and not rehash past mistakes."

Brom rubbed his temples. "I will locate Rhen and assist with your return home. But, and there is a big but, LOUT controls all airspace and communications. So somehow, we need to disable that control. I will send Flynn to locate the meat eaters. I believe there is a good chance they have Rhen, and it would be advantageous to form an alliance. Perhaps, they have skills they can bring to the table to defeat LOUT."

Mila stood, rinsed the two empty glasses and placed them upside down on the sink. "I need to shower, change, and find some clean clothes. Because these might stand up on their own, given half the chance."

"Of course," Brom replied. Embarrassed that he hadn't thought of it earlier. In his defence, he had a lot weighing on his mind. "I still have my sister's clothes; she was about your size. I will leave them on the bed for you."

She nodded and left him alone with his thoughts.

The woman unsettled him and occupied his mind when duty should be his first thought. And he needed time to think. Finding Rhen was a priority because he didn't want another death on his conscience. After leaving Mila a selection of clothes, Brom made them both a hot kaff after their sleep-deprived night.

At the sound of heavy footsteps ascending the stairs to his home and a rapid knock at the hatch, he stopped what he was doing. "Hold on," he bellowed, dropping his kaff on the table.

Seconds after he opened the hatch, Darrold rushed past him, breathing heavily. "There's been an accident," he panted.

Brom placed a comforting hand on his shoulder. "Slow down and take a deep breath."

Flynn. He's hurt. Bad." The words came out in short, ragged bursts before Darrold paused, gasping for breath.

Brom swallowed the surge of fear rising in his throat.

"Shaman Oldson... told me to tell you," he panted.

Despite wanting to press for answers, Brom guided a red-faced Darrold into a chair while Mila stepped in from the corridor, placing a cup of water in the young man's trembling hands.

Darrold exhaled slowly, his shoulders sagging. "Shaman Oldson was foraging for herbs near the monastery when he heard a sharp cry from the cliffside. He looked up in time to see one figure collapse while another fled. Oldson found Flynn unconscious, blood spreading across his chest as if he'd been shot. He was brought to the monastery and placed in a medbed."

"What about the person who fled?" Brom asked.

"I don't know."

Brom was pretty sure Flynn's companion was Danelda. "Darrold, please locate Danelda. I want to know if she witnessed the attack. Meet me back here as soon as you can."

"Yes, Brom," Darrold replied, flying out the door.

Mila stood and dropped her cup in the sink. "I'm coming with you."

Brom's gaze flicked to her hands, steady and capable. He should have argued, but he trusted her. "Stay close," he said.

"Is this the same Flynn who was to locate the meat eaters?"

"Unfortunately, yes."

"Luck is not on our side, is it?"

He wasn't going to answer that because she was right. "Rex is our next best tracker. While he is talented, he can be a little quirky and unpredictable."

Mila folded her arms. "I get that Rex has unique tracking skills, but he doesn't sound like the right fit. We need someone who can be cautious, deliberate and strategic."

"I'll pair him with two seasoned, level-headed partners who can keep him in check."

"I'm just not sure we can afford to let his impulsiveness jeopardise the operation."

"Trust me."

She nodded. "What sort of medical facilities do you have in Gromwell?"

He drew a deep breath. "We have a medical facility run by a healer with several medbeds."

"Given what I have seen of your community, I am surprised."

"The ship transporting our ancestors contained the latest technology, including technicians and medical professionals, many of whom survived the crash. Additionally, we salvaged similar technology from the buildings and ships left behind. The monastery has the same technology and is a repository for all data and historical recordings."

Mila's gaze sharpened. "So, Flynn is in good hands?"

"Yes. We have shamans who specialise in training our healers and information technology technicians. While Gromwell relies heavily on their support, many other communities use Atmos physicians for treatment, no longer trusting their own."

Mila crossed her arms and gazed out of a porthole.

It was a difficult silence as they waited for Danelda's appearance. He hoped it was an accident, not another play from LOUT.

Mila's reflection hovered in the porthole glass, all sharp angles and control, but Brom could see fatigue pulling at the edges. He wanted to reach for her, to steady her, but he kept his hands to himself. Wanting her was a liability, and the most honest thing he had felt in years.

CHAPTER 5

After hours suspended over the canyon, dehydration set in, then despair. How long would they leave him there? Long enough to watch him suffer, long enough to die slowly. By his calculation, it would not take much longer; the heat and humidity were stripping the last of his moisture. He could no longer shout. His throat had narrowed to a rasp, his tongue felt swollen, and his skull pulsed with each heartbeat. Soon he would black out, and by all accounts, that would be a mercy; he did not want to be conscious for the end.

Voices cut through the haze. A squealing pulley strained above him, the cargo net jerking upward in harsh, metre-long lifts. The cliff edge swung into view, then the sky, then the cliff again. When they hauled him onto the top, he hit the ground face-first. Dirt packed his mouth. Hands yanked at the knots, and when his wrists and ankles finally came free, every stiff muscle flared as blood returned in needles and fire. He rolled onto his back, chest heaving, squinting against the sun.

He spat grit and pebbles, then forced his throat to work. "Can I have some water, please?" he rasped, lips cracked, eyes half closed against the glare. A flask was shoved into his hands. He drank until it was empty, then levered himself upright, dizzy and nauseous, trying to keep the water down.

"Astrea's awake," one of them said. "She wants you. Now." He was marched onto what remained of the ship's bridge and dumped at Astrea's feet. Relief hit first; she looked whole, steady, furious, then fear followed. He could not afford another mistake.

"Leave us," Astrea ordered.

The others withdrew.

She turned her full attention on him. "What did you do to me earlier. I want the unvarnished truth."

"I forced your neural implant into safe mode," Rhen said. "Temporary, unless it is removed surgically. I did it to show you what Command has done to all of you, not to harm you."

"That excuse," she said, "usually comes after a crime."

Outside the shattered viewport, wind shoved rain across the compound, turning dust into slurry. Rhen swallowed, steadier now that she was listening instead of looming. "What are your plans for me?" he asked.

Astrea's jaw tightened. "I dreamed about my family. That has not happened in a long time. Duty has been first and foremost."

"That was not duty," Rhen said. "That was programming."

Her chin lifted, hands on her hips, defensive and dangerous. "Or perhaps you want to control us now, so we do your bidding."

"Remember," he said, "you insisted I return with you. I did not seek you out."

"Perhaps."

He exhaled through his nose, sick of the word, sick of her uncertainty. "Give me supplies and point me toward Gromwell, and I will leave."

"Or lead the enemy here."

"Blindfold me, drop me near the settlement, and I will walk."

Astrea studied him, then looked back out at the rain as if weighing the shape of betrayal. "At this point," she said, "you stay. You will disable every neural unit in this compound, with Orella's assistance, and you will report to me."

Relief loosened something in his chest. She did not trust him, not yet, but she was willing to test the truth. Rhen sat at the cracked interface, fingers moving with practised speed. "My wrist unit can push an implant into medical safe mode," he said. "But only at close range."

"So we amplify it," Astrea said, "Orella, you will work with Rhen. You do not get clever. You do not get deviate. You follow my orders."

Orella's expression barely shifted. "Yes, Commander."

They scavenged what the crash had not cooked, an emergency beacon casing, two intact induction coils, and enough signal conditioning hardware to stitch together a broadcast stage. Rhen kept it ugly and simple; the beacon's job was to saturate the hull with a pattern, he just needed it to scream a different one.

When the shield feed came online, the makeshift assembly hummed against the bulkhead. Status lights blinked, then held. Rhen jacked his wrist unit into the port and brought up the failsafe routine. "We test one implant first," he said. "If it behaves, we widen the range."

Astrea stepped forward. "Status update," she ordered, directing her question to Orella.

"We have an amplifier tied into the internal loop. Rhen believes it can broadcast a shutdown pulse and neutralise the control routines. He wants a single-target test."

Astrea's gaze snapped to Rhen. "Risk."

"Low," he said, "not zero."

Orella stood very still, eyes on the diagnostic panel, not the device. Not him. Her jaw worked once, as if she wanted to speak, then the moment passed.

Astrea watched her, then made the decision without looking away. "Orella, you're first."

A flicker crossed Orella's face, something human and fast, swallowed by training. "Commander, that is a risk to our mission and not within allowable parameters."

"It's an order," Astrea cut in. "Mission parameters assume secure command authority. We no longer have that. If the link can be reached, it can be turned. That makes us compromised. You will comply. Protocol Theta, compromise containment," Astrea said. "If command authority cannot be authenticated, the field commander assumes cognitive integrity measures."

Orella's throat bobbed. Her fingers rose toward the port at the base of her skull, hesitated, then moved again, as if dragged through thick water. A faint tremor ran through her hand.

Rhen saw it, the tiny delay, the implant fighting to keep the rails intact.

Astrea stepped closer, voice dropping into something colder than an order, something that belonged to Command's own language. "Execute."

Orella's hand completed the motion. She braced one palm on the console, shoulders squared, eyes fixed forward. "Ready," she said, but the word sounded like it had been taken from her, not offered.

Rhen swallowed, keyed the routine for a narrowcast, locked it to Orella's signature, and armed the emitter. The status field slid from idle to armed, a soft tone confirming the link to the internal loop.

He sent the pulse, keying the routine for a narrowcast, locking it to Orella's neural signature. The emitter's status field slid from idle to armed, a soft tone confirming the link to the internal loop. He sent the pulse.

The amplifier thumped as power surged, and Orella stiffened, eyes flaring for a heartbeat, one hand snapping out to brace against the console as a wave of vertigo washed over her. On the diagnostic panel, her implant's telemetry spiked, then flattened.

She sucked in a breath, blinking hard. "Everything just tilted," she said, voice unsteady. "Like gravity couldn't make up its mind." She closed her eyes for a moment. "The interface is still there, but it's quiet. The prediction cues are gone. I feel slower. Heavier. And..." She touched her temple, surprised. "Clearer. The background noise is gone. Why didn't I collapse as Astrea did?"

Rhen watched the new pattern hold on the display. "I ramped the signal down for you," he said. "Astrea got a hard cut, that's why she dropped. This time, I let the implant bleed off the overload instead of dumping everything at once. Your sensory systems are now running on you alone."

Orella flexed her fingers, then rolled her shoulders, testing how her body responded. Muscles fired a fraction too slow, balance a shade off. "I feel different," she said at last. A faint, humourless huff escaped her. "But at least the thoughts in my head are mine."

Rhen let out the breath he'd been holding. "There's something else," he said. "The nanites in your blood, the ones that handle rapid repair and load-bearing enhancements, were slaved to the implant's command layer. With that gone, they'll revert to passive mode. No more boosts. No more combat-grade regeneration."

Astrea's eyes snapped to his. "I don't recall you mentioning that before."

"I didn't," Rhen admitted. "If I had, you might have said no. Once we get out of here, I can look at reprogramming the units to run independently and reactivate the nanites."

For a heartbeat, the only sound was the low hum of the improvised emitter.

"Next time," Astrea said, her voice very calm, "you tell me everything. I assumed what I felt was just a temporary side effect, not a permanent downgrade."

Rhen let out the breath he'd been holding. His legs felt weak; he ignored it and met Astrea's gaze, refusing to look away. "That was one," he said. "Now we tell the rest of the implants to stand down, if you're still in agreement, Astrea. Do you want to warn them, or keep them in the dark about what's coming?"

She held his eyes for a long, sharp second. "We neutralise them first," she said at last. "Then I explain."

Rhen frowned. "You don't trust them to choose?"

"It's not them I don't trust," Astrea said. "It's what's riding behind their eyes." Her jaw tightened. "Protocol Theta is a blunt instrument. If I announce it, the loyalty routines will spike, half of them will panic, and the other half will try to restrain anyone who hesitates, because the implant will interpret hesitation as compromise. I am not turning my people on each other before we have a chance to pull the hook out cleanly. I need their units quiet first, then I can speak to the women I actually lead, not Command's ghosts.

Rhen nodded, expanded the target range to include every implant signature in the area, recalculated the checksum, and armed the emitter again. The improvised relay hummed, hungry for power, and he hit send.

The amplifier flared, filling the internal comms loop with the shaped pulse. On the diagnostic display, neural IDs blinked as the signal rippled through the squad: spikes of activity, then the same calm baseline appearing beside each one as their control layers collapsed into safe mode.

"Done," Rhen said quietly, more to himself than anyone else. "Command isn't calling the shots anymore." He knew it would take some adjustment now that the artificial cohesion that had guided their movements was severed, replaced by a raw, unfamiliar isolation. And for the first time in a long time, they were truly on their own.

"Until I can reprogram the neural units, you need to be careful because your body won't heal as quickly without the nanite repair." Thankfully, most women remained on their feet, but some looked dazed, and others needed time to deal with the emotions bubbling to the surface.

"Now that it's over, could I have something to eat and drink? I worked up quite an appetite swinging in the breeze."

Astrea shook her head. "We will break our fast as soon as I know everyone has recovered."

Rhen was about to agree when a commotion drew them outside. Several women escorted two pale green men into the compound. "We found these two lingering outside the perimeter."

After approaching, she commanded the men to kneel. "Explain the reason for your intrusion, plant eaters."

"The elder of the two sighed loudly. "I am Worren, and this is Rex," he said, pointing to his companion. "We were not lingering but trying to get your attention. You only saw us because we wanted to be seen. Brom, the leader of Gromwell, sent us. We are looking for a man called Rhen."

Rhen leapt forward. "I am Rhen. Is Mila with you? Is she alright?"

"Yes, to both questions," the man responded.

Worren turned his attention to Astrea. "Our leader, Brom, requests a meeting."

"Why, what would we discuss?"

"LOUT and its downfall."

"I am not naive. You are in concert with them."

"Some of our settlements are, but Gromwell isn't one of them. We want them removed from the planet."

Rex, unable to contain himself any longer, unleashed his enthusiasm. "This rainforest just got a serious upgrade in beauty. I've chased rogue animals and tangled with storms, but nothing compares to tracking down a squad of celestial sirens! Ladies, you light up the jungle like a supernova!"

Astrea crossed her arms, her gaze focused on both visitors. "You send an envoy who acts like a child on a sugar high and expect us to believe you are serious? Why should we work with a group of idiots like this one?" she said, pointing to Rex. "Perhaps you should tell Brom that if he wants our cooperation, he'll need more than a simpleton with a big mouth and a shaky sense of responsibility."

Rhen stepped forward, ready to intervene, but Astrea gave him a look that said, 'keep quiet or else', before she redirected her narrowed gaze to the two men.

Rex cleared his throat. "I might come off as a bit unorthodox. But I have a clear mission."

"We will discuss your proposal." She waved two of her soldiers closer. "Take these two and lock them up with Rhen."

Rhen couldn't believe his ears. After everything that had happened, she still had trust issues. Hopefully, he wasn't headed for the net again. He was done being the insect in someone else's trap, especially when all he wanted was a clean escape.

CHAPTER 6

Half an hour later, Darrold escorted Danelda into Brom's home.

Her gaze flicked across the room, fast and calculating, until it landed on Brom. "What is the meaning of this?" she snapped. "Why have I been dragged here?" She tore herself from Darrold's grip, strode to the table, and slammed her basket down hard enough to rattle the cups. "Brom, explain. Now." Then she took in the faces around her, the silence, the set of their shoulders, and her expression melted into a pout. "You're scaring me."

Brom met her gaze. "Where were you a couple of hours ago, Danelda?"

"Doing errands for my mother."

"So, you were not with Flynn?"

"No, of course not. Why are you asking me this?"

"Flynn was picnicking near the monastery today when he was injured. And he wasn't alone."

Tears pooled in her eyes. "Oh, poor Flynn. How is he?" she cried.

"So, you weren't with him?"

"I said I was not." Her lip curled.

Mila entered the fray. "Was he seeing another woman then?" This was a trick question because it was unclear whether the person who fled the scene was a man or a woman.

Danelda shrugged and then looked away. "He is free to do as he pleases."

Brom's fists tightened at his sides, the knuckles white with restrained anger. The room felt like it held its breath.

"Perhaps you were frightened, Danelda, and that's why you fled?" Mila said.

"Don't speak to me, bitch," she snarled with an aura of violence. "You have no right to be here. Return to where you came from. We don't need you, and we don't want you. LOUT will look after us. Brom, you must see the logic here."

The dam burst, and Brom slammed his fist down onto the table so hard that Danelda's basket jumped. "Enough, Danelda! We have been over this a thousand times. I will not change my mind. I invited Mila here."

A sob snagged in Danelda's throat, but Brom didn't buy a second of it. She'd missed her calling, he thought, the theatre's loss was now everyone else's problem. He dragged a hand down his face, fighting the old, stupid flicker of memory. How had he ever been drawn to her? "Enough," he said, voice level. "Tell us the truth. You're not in trouble, but we need to know what happened. If you were scared, that's understandable."

He pulled out a chair and nudged it toward her. "Sit down, Danelda. Start from the beginning. We already know it wasn't your fault. I need the facts."

Danelda's shoulders dropped, and she released a long breath, falling into the chair. "Okay." She tucked a strand of hair behind her ear and looked up at Brom as though butter wouldn't melt in her mouth. "We were enjoying a picnic when Flynn suddenly pitched to the ground." A sob escaped her, and she covered her face with shaking hands. A red stain blossomed on his chest." She wiped her cheeks. "I panicked and ran for cover, worried that I might be next."

Brom glanced at Mila and shook his head. Both knew they would get nothing more from her, and certainly not the truth. "Darrold, please take Danelda home," Brom said.

The young man hurried to Danelda's side, helped her up from the chair, grabbed the basket, and guided her toward the front hatch.

But not before Danelda cast a cold, emotionless stare at Mila, her narrowed red eyes hard and unblinking.

After the hatch closed, Brom said. "Let's head to the monastery and check on Flynn. I believe that our healer, Tussold, is already there. We'll take my transport."

ENTERING THE MONASTERY, Brom's eyes drank in the familiar majesty of the stone foyer, which rose several stories before narrowing to a peak at the summit. Although he remembered his time here with fondness, seeing it again was overwhelming. He had enjoyed the austerity and predictability of life here, which contrasted sharply with life now.

After leaving Flynn in the capable hands of Mila and the other healers, he'd listened to Shaman Oldson's story. On reflection, he felt more off-balance than enlightened because he'd learned nothing new. To him, the attempt on Flynn's life seemed too obvious to ignore. It wasn't an accident. It was another targeted attempt to threaten him and his community. But what was Danelda's role? Was she an innocent bystander, or was she involved? Her passionate plea to accept LOUT provided evidence in favour of the latter. The question was, had she been corrupted after living in Atmos? She'd spent several orbits there before returning to Gromwell without an explanation and acting as though she had never left. Perhaps they should have delved more deeply into her return. After he returned home, he would question Danelda again. And he would get the truth out of her before anyone else was harmed.

CHAPTER 7

Hours crawled by as Rhen, Worren, and Rex sat in a shed shoulder to shoulder on the dirt floor, legs outstretched, the heat pressing down on them. Rhen used the time to pry what he could from the men about the planet's tangled politics and history. It was so hot, Rhen mused, the jungle fowl outside were probably laying hard-boiled eggs.

The sound of footsteps and the rattle of a chain came just before the door opened, flooding the dark shed with light so bright that Rhen was forced to shield his eyes.

"Astrea wants to see you," one of their jailors announced.

At this stage, Rhen could cope with anything as long as he didn't have to spend more time incarcerated. Outside, the sun was lowering in the sky. Nudged forward, the three men were paraded before Astrea and her soldiers, seated in the courtyard at long tables, eating more of yesterday's kill. Rhen's mouth watered at the food on offer. In contrast, the two men beside him didn't appear to be affected by the display.

Astrea took a pull from her tankard. "We have discussed your proposal and will consider a meeting with Brom."

Inside, Rhen jumped for joy.

Chewing a piece of meat, she added, "We leave at first light. Sit."

Rhen didn't need to be asked twice, but Worren and Rex waved the offer aside. "We prefer to forage in the rainforest for our meal."

"Fine, but two of my soldiers will accompany you."

After they nodded and disappeared, Rhen sat in the spot vacated by the two women tasked to supervise the plant eaters and ate with gusto until his stomach groaned in protest.

Half an hour later, they returned from the rainforest with a bulging bag of edibles, which they consumed under everyone's watchful eyes.

Rhen had been bursting to ask a question about tomorrow and decided now was the time. "Astrea, would it be possible to check on my ship and then proceed to Gromwell?"

"Perhaps."

By the Elders, he hated that word. "I think it's important to ensure it is a viable escape option."

Astrea sat for a moment to consider the issue, "I see the logic, Rhen, and I will allow it. Perhaps we can discuss this further in my quarters?"

Maybe 'perhaps' was not such a bad word, he thought. "Ah... yes." He wasn't sure what else to say because he was caught off guard by the offer. He hoped it would involve more than a discussion about tomorrow. And with the looks the other two men were receiving, he didn't think they would be lonely tonight either.

CHAPTER 8

The sun had set when Brom and Mila returned home after leaving Gromwell's medical facility, where Flynn was now being treated. Mila reassured Brom that his friend would recover, but it would take time, given the extent of his injuries. However, they hadn't discussed Danelda or the information Brom gleaned from Shaman Oldson.

Entering the meal prep area, Mila was relieved to discover fresh bread and a hot, thick, hearty vegetable soup in an insulated container. Brom sliced the bread while Mila ladled the soup into two bowls.

Before they had a chance to eat, they were interrupted by a knock at the hatch. Brom let out a deep breath and greeted their visitor. After a brief discussion, the man disappeared, and Brom returned.

"Good news, Mila. It appears that our envoy to the meat-eaters' camp was successful. I sent three men. One remained outside, while the other two gained entry. This allowed the two men inside to get a message to the third. They reported that Rhen is with the meat eaters, who are willing to meet with me. They should arrive tomorrow evening."

With the news, Mila's furrowed brows relaxed, and the slight wrinkle between her eyes softened into a look of relief. Overcome with emotion, she stood and wrapped her arms around Brom. He was at least a head taller than her, and she wasn't a short woman. Tilting her head up, she met a pair of intelligent eyes, which seemed to scream 'deer in the headlights.' Honestly, she probably shared that look because this was something she hadn't planned.

Brom lowered his lips to hers to deliver a 'toe-curling' kiss. In addition to the heat, unexplained comfort washed over her soul. Without conscious thought, she relaxed against him. Large hands threaded into her tresses, and she tilted her head to deepen the kiss. Still acting on instinct, she lost the ability to think until he finally released her and stepped back. Unexpectedly embarrassed, Brom cleared his throat and looked away. "I'm sorry, Mila."

She looked away. "Let's finish our soup before it gets cold." What was I thinking? Mila's mind raced as she sat across from Brom, the taste of that kiss still lingering on her lips. She prided herself on being rational, always in control, but something about that moment shattered her usual restraint. Maybe it was the stress of the day, the emotional toll of everything they'd been through, or the unexpected warmth in his eyes that made her feel safe. She was embarrassed, though she'd never admit it out loud. Regret? Not exactly. But kissing Brom wasn't part of any logical plan, and the fact that she had let it happen so easily gnawed at her, especially when she hadn't forgiven him yet. Brom nodded and sat at the table, unwilling to meet her eyes, so Mila dived into the breach. "What are your thoughts about the events surrounding Flynn?"

"Unfortunately, I don't have sufficient information. I will speak to Danelda again tomorrow and get the truth. Given her lack of interest in Flynn's recovery and her performance, I suspect she was involved. And if that is the case, I have some hard decisions to make."

"I think you should sleep on it. Let's hope that Flynn wakes tomorrow and fills in the gaps."

After finishing their soup, Brom stood and collected the bowls, his movements a little too careful. The clink of ceramic in the sink echoed louder than it should have. "Agreed," he said at last. "I'm exhausted, after last night's explosion, and everything since." He rubbed his eyes, not quite meeting hers, then gestured to a door across the room. "The second bedroom is set up for visitors. You should be comfortable there."

A pause hung between them, thick with everything unsaid.

"Goodnight," he added quietly, before turning away and disappearing into the opposite room. The soft click felt final.

Mila tilted her neck from side to side to release the tension in her shoulders, wondering what had just happened. She was conflicted. Attraction warred with common sense. But common sense prevailed as she made her way to the guest bedroom, wondering what tomorrow would bring. Hopefully, Rhen's return. Exhausted, Mila quickly fell into a deep sleep.

MILA WOKE WITH A START. She had no idea what had woken her or how long she'd been asleep. Sitting up, she heard faint scuffling noises in an adjoining room, and the hair on her arms rose to attention. Swinging her legs from the bed, she quietly made her way to the door and cracked it open. The empty living and meal prep area was bathed in darkness, and everything appeared in order except for the noise coming from Brom's bedroom. Indecision gripped her as she hesitated at his door. Heart racing, she knocked softly before calling out, "Brom, is everything okay?"

A grunt, followed by a sharp crash, was all the answer she needed. Heart pounding, Mila gripped the doorknob and flung the door open. Inside, chaos exploded into motion. Two figures wrestled with Brom, one of them forcing a pressure injector against his neck. Terror surged through her like a lightning strike as one of the attackers broke away and turned toward her. She barely had time to react before the assailant, little more than a shadow in the gloom, raised a pistol and levelled it at her head. Too late to run. Too late to scream.

"I'll handle this one," a woman said coldly.

Mila recognised that voice. "Danelda, what's going on?"

"Shut up, bitch. One wrong move, and I'll gladly end your pathetic excuse for a life. You're coming with us."

The man beside her cut in. "Waylan instructed us to take Brom."

"I'll speak to him," Danelda snapped, her voice a snarl.

"We should check with him first," the man insisted.

"No. He owes me."

Mila wondered how long this argument would drag on. Meanwhile, Brom now lay unnervingly silent on the bed.

Suddenly, something cold pressed against her neck, and everything went black.

TERAWATTS OF VIOLENCE unleashed from the sky in a deafening CRACK, RUMBLE and BOOM, jolted Mila awake. And if that wasn't bad enough, a massive, ear-popping, stomach-ruining drop followed. A crushing headache, nausea and blurred vision clouded her recall of the kidnapping, and her brain felt like a flat battery. Given the engine noise and vibration, she guessed they were airborne.

Bracing herself, she opened her eyes as another bolt of lightning unleashed a deafening BOOM! Outside, the surrounding clouds flickered and flashed with reflected lightning, intermittently lighting up the dark cabin. Thankfully, the restraints across her thighs kept her secure in her seat.

The craft shook violently, turning loose objects into deadly projectiles that ricocheted off the walls and careened around the cabin. The whoosh of a panel rocketing overhead, then shattering into a million pieces against the back wall, further tested her frayed nerves.

Moments later, the craft jolted violently as it navigated through more choppy cloud layers. Fear had her plastering her gaze on an unresponsive Brom beside her before turning to the porthole in a futile attempt to find reassurance. But to no avail. The knot in her stomach twisted tighter as they descended sharply, her trembling hands scrabbling for purchase on the armrests. Their kidnappers must have been desperate to fly in this weather, and in a small craft where corrosion ravaged the walls like a bad case of scurvy, which she had only glimpsed. No doubt, it was worse in the light of day. Would she and Brom pay the ultimate price? What was Danelda's game?

Danelda stumbled around the cabin armed with a large knife, anxiously peering out of every porthole she passed. Unsurprisingly, the next jolt sent the woman diving into a seat in the front row.

Amid the chaos, the cockpit door flew open, revealing a storm of flashing red warnings that bathed the cramped space in a sinister glow. Klaxon alarms screamed through the hull, vibrating through the metal. Mila caught a glimpse of the pilot's hands darting over the flickering virtual controls, his face tight with grim focus as he fought against the storm and failing systems, every tap an urgent search for a miracle.

Suddenly, the pilot's voice cut through the cacophony. "Danelda! Comms are dead and the AI's offline!" His fingers clenched the steering column, knuckles white. "Strap in, now!"

During a flash of lightning that briefly transformed the shuttle's cabin into a harsh tableau of light and shadow, Mila caught a glimpse of the pilot's terrified face. Taking advantage of the next BOOM! Mila swallowed her fear and checked on Brom, who was breathing normally. She was thankful that the experimental nanites she'd injected into her body a couple of months ago had paid off. Evidently, they'd neutralised the drug quickly, unlike Brom, who was still reeling from its effects unless she could find something to bring him out of it. If there were a medical kit on board, it might hold something that might help. But tracking it down in this chaos felt impossible. Frankly, she'd be shocked if this flying coffin had any safety equipment at all.

From Mila's vantage point, Danelda ignored the pilot's advice to strap in. Instead, she remained preoccupied with the raging storm, nervously clenching and unclenching the knife's hilt in her right hand.

Another CRACK, RUMBLE and BOOM! Plunged the craft into a nose-dive, and the deep roar of the engines filled the cabin as they fought to remain airborne. Through Mila's porthole, the wing shuddered violently in the turbulent wind, its frame trembling as if barely holding together. One of the engines belched thick, black smoke in wild spirals. The sputtering roar of the failing engine deepened into a metallic groan, and then a deafening rumble. The entire craft shivered with the force. Every rusty bolt and seam was vibrating in protest, threatening to come loose at any moment. Glancing out the porthole, the ground rushed towards them. It was scary sitting there, unable to do anything except watch a mad woman wield a knife and pray that the pilot knew what he was doing. She had never been so scared, wondering if she would die. And if she did. Would it be painful?

She envied Brom. Ignorance was bliss at this point. If they went down, he wouldn't feel a thing. She, on the other hand, would experience the terror firsthand. She leaned over and grasped one of his hands, praying to the Elders that they would be spared. Brom's community needed him. In truth, although he had much to answer for by dragging her and Rhen to this forsaken planet, he was still a good man who didn't deserve to die.

It all unfolded in a blur. One moment, Mila was bracing herself, and the next, a violent jolt slammed her forward into the seat ahead, the impact so forceful it knocked the breath from her lungs. Everything around her seemed to slow, a surreal detachment settling in as if she were watching from a distance, her body numb to the chaos. Through her blurred vision, she saw the shuttle's nose crumple and peel away from the fuselage, metal twisting and shrieking as the craft skidded and bounced across the dense rainforest floor, ripping through trees and foliage. The world outside spun, flashes of green and smoke swirling in her periphery.

After what seemed like a long time, they finally stopped. There was almost complete silence, except for the crackling of fire and groaning of metal. What was left of the cabin resembled an egg cracked in two. At least they wouldn't asphyxiate from the smoke billowing from the back of the cabin, given the fresh air entering from the front.

Amidst the dwindling rain and cloud cover, the sun inched over the horizon, spreading gently diffused light. It struck her then that the thunder and lightning had thankfully abated.

Taking stock of her body, Mila catalogued a few cuts and bruises. Thankfully, nothing was broken. Groaning, she dragged a shaky hand through her tangled brown mane, raking it away from her face before she unclipped her restraint. She was still in her nightclothes, the thin fabric and bare feet a brutal reminder that they had been taken from sleep, not prepared for survival. Gripping the armrest, she tried to rise, but a wave of dizziness pinned her to the seat. She closed her stinging eyes, forced a slow breath, and pulled herself together. Heart hammering, she turned to Brom. He was slumped in his harness, still in what he had been wearing when they were dragged from his home, rumpled nightclothes. Mila checked his pulse and breathing, relieved to find them steady, if faint, then scanned the cabin for anything useful, which was probably a big ask.

She got one foot down onto the uneven floor, and the fuselage groaned in protest. She flinched, steadied herself, and moved carefully through the wrecked cabin, stepping over torn webbing, fractured panelling, and scattered personal effects. Near the rear bulkhead, half buried under a collapsed section of wall, she spotted a locker marked with medical insignia. Wrenching it open, she rifled through the strewn contents, fingers shaking as she pushed aside bandage packs and sealant strips. No full kit, but enough to matter. She found a pressure cylinder, the kind used for fast-acting stimulants and emergency recovery, and exhaled hard.

Before she returned to Brom, she checked the storage lockers along the port side, searching for anything that could pass as clothing. Shuttles like this were often stocked with utilitarian extras, emergency coveralls, thermal layers, basic boots, the kind of gear meant for crew and passengers caught in a hard landing. She found a sealed pack of charcoal-grey, durable jumpsuits with reinforced knees and forearms, sizing straps, and a simple insignia on the chest. Next, she found boots, heavy-duty and scuffed, the kind designed for traction and protection rather than comfort. Mila hesitated, eyeing the sizing marks, then took them anyway. Too big was better than bare feet, and too small was a problem for later.

She bundled the clothing under her arm and scooped up the boots, one by one, along with a pair of thin utility gloves, then turned back toward Brom.

She knelt beside him and pressed the pressure cylinder to his neck.

Seconds later, Brom inhaled sharply. His eyes opened, unfocused at first, then snapped to her face. "What happened?" He dragged a hand over his mouth and jaw, as if checking he was still whole. "Where are we?"

Mila popped his harness release and offered him her hand. "Unfortunately, I don't have time to answer," she said, keeping her voice steady, even as her legs started to tremble now that the adrenaline was bleeding away. "We need to get out of here before what's left of this shuttle goes up in flames." She tightened her grip, braced, and helped him to his feet. "Take it easy."

Brom swallowed, nodding once. "Understood," he muttered, gaze sweeping the twisted cabin. "It is a miracle that we survived."

"A few cuts and bruises are nothing compared to what might have happened," Mila said. She shifted the clothing higher under her arm, handed Brom the medical kit and pushed forward, guiding them through the debris. "As soon as we're clear, we're climbing into these jumpsuits."

They stumbled down through a breach in the fuselage, the rainforest air hitting Mila like a wall, wet heat, leaf rot, and smoke. They quickly pulled on the clothing and boots, and Mila headed toward the front section of the wreck, forcing herself to move with purpose, not panic. "Now the doctor in me needs to check for survivors," she said, voice tight.

At the shuttle's forward end, she peered in from outside and saw the pilot, motionless in his seat, impaled by splintered branches that had punched through the torn hull, the impact finishing what the crash had not. Mila's stomach clenched, but she kept her calm. When she returned to Brom, she lowered her voice. "I didn't see Danelda," she said. "She could be anywhere, and she wasn't using a seat restraint."

"Why am I not surprised?" Brom shook his head.

Picking their way across the debris field, Mila stayed close to Brom, the medical kit clutched in her hand. Twisted plating lay half-buried in the earth, and shards of torn hull metal glittered between splintered branches and scattered components.

They spotted her a few metres ahead, wedged against a fallen section of framing, shock-pale and still conscious, one hand braced on the ground, the other trembling near the knife buried to the hilt in her abdomen.

"Danelda, look at me." Mila dropped to her knees, the medical kit hitting the ground with a dull thud as she snapped it open with shaking fingers she refused to let show. "Stay with me and keep your eyes on mine."

Danelda's breathing hitched, wet and sharp. Each inhale made the blade tremble, and dark blood bubbled around the hilt with a soft, horrible hiss, as if the wound itself were breathing.

Mila's stomach turned. No proper surgical bay, no extraction team, no time. Just wreckage, smoke, and the awful certainty of what she could not fix. "You're not alone," Mila said, forcing her voice steady as the world narrowed to Danelda's face. "I'm right here. I'm going to take the pain away, and you're going to keep breathing with me, one breath at a time. Do you hear me?"

She drew up a dose of pain medication and injected it with practised speed, then sprayed a layer of bio-gel over the exposed tissue. The compound reacted instantly, foaming, then sealing, hardening within seconds to coagulate the bleeding and hold what it could in place.

Brom knelt beside Danelda, gently taking her hand as her pain-filled eyes fluttered open. She managed a strained smile, one corner of her mouth lifting. "I need to tell you something," she whispered, her voice barely audible.

"Later. Save your energy, Danelda."

Mila shook her head at Brom to indicate that there would be no 'later'.

"I need to confess," Danelda said, taking a shallow, rattling breath before she continued. "I am sorry, Brom. Sorry for your father, brother and Flynn's injuries."

"They weren't your fault."

"Yes, they were," she whispered, closing her eyes briefly.

The crease between Brom's eyes deepened.

"But that isn't all," she murmured. "You have a daughter called Oxana who is fifteen orbits old and resides in Atmos. I haven't been a good mother. Waylan has her in a special school for students with potent Kesk powers." With that said, she closed her eyes and took her last shallow breath.

Brom let go of Danelda's hand, stood and panned his eyes over the rainforest. "Do you think she was telling the truth, or was she delirious?" he asked.

Mila pushed aside her disappointment that she didn't have the tools to save Danelda. "From my experience, deathbed confessions tend to be truthful."

Brom opened his arms in invitation. She didn't need any encouragement to fall into his embrace. It was just what they both needed.

THEY CARRIED DANELDA'S body to an empty engine casing nearby and eased her inside, then sealed the opening with a sheet of metal. After a few quiet words, Mila removed the necklace engraved with Danelda's name and draped it over the casing, letting it rest against the scorched hull like a marker.

Afterwards, Brom sat down between two trees, placed his hands against the trunks, crossed his legs and closed his eyes.

"What are you doing?"

"Absorbing energy from the trees. They have agreed to give me some of their life force."

Obviously, she had questions, but now was not the time. Returning to the smouldering fuselage, Mila searched the surrounding area for anything useful. But besides the medical kit, she came up empty, so she returned to Brom, who was now on his feet. "Feeling better?" she asked.

"Yes," he said, smiling. But the smile didn't quite reach his eyes.

"I couldn't find anything useful in the wreck," she said, desperately wanting to ask about the energy transfer.

"We have the rainforest. That's all we need," Brom said.

Although a protest wavered on Mila's lips, she remained silent.

CHAPTER 9

After locating the Halo Insurgent III, Rhen tried to bring her systems online, only to hit a hard lock when his startup codes were revoked. Someone had changed them. He would have to hack his way back into control, which meant wading through layers of security protocols that could swallow up precious time. Still, the vessel was intact, powered, and flight-ready.

He, Astrea, three of her soldiers, and Rex and Worren arrived in Growmwell by mid-afternoon just as the town residents were assembling.

Worren recognised Tussold, the local healer, and pulled him aside. "What is going on?"

It was then that Tussold noticed the strangers.

"Don't be alarmed," Worren said. "Brom requested we bring them here."

Worren's eyebrows lowered. "Where is Brom?" he asked.

The healer rubbed his eyes.

"Tussold?" Worren snapped.

"He's missing, along with the doctor. Judging by the state of Brom's home, there was a struggle. The gate sentries had also been drugged."

Rex shook his head. "This has LOUT's name written all over it."

Rhen pushed forward then. "Is Mila missing?"

"I'm afraid so," the healer replied.

Rhen dropped his head, and disappointment tightened his chest.

Tussold waved them towards the gathering. "Join us. We are about to discuss the way forward."

CHAPTER 10

Events took an unexpected turn when Mila and Brom caught sight of a shuttle hovering above the rainforest canopy. Against the backdrop of a cloud-streaked sky, dark figures descended from its underside on cables, their movements swift and deliberate as they rappelled into the rainforest.

Brom waved Mila into the undergrowth. "It's not one of ours. The pilot must have activated an emergency beacon or sent a message to LOUT before impact."

Unbeknownst to Mila, she'd picked the wrong place to hide. Ants flowed around her feet like water, which hadn't initially concerned her. But within seconds, they splashed over her boots and scaled her legs in earnest. She quickly learned they were weaponised. Normally, she would have run, but one movement, one scream, one involuntary gasp, and it would all be over.

Brom's eyes widened as he understood her dilemma and the tears streaming down her cheeks.

At breaking point, she gave him one last look, then sprinted deeper into the rainforest, snapping branches and slapping at the ants as she crashed through the undergrowth.

Brom stayed on her heels, and the shouts behind them told her the men were gaining ground. He vaulted a narrow stream, and she scrambled after him, her footing skidding on the slick bank. She went down hard. Brom was back in an instant. He met her eyes, steady, encouraging, then reached for her hand and hauled her upright.

"You might have guessed that cross-country running is not my forte," she whispered between gritted teeth.

"It's not my favourite pastime either, especially in these circumstances."

"Do you have a destination in mind?"

"I do. There are caves nearby. Unfortunately, the rainforest has reclaimed the entrances, making them hard to locate, but that could also work to our advantage. I am looking for a specific tree species. Once I locate it, the caves will be close by."

Mila felt intense dread and panic as her boots pounded the damp earth beneath her while her arms wrangled with the dense foliage. Her heart raced, and her breathing came in short gasps as she ran to the sound of the enemy on their heels, their heavy footsteps and menacing shouts closing in. Tearing through the dense rainforest, leaping over fallen logs and weaving around broad tree trunks, Mila was becoming exhausted, but she wouldn't let that stop her.

Ahead, Brom's body moved with a strength and agility that she envied. As the enemy marched closer, she heard the rattle and clang of their weapons, along with threatening shouts. Brom's determination to keep going spurred her on. So, she drew on the last of her energy and kept running, pushing her body to its limits, praying that they would make it to the caves.

Mila felt immense relief when they finally stumbled upon one of the caves Brom had been searching for. After running through the dense rainforest for so long, she'd lost hope of finding safety. But upon seeing the cave entrance, she let out a relieved breath.

With the enemy still hot on their trail, Brom waved her safely inside before touching the vines hanging near the cave entrance and closing his eyes. She watched as they quickly entwined themselves around the opening, creating a thick wall of greenery that blocked their hiding place from view and provided perfect camouflage. Mila experienced deep awe for Brom's mysterious powers, which seemed endless. With a newfound sense of security, she took several deep breaths.

Brom's lips curved into a satisfied smile as he surveyed his work before leading her deeper into the cave, guided by shafts of weak morning sunlight streaming through the interspersed oculus vents. Brom traced the walls with his hands, navigating the twists and turns with precision, while Mila concentrated on finding her footing, carefully avoiding jagged rocks and crevices. Together, they made their way through the darkness, following the occasional rays of light illuminating their path.

They descended further into the cave, where the muted echo of their movements reverberated through the walls, along with the gentle dripping of water and the flutter of wings from the cave's inhabitants. Outside, all sounds of the enemy had disappeared.

Exhaustion prompted Mila to ask, "How much further, Brom?" She shivered. The chill was deep in her bones, no doubt exacerbated by her damp clothing, which also hampered movement. Her heart pounded as she forced herself to focus on the task at hand, fighting the rising dread that something was lurking in the depths of the dark cave.

"From memory, we are nearly there."

"You're not leading me on, are you?" she teased, the lightness in her voice masking the tight knot of anxiety inside. Humour was her last defence, and a fragile shield.

"Believe me. You will know when I am leading you on. There won't be any doubt." He held her gaze for a few moments, then gave her a seductive wink before turning back around.

Mila felt a flutter of excitement in her stomach at the swift and unexpected exchange.

Brom cleared his throat. "It was part of the school curriculum to camp out here for a few days and replicate the early settlers' experience. Later, Flynn and I visited for fun." He stopped suddenly then, causing Mila to slam into his back. She hadn't noticed because her eyes were focused on the ground while her mind pondered his flirtatious remarks.

"We have arrived," Brom said. He turned, caught her by the upper arms, and steadied her before her knees could betray her. His grip was firm, warm through the fabric, thumbs anchoring just enough pressure to bring her back into her body. He dipped his head, and when she lifted her face, his eyes held hers, intelligent, intent, and openly wanting. She probably wore the same look. Brom groaned once, low, controlled, then forced himself to slow, like he was memorising her while he still could. His hands framed her ribs, not claiming, not yet, just holding her steady as the world outside hunted them.

In addition to the heat, unexplained comfort washed over her soul. Unable to resist, she answered his demands and relaxed into the experience. Without conscious thought, she found herself clinging to his shoulders and breathing in his earthy scent.

His warm lips and hands invoked an answer that resonated deep within her. Large hands traced and caressed her mud-caked back before sliding down to learn her contours. Her senses rocketed to overload when her nipples brushed against his solid chest as it rose and fell, puckering them into hard points as they chafed against their confinement.

Totally immersed, it took Brom a moment to realise that Mila was wet and shaking from the cold. Withdrawing his lips, he stepped back to examine her in more detail. "We need to get you out of those clothes."

"Well, that's straight to the point."

His face reddened. "I meant to get you dry, not to...."

"What?"

"Make love to you." His eyes darkened. "Even though that is on the top of my list."

Pleasure hummed along her skin. She wasn't shivering with cold so much as desire now.

Brom cleared his throat. "Unfortunately, the ocular above us won't provide this chamber with sufficient light." He quickly set about lighting a campfire, his hands deftly gathering wood from a stack in the far corner. Mila watched as he found an old fire-starting device and efficiently coaxed a flame to life beneath the ocular. He stepped back with a satisfied smile, waiting for the fire to catch.

Worried, she asked, "Won't the enemy see the smoke?"

"We are very deep in the cave system." He smiled then. "Would you like a bath?"

"This is no time to joke, Brom. There is nothing I would like more."

He scooped a small metallic object from the corner. With a swipe of his hand over its sensor, the device activated, casting a soft, bluish light that pulsed gently. The ambient glow illuminated the space as he beckoned her to follow through an aperture only slightly larger than their bodies, into the adjoining area, where a bubbling spring fed into a rock pool. Its waters glistened in the faint light, forming a small current that lapped against the edges. A smell of sulphur filled the air, mixed with a faint scent of moss, carried by the wisps of white steam rising from the pool and escaping through another ocular above.

Tears of joy pooled in Mila's eyes as she witnessed light bouncing off the bubbles and exploding to the surface.

"Your own private hot tub," he stated with pride.

Her weary muscles and the numerous ant bites silently thanked him.

"I will leave you to your bath, my lady," he said, bowing before spinning on his heels and walking away.

"Wait, Brom. I think there is room for two." She heard the tremble in her own voice.

Brom turned back. His face broke into a smile. "Are you sure, Mila?"

"Yes." She presented him with a seductive smile before slowly removing her boots, then her jumpsuit, and finally her pyjamas. Next, she loosened her ponytail and shook out her long hair.

Mesmerised, Brom padded across the dirt, lifted her hand to his lips and placed a tender kiss on her knuckle, which sizzled up her arm.

"Brom," she whispered, her eyes locked onto his unfaltering ones. No one else had gotten this close, especially someone she hadn't known for long. Their time together had been fuelled by adrenaline and danger, so she couldn't help wondering whether the attraction had been fuelled by circumstance or if it was the start of something more profound. For now, she just wanted him.

In slow motion, his hand released hers, sliding up to cradle the back of her neck and draw her close. His mouth brushed the silken seam of her closed lips, teasing them apart, and after the first fierce claim, the kiss gentled, turning warm and sure.

Mila closed her eyes. Her hands travelled over Brom's back, over the damp fabric of the jumpsuit, tracing the hard lines beneath it, before she leaned into his heat with a soft, breathless sound.

In one smooth motion, he slipped an arm beneath her knees and the other behind her back, lifting her as if she weighed nothing, angling toward the pool as though he meant to carry her straight in, boots and all.

Mila caught her breath, half laughing, half desperate. "I think you have way too many clothes on, Brom."

He stopped, set her down gently beside the water, and held her gaze, the corner of his mouth twitching as if he had been waiting for permission. Moving with his natural grace, he sat, tugged off the boots first, then rose and peeled the wet jumpsuit and his pyjama pants down his torso, shoving them past his hips and stepping free.

The fabric hit the ground with a damp slap. He did not look away from her as he hooked his thumbs into his underpants and lowered them, baring the thick, straining line of his erection. Finally naked, he offered her his hands, guided her into the water with steady care, then followed, sinking in behind her and pulling her close. His mouth found hers again, deep and sound, as his hands slid over her skin, claiming what the water could not hide. His restless fingers found her nipples, already tight, and his calloused palms grazed over the peaks.

The sensation sparked through her, sharp and hot, igniting everything inside her until she arched into him, needing more. Mila closed her eyes to savour the experience.

"Open your eyes, Mila, and look at me. I want you to know who is making love to you."

"Is it the shaman or the leader of Gromwell, or both?" she asked.

"It is the man. A simple man who has led a spiritual life of discipline and self-control for the most part." He kissed her again.

Mila felt the gentle caress of his fingertips on her bare skin as he brushed them lightly over her neck and shoulders. His soft and tender touch sent a wave of pleasure down her spine. His lips trailed along her jawline, his breath hot against her skin. His hands moved lower, exploring her curves, and Mila felt her body hum in response. His touch was featherlight and gentle, igniting a fire within her that curled her toes. He worshipped her body with his hands, lips, and eyes, and Mila felt her heart swell with desire.

Mila allowed his lips to gently explore her neck and shoulder.

Between kisses, Brom whispered. "You are an amazing woman, and I am a very lucky man after everything I did to you. And for that, I am sorry. But I plan to make it up to you now," he growled.

Mila's approval came in the form of a smile. "Big promises, Brom. I hope you are up for it. Pun intended."

"I think the evidence speaks for itself, don't you?" he said, enclosing her hand within his own and wrapping it around his straining erection. "I am at your command, dear lady." Brom lightly pressed her back against the edge of the rock pool and crushed her lips against his. "The atmosphere almost makes it a spiritual experience, don't you think?" he murmured before deepening the kiss and sliding his tongue inside.

Unable to resist, she opened up to him and quickly became a spirited partner. Sliding her hands over his muscled shoulders, she moved them to his head, redirecting his lips to her nipples. Mila was mesmerised by this strong but gentle man, so different from other men she had met. It was too early to label it, but he was unique, and that thought gave her pause. She wasn't looking for a serious relationship, but this man made her question that. She had a life and career on Rotari, and she couldn't think beyond returning home.

Needing no encouragement, Brom lifted her slightly and curled his tongue around one stiffened nipple at a time, his teeth tugging lightly on each in turn. "Beautiful," he whispered, worrying one with his tongue before lavishing the other to prove his point.

She closed her eyes briefly and shivered at the sensation of his lips sucking and pulling on her sensitised nipples, made more so by the scrape of his whiskers.

Brom ran his nimble fingers through her folds and parted her carefully. His eyes were almost black in the dim light, burning with lust and emotion as she felt his shaft press against her tender opening before he forged slowly into her welcoming heat. A flush of warmth had her lips gravitating to his again as she subtly adjusted her position to accommodate his thick shaft. He played her like a master magician who had been given a precious instrument. While his warm lips and hands invoked an unfamiliar cord of response, his shallow thrusts promised something more. But not yet. Despite her protests, he maintained the pace and shimmied his hands to cup her bottom.

Mila groaned.

Brom's hips began to thrust his shaft inside her with deep, hard movements as he quickened the pace.

All Mila could do was cling to his shoulders and hang on for dear life. She was so close to coming. She could feel the fire sizzling in her core and the tremors trying to break free as she rode Brom with wild abandon. Desire burned hotter and higher with each pass of his shaft, and Mila knew she wouldn't last much longer. To add to the sensual onslaught, her flushed, swollen breasts danced over the water's surface. Each time he rasped her inner core, flames ignited her body. She didn't think it was possible, but his thrusts reached deeper, and she felt electrical sparks run through her nervous system. Reaching down between their bodies, he stroked her firm pearl until he was rewarded with a shiver and a sharp inhale. The detonation consumed her mind, body, and soul; it took a moment before she could breathe again.

Three more fierce thrusts heralded his release. Weaving his fingers into her wet tresses, he dropped his forehead against hers and took a deep breath.

Mila blinked up at him, breath unsteady. "I could get addicted to this."

Brom's mouth hitched, then he pressed his forehead to hers. "You're late."

Her brow lifted.

"I already am." He tipped his head back and released a lusty laugh. "Your bedside manner is going to get you into trouble." His gaze held hers. "With me," he whispered, nuzzling her throat, unaware of the effect of his prophetic words. Still breathing heavily, he shifted Mila in his arms and held her tightly against his chest in the warm, bubbling water.

Mila's lips curved. "I'll write it up as a complication." She paused for effect. "Exposure to Brom: heightened heart rate and impaired judgment."

"So what's the treatment, doctor?"

Mila's eyes flicked to his mouth, then back up. "Avoid exposure."

Brom's thumb traced her lower lip. "Careful, Doctor. You're the one self-prescribing."

Mila listened to the cave's silence for a beat, letting the afterglow drain into focus. "Brom." Her voice dropped. "Before we move, I need answers." She held his gaze. "You've already shown me some of your skills." A faint curve touched her mouth, then vanished. "Now tell me what else you can do, especially with flora. What is that connection, and how far does it go?"

"All plants, including trees, have life running through them as we do, but it's slower, more patient. When I'm in pain or tired, I can take a bit of that energy and let it flow into me. It's like drinking from the tree of life."

Mila watched him, her brow furrowed in curiosity. "And they just give it to you? Doesn't it harm them?"

"Not if I'm careful. He closed his eyes. "They feel it, sure. But it's more about sharing than taking. The trick is knowing when to stop. If I take too much, they start to wither. And that's on me." His eyes opened, a shadow crossing his face. "It can drain them just like they can drain me. When I was younger, I didn't understand the balance. I thought having this gift meant I could take whatever I needed whenever I wanted. Unfortunately, I killed the first tree I tried it on." His voice grew quiet as he ran his hand over his face. "That's when I was sent to the monastery. Their teachings weren't just about trees but control and understanding. You see, there's power in everything around us, in the earth, the sky, and even in ourselves. But if you can't control that power, it controls you. And the cost is always higher than you think." He looked at her, his gaze heavy with the weight of memories. "The shamans also taught me how to listen, to feel the ebb and flow of life around me." He paused, his expression softening as he spoke of the place that had clearly shaped him.

"The training included days of silence, sitting with my back to a tree, trying to feel its pulse. Hours spent meditating, learning to keep my own energy in check. They pushed me to my limits because if you can't control your own power, you end up destroying everything around you. It wasn't just about protecting the trees; it was about protecting myself and those around me. The shamans understood that power without control is just as dangerous as no power at all."

"That sounds... intense," she said. "But what happens if someone can't master their power?"

"They leave." His voice dropped, tinged with a trace of sadness. "Not everyone can handle it. Some are too impulsive and too desperate to use their abilities without thinking, and become dangerous. A few never return from the rainforest. The trees don't always give you what you want. If you take too much, too quickly, you lose yourself to them. You become part of them." He sighed, glancing up at the ocular above them. "That's why the training is so important. You must respect the power, or it'll consume you."

"It sounds like the shamans weren't just teaching you how to control your power. They were teaching you how to respect it."

"Exactly. Power isn't just about what you can do. It's about knowing when not to use it. That's the hardest lesson of all."

"It also sounds dangerous."

"It is. And that's where specialised training comes in. It's a delicate balance. And sometimes, the rainforest needs me more than I need it."

"But you're different, aren't you? There's more to it... more to you. What else can you do?"

Brom's eyes narrowed, and a faint smile tugged at the corners of his lips, but there was something guarded behind it. "For now, let's just say the Kesk abilities run deep in my family. As such, one family member from each generation studies at the monastery with the expectation that they will become the head shaman. Currently, my uncle, Shaman Oldson, holds the title. If I had been left in situ, I would have been content to continue my training."

Mila studied him closely, catching the subtle change in his tone and the careful way he dodged her question. It was clear he was holding something back, not ready to reveal more. Maybe he didn't trust her with it yet or thought she wouldn't understand. Either way, it didn't matter. She could sense there was more to uncover, but she wasn't in a hurry. There would be other moments, she thought, content to let it slide for now, knowing patience was key with someone like him. There was a time and place for everything, and she'd push further when the moment was right. For now, she'd let it rest, satisfied that she'd at least caught a glimpse of something deeper beneath his guarded exterior. With a quiet nod, she mentally filed away her curiosity for later, knowing this topic was far from over. Taking a more general approach, she said, "So, you have a new path now."

"I don't have a choice. Not until Gromwell votes in another leader."

"What if they want you to stay on?"

"They will be disappointed because I am not my father or brother. They were real leaders."

"But you were going to take over the monastery."

"Yes, but that's vastly different to leading five thousand people who don't always agree with you, and your prime directive to keep them safe."

"I think you are more suited than you think. They look up to you. From what I can ascertain, they don't want anyone else."

"Well, it's a moot point. I have to beat LOUT at their game, and Gromwell doesn't stand a chance until I do that. And there is the issue of a daughter whom I knew nothing about until today. The only option I see is to destroy the organisation from the inside and rescue my daughter. And to do that, I need to get into Atmos. I can see I was a little delusional, thinking that you and Rotari would be the answer to my problems. Now I have drawn you and Rhen into our conflict, and to what end? In truth, all I have done is put you both in danger."

"Stop beating yourself up. We will think of something. Get some rest. Tomorrow's problems can wait.

AFTER A FITFUL NIGHT on a slatted pallet topped with an old canvas bedroll, stale with smoke and someone else's sweat, Mila and Brom rose at daybreak and climbed into their washed but not yet dry clothing to forage for food. Mila was fascinated by Brom's knowledge of edible plants and their healing and nutritional properties. Following Brom's lead, Mila ate her way through the nearby area until the sound of a shuttle overhead brought reality back.

"They have returned," Brom snapped.

"They must see you as a threat. Otherwise, why would they bother?"

"LOUT must have a bigger plan in motion, and they want me out of the picture." He walked towards her and enclosed her hands in his. "Perhaps I should let them capture me. That's the easiest way to get inside Atmos."

"That is madness, Brom. Don't."

"Maybe, but I need to confront the enemy head-on. Without putting others at risk."

"Why don't we wait for rescue and then devise a plan?"

He leaned down and kissed her. "Sorry, Mila, my mind is made up. Please go back to the cave. Flynn and the others will find you within a day or so. I left a trail from the crash site for them to follow, and you know enough to feed yourself now." With that said, he gave her one last look before sprinting towards the landing shuttle and into danger. Not one for following orders, Mila trailed behind but remained out of sight.

The sound of a whirring engine powering down filled the air, and Mila's heart sank. She knew what was coming, and all she could do was stand and watch in terror. Armed soldiers leapt out of the craft, and Brom lifted his hands in the air. Despite surrendering, he was stunned and quickly hit the ground before being carried away. All rational thought evaporated, and Mila ran towards the soldiers who met her with the cold barrels of their guns and a set of cuffs before she was herded into the shuttle. She wasn't going to let Brom execute his plan alone. "Where are you taking us?" she asked.

"You will find out soon enough," one of them answered.

She wished she could help Brom. "I am a doctor. Can I check his vitals?"

"He will be examined as soon as we arrive in Atmos."

"Why did you tranquilise him? He was surrendering. He wasn't going to harm you."

"I beg to differ. The green people are dangerous, particularly this one. One touch from him could stop your heart."

That was a new and slightly alarming fact. From her perspective, the only damage Mila foresaw was Brom breaking her heart, a revelation in itself that required more soul-searching. Be that as it may, what else was Brom capable of? She regretted not pressing him for answers earlier.

About fifteen minutes later, she spied a circular structure in a hub-and-spoke configuration at least half a kilometre wide, supported by a central column that descended into the lake below. The structural column was so tall that it rivalled the surrounding mountains. She assumed this was the famed Atmos.

Without warning, the shuttle executed a sudden vertical descent, plummeting toward the mountains that ringed the shimmering lake.

It then levelled out, gliding smoothly into the mouth of a massive rock-carved entrance. The large passage swallowed the craft as it descended deeper beneath the lake; its sleek and cold walls were lined with running lights to guide the way. Soon, the passage opened into a sprawling underground hangar beneath the lake's surface. It must have been hewn from solid rock first, carved on a scale that stole her breath, then tamed with a massive ribbed framework and utilitarian cladding that wrapped the chamber like a skeleton in armour. Arched supports marched away into the distance, vanishing in repeating curves.

A marshal waved them into a marked bay. The shuttle glided in and settled. Landing struts hissed as they took the weight, and a burst of steam vented from beneath the hull, enough to make nearby workers flinch back and shield their faces as grit and damp dust skittered across the deck.

In front of her, Brom was loaded onto a hover trolley, which silently glided towards a wide, circular foyer. Around her, a restless crowd gathered, waiting in front of massive vac lifts that serviced the city above. One of the lifts opened with a quiet hiss, depositing passengers who quickly dispersed. After a push between her shoulder blades, she entered an empty vac lift along with Brom and the guards.

The three guards exchanged a few quick words, and the doors closed. A high-pitched whine followed, then a brief wash of white light as the vac lift engaged. Mila closed her eyes, then opened them again as the whine fell away and the lift eased to a stop at their destination.

Waiting was an armed guard who issued instructions. "Take him to the infirmary," he said, pointing to Brom. "Take the woman to the interrogation room."

Now, Mila was really worried; she didn't want to be separated from Brom. "I'm a doctor. He needs my assistance," she pleaded.

"Atmos physicians will take care of him now," the same guard said.

Just as she was ready to make a break for it, one of the guards wearing a face set in serious lines grabbed her arm and shook his head. "I don't want to hurt you."

While she subdued the impulse to give him the bird, she vowed to find a way to escape.

CHAPTER 11

Back in Gromwell, Tussold mounted the podium and Rhen and Astrea pushed their way to the front of the crowd.

Tussold lifted his right hand, and silence fell like a shroud over the gathered faces. Every breath seemed to catch. "I know you are all wondering what transpired last night." His voice cut through the quiet, low and steady. He let the words hang, eyes scanning the assembly as if pulling each soul closer.

"Hoark and Auna were on gate duty when the assailants hit. Even drugged, Auna managed to get an alarm out before she went down. I reached the gate a few minutes later and found them both unconscious."

Murmurs rippled through the crowd.

Tussold's jaw tightened. "I'm relieved to report that both are recovering. But that isn't all, dear friends." He drew in a deep breath before delivering the next blow. "Brom and his visitor, Mila, are missing. We believe it is the work of LOUT."

A roar of demands swept the plaza, every shout sharper than the one before. Tussold raised his arms in a plea for calm, but the tide of anger swallowed his gesture. Ripples of dissent pulsed through the crowd as they pressed in, each footstep a drumbeat of impatience. His unshakable authority now felt fragile. In desperation, he pointed to Rhen, who looked around to find all eyes focused on him. "Rhen and the meat-eaters will forge a plan to free Brom and Mila. It's time we rose against LOUT!" he thundered.

A sharp voice from the crowd sliced through the uproar. "Why not accept their offer?" In an instant, hesitant murmurs swelled into full-throated assent, like an oncoming tide.

Astrea mounted the podium, her eyes flashing with defiance, amidst a ripple of surprised murmurs. "LOUT won't rest until you're nothing more than slaves on your own soil. What glitters from afar is a gilded cage up close. Do you really want to bow to someone else's rules and be trapped in a ruthless regime? I, for one, do not. Don't you want the freedom to move about this planet and come and go as you please? LOUT shot down my ship because they don't want any interference with their plan to exploit you and your gifts. I know what it's like to be under someone else's control and be complicit in their agenda without knowing it."

Rhen was taken aback by her ability to motivate the crowd, not to mention her relaxed relationship with the truth. She failed to mention why she and her charges were on the planet. But reminded himself that it was before her neural controller had been disabled. Perhaps she had a change of heart now that she and her soldiers were clear of interference and manipulation.

She glanced at him, and he gave her a smile and a thumbs-up.

Satisfied with the response, she continued. "Your time is limited, so don't waste it living by someone else's code. Don't let the noise of outsiders drown out your own inner voice. And most importantly, dare to follow your heart and intuition. Everything else is secondary," she shouted, punching her left hand into the air, prompting a shout of approval from the crowd. "Now, go home. We will call another meeting when we know more."

A few clusters of listeners broke away into whispered huddles, while others drifted away. Rhen stood rooted, jaw slack, thinking that Astrea had a future in politics.

Tussold, still blinking in disbelief, strode forward and clasped her hand. "Outstanding work, my girl. That's exactly the kind of rallying cry that we needed."

In response, Astrea snapped. "I'm not a girl, Tussold, remember that."

"I'm sorry, it was not meant to be an insult." He bowed his head. "Let's meet at the medical centre to plan our next move. Flynn is awake now, and as Brom's deputy, he needs to be part of this," Tussold said, falling into step beside her.

They moved through the town, footsteps echoing on stone streets. Rhen glanced at Astrea, curiosity aflame. "What drove you to climb up there and deliver that speech? You've got the heart and the voice of a born leader."

"I remembered that my father was a politician. I used to attend rallies with my mother and listen to him speak. He was running against the government."

"What happened to your parents?"

"I don't know, but I intend to find out. You were right about our memories being blocked. I suspect my parents might have paid a high price for their political views."

"Gaia's parents vanished without a trace. She hasn't had the chance to learn what happened to them. Do any of your soldiers bear similar stories?"

"If they do, the Krylan government will answer for it."

Before he could stop himself, Rhen replied, "I believe they already have."

Astrea whirled, halting so abruptly that the others streamed past her. Her eyes blazed. "What do you mean?" she demanded. "It's past time you told me everything. And this time, I want the unvarnished truth."

Her eyes burned with betrayal as Rhen spoke and explained where he was from and how Krylan had lost the war. In one swift motion, she snapped her gaze away and pivoted on her heel. Her shoulders locked, and her jaw clenched, every muscle coiled as she backed away, putting several paces of icy distance between them. The cold set to her posture, spelling out her fury.

"That went well," he said aloud before he followed at a distance, unsure how to regain her confidence. Perhaps more than that, if he were honest. He finally understood the draw of these formidable women, their steely confidence and effortless command. No wonder his half-brother, Dane, had found happiness with Gaia.

After meeting at the medical facility, Flynn suggested that Rhen visit the monastery archives as he believed they might contain useful data.

THE FOLLOWING DAY, Astrea left two soldiers on Gromwell's front gate, then set out with Rhen for the monastery. Approval had come through the day before, and they intended to use it. If the archive contained anything on Atmos or LOUT, they would use it.

A shaman met them at the entrance and then led them below, down through cool stone corridors into the archive's data vault, where the air felt stale. Rhen took in the derelict room, shelves lined with ageing equipment, everything filmed beneath several layers of grime, even the flagstone floors. Cobwebs sagged from the overhead beams, dusted so heavily they looked as though time itself had been hanging there, undisturbed.

A man sat at the main console, shoulders hunched, sleeves rolled to the elbows, fingers hovering over an antiquated keyboard that looked too stubborn to wake. In the grey light, the screen's thin glow carved his face into hard angles, focused and unreadable. He finally turned, eyes locking on them without flinching. "Hi, I'm Novak," he said, voice even. "Lorax sent for me. He said you needed someone who could coax this relic into giving up its secrets."

The shaman-in-training hovered near the doorway, hands clasped, dust clinging to his robe. "Yes, sir," Lorax said, then corrected himself quickly. "I thought it would be faster if Novak assisted. We do not have many who understand the data systems."

Astrea stepped in behind Rhen, her presence filling the room, her eyes scanning corners and shadows as if expecting trouble to rise out of the grime. "If he slows us down, he's out," she said.

Novak's mouth twitched, but his hands kept moving.

Every step they took stirred the stagnant air, dust motes lifting into the thin shafts of sunlight that slipped through cloudy, stained glass. Rhen tried not to cough, failed, and waved a hand toward the windows. "Lorax, can you open them?"

Lorax struggled with the stiff latch. Astrea nudged him aside and forced it open with a single impatient shove.

Rhen moved to stand behind Novak, close enough to read the screen over his shoulder. The keyboard beneath Novak's hands was oddly clean compared to the rest of the room.

"What happened here?" Rhen asked, voice roughened by dust.

Lorax kept his eyes lowered. "After most of the other communities sided with LOUT, we lost many of our shaman initiates. Gromwell is the only community currently providing candidates, and we are severely understaffed. There is no one left to maintain the technology or manage the data storage. We are stretched thin."

Rhen watched Novak work. He was fast, efficient, and familiar with the machine. Strings of old code rolled past, an interface from a different era, stubborn menus, and nested security prompts that did not forgive errors.

"How far in are you?" Rhen asked.

Novak tapped a sequence, waited for the system to respond, then slid to the side so Rhen could see more clearly. "Past the first layer," he said. "The indexing is terrible. Whoever set this up intended it for people who knew where everything was stored."

Rhen frowned. "Or for people who did not want outsiders to find anything."

Novak did not react. "Possible."

Astrea shifted behind them, arms crossed, impatience radiating off her. Rhen could feel it, the pull toward action and plans you could draw on a map. Research required patience, and patience was not Astrea's natural state.

Novak's fingers paused, then moved again, precise. The screen flickered, stabilised, and a directory tree unfolded, dense with file clusters, schematic tags, and archived image strings. "There," Novak said quietly, as if he had been expecting it. "That's the structural category you mentioned, hub and spoke, central spine, vac lift arrays."

Rhen leaned in, and his pulse quickened despite himself. "Open it."

Novak clicked through. The system hesitated, then complied, coughing up a set of blueprints and schematic overlays.

Rhen stared. The layout on the screen was unmistakable: a circular hub, radiating spokes, a core spine, the same geometry he had been building in his head from fragments and hearsay. Only this was not hearsay. This was a design with a lineage. His breath left him in a slow exhale. "By the stars."

Lorax edged closer, eyes wide. "Is it what you were looking for?"

Rhen did not answer immediately because his mind sprinted ahead, mapping weaknesses, imagining access points, imagining failure modes. The thrill of discovery hit like a drug. "It is more than I hoped for," he said at last, voice low. "Atmos, it is not a new design. It was built on something older, a design that has been used before. The core structure is here, the original plans, or close enough to them."

Novak's profile stayed composed, his gaze fixed on the scrolling data as if he were simply doing a job. "You can export it," he said. "If you have a datapad."

Rhen drew out the loaned device Lorax had given him and connected it. Novak initiated the transfer. File bars crawled across the screen, and Rhen forced himself to keep watching, to remember that information was only useful if you could trust the path it took to reach you. When the upload completed, Novak powered the console down, like a man who knew exactly which doors to close behind him.

Astrea pushed off the wall. "Done?"

Rhen slid the datapad into his pocket. "I won't know until we analyse this properly." They left the archive and followed the corridor toward the monastery kitchen, Lorax peeling away to his duties. Rhen's thoughts stayed on the schematics, on what they implied, on what they might make possible.

The kitchen was scented with boiled herbs and old smoke. A shaman at the hearth glanced up and motioned them in, already reaching for cups. "You'll want something before you go," he said, voice mild, as if trouble was not stalking their doorstep.

Astrea claimed the table first, sitting with her back to the wall out of habit, eyes tracking every doorway. Rhen took the seat beside her, keeping a clear line of sight to Novak, who sat opposite, shoulders squared.

The shaman set down three cups of steaming, dark tea, medicinal and sharp. Rhen wrapped his hands around his, letting the heat bite his palms.

Astrea did not touch hers. She leaned forward instead, gaze fixed on Novak. "Lorax says you're a font of knowledge," she said, the words polite, the tone anything but. "Tell us about LOUT."

Novak's eyes flicked to the cups, then back to Astrea. He nodded once. "LOUT has a long history with this planet," he began. "Eania hosted a thriving mining colony owned by an earlier iteration of the organisation. The decline started after the onset of an intergalactic war in this sector, and a drop in profitability. The mines closed, and the workforce was uplifted to another off-planet operation."

Rhen eased into a chair, keeping Novak in view. "And the Kesk?"

"I'm getting to that," Novak said, tone calm, controlled.

Rhen listened. Novak didn't sound like he was guessing.

Hundreds of orbits back, the Kesk and other humanoids passed through with a seed bank big enough to outlast any war, a cargo that could restart a civilisation. They'd been forced to salvage the old mining machinery first, stripping the abandoned works under guard, before being transported on to wherever they were meant to disappear. But the convoy was hit on departure, and what was left of them populated this world."

He paused. "Ten orbits ago, LOUT stumbled onto the survivors and the vault. The first proposal was relocation, shift them to a controlled world, put them under horticultural oversight. Then LOUT saw the numbers. The Kesk were flourishing. So LOUT did what it always does: it planted a flag and called it stewardship. They built a city to monetise the ecosystem, and the truffles were the first product line."

Astrea watched him the way she watched an enemy, alert for movement, for weakness, for any sign of deception.

"Hence Atmos," Novak continued. "Nestled in a lake, surrounded by mountains. LOUT engineers spent two orbits excavating a tunnel through the mountains and under the lake, building a hangar system. From there, they erected a massive central spine with vac lifts connecting submerged infrastructure to a hub-and-spoke ship configuration stationed above. It is designed to touch down on new worlds and seed them with fully formed cities. And if necessary, the ship is comprised of modules which can disengage and leave at a moment's notice."

Rhen kept his face neutral, even as the details clicked neatly into place alongside the schematics. "How do you know all this?" Rhen asked.

"My role was to supervise the programming and tasking of maintenance droids," Novak replied. "That gave me access to most of Atmos."

"Why did you leave?"

A flicker crossed Novak's eyes, then quickly vanished. "I was tasked with a job in the restricted laboratory division. Unusual. It was meant to be routine, but what I saw changed things." He brushed his moustache absently, the gesture slight, almost unconscious. "I spoke to my superior. He reported me. When I learned the enforcers were looking for me, I escaped and found refuge here."

Astrea's voice cut in. "And you have been doing what, exactly, in a monastery, for months?"

"A bit of everything," Novak said. "I am a deft hand at most things."

Rhen's gaze caught on the intricate tattoos winding down Novak's arm. The ink had the look of old unit markings, not decorative work. "That's serious ink."

Novak glanced at his arm, jaw tightening for a beat. "A long time ago," he said. "Back when I was still a combat engineer on Atreos. A rite of passage. Before I earned a scholarship with LOUT."

Astrea's expression did not soften. "Your talents are wasted here."

Novak's eyes tracked to the window, then back to Rhen. "I do not plan to stay here forever. Not without a plan." He paused. "I can assist you," he offered."

Rhen held his gaze. "Your understanding of Atmos's layout is what we need," he said evenly. "And your military training, when the time comes."

Novak extended his hand. "Count me in. I will help bring LOUT down and return the planet to the Kesk people."

Rhen shook his hand. "Welcome aboard. Can you join us in Gromwell?"

"Of course."

Astrea rose and walked straight past Novak's outstretched hand as if it did not exist. "Let's go," she snapped.

Rhen looked at Novak with a small shrug. "It takes her time to warm up to people," he said, with a hint of humour. "Be thankful she didn't tie you up, hang you over a ravine like an insect, or lock you in a storage unit."

Novak managed a tight smile, but his gaze dropped to his unshaken hand before he slipped it into his pocket. He fell in behind them, shoulders rigid, eyes unreadable.

CHAPTER 12

Mila was led into a room where two men watched her every move. Their stiff postures and tightly crossed arms spoke volumes. She let her gaze linger on them, her lips twitching in amusement. After years of working for the Krylans, who were masters of intimidation, it would take more than these two to shake her.

Mila replayed the series of events that led her here. Once again, she'd landed in trouble. She forced herself to relax through well-practised breathing exercises, and until she knew LOUT's intentions, she would need to be on her guard. She had to remind herself that there were people who cared about her and Brom.

Moments later, the interrogation began, including rapid-fire questions about her purpose, plans, and connections. One of the men introduced himself as Waylan. The other, however, remained nameless and silent, his presence more unsettling for the mystery it carried.

"We already know who you are, Doctor Mila Doray. We want to know why you are helping Brom and his followers."

"The Zoldacks captured my ship on its return to Rotari," Mila said, her voice low and steady. "One minute we were cruising, and then all our systems went dark." She didn't add how easily it had happened or how unprepared they had been. That part, at least, was true.

"They stole the cargo. Energems." She let the word land. Everyone knew Rotari was rich in them. It would sound plausible enough, and that was the point. She paused, letting a flicker of tension cross her face, jaw tightening just enough to read as pain. "Then they dumped us here. Like trash." She dipped her head, eyes closing briefly. Just long enough to look like the memory hurt. "My pilot didn't make it." Her voice softened into practised grief. "Maybe that was mercy." A beat of silence. She let them think she was alone. If they suspected the ship was still out there, or that Rhen had survived, they might start hunting. And she couldn't let that happen.

The man who hadn't introduced himself let her finish without interrupting, but now his voice cut through the silence like a blade.

"Touching story," he said flatly. "But it doesn't explain why you're helping Brom." He didn't blink. "Or why you care what happens to Gromwell. You're not one of them." A pause. "So what's in it for you? Or are we supposed to believe you just stumbled out of the rainforest and grew a conscience?" The man scoffed. "The Zoldacks don't dump cargo. If you were left alive, it was for a reason."

Waylan studied her like a puzzle missing a few pieces. "You're hiding something, doctor. Let's not waste time pretending you aren't. Why were you helping Brom?" he asked.

Mila didn't flinch under the scrutiny. She met Waylan's gaze with weary defiance, letting just a trace of exhaustion bleed into her voice. Her expression tightened, just enough to suggest she was debating whether to speak. "I've wondered that myself," she said. "Why didn't the Zoldacks finish the job?" She hesitated, then gave them something, not the truth, but something that felt close enough. "My guess? They didn't want more trouble with Rotari. Killing a civilian from a neutral sector might draw too much heat. Especially if news of it got out." She let her gaze drop, adding a note of bitterness. "So they dumped us here instead. Fewer questions that way." She didn't mention the payment. Or Brom. Or the deal made behind the scenes. That part stayed buried. "Whatever the reason," she added, "Gromwell was the first place I came across after the rainforest." She shrugged lightly, as if the choice had been purely circumstantial.

"They gave me water and food. That's it." She let a breath out slowly, as though this conversation was wearing her down. "I'm not interested in their cause or their politics. "I've been busy keeping people alive. You know, after your little fireworks show. As a doctor, it was the least I could do until I found a way off this planet." Another shrug, this one more resigned. "Doesn't make me one of them."

Despite her reluctance to answer further questions, they were relentless. Making her wonder if Brom was undergoing the same interrogation, assuming he had regained consciousness.

Frustrated, Waylan stepped in a little too close and lowered his voice. "Atmos has no further use for you. But given your high connections to Rotari, we will let you live." With that, he turned to his silent partner and ordered. "Drop her at the agreed location."

Mila felt a chill run up her spine.

Waylan pressed a pressure injector against her neck, and she blacked out.

IN ANOTHER PART OF Atmos, Costa, a Professor of Horticulture, sat in his office staring at the surrounding mountains, contemplating how to use the information he'd gleaned at last night's card game. One of his cronies bragged about the capture of Brom, a Kesk leader and thorn in LOUT's side, along with a female companion.

Despite his position, Costa was little more than an indentured servant, working off a gambling debt that kept him bound to LOUT. For the next ten orbits, he would remain an unpaid worker, fed, clothed, and housed by the League. At the time, it was a better option than being incarcerated for an orbit, but now, he wasn't so sure. In choosing freedom from a cell, he had traded confinement for a longer sentence. Despite this, his appetite for gambling hadn't faded. Instead, Costa sharpened his skills to acquire credits and valuable information quietly. Valuable assets if he played his cards right.

With Atmos's leadership locked in talks with the Kesk chiefs and the city's guard preoccupied, the moment to strike had arrived. It didn't take a rocket scientist to know that LOUT wanted to keep Brom in the dark about the meeting. Without Costa's intervention, Brom was a dead man walking. So, he was doing the man a favour, wasn't he? Costa needed someone with external contacts, and this man might be his ticket to freedom.

Costa glanced at the mirror, a flicker of satisfaction crossing his face. The reflection that greeted him was no longer the familiar sight of a tall, middle-aged man with dark, thinning hair. Instead, staring back at him was the face of a young, attractive man with a full head of hair, just one of several programmed disguises he had acquired with his winnings. With the help of face-altering technology and a few trial runs, he was now unrecognisable to anyone who might know him.

Next, he had to extract the tracker embedded in his forearm. LOUT only trusted their indentured employees up to a point, and that point did not extend beyond Atmos's walls. Determination boiled through Costa's veins as he located the tracker with a scanning device and then anesthetised the site. Gritting his teeth, he took hold of the laser scalpel on his desk and sliced open the skin above the small, circular object. He took a deep breath and tugged at the device with thin-nosed medical pliers, agony erupting in his arm as the metal prongs burrowed deeper, ripping through nerve endings and muscle. After yanking the tracker free, blood trickled from the wound and pooled onto the floor. Clenching his jaw, Costa dropped the device into a metal tray and stared at it, feeling satisfied that he was on the road to freedom. After placing a healing synth skin patch over the wound, he washed the device, dropped it into his desk drawer and cleaned the blood from the floor. Let them think he was still at work. Luckily, the technology was basic and unable to determine whether it was still housed in a living organism. Obviously, LOUT didn't think their employees were smart enough to work that out, and he would use that to his advantage. The thought that he might have to do the same to Brom turned his stomach. While he was comfortable slicing and dicing plants, flesh and blood were another matter.

Taking advantage of the lunch break, he ducked into the cleaners' storeroom, donned a janitor's uniform, and loaded cleaning chemicals and his tray of medical supplies onto a hover trolley. The autowalks and corridors had been easy. Getting an access pass would take more finesse, he thought, as he studied the reception node of the low-security detention facility just a few steps ahead.

Swallowing his apprehension, he stepped up to the reception node to speak to the only person in sight, a young woman immersed in a shimmering holo-interface that floated inches above her desk. Her fingers flicked and pinched the air, navigating layered social feeds and filtering through augmented selfies with practised indifference. She seemed far more engaged in broadcasting status updates to her public stream than acknowledging arrivals or monitoring the facility's security feeds. Naturally, it took a moment before she registered his presence.

And as soon as she did, he smiled. "Hi, I am here to clean the Chief's Office. Is he in?" he asked, well aware the man had been invited to the Kesk talkfest.

"No," she replied, returning her attention to the holo-interface. "Return tomorrow."

"My boss said that the Chief was adamant that it be done today and on the quiet." He leaned over the desk and whispered. "Things got out of hand last night after he gave a friend," he used finger quotes around the last word, "a tour of his office." He tapped his nose. "If you know what I mean." He'd gleaned the useful information from his gambling cronies in the hope it would pay off someday.

As soon as she rolled her eyes, he knew he was in the game. She knew her boss's after-hours reputation and clearly wanted him gone fast.

"Fine. Make it quick. I'm busy."

He swallowed the urge to say "I can see that" and offered a smooth, "Thank you" instead. With a convincing frown, he patted down his pockets, each movement deliberate. "You've got to be kidding me," he muttered, just loud enough for her to hear. "My access pass is gone. Must've dropped it at my last stop." He let the frustration linger in his voice, then looked up with practised helplessness. "Any chance you've got a spare I can borrow? So that I don't have to backtrack."

She let out another theatrical eye roll, fingers still flicking through glowing icons on her holo-interface. "I'm only authorised to issue passes to pre-approved visitors," she said, not even trying to sound sincere. Her eyes flicked to a warning notification pulsing amber in the corner of her display, and for a brief second, she hesitated, lip caught between her teeth. Then, with a quiet sigh, she slid open a lower drawer, keeping her posture casual as if reaching for something routine. Her hand dipped below the desk, and when it reappeared, a slim electronic visitor pass was pinched between her fingers. She dropped it into his open hand with a firm slap. "You're lucky my supervisor's at lunch," she muttered, still not looking at him. "If anyone asks, we never spoke. Do what you need to do and have that pass back here before he's breathing down my neck."

Without waiting for a reply, she dismissed him with a flick of her hand, already absorbed in the glowing lattice of her holo-interface. Notifications cascaded past her eyes like rain on glass, her focus locked on anything but him. Costa didn't linger. He slipped into the corridor, heart drumming against his ribs. The facility's lighting pulsed with a sterile, synthetic glow, and silent security drones drifted along the ceiling tracks like lazy predators. Every footstep echoed too loudly in his ears. Keeping his posture casual, he moved with purpose, scanning room identifiers projected along the glass-panelled hallway. Then he saw it: Treatment Unit 3. Brom's name glowed beneath in digital script, tagged with a red warning: "RESTRICTED ACCESS. DO NOT ENTER." They might as well have drawn him a map.

He palmed the borrowed pass and slid it across the wall reader. Following a quiet chime, the lock disengaged, and the door slid open. Inside, the lights were dimmed, casting the room in soft blues and pulses of bioreadouts. Brom lay motionless in a medbed, his vitals displayed in a virtual overhead panel. The coma was chemically induced, just as Costa had been told. From a hidden pouch, he withdrew a sleek, untraceable, and illegal injector, smuggled in by contacts who asked no questions. He didn't waste time. One press against the neck. A whisper of compressed gas. Done. He stepped back, watching the overhead panel's readouts register subtle fluctuations in neural activity. Time was moving again, and it wasn't on his side.

BROM INHALED SHARPLY and slowly opened his eyes to a white-walled room populated with virtual monitors and a man standing attentively by his bedside. Confused and disoriented, Brom felt weak and exhausted as his body adjusted to consciousness again. He felt muscle soreness and wondered how long he had been strapped to the bed. Looking around, he tried to make sense of his surroundings and understand what had happened after surrendering. Slowly, he tried to raise himself onto his elbows, but resistance prevented him from going any higher. "Where am I?"

"We don't have time for a question-and-answer session," the man muttered as he unstrapped Brom, reached into his satchel, extracted a coat bearing a medical insignia, and shoved it into his hands.

Brom swung his legs over the side of the bed. "Where are my boots and clothes?" he asked, flinching as his feet hit the cold floor. "What the hell am I wearing?"

"A hospital gown, which, if you ask me, was designed to reduce one's dignity to zero."

Brom let out a harsh breath.

"First, I need to determine if LOUT tagged you." Costa extracted a small device from his satchel and ran it over Brom's body, scanning for signs of a subdermal tracking device. Brom felt a slight tingle and heard a faint beep when it passed over his left shoulder.

"Sorry, this is going to be unpleasant but necessary," Costa said.

Brom backed away. "Who are you, and why are you helping me?"

"My name is Costa. That's all you need to know for now. I will fill you in later. For now, you need to trust me."

After several agonising minutes, Costa sprayed his hands with a sterilising solution, extracted the tracker and finished the procedure with a strip of synthetic skin. "Slip the coat over the hospital gown while I rinse the tracker and attach it to the underside of the medbed."

Next, Brom watched as Costa bunched the pillow and bottom sheet into the shape of a body. Then he covered it with a top sheet. "This won't fool them for long, but it will give us a head start."

"This garment is an accident waiting to happen! How can I defend myself dressed like this?" Brom asked, unnerved that he was still slightly light-headed.

"You don't. We need to move because the lunch break is almost over," Costa said, slipping a small box from his pocket and placing it in Brom's hand. "This is face-altering technology. Hold the box at arm's length in front of your face and press the triangular button to create a 3D head map. After you hear the beep, hold it steady while it completes the transformation."

"This is not permanent, is it?"

"No. It only lasts an hour. What are you waiting for? Do it now!"

Brom glanced down at his bare feet. "I need shoes."

A few minutes later, both men emerged from the medical centre, their disguises in place, and Brom wearing shoes that pinched his feet. They stepped onto the auto walk along with a crowd of shoppers. Negotiating the main thoroughfare, Brom was astounded at the diversity of entertainment available. It would take weeks to experience everything on offer, including the gardens on the upper level. Lifting his gaze, he was hit by the sight of the mountains in the distance framed by large circular glass panels. So, this was Atmos. Now he understood the lure.

Brom's gaze swept over the crowded plaza, lights flashing from every surface. But then he stopped, eyes locked on a massive holoboard. It wasn't the ad that caught him. It was her. A stunning woman with luminous pale-green skin and a cascade of midnight-black hair that shimmered as she moved. Her sapphire eyes sparkled even through the projection, almost too vivid to be real. High cheekbones, a bold mouth painted crimson, and a sleek white dress that hugged her form like liquid silk. She radiated elegance, unreachable and unforgettable. The ad cycled through visual layers, flickering between glamour shots and the brand name, Keskara Botanics. Brom took an unconscious step forward. "Who is she?" he asked, pointing at the screen.

Costa followed his gaze and let out a chuckle. "You seriously don't know Kimmy K, the face and the brains behind the brand?" He shook his head. "Our most famous export. She started as a social correspondent, then caught the eye of Waylan, the president's son. Now she runs her own cosmetics empire, built on rare plant compounds. Trade secret formulas and all that."

Brom didn't answer. His hand had dropped to his side, fingers twitching slightly. His mouth had gone dry. His pulse thundered in his ears. It couldn't be. Not here. Not like this. The image shifted again, her smile blooming across the screen. Too familiar. Too perfect.

Costa finally noticed his expression and frowned. "You okay?"

Brom's voice came out hoarse, barely above a whisper. "It's her."

Costa blinked. "Her?"

A long pause. Then, with effort, Brom said, "My sister."

Costa's eyebrows shot up. "You're serious?"

Brom nodded once, still staring.

"Do you think she'll help us?"

Brom's jaw tightened. "I don't know. When she left Gromwell, we didn't exactly say goodbye."

Costa gave a low whistle. "From a purely professional standpoint, I'd love to meet the woman who built an empire from plants." He grinned. "Family reunion or not."

Moments later, a group of Kesk men joined them on the auto walk. Brom was surprised that the group consisted of Kesk leaders from other settlements. Curious, he tapped Costa on the shoulder, "What is going on?" With the amount of adrenaline running through his veins, he felt ready to run a marathon or shoot something.

"Later," Costa whispered over his shoulder. In unison, they stepped off the auto walk into the residential sector. Several corridors later, Costa stopped and pressed his thumb against a wall panel. The door slid open to a small, neat, sparsely furnished living space. Directly ahead was a small, well-equipped kitchen and dining area. Across from the kitchen, a single armchair was positioned beside a large window, facing a small bed. Costa motioned for Brom to sit, glancing both ways down the corridor before the sliding door closed. "We're safe," he said softly, "for now."

"Start talking and tell me what's going on," Brom said.

"Okay," Costa replied, pulling up a dining chair.

Brom rubbed his face, contemplating all he'd been told by the man, particularly the meeting in progress between Kesk community leaders and LOUT to finalise details of a trade agreement. The other bombshell was that Costa was relying on Brom's help to escape.

Costa, his face now older and more lined, looked at him carefully. "Who was the woman captured with you? I heard she wasn't Kesk."

Brom froze. His mouth parted in disbelief. "What? And you're only telling me this now?"

Costa shrugged, not unkindly. "I didn't think it mattered."

Brom's voice sharpened. "Do you have a name? A description, anything?"

Costa shook his head. "Just that she was taken with you."

"It has to be Mila. She wasn't meant to be captured." Brom's voice tightened, worry gnawing at him. "This complicates everything. I have to discover where they've taken her."

Listen," Costa snapped, his voice sharp with frustration. "I already risked everything getting you out. We need to move. Now. Her fate isn't my problem."

Brom leaned forward, jaw tight, fists clenched on the chair's arms. "But it sure as hell is mine." The words came out like a growl, raw and unfiltered. His pulse pounded in his ears. The image of Mila flashed through his mind like a wound. Damn it, why didn't he say something sooner? But even as fury burned in his chest, Brom knew the truth. This wasn't the moment. The fight for answers, and for her, would have to wait. He forced his voice down, jaw flexing. "Let's go. But we're not done talking about this."

"So, you're related to Kimmy K." Costa shook his head. "I still can't quite believe it. After thinking it through, I don't think we should involve her."

"Why?"

"She is close to President Aivel and his son Waylan. Also, the fact that you aren't on good terms does not inspire confidence. She also has a teenage son to consider. Xander is the spitting image of her."

Wow, that gave Brom a lot to think about. Kihm, or Kimmy K as she was known in Atmos, had only departed Gromwell two orbits ago. The boy must belong to Waylan. "Do you have a picture of them?" Brom asked.

"I'll pull up one of the socials," Costa said, scrolling through various screens on his holo-interface.

"Moments later, Brom was staring at his sister and Xander. The boy was Kesk. Adopted? Another mystery to be solved, and one that solidified his resolve to speak to his sister. He also needed information about Danelda's claim that he had a daughter.

Costa stood. "Do you honestly think that Kimmy K will turn a blind eye and help a brother she hasn't seen for years?"

"To be honest, I don't know," Brom responded.

"Let's eat, and then we will plan," Costa suggested.

Brom nodded.

CHAPTER 13

Mila woke to the sound of rain falling, piercing through the thick humidity that hung in the air like a heavy veil. Her head pounded with unfamiliar grogginess, and her body shivered. She had no recollection of arriving here.

Lying in the mud, her head swam with confusion and fear as she tried to make sense of her surroundings. Her heart beat faster and faster, and her breath came in short, shallow gasps as a wave of panic washed over her. Then she remembered a familiar saying from one of her lecturers. 'Fear is false evidence appearing real.' Unless, of course, you were actually in a life-and-death situation. She could do this. Mila took a deep breath, and then another, and her fear lessened each time.

Summoning what little strength she had, Mila pushed herself upright, her limbs heavy and uncooperative. She staggered to her feet, the world tilting slightly as she fought to steady herself. The alley reeked of damp earth and rotting garbage, and the cloying air pressed in from all sides. And apart from the occasional figure trudging through the mud in the adjacent street, she saw few people. Where was she? She had no answers, only more questions.

She stumbled forward, feeling lost and alone, and stepped out of the alley, her eyes taking in the dilapidated, crumbling buildings. The paint that once covered them was now reduced to tiny flecks and fragments. She shivered in her wet and very stale-smelling jumpsuit, and a chill ran down her spine as she catalogued the potential dangers that lurked around every corner.

Despite her dizziness, Mila remained alert as she scanned the area, taking in the chatter of people and the sound of their boots squelching through the mud, creating a soft, muted splash with each step. The locals, who appeared to be predominantly Kesk, ignored her, which was fine for now. At least she was still on the same planet, so there was hope.

The town seemed so desolate and unwelcoming, except for the smell of spicy food wafting from a small, unassuming eatery. Despite the dirty windows, stained counters, bare walls and tables worn from years of use, it was bustling with people.

Finally, after what felt like an eternity, Mila saw a faded sign in the distance that, on any planet, read 'medical facility'. She approached the building with hope that she might find answers or someone willing to help her. Taking a steadying breath, she stepped toward the door, fingers closing around the handle, when someone seized her arm. A man in a hooded rain jacket loomed close, his voice low and threatening. "Who the hell are you?"

She blinked, caught off guard.

"Release me!"

He leaned in, eyes narrowing. "You're new. Let me guess, a runaway from Atmos?"

She hesitated. "No." Technically a lie, but close enough.

"Then where?"

"Gromwell," she said, voice clipped. No need to mention she was from off-planet.

The man gave a slow, mocking grin, his grip on her arm tightening just enough to make her muscles tense.

"Gromwell, huh?" He leaned in closer. "That's a long way from here. People don't just stroll in from Gromwell unless they're running from something. So, which is it?" His voice dropped to a near-whisper. "Theft? Revenge? Or did you leave a body behind?"

Mila's eyes flashed, and she yanked harder at her arm. "That's none of your business," she said, steel threading through her tone. "Let. Go."

But he didn't, not right away. Instead, his gaze narrowed, lingering on her face like he was trying to pin a memory in place.

"You look familiar," he muttered. "Like someone I've seen on a watchlist."

Her pulse spiked, but she held her ground. "You're making a mistake," she said, forcing calm. "Now, unless you want trouble, I suggest you forget my face."

A tense moment passed. Then, finally, with a grunt, he released her arm.

His hair was grey, peppered with white, and his eyes were a cold, transparent green. His pale green face was weathered and lined with wrinkles, revealing years of hard living. Under his rain jacket, he was well-dressed in a dark suit, topped off by a black hat. He spoke in a gruff, authoritative voice, with a commanding presence that made Mila uneasy.

"I am the law around here. My name is Dram, and you would be wise to remember it. Blackwell is a hive of scum, home to an eclectic mix of criminals and fugitives. Nobody sneezes without my say-so," he snarled. "Everybody here is running from somewhere or someone. This is the garbage dump of Eania. So why don't you tell me the truth? I will find out eventually, one way or another."

"I was kidnapped and dumped. I am a doctor." She blurted out, trying to wrench her arm free.

"Yeah, and I'm the local librarian. You are coming with me."

"No."

Despite her resistance, he dragged her down another alleyway and pushed her inside the back door of a building. The place was dark, smoky and filled with the smell of alcohol. She looked around in shock. "I know my rights. You can't do this," she protested.

"The only rights you have are the ones I give you," he said, laughing. "You look fit and healthy. We have a profitable enterprise that could use some extra workers."

She tried to leave, but he stepped into her path and blocked the doorway. "There is no escape," he said.

She scanned the dark, smoky room, and her stomach clenched. On the stage, girls danced under harsh lights, while others, eyes flat, led customers toward the stairs. Mila shivered. Since arriving on this planet, she had not had a single clean choice; her body and her future had been pushed and pulled by other people's decisions. The thought landed like a bruise. No doubt these women understood that kind of helplessness, controlled, cornered, doing what they had to because there was no safe alternative.

A big, heavy-set man with sagging jowls stepped from behind the bar. "Who do you have here, Dram?"

"A new recruit, Vek."

"I can't take on any more ladies, especially one so mature." He grabbed Mila's chin and asked, "What happened? Fall face-first into a scrap heap?"

"Close," she replied tightly. "Got kidnapped and dumped in Blackwell. What's your excuse?"

He snorted. "You've got spunk. That won't last long around here. Wherever you came from, you look like hell. Dirty and barely passable." He gave her a once-over, then shrugged. "Still, I've seen worse. He released her with a flick of his hand.

While Mila didn't want to work in the bordello, the thought that she was too old at thirty-seven was insulting, to say the least.

"She's not for you. Too headstrong. I'm looking for Sorn. This is his second home, if I'm not mistaken."

"She doesn't look like she's got what it takes to survive his operation."

"I didn't ask for your opinion, Vek. Is Sorn here?" he growled.

Vek pointed to the far end of the bar. "Over there."

Mila felt Dram's grip tighten on her arm as he pulled her toward the looming figure of Sorn. She kept her face composed, forcing herself not to recoil as they stopped in front of him. The stench of sweat and metal hung around him like a warning. One that said, run for your life, though the woman draped over his lap looked like she'd missed the memo. Whatever Sorn's operation involved, it couldn't be worse than playing decoration on his lap, could it?

Sorn looked her over, eyes narrowing. "Well, who have you got there, Dram?"

"Another resource for you."

Sorn lifted an eyebrow. "Let's have a look at 'er then! Come on, lady, show the boss whatcha got."

Mila took a deep breath, trying to hide the rising wave of revulsion. She didn't belong here. As soon as she could, she'd run.

Sorn's eyes narrowed as if he sensed her reluctance. He leaned in, lifting her chin with a rough hand. "What's your name, girl?"

She paused, weighing the risk of giving her real name. If someone were searching, it'd be the first thing they'd use to track her. After a moment's hesitation, she replied quietly, 'Mila.'"

Sorn smirked, letting his hand drop. "Mila, huh? You don't look like you'd last a day in the Blackheart Mine. The place isn't exactly a walk in the park."

Mila clenched her jaw, swallowing the bitter reply that lingered on her tongue. "I agree. I'm a doctor," she said, choosing her words carefully, hoping he'd dismiss her without much fuss. "I'm just passing through."

Sorn chuckled, clearly amused. "Oh, I'll bet you are. But let me tell ya something: there ain't no 'passing through' in this town unless you can prove yourself useful. You'll do your time in the pit like everyone else who needs food and shelter around here."

Mila forced herself to remain calm, even as her mind raced. Her years of medical training meant nothing to him. He only saw another set of hands. She needed a plan, a way to slip out unnoticed, but Sorn's sharp gaze told her he wasn't going to let her disappear that easily. She nodded stiffly, keeping her expression neutral. "Understood."

Sorn motioned to the man beside him with a jerk of his thumb. "Get her set up for the morning shift. Make sure she's tagged. If she makes it through one day, I'll be surprised."

As Sorn turned away, Mila's heart pounded. She wasn't about to descend into the mine. She'd need to find a way to escape this grimy trap before dawn. She was a doctor, a healer.

The second man gave a curt nod and seized her arm before she could bolt. With his free hand, he flicked open a small metal case, retrieving a bulky pressure injector that gleamed ominously in the dim light. Without a word, he pressed it firmly against her arm and pulled the trigger. Mila felt the sting radiate up her arm, and a cold sensation followed, settling deep into her arm. Before she could protest, the man gave her a sly grin.

"Insurance," he said, waving the pressure injector lazily. "That's a subdermal tracker, sweetheart. As long as you're in the designated work zone, you're just fine. But step outside the restricted area, and... well, let's say you won't be taking another step anywhere." He leaned in closer, voice dropping to a low whisper. "It's rigged to detonate if you cross the boundary."

Mila's heart sank as she glanced at her arm. Escape just became a deadly gamble.

AS THE SUN CRESTED the horizon the following day, Rhen, Novak and Astrea set off on hover scooters to the Halo Insurgent III to utilise its technology to help locate Brom and Mila. Rhen planned to track ion trails between Gromwell and the most likely destination, Atmos.

Kneeling in the leaf litter beneath the hull, sweat prickling in the searing, humid air, Rhen jacked his wrist rig into a concealed maintenance port and let it listen to the ship's idle power chatter, hunting for a timing flaw in the Zoldacks' fresh lockout while the others watched from the shade of the rainforest. Brom had vanished with the codes, so Rhen built a spoofed access signature on the fly, riding the tiny glitch he'd found until the security grid finally blinked open to him. After cracking the ship's security and rolling back the lockdown codes, they boarded. On the bridge, Rhen's fingers danced over the hovering holo-keys, and streams of data spilled across the virtual console as the systems came alive.

Astrea stood behind him, eyes tracking each swift command. "How do you plan to find them?" she asked.

Rhen's hands stilled, and he glanced over his shoulder. "You track a craft with an ion-trail antenna, a specialised receiver that picks up the ionised particles it leaves behind. The system filters those from all the other junk in the area, then the nav suite uses particle density, speed, and time to determine the craft's course and current position." He tapped the display. "Which the AI is doing."

Astrea rolled her eyes. "That was more information than I needed."

"I'm a tech head, so I'm incapable of giving you the short version," he joked. "The analysis will take a few minutes. Sufficient time for us to return to Gromwell before sundown. Where is Novak? I haven't seen him for a while."

"Come to think of it. I haven't, either." She lifted an eyebrow. "I am becoming suspicious of him," she whispered. "His vibe is off."

"He has been very helpful."

"Yes, but why? What is his motivation?" she asked. "My gut is telling me we need to watch him."

A soft beep pulled Rhen's attention to the nav screen. "Only one trajectory intersects with Atmos. That's our starting point." He tapped the screen, frowning. "But it doesn't reach Atmos. Either the craft dropped them mid-flight, and they switched to another transport, or worst case, it had an unscheduled landing." Rhen exhaled through his nose, the weight of the implications settling heavily on his chest. "There's something else," he said, eyes narrowing. "An ion trail made a full round trip, same departure point, same return vector. Back to Atmos."

The bridge doors hissed open. Novak strolled in, one hand buried in his coat pocket. He glanced around, eyes briefly landing on the screen before forcing a smile. "So," he said lightly, "what'd I miss?"

Astrea didn't return the smile. Her gaze sharpened, mouth tightening to a thin line.

"Where were you just now?" she asked, voice flat and cold.

Novak gave a loose shrug, but his eyes didn't meet hers. They flicked past her to the console, the ceiling, anywhere else. "Just admiring the ship," he said, tone light but a beat too late. "She's impressive. Wouldn't mind poking around her systems, see how she ticks."

Astrea's reply came fast, edged like a blade.

"This isn't a sightseeing cruise, it's a rescue mission."

Rhen cut her a sideways look, eyebrow lifting.

Astrea ignored it.

"Let's go," Rhen said, powering down the onboard systems. Once they'd disembarked, he keyed in the ship's cloaking sequence. With a soft hum, the hull shimmered, light bending and dissolving around it until the Halo faded into near invisibility. Only a faint distortion in the air marked where it had been. Rhen gave a small nod, satisfied. He swung a leg over his grav-scooter, the magnetic stabilisers whirring to life beneath him. As he settled into the saddle, he cast one last glance behind him, reassured that the ship was beyond the reach of LOUT surveillance.

"I'm heading back to Gromwell," Novak called out, already mounting his own scooter.

Astrea's eyebrow arched, and her gaze sharpened. "There's still plenty of daylight, Novak. Why not join us in the search?" Her voice held an edge, probing. "Other than Flynn, you are familiar with the terrain."

Novak paused, rubbing the back of his neck as if he hadn't anticipated the question. He gave a casual shrug, eyes drifting past her as though something out there demanded his attention more than the task at hand. "I've got some critical groundwork to handle. As you said, we don't have much time, and I need all the time I can get." He offered a faint smile.

Rhen gave a slow nod, and his lips pressed into a thin line. He'd have preferred Novak to join them. Having his local knowledge would've been invaluable. Looking over at Astrea, she clearly wasn't buying it. Perhaps she had a point. They knew little about the man and his motives, which were starting to look suspicious even to him.

USING A LOCAL SHUTTLE, Rhen, Astrea and Flynn followed the ion trail until they arrived at a site strewn with wreckage. Rhen's heart dropped to his stomach, and he dragged a hand down his face. Whiskers he hadn't had time to shave abraded his palm.

Disembarking, they methodically searched the wreckage and discovered the grisly sight of the pilot, impaled and slumped over the shuttle's console, along with a marker denoting Danelda's resting place.

Rhen bent over to rest his hands on his thighs, a cold chill gripping his heart. Where were Mila and Brom? He imagined the worst.

"Over here!" Flynn shouted.

Rhen and Astrea pushed through the thick undergrowth, branches clawing at their clothes as they followed him toward a dark break in the greenery, a cave entrance, half-hidden by moss and shadow.

Rhen's heart hammered as he stepped closer, bracing for what they might find.

"They made it," Flynn said, pointing to a message etched into the stone wall, rough, hurried lettering. "They're alive. The only thing missing is where they are now."

A rush of relief surged through Rhen, loosening a knot he hadn't realised was in his chest. In its place, a spark of hope flared.

Astrea, as always, was the voice of reason. "It appears that all roads lead to Atmos, so that's where we start. Now, we need a plan to get inside."

Rhen nodded in agreement.

About to board the shuttle, the underbrush stirred. Shadows shifted. Figures emerged, and armed soldiers stepped into view, weapons drawn, encircling them with silent precision. Their armour was matte black, their helmets featureless, faceless masks. Rhen's gaze darted from visor to visor, heart thudding. No sign of Flynn. Smart, he thought, a flicker of envy biting through his fear. He must have melted into the rainforest the moment things turned.

Astrea locked eyes with the nearest soldier, her stare unwavering and her lips pressed into a razor-thin line. Every centimetre of her radiated coiled tension, like a storm held barely in check. Rhen's breath caught. He knew that look. She was ready to fight. If Astrea made a move, the whole jungle would explode in gunfire.

Just then, a familiar face rounded the front of their shuttle. "Astrea, stand down. It would be foolish to resist. Even you should realise this."

Rhen's face felt frozen in shock, his mind racing with a thousand questions, as two soldiers forced them to their knees, wrenched their arms behind their backs and snapped plascrete cuffs around their wrists. Next, they were patted down for weapons or contraband. Rhen couldn't hold back any longer. "Why, Novak?"

"You look surprised," Novak said smugly. "Astrea was already suspicious, so I was forced to step up my plans."

Astrea's eyes narrowed. Her tone was razor-sharp. "So, you're working for LOUT. I should have followed my instincts, which are rarely wrong. What was your plan?"

Novak shrugged. "My mission was to eliminate or detain Brom, determine your threat level, and make sure Flynn didn't survive another attempt on his life," he said with a chuckle and satisfied smile. "Speaking of Flynn, where is he?"

Astrea snorted, her voice dripping with sarcasm. "Funny, I thought rodents preferred sewers. Guess you like open spaces."

"Flynn didn't join us," Rhen said.

"Try again."

Rhen shrugged, feigning indifference. "It's the truth. So, what's the grand plan for us?"

Novak's mouth curved into a sly smirk. "Well, that all depends on you," he replied, his tone laced with quiet menace. "Let's just say... it doesn't usually end well for those who don't cooperate."

Rhen snorted. "Cooperate? You're joking, right? That ship sailed long ago."

Novak's smile didn't falter. "I'd prefer to keep things civil."

Astrea shot him a withering look, her patience long gone. "You're delusional," she said. "Now, what do you really want from us?"

Novak's smile faded. "To take you out of the picture. Once the troublemakers in Gromwell are eliminated, the other inhabitants will quickly fall into line. And while Flynn survived one attempt on his life, I do not expect him to survive another." He smiled then. "But it doesn't have to be this way. If everyone cooperates, we can work together for the greater good."

"You mean LOUT's greater good," Astrea snapped.

Novak scowled at her but directed the following statement to Rhen. "Lucky for you, LOUT would prefer not to alienate Rotari. In fact, it plans to establish a trading partnership. As such, the organisation is prepared to offer you a deal. You will be escorted to your ship unharmed and then allowed to leave. We will also tell you where to find Doctor Doray. The same goes for you and your soldiers, Astrea." He looked at her directly. "Yes, LOUT has known about your little band for some time. But now that you are involved in this conflict, we can't ignore you any longer. I believe the Rotari ship will accommodate everyone. How does that sound?" he asked with a sly smirk.

Astrea's eyes narrowed, and her lips formed a thin, pressed line. "What if we don't accept your generous offer?" she sneered.

"You have no bargaining power, Astrea. LOUT has no ties with Krylan and no plans to establish any. You and your soldiers are expendable." He shifted his attention back to Rhen, and his mouth curved faintly.

Rhen caught a flicker of motion beyond the line of soldiers, a subtle ripple in the undergrowth. Vines, thick and sinewy, slithered from the shadows, weaving soundlessly through the leaf litter. His heart stuttered, but he kept his expression unreadable. In a sudden blur of motion, the vines struck and coiled around the soldiers' ankles with unnatural precision, quickly tightening. One by one, the men were ripped off their feet and slammed to the ground, weapons clattering into the soil. No warning. No sound. Just the rustle of leaves and the dull thuds of bodies hitting earth. Rhen's eyes flicked to Novak, already struggling in a tightening web of green, face contorted in panic. The vines wrapped tighter, locking down limbs with deliberate, inescapable force. They weren't just captured. They were claimed.

Rhen's thoughts whiplashed between shock and relief. One moment, they were powerless, and the next, their captors lay immobilised, ensnared by something as silent as it was merciless.

The vines still writhed slightly, as if savouring the aftermath. A shiver crawled up Rhen's spine. Their touch hadn't been loud or violent, just precise, and that made the situation all the more unsettling. It was a visceral reminder. They were fragile things in a world full of quiet power.

Then, breathless, Flynn burst from the treeline, kneeling beside them and cutting the cuffs away with quick, practised slices.

Still in shock, Rhen rubbed his chafed wrists, muttering, "Thanks. I don't know how you did it, but I appreciate it," he said, gathering the soldiers' scattered weapons and handing them to Astrea and Flynn. Rhen quickly looked at Astrea, "I'm not giving up on Gromwell and its people, are you?"

"Hell, no," she replied as she approached Novak and pressed the muzzle of a siezed weapon against his temple. "So, what do you have to say for yourself now?"

The terror in his eyes was palpable.

"What. Nothing to say?" Her eyes narrowed. "But you were so talkative a few minutes ago." She nudged him with the muzzle again. "What do you think we should do with him, boys?"

"Leave him for the snarks," Flynn replied."

Novak's eyes went wide, the whites stark against his pale face. "No, please. I could be useful," he stammered, desperation creeping into his voice.

Flynn pointed to the setting sun. "Whatever we decide to do, it needs to be done quickly."

Astrea stepped forward, voice crisp with command. "Flynn, cut the soldiers loose. Let the jungle deal with them," she said with a faint smile.

He gave a silent nod and moved to obey.

Then her gaze shifted to Novak, steely and unblinking. "But he's coming with us. We've also acquired a LOUT shuttle now, and a way into Atmos."

Moments later, the vines retreated, and the soldiers were sent packing, wearing only their undergarments. Novak was cuffed and herded towards the Gromwell shuttle by Astrea and Flynn, who assumed he would go quietly. But that wasn't to be. Novak kicked Astrea with a force that had her body instantly recoiling to avoid the worst of it, but not all. Annoyed, her hands clasped his head, and with a single, swift movement, her kneecap collided with his nose, the sharp crack ringing out like a gunshot. Blood now trickled from his crooked nose and over his lips and chin. The pain and the salty taste of iron would remind him of his mistake.

With Novak locked into a crash seat aboard the Gromwell shuttle, Astrea and Flynn slammed their hatch closed as Rhen slipped into the LOUT shuttle, killed the comms, scrubbed the tracking signature, and shifted the systems into stealth. The shuttles leapt from the rainforest floor in clean arcs through the canopy, bound for home.

CHAPTER 14

Kihm stood in her luxurious apartment, staring out at the sweeping view of the mountains surrounding Atmos, but the landscape's beauty offered no comfort. Waylan's obsession with fathering a child had deepened, driven by pressure from his overbearing father, Aivel, president of Atmos, who wanted a direct genetic link to the Kesk to cement his position. To keep Waylan from uncovering the truth, she always claimed they needed just one more test, one more opinion. And it was becoming increasingly difficult to distract him. Her stomach clenched as she recalled last night's revelation: Aivel had arranged for a renowned fertility expert to visit Atmos in the coming weeks. That could not happen. One blood test, and everything would fall apart. The plant-based compound she'd been slipping Waylan would be discovered. Then the lies would unravel, and with them, everything she'd built to keep her family safe. She needed to act just as she'd protected Brom in Gromwell. Just as she'd kept her father, her brother, and Oxana and Xander alive in Atmos, this was just one more secret to manage.

Kihm had kept close tabs on her niece, Oxana, chosen for an elite group under LOUT's observation. In their line, the Kesk gifts ran especially strong, and Oxana was no exception. With the Kesk's uncanny ability to manipulate plant life and draw energy from it, or imbue it with their own, and the chameleon-like skin that shifted to match surrounding greenery, she had quickly attracted the organisation's interest. The Kesk people had always been extraordinary, coaxing life from the barest soil.

But at the moment, she had bigger problems, such as Waylan, who marched through the door like a storm cloud, his face contorted with rage. He viciously threw the contents of his pockets onto the hall table with a force that made her wince. She had seen his mood swings before, but this time, they seemed more intense. His presence filled the room with oppressive dread, as it always did. Thankfully, he kept that side hidden from Xander, who was at Blast Ball practice for another hour.

Plastering a smile on her face, she kissed his cheek and steered him to the lounge. "Sit down and tell me what is bothering you." She found that when he was angry, he tended to blurt out more than he intended.

"You aren't going to like this, Kimmy K. We had no choice."

Her blood turned cold. The 'we' always meant Aivel. Waylan was a pawn in his father's game and an unpredictable one at that.

"Tell me," she said calmly.

"Brom has been captured, along with an off-world doctor."

"That was never part of our deal, Waylan. You and your father agreed to leave my family alone if I built the cosmetics business into a high-value intersystem enterprise. I delivered. You've already received a substantial return on your investment." Every word burned, but she forced her voice to remain even.

"Brom was asking for trouble, and now he has found it. Gromwell will now fall into line with the other settlements."

"What do you mean?" she asked.

"You know exactly what I mean." Waylan was talking in rapid bursts now and seemed on the verge of losing control. His body shook with anger, and he clenched his fists. "I don't care if he's your brother; this is all his fault! If he'd just fallen into line, if he hadn't stirred things up, none of this would've happened!" Waylan's voice cracked, his frustration spilling out. Standing, he nervously paced the room. "Now I must deal with the mess! Brom forced our hand!" His voice echoed off the walls, desperate and accusatory.

She couldn't believe it had come to this. "Sit down, and I'll make you a drink," she suggested. Of course, she would add a calming herb. Moments later, she returned with the doctored hot beverage. "Drink up." She sat beside him and forced a smile as he sipped the drink. "Can I speak to Brom and try to talk sense into him?"

"Too late," he blurted.

Her breath caught. "Why is it too late?"

"He's in a drug-induced coma in the detention centre," he replied, carefully avoiding her gaze. "He's not speaking to anyone."

A sense of unease prickled at the back of her mind. He was holding something back, she was sure of it. Somehow, she'd have to visit the centre to uncover the truth. But for now, she shifted her approach, keeping her voice steady. "What about the off-world doctor who accompanied him?"

"I did some digging on her," he said. "Doctor of Medicine, Institute of Research on Krylan. Master of Science in Genetics and Molecular Biology. Universal Society of Human Genetics, a publishing record that keeps repeating, invited talks at high-level events. In other words, she's not ordinary." His gaze narrowed. "Then, out of nowhere, she pivots to Rotari, starts turning up where she shouldn't, and ends up speaking on behalf of their President like she's been here her whole life. So tell me, what's she doing on this planet, and why is she tangled up with your brother?"

Inspiration struck like a spark in the dark. If getting permission to speak to Brom was a dead end, then reaching out to the doctor would be her next best move. "This is just a thought, but do you think she could help with our um... problem?" Her eyebrows lifted in enquiry.

"I hadn't thought of that. Unfortunately, she isn't here." His fingers moved to trace Kihm's face and its contours, sending a shiver up her spine.

"Where is she?"

"Blackwell."

"Blackwell! That's not a safe place," she cried.

"LOUT doesn't want a conflict with Rotari."

"Well, they might very well have one if something happens to her, which is more than likely."

"I'm told she will be fine."

Kihm shifted her questioning to the things that always hooked him, profit and his father's approval. "She could be useful to my business, too. With the right genetic manipulation, there are products I could produce that would be far more profitable." She let that hang, then added, soft as a promise, "Your father would be pleased, seeing that kind of ingenuity and forward thinking from you."

"Again, I'll have to speak to Father."

"Why don't we get ahead of it?" she said. "Collect the doctor, secure her cooperation. Then, when you take the plan to your father, it's already packaged." She swallowed, aware she'd stepped into dangerous territory, and forced herself to hold his gaze. "Wouldn't your father be impressed if you turned a problem into an advantage?" Her voice dropped. "And if she refuses, we still control the outcome. A subdermal tracker, something discreet, so she can't slip past the confines of Atmos."

"You may be onto something there, Kimmy K. I will speak to my pilot."

"Can we take your father's new yacht?" I want to bring a few of my new botanists. Your shuttle isn't large enough, and some of the herbs and plants we need grow near Blackwell. It would be ideal if they could collect them while we track down the doctor."

"I suppose we could use his yacht."

Her time in Atmos was running out, which meant it was time for bold moves. Xander knew Waylan was his adoptive father, but lately he had started watching Kihm whenever anyone mentioned her resemblance to him. The shared green skin was the easy explanation, the one everyone accepted, but Xander was not everyone. He was a smart boy, too smart, and she could see the questions lining up behind his eyes, waiting for the first crack.

"Brains and beauty. How did I get so lucky?" Waylan said, glancing at his timepiece.

She knew the answer to that: threats and intimidation.

He leaned in closer. "We have half an hour until Xander returns home. Why don't we take advantage of that?" he asked, his eyebrows wiggling like angry caterpillars.

Although Kihm desperately wanted to say no, not in this lifetime, she had to maintain her persona. "Of course, darling, there is nothing I would like more."

Kihm knew that with the herb in his system, he would fall asleep quickly afterwards, giving her time to visit her father and brother and devise a plan to free Brom. Hopefully, her ruse to retrieve the doctor would be fruitful.

AN HOUR LATER, ONCE Xander was fully immersed in his neuro-interactive simulation rig, a high-fidelity game environment that synchronised directly with his sensory cortex, she slipped quietly out to meet her family. With the sedative compound discreetly laced into Waylan's drink, she calculated at least another hour before he would wake. Before leaving, she paused briefly at Xander's doorway. "I'm heading out for a bit," she said, keeping her voice casual. "One of the augmented reality photo campaigns is glitching, something with the lighting shaders and the volumetric projection. Your favourite meal is queued in the replicator. And don't disturb your father. He had a rough day and needs the rest."

"Sure, Kimmy K," he responded distractedly, more interested in his game.

Before slipping into the service corridor, she activated a mist from one of her best-selling chroma-serums, layering temporary blonde and red highlights into her dark hair with a soft hiss. A second spray released a micro-curl infusion, sculpting her strands into perfect waves, another top seller in her line. Now, the outfit. Fortunately, she was already wearing a transformation dress; with a subvocal command, its fabric shimmered and began to reconfigure. A present from Waylan, who had ordered it from Solaris Prime, a holiday planet known for its high-tech fashion.

She dialled the chroma-fibre to a dull brown, then increased the volumetrics, prompting the smartfabric to swell and slump until it resembled a worn utility sack, exactly what she needed. Next, she misted away her makeup with a quick-dissolving spray, then used her magi-wand eyeliner to add dark smudges of fatigue beneath her eyes. A pair of adaptive contact lenses, tinted brown, slipped into place, completely masking her natural eye colour.

Ready, she took a deep breath and exited the apartment via the service entrance, hunched over and limping slightly. The disguise fooled the paparazzi who regularly camped outside her front door. She boarded an orbital shuttle circling Atmos and disembarked a block from her father's residence.

Ten minutes later, she activated the door chime, an old analog model he refused to upgrade, and her father, Andar, answered, his expression tight with concern. He had every reason to be uneasy. She only ever arrived in disguise, unannounced, when trouble was brewing.

"Come in. Your brother is here." He stepped aside to let her in, then cast a glance up and down the corridor before the door slid firmly behind her.

"Good. I need to speak to both of you." After briefing them on Brom's capture, she dropped the final bombshell. "I think they mean to kill him this time. Our agreement with Aivel and Waylan appears to be over, so we need to leave Atmos." As much as they wanted to blame Brom for pushing things this far, they'd all known that this day was coming.

"What about Xander?" Andar asked.

"He's coming with us," she said at last. "But it's going to be tricky." She exhaled slowly. "I wish I could include Oxana, too. The girl probably doesn't know she has family here. Danelda made sure of that. And Xander's just as much in the dark." Her gaze hardened. "That has to change. They both need to be told who they really are."

Vrack nodded once. "So, sis, how do we make this happen?"

"I have a plan," Kihm said. "I've talked Waylan into letting me rescue Doctor Doray, the one they took with Brom." Kihm's mouth curved, but it didn't reach her eyes. "Luck dropped her in our lap; they dumped her in Blackwell. I've already planted the narrative that she needs to be returned to Atmos, that she'll be useful to Keskara Botanics." She paused, letting the logic settle, each piece clicking into place."If we use Aivel's new yacht, which features state-of-the-art cloaking tech, we can escape cleanly. You fly it, Vrack. We launch a 'search' for the doctor, and that becomes our cover." Her eyes sharpened. "The hunt gives us a reason to leave, and a reason not to return." She gave a small, confident shrug. "Easy."

"And Waylan?" Andar asked.

"Don't worry, I will take care of him," she said. "I know this escape is a risk, but it is a risk we need to take." Kihm activated her datapad, fingers dancing across the interface. "I'm dispatching a series of anonymised bursts to the more volatile Kesk faction leaders attending the conference, subtle hints suggesting their rivals are cutting secret deals for better terms," she said. "It'll trigger paranoia, make them think they're being outmaneuvered. That kind of distrust should destabilise their internal channels, just enough for me to slip into the detention centre and locate Brom." She paused, scanning their faces for any sign of doubt. "If I synchronise my visit with the timing of the arrests, the confusion might create the perfect blind spot." She handed the datapad to her father and brother. "Read it. Tell me what you think."

Andar was the first to react. "This is risky, Kihm. Are you sure it will work and can't be traced back to you?"

"From what Waylan said, this is exactly what LOUT plans to do anyway. Do you have a better idea?"

Andar and Vrack shook their heads in unison.

"What is your plan, Kihm?" Andor asked.

"You'll pose as xenobotanists conducting a survey of endemic flora, a species that only propagates in the Blackwell region," she said crisply. "Before we deploy, I'll upload fabricated personnel files into the central registry, complete with credentials and work histories, so everything checks out." She rummaged through her large bag and extracted two sleek, monogrammed lab coats embedded with ID-threading. "Wear these tomorrow. They will be encoded with your aliases and department tags."

Andar smiled. "What do I always say? Aim for the stars; even if you miss, you'll land somewhere wonderful."

"I'm not twelve anymore, Father," she said, leaning over to place a kiss on his cheek.

"I know, but my advice doesn't change, no matter how old you are. Now, go catch those stars, my girl."

NEAR THE PERIMETER of the detention complex, she ducked into a maintenance alcove embedded between two sensor-blind zones. With a subtle gesture, her adaptive garments reconfigured, and nanofibers unravelled their botanical camouflage, restoring her default urban attire. She wiped off the dermal pigment mask and retrieved her magi-wand, initiating a rapid follicular reset. In seconds, her hair resumed its original hue and biometric signature.

Crouched in the shadows, she monitored the encrypted comms feed. The false intel she'd seeded into the Kesk network was spreading fast, triggering exactly the kind of fracture she'd planned. Moments later, a cluster of guards stormed into view, struggling to contain the first wave of detainees. Perfect. The chaos she'd engineered was unfolding on schedule.

That was her signal to move. She straightened, shifted her stance, and activated the polished persona of Kimmy K. With calculated ease, she strode toward the detention centre's reception node, radiating confidence. A faint smile tugged at her lips. The distraction had unfolded exactly as designed.

As Kihm approached, the receptionist straightened abruptly, her eyes widening with recognition. A nervous smile tugged at her lips, and though she opened her mouth several times, nothing came out. Clearly starstruck, she blinked rapidly, visibly trying to gather herself. Finally, in a breathy rush, she said, "Hi, I'm Wilma. I'm a huge fan!"

"I saw the commotion outside and wanted to know what was going on."

The receptionist's gaze remained fixed on her idol, her expression caught between awe and anxiety. "I... I'm sorry," she stammered, clearly torn. "I'm not really allowed to talk about it."

Kihm offered a gracious nod, masking her frustration behind a polished smile. She'd need a different angle.

The receptionist worried her lower lip, eyes bright with barely contained excitement. "Would you mind if we capture a holo together? My friends won't believe you stood here otherwise."

"Sure," Kihm replied.

Off to the side, chaos erupted. Detainees shouted and thrashed against the guards, refusing to comply. "Let us go! We didn't do anything wrong!" they yelled, voices raw with defiance.

The guards shouted over them, struggling to maintain control. "Stop resisting! Get on the ground! Put your hands behind your back!"

But the detainees weren't listening; they fought back with curses and flailing limbs. More guards poured in, barking orders as they tried to contain the scene.

Kihm watched from a distance, tension coiling in her chest. No one was backing down. If this spiralled further, someone would get hurt. And it would be her fault. Trying to ignore the chaos exploding in the adjacent area, Kihm offered Wilma a warm smile, then casually reached into her purse, drawing out a sleek makeup kit and holding it up like a precious gem. "This is from my new Alure range," she said, letting the receptionist catch a glimpse of the exclusive product. "It's not on the shelves yet. You'd be one of the first to have it."

Wilma's eyes widened, and her fingers twitched with the impulse to grab it, but she hesitated, torn between polite restraint and fangirl excitement.

Kihm watched her carefully, reading every micro-expression. "I heard there's already been an arrest," Kihm said casually, as if making small talk. "One of the Kesk leaders, Brom, I think his name was?"

Wilma's eyes lit up at the mention, and her hand extended instinctively, eager for the promised prize. But Kihm didn't release it. Not yet. "Brom?" she repeated, her tone soft but expectant.

Now they were locked in a subtle standoff, celebrity charm versus guarded protocol. Kihm held the kit just out of reach, her fingers curled tightly around it, the smile on her face not quite reaching her eyes.

Wilma glanced nervously around before lowering her voice. "He disappeared. They haven't found him, or whoever helped him escape."

Now, Kihm knew why it was 'impossible' to speak to Brom. She smiled and placed the gift into the girl's waiting hands. "Thank you, Wilma, you have been most helpful."

The receptionist took the case and caressed the transparent lid before pointing to one of the lip shades, "Is that your new Rouge Nights lipstick?"

"Yes, it is."

"Could I get that holo now?"

"I'm sorry, Wilma, I really must go. Perhaps, another time."

"Okay," she replied, clearly disappointed.

The noise had died down. Which meant it was time to go before she was noticed.

MEANWHILE, BROM AND Costa sat at a café across the plaza from the detention centre, casually sipping café, just another pair of locals enjoying the afternoon. Both were already operating under different face-altered identities for this phase of the plan, their features subtly modified to slip past biometric scans.

Brom's eyes remained fixed on the facility. He was convinced Mila was being held inside, and every second that passed only tightened the knot in his chest. Then he froze. His sister, Kihm, had just walked through the front entrance. He stared, momentarily stunned. What was she doing there? Within minutes, she reemerged, calm and composed, disappearing into the crowd as if she had never been there at all.

"Stay here," Brom said to Costa as he slipped the comms unit the man had given him from his pocket and quickly dictated a message. Now, he had to get it to Kihm before she disappeared. He hoped that she wouldn't sit on the sidelines if he needed help, even if the last time they'd parted hadn't been on the best of terms.

Brom followed at a measured distance, eyes sharp, waiting as she headed for a private transport module parked discreetly outside a row of boutique clothiers. When the crowd shifted in his favour, he moved, crossing her path with casual ease, brushing against her just enough to seem accidental. In that instant, he slipped the small comms device into her shoulder bag. Then he vanished, folding into the stream of passersby like smoke into the air. A storm of emotions churned beneath his calm exterior. He hoped she'd find the device soon. He wanted to believe she'd listen. What hurt most wasn't her secrecy, it was the silence. The not knowing. Why hadn't she returned to Gromwell? Why hadn't she reached out?

BACK HOME, KIHM REACHED into her large bag and retrieved her comms unit, only to pause, her fingers brushing against something unfamiliar. She pulled it out slowly, frowning at the smooth, high-density alloy surface and subtle pulse of its inactive display. It wasn't hers. Curious, she whispered, "Activate device." The screen shimmered to life without resistance. No biometric scan. No encryption barrier. That alone was enough to raise suspicion. This wasn't an oversight. It was intentional. "Open messages," she said, her voice steady despite the growing tightness in her chest.

A heartbeat later, a familiar voice filled the room, deep, grounded, unmistakably Brom. "Kihm, I need to speak to you urgently. Use this device. It is untraceable."

Luckily, she was alone. Xander and Waylan were out for dinner, and she had conveniently claimed exhaustion. Kihm was moments from initiating the call when her AI interrupted. "You have a visitor at the door."

She froze. She wasn't expecting anyone. Fortunately, her front door was equipped with adaptive smartglass and an integrated AI security system. "AI, show me who's at the door," she instructed.

On cue, the door's surface, usually opaque and armoured, shifted into a transparent display. Facial recognition kicked in immediately, cross-referencing the image against her private registry, household contacts, and Atmos building access logs.

To her surprise, it was Uncle Roddick. He had been estranged from her father five orbits ago after a heated dispute. The rift began when Roddick's community formed a partnership with LOUT, a move he spearheaded, and her father couldn't forgive. Kihm's pulse quickened. If Roddick was here, unannounced, on her doorstep, then either he was desperate, or someone had sent him. Intrigued, she instructed the AI to open the door. "Hello, Uncle."

"Hi, Kihm, or should I call you Kimmy K now."

"Kihm is just fine."

"It's been a long time," he said, and his smile looked practised, not quite reaching his eyes. "I came to say I'm sorry for not being there these past few years. I wanted to make things right, but the timing never felt right. Then too much time had passed."

She remembered her father saying that his older brother had a distinctly relaxed relationship with the truth when it suited him. "I appreciate that, Uncle. I'm glad you came by."

His voice lowered as he looked both ways along the corridor. "Can I come inside?"

Despite her reservations, she stepped aside and waved him in. His eyes lingered on every shadow as if expecting something, or someone, to emerge. His movements were controlled, but beneath them lay a sharp edge of tension.

"We're alone," she said, and let a little bite creep into her tone. "This apartment is shielded and off the building grid. I assume you don't want anyone to know you're here."

"It's not what you think, Kihm."

"Is that right?"

"May I sit down?"

"Of course," she replied, waving him toward the couch.

Roddick avoided her gaze, his hands twisting together until his knuckles blanched. The fine lines she remembered had cut deeper, etched into his face as if time had taken a blade to him and not bothered to be gentle. Whatever softness he once carried was gone. This man had been worn down and sharpened.

"I don't know where to start," he admitted, still not meeting her gaze.

"Perhaps you can start by explaining why you are here."

He cleared his throat. "I might have made a mistake partnering with LOUT."

"Might or have."

"Okay, I have." He finally met her gaze, and his eyes radiated unease. Real unease, not the kind men performed to disarm you.

"So, what are you planning to do about it?" she asked. "Or, more importantly, what do you think I can do about it?"

"That's just it. I don't know," he said, then his gaze flicked past her shoulder, a fraction too fast, to the living room console, to the comms dock, to the sleek privacy modules her cosmetics company insisted she keep in every residence. "I know your family paid a high price for defiance, but you have influence in Atmos."

Now she had a decision to make. Did her uncle have an agenda, or was he genuine? What would happen if she told the truth? Would she put their family in danger? Would her uncle use the information against them? Had someone sent him to gather intel. Did he know Brom had been captured and escaped? Was she under suspicion?

Surveying the situation anew, she couldn't risk it. Perhaps they could reconcile after she had saved her family. "This is a radical departure from your previous stance," she said, keeping her voice even. "The stance that divided our families."

"My community has lost its identity," he said. "Most of the younger generation have already left, drawn away by LOUT's promises and opportunities off-world. I don't think it's accidental. They've left just enough of us behind to preserve the knowledge they want to extract for their own researchers. The signs have been there for a long time. I just refused to see them."

His words landed with a dull weight, because she could hear the truth inside them, and still she couldn't afford to trust it.

"I'm sorry, Uncle," she said at last. "I understand your worries, and I wish I could help you, but I have a successful cosmetics company to consider."

"I see," he snapped, pushing himself to his feet, the practised softness dropping away. "I suppose there is nothing left to say but goodbye."

She rose too, wishing things could be different. "I wish you well, Uncle."

"You too." He paused at the door, eyes narrowing slightly, as if taking one last measurement of her. "I knew this was a long shot, but I had to see for myself."

The words pricked. See what. Before she could ask, he stepped into the corridor. The door sealed behind him, the smartglass turning opaque again, leaving Kihm alone with Brom's untraceable device in her hand, and the sudden, unpleasant certainty that Uncle Roddick had not come here only to apologise. She rested her forehead against the panel and closed her eyes. She hadn't wanted to lie, but the truth was a blade pointed at her throat. A slow breath left her, tension draining with it. The last few minutes had been all tight breath and clenched nerves, and only now was the relief of his departure beginning to register. The visit did not just unsettle her; it snapped her into motion, hardening her resolve. If they were onto her, the window was closing, and she could not afford another mistake. She called Waylan and started laying the groundwork. He answered almost at once. "Waylan. I hope you and Xander are enjoying your evening."

"Yes, I'm having an after-dinner drink with a few friends, and Xander is enjoying the virtual gaming consoles."

Kimmy K knew what he meant by friends. She didn't care about his infidelities anymore. It was water under the bridge. Instead, she remained upbeat. He would discover the truth soon enough. "That's great. Did you manage to secure your father's yacht for our visit to Blackwell tomorrow?"

"Why can't you use the company shuttle?" he countered. Once again, she heard the annoyance in his voice.

"You know why. I explained yesterday. Your father's yacht has more capacity. Don't forget, he will be very pleased if we pull this off. We can also ramp up operations on new product lines. Which would, of course, mean more profit." Appealing to his vanity and the bottom line always hit the mark. He was an easy target.

"Listen, I don't want to interrupt him while he's working on reestablishing negotiations with the Kesk leaders, so I'll approve your request and update him afterwards."

"Can you contact the hangar manager with the approval and have him ready the yacht for 0800 tomorrow? One of my regular pilots is building up his flying hours and is eager to be promoted to captain. Rest assured, he is more than capable. Oh, before I forget, can Xander join us? He would benefit from learning the ground roots of the business so he can take over one day." Aware that the last statement would seal the deal.

"I will lock it in now, and yes, Xander can join you."

"Excellent. Thank you."

"Bye," was all she got before he hung up. She could have jumped for joy because clearing the first major hurdle felt like a personal victory. That yacht wasn't just a luxury vessel; it was the only one in LOUT's fleet that wasn't hardwired with telemetry beacons. Better still, it was outfitted with a phased cloaking array and a next-gen ion dispersal system, capable of masking its propulsion signature across most standard tracking grids. Aivel's obsession with privacy was finally working in her favour.

Next, she called Brom using the number he'd left in his voice message.

He answered on the first ring. "Hi, sis."

The word sat awkwardly between them. "Brom," Kihm said, her voice coming out more formal than she intended. "It's... been a while."

"Yeah. A while." A pause crackled down the line. "I didn't think you'd actually call."

"I heard you'd been captured," Kihm said. "And discovered for myself that you'd escaped. I gather you are still in Atmos."

"Yes," he replied.

She took a breath, then lowered her voice, instinctively glancing at the smartglass door even though it was opaque again. "Before I say anything else, Roddick came to my apartment tonight."

On the other end, the silence changed, sharpened.

"He was sniffing around," she continued, choosing her words with care. "Apologies, regret, talk of LOUT, but his eyes kept tracking my comms, my security, everything. It didn't feel like family. It felt like an assessment."

Brom's exhale was slow and controlled. "He's never done anything without a reason."

"That's what I'm afraid of," she said. "So listen closely."

She steadied herself. “I have an escape plan using the president’s private yacht. Meet me in the shopping district vac-lift lobby at 0730 tomorrow.”

Another silence. When Brom finally spoke, his voice was tight. “I can’t leave without Mila.”

“She isn’t here, Brom, she’s in Blackwell,” Kihm said, keeping her tone firm. “Other lives are at stake, and we only have a small window of opportunity.”

“Okay, but I’ll need to rescue Mila as soon as possible. Is there room on the shuttle for one more?”

“Who?”

“Costa, who risked his life to free me from the detention facility.”

“Can he be trusted?”

“Yes.”

“I didn’t spot you yesterday, so you must be using face-altering tech.”

“Correct,” he replied.

“You’ll pose as xenobotanists,” she said crisply. “Before we deploy, I’ll upload fabricated personnel files, complete with credentials and work histories, so everything checks out.” I will have two monogrammed lab coats embedded with ID-threading ready for you to wear tomorrow. “I’ll transmit your new identities once they’ve been embedded in the system, along with everything else you’ll need. There’s a chance you and your colleague have been fitted with subdermal tracking implants. If so, they’ll need to be extracted.”

“Costa has already seen to that.”

“Excellent.” After hanging up, she used Brom’s undetectable device to call her father and brother to confirm the meeting time. Vrack’s role was crucial, as he was piloting the state-of-the-art yacht. Before ending the call, she reminded them to remove their subdermal trackers before leaving home. Sitting on the couch, she smiled with a sense of accomplishment and satisfaction. She had a lot of work to do between now and tomorrow, but she might just pull this off.

THE NEXT MORNING, WAYLAN had already left for work, and Xander was in his room, waiting for her to announce they were leaving. He'd been excited last night when she'd asked him if he wanted to skip his studies today for a ride in his grandfather's new yacht. She felt immense guilt for betraying Xander's trust and taking advantage of his vulnerability. Ultimately, it was her responsibility to make things right, even if it meant facing inevitable difficult conversations. And then there was Brom. She didn't know how much, if anything, he knew about Danelda's children.

The crystal earrings in Kihm's hand glinted in the light. Taking a deep breath, she looked at her reflection in the mirror, lifted one earring at a time to her earlobe, and pushed the wire through the piercing. Stepping back, she admired how the light caught the crystals, dancing and dazzling in the reflection. No one realised the crystals were embedded with micro-encoded biotech, housing her existing cosmetic formulas along with prototypes for a next-gen line of bioactive, plant-based pharmaceuticals. Her departure would trigger the termination of LOUT's access to her product line, as all proprietary data, including molecular blueprints, synthesis protocols, and bio-compound schematics, was scheduled for a full-system purge at 0815 tomorrow, unless she stopped it. The servers would be scrubbed by quantum-grade erasure protocols, leaving nothing retrievable. She would love to see the look on Aivel and Waylan's faces when they realised they had nothing.

With her packing complete, she took one last look around the apartment, barely able to believe she was leaving it all behind and stepping into uncertainty. Yet beneath the ache of goodbye, she knew this was the right path. And she was ready to walk it.

Kihm took a steadying breath, summoning her best 'nothing-to-worry-about' tone as she approached Xander's room, keeping her movements casual. "Hey, I got a system alert about your subdermal tracker," she said casually, her tone light, like this was just another minor routine fix. "Looks like the unit's glitching. They flagged it as a potential systems interference risk, so I'd best extract it now before it starts scrambling your bio-signals. Won't take more than a minute." She offered a reassuring smile, holding a slim, pen-like dermal anesthetizer in one hand and a precision-coded extraction tool in the other. "We'll pop it out, clean and easy. You can have a fresh implant fitted once we return."

He glanced up, brow furrowed. "Why don't we visit the clinic?"

She smiled, masking her urgency behind a nonchalant wave of her hand. "You don't want to miss out on today's trip, do you?" She gestured for him to extend his arm, keeping her tone light and easy. "I've done this before. You won't feel a thing. It's no worse than pulling out a splinter." She spoke from experience after extracting her own tracker.

At 0730, she and Xander waited at the designated location. And while Xander bounced with excitement, she was a bundle of nerves, chanting calming mantras to herself until everyone arrived. Her father and brother arrived first, dressed appropriately, followed by Brom and Costa, who introduced themselves to the group to reinforce the ruse.

Brom's eyes widened, his normally steely expression cracking as he stared at his father, Andar, and his brother, Vrack, whom he had long believed to be dead. His gaze flicked between them in disbelief, lingering on their faces as if trying to confirm they were real. When he finally looked at Kihm, his eyes burned with questions, the unspoken demand for answers clear in their intensity. No words were needed; the weight of his stare alone made it clear that explanations were not only expected but long overdue.

Heart racing, Kihm shook her head, grabbed Brom's arm, and handed him and Costa lab coats, which they quickly put on.

Although Xander was the main reason for the subterfuge, she didn't want her father and brother to know who the other two men were until they were underway. The less they knew, the less chance of a slip-up. After exchanging pleasantries, they boarded a vac lift down to the underground hangar.

Minutes later, they headed for the private yacht, where final preparations were being made by ground staff and Aviel's pilot. Schooling her face into a blank expression, Kihm approached him. "Hi Prem, you're off the hook today. I have my own man."

Prem lifted an eyebrow. "Only I fly this beauty, and that's on the boss's orders."

Kihm cursed Waylan, who had been too spineless to tell her. Her hands trembled, and she closed her eyes briefly. She would have to deal. "Prem, I would like to introduce my Xenobotanists Brommel, Carlos, Vox and Zor. Xander, you already know."

Prem ruffled Xander's hair. "Looking forward to some adventure and skipping your studies today, young man?"

"Too right!"

"My pre-flight check is complete, so let's get going," he said, waving everyone inside. "Xander, do you want to sit beside me?"

"Can I, Kimmy K?"

"Ahh, I would like you to sit with me." His crestfallen expression said everything. "Perhaps, you can sit with Prem on the return?"

"Okay."

She was relieved. She needed Vrack in the cockpit so he could take over when she drugged Prem, which hadn't been part of the plan, but she could pivot.

Xander didn't waste any time asking Brom about his home. Thankfully, Brom was able to give the boy a very detailed description of a planet called Rotari. She paused, taking a moment to really study

Xander. The resemblance to Brom at that age was uncanny, almost haunting. It wasn't just the same sharp jawline and the dark hair, but in the way he carried himself, with that same quiet intensity. It was like looking at a thread that connected past and present, weaving through time. Without Brom's disguise, there would be no question they were father and son, mirrors of each other in ways that went far beyond appearance.

A pang of emotion stirred deep within her, an ache that resonated with the weight of everything father and son had lost. The years, the moments that had been stolen from them, and she couldn't shake the gnawing guilt that it was, in part, her doing. She had been the one to weave those walls of secrecy, to keep them at arm's length. And now, looking back, she wasn't sure it had been the right call. Perhaps there had been another way. But now was not the time for introspection. There would be plenty of time for that later.

After passing over several settlements, Kihm made her move. "Excuse me for a moment," she said, grabbing her backpack on the way to the bathroom. Once inside, she opened her medicine cassette, which stored her precious vials and extracted a potent tranquilliser that would cause no lasting harm to Prem. After loading the liquid into an empty pressure injector, she palmed it, entered the cockpit and pressed the high-pressure injection against Prem's neck. "Sorry, Prem," she said as he slumped in his seat beside Vrack.

"A heads-up might've been nice," Vrack muttered, fingers flying over the virtual controls as he wrested command back to his side. The sleek display flickered under his grip, responding to the shift in authority. "Now, what's the plan, sis?"

"Initiate cloaking and fire up the ion diffuser," she instructed, keeping her voice steady. "We are heading to Gromwell."

Vrack nodded, eyes narrowing as he keyed in the location.

She flexed her fingers, giving her hands a quick wipe on her pants as if the gesture could banish her guilt. "I'll extract Prem's subdermal tracker and cover the wound with synth skin." She sighed. This is the easy part," she murmured, as much to herself as to Vrack, as she removed the device quickly and efficiently and sealed the wound. Lacking a dampener, she acted fast, crushing the tracker underfoot, grinding it into the floor until the casing cracked and the internal circuitry sparked and died. "The hard part starts when I have to go back in there," she said, pointing to the main cabin.

Vrack glanced up, a smirk tugging at the corner of his mouth. "The hard part, huh? And what exactly would that be?"

Her eyes shifted away, avoiding Vrack's knowing gaze. "Telling the truth," she said, her voice barely a whisper yet heavy with dread.

Vrack caught her gaze, his hand resting gently on her arm. "You weren't alone in this," he murmured. "The guilt's not yours to carry alone."

"I know," she whispered, the words thick with regret. "But it was my idea, and you warned me about the consequences."

"Brom and Xander will forgive us once they hear the story. But you'd better hurry. We're about ten clicks out from Gromwell. I'll hide the yacht in the underground caves. Unfortunately, it is a hike to Gromwell from there."

Kihm nodded, letting the cockpit door close behind her with a quiet hiss. She paused, exhaling slowly as her eyes settled on Brom and Xander, who looked back at her, their expressions sharpening under her steady gaze. She clenched her hands, feeling the words press against her throat like a storm ready to break. "There's something you both need to know."

Curious, Xander asked, "What is it?"

"The man sitting beside you is not from off-planet. He is your biological father." Brom's face was a mask of shock and disbelief. His mouth hung open, his eyes widened, and his brow furrowed.

Meanwhile, Xander stared back in disbelief. His face was a mix of emotions as he tried to make sense of her statement. "You seriously expect me to believe that, Kimmy?" Xander scoffed, eyebrows raised. "He looks nothing like us."

Brom deactivated the disguise, masking his green skin. "Kihm, Danelda said I had a daughter. She said nothing about a son."

"Danelda had twins, but was kept in the dark about her son. Waylan saw an opportunity to claim a Kesk offspring. Sorry, Xander, I know this sounds far-fetched, but Waylan is not the person you think he is. The other man in the cockpit is Vrack, your uncle and my brother, and the older man sitting behind you is your grandfather, Andar."

Although the evidence was staring him in the face, Xander responded with, "I don't believe you. Take me home, now!"

"No. We are heading to Gromwell. Our real home."

While still shocked, Brom turned to the young man. "I am as surprised as you. But you can't deny the resemblance."

Xander's expression remained angry. "If it's a ransom you want, my father will pay."

Brom shook his head. "No, I believe it's true, and deep down, you do too."

"How? It doesn't make any sense. Who is my mother?"

Brom's face softened. "It's complicated. After we arrive in Gromwell, we will sit down and piece the story together. You and I need to know everything that led us to this point." He glanced from Kihm to his father and brother.

Xander was silent for a moment, then slowly nodded. "I see. So, what does this mean for us now?" he asked.

Brom's smile faded slightly, but his eyes were warm. "It means," he said slowly, "that we are family, and we stick together."

Kihm could see by the look on Xander's face that he wasn't entirely convinced. He would need to be watched closely because she wouldn't put it past him to run back to Atmos.

THE HORIZON DARKENED as thick, bruised clouds rolled in, swallowing the last traces of clear sky. A distant rumble of thunder trembled in the air, its low growl a warning of the storm about to be unleashed. As the group walked through the gates of Gromwell, the smell of rain, earthy and electric, hung in the air.

Despite the welcoming party hastily covering their heads with anything they could find to shield themselves from the now-steady wind and rain, the atmosphere was almost electric with anticipation. Brom's friends and neighbours, unfazed by the sudden shift in weather, welcomed them with open arms. But it wasn't just the rain or the unexpected gathering that caught them off guard. It felt like old ghosts walking back into their lives, Andar and Vrack, believed dead, and Kihm, gone for many orbits.

Rhen's eyes scanned the crowd, desperately searching for Mila. The rain beaded on his skin, forgotten in the rush of emotions. Just as he was about to push through, Brom stepped forward and extended his hand.

"Hi, I'm Brom," he said, his voice steady despite the storm building around them. "You must be Rhen. Mila spoke of you often." Brom watched Rhen search for her, barely seeming to hear his words. The question was inevitable, but when it came, it was raw.

"Where is she?" he asked, his voice strained.

Brom could see how much Rhen needed the answer, but was terrified of what it might be. The tension between them was thick, and Brom felt a pang of sympathy, knowing that whatever he said, it wouldn't be the answer Rhen was hoping for. Brom wrapped an arm around Rhen's shoulders and steered him towards his home. "Unfortunately, she is in Blackwell. Join us so we can put a rescue plan together."

Rhen gestured toward a woman standing beside him. "Astrea should be part of this. She commands the Krylan soldiers. Or as you call them, the meat eaters."

Brom nodded, intrigued by the chance to meet the elusive strangers from the rainforest. "Of course," Brom said as more people gathered outside his home to greet him and his family.

Flynn pulled him in for a solid hug. "Welcome home, Brom," he said above the chatter. "I don't know how you deal with all the issues here and remain sane."

Brom broke the news to Flynn that Danelda had given birth to twins, who were now teenagers. Although Flynn's reaction mirrored his own initial shock, he was more surprised than deeply shaken because Danelda had played a key role in the plot to take his life.

Home was a heartwarming sight. People arrived in droves carrying a variety of dishes, ranging from hearty vegetable casseroles to freshly baked pies and cakes. As they filled his home, the aroma of homemade food wafted through the air. Before long, the kitchen table overflowed with a colourful array of steaming dishes and bowls. There were smiles, laughter, and words of gratitude for their safe return. The atmosphere was one of joy and relief.

Brom was feeling a mix of emotions as he watched the celebration unfold. Although he was overjoyed to be home, he was eager to end the festivities and discuss Mila and Oxana's rescues.

Just then, Shaman Oldson approached him. "Brom, how are you?"

"All things considered, not too bad, Uncle. But I feel the weight of responsibility."

"Remember your training. Meditate and listen to your intuition. It is stronger than you think, especially in our family." He put his hand on Brom's shoulder and leaned closer. "I've come to remind you of the warning I gave you many years ago. Do you remember?"

"Yes, of course."

"Good. Be careful."

Brom nodded. "Can the family stay in the monastery for a few days? I want them out of sight and away from Gromwell."

"Yes, of course," he replied, pulling Brom into a quick hug before turning to the others: his brother Andar, his nephew Vrack, his niece Kihm, and Xander. One by one, he drew them in, welcoming them home.

An hour later, Brom forced a smile, nodding along with the conversation swirling around him, though his mind wandered to Mila and his daughter, Oxana. His thoughts churned with rescue plans. Now and then, he caught Rhen's sharp, restless gaze. The impatience in his eyes was hard to miss, a sentiment Brom echoed. No amount of small talk could distract him from the urgency hanging between them.

And with that in mind, he cleared his throat to quieten the group. "Thank you, everyone, for your warm welcome and support. I am sure you are as pleased as I am to welcome my family back. But we still have work to do to defeat LOUT."

The group cheered.

Then, Brom looked over at Xander, whose face spoke a thousand words. He knew winning over the teenager whose world had just been turned upside down would take time. Unfortunately, that would have to wait as he had bigger fish to fry tonight.

A FEW MINUTES LATER, Xander slipped outside, fingers shaking as he activated the comms unit stashed in his pocket and contacted Waylan. One tiny stroke of luck in this whole insane mess. All he wanted was to return home, where things made sense. "I've been abducted."

"I know all about Kimmy K's little escapade."

"When are you coming to get me?" he asked, his voice wavering with an edge of desperation.

"Soon. Where are you?" Waylan's voice came through, sharp and devoid of warmth.

Xander swallowed. "Outside Brom's residence." He then heard a soft ping in his earpiece, confirming that Waylan had just received his coordinates.

A beat of silence. Then Waylan replied, his tone icy and precise. "Good. But first, I need to know where they're holding Novak and Prem."

"I... I don't know." Xander hesitated, anxiety tightening his chest. He'd expected Waylan to offer reassurance, not make demands.

"Then find out," Waylan snapped, each word a command, before he softened his tone. "You want to return home, don't you?"

Xander swallowed hard. "But if I ask, they'll get suspicious."

"Use your initiative, boy," Waylan said sharply. "You're not a child. I taught you to think on your feet."

Xander shifted uncomfortably, the weight of the situation pressing down on him. "I suppose I could try..."

"Not 'try,' Xander. Do it," Waylan pressed, his tone sharp and unyielding. "Once you confirm the location, I'll create a diversion, and you'll get them out. Simple."

Xander swallowed, his voice wavering as he asked, "What kind of diversion?" The edge of doubt was clear.

"That's not your concern," Waylan snapped. "You'll recognise it when it happens. Do exactly as I say. No deviation from the plan, no second-guessing. After that, I'll bring you home."

Xander hesitated, the fear creeping back into his voice. "It sounds risky. I don't know if I can."

"You can and you will," Waylan interrupted. "Failure isn't an option, boy. If you want to return home, you'll follow my orders. Understood?"

"Yes," Xander said, knowing he had no choice.

"Before you go, Kimmy K said that Brom is my real father. Is it true?"

"You shouldn't believe anything that witch tells you."

"Okay," Xander responded uncertainly.

"And Xander, when you free my men, give Novak your comms unit. I need to speak to him urgently. Understood?"

"Yes, Father."

"Now go," Waylan said before hanging up.

Returning to Brom's home, Xander was surrounded by a strange mix of voices. In the corner, two men discussed a business deal, while across the room, a woman laughed. Xander stood in the middle of it all, and although he resembled those around him, he felt out of place. Moving across the room, his eyes flitted from one person to the next. He nodded at one, exchanged a few words with another, and then stopped to listen to a third, which just happened to be the jackpot. He now knew the men were being held inside an old prison ship on the edge of town. After freeing Novak and Prem, he intended to return to Atmos. Like a ghost, he slipped out into the evening to do reconnaissance on the location with no thought to the retribution that LOUT would rain down on Gromwell. That revelation would come later.

AFTER MANY OF THE OLDER visitors shared stories, laughter, and a few tears, they said their goodbyes, leaving only Brom, Kihm, Andar, Vrack, Costa, Shaman Oldson, Flynn, Rhen, and Astrea behind.

Kihm asked, "Has anyone seen Xander?"

A chorus of silent headshakes confirmed her worst fear. "I hope he hasn't taken it into his head to return to Atmos."

"He is probably outside clearing his head," Flynn said. "He's a teenager, and it's a lot for him to absorb. Hell, it's a lot for us adults."

Kihm bit her lip. "You're probably right. I'll give him another half hour before I go looking."

Brom rubbed his eyes. "We should regroup tomorrow. I need to speak with Novak in the morning and gather more information."

Flynn shook his head. "Good luck with that. I doubt he'll cooperate."

Just then, Xander wandered over with his hands firmly planted in his pockets, his mouth set in a thin, hard line, and his eyes narrowed in a sulky expression.

"Xander! We were worried about you," Kihm said.

"I'm fine," he bit out. "I'm not a child."

Brom directed his next comment to his family members. "Shaman Oldson will take you all to the Monastery for the next few days. I don't want any argument."

"I think you should join us, Brom," Kihm said.

Brom shoved a hand through his hair. "No. I'm staying put. Go."

After the group departed, Brom, Rhen and Astrea sat around the table, and Brom broke the silence with a calm urgency. "We need to talk about rescuing Mila from Blackwell. Rhen, I need you to pilot the yacht and drop me outside of Blackwell."

Rhen's brows creased. "What's the extraction plan?"

"Stay close, but keep the phased cloaking array active. I'll be in touch when I'm ready. In the meantime, Astrea, please take a secondary shuttle, load your gear, and start transporting your entire team to Gromwell. I know it'll take multiple trips, but I need them in Gromwell to look after the town while we strike Atmos tomorrow evening."

Astrea leaned back. "Are you sure you don't need extra firepower in Blackwell? You'll be on your own."

"I'm sure," Brom replied confidently. "If I keep a low profile. Blackwell residents are naturally suspicious and don't usually talk to strangers."

Rhen's jaw tightened, but his eyes stayed on Brom. "Got it."

Brom reached across, clasping Rhen's forearm in a show of solidarity. "We will finalise our preparations at dawn. We will bring Mila back safely."

Rhen nodded. "I'll be ready. Astrea and I will spend the night prepping the yacht and catch some sleep there," Rhen said, his tone decisive.

Finally, alone, Brom entered the quiet solitude of his cellar, buried deep into the ground beneath his home, to collect the supplies he needed. He knew sleep wouldn't come tonight because his heart ached with the weight of regret, each second ticking by feeling like a lifetime. The thought of delaying Mila's rescue clawed at his soul. She hadn't asked for any of this; he had pulled her into a web of danger and uncertainty. Yet, she'd risked everything for him. He cared for her more deeply than he wanted to admit, and the thought of her getting hurt was hard to bear.

And then there was the bitter truth he kept shoving to the back of his mind: when all of this was over, she'd return to Rotari, the home she loved. He tried to picture life without her, the hollow silence she'd leave behind. But he couldn't. And deep down, he didn't want to. The idea of her leaving felt like the ground slipping from under him. The possibility of leaving Eania, especially now that he had the twins to think about, was probably not an option. Perhaps his father could lead Gromwell again. All he could do now was hope that fate wouldn't be cruel enough to take her from him before he had the chance to tell her what she meant. Instead, he rummaged around in the dimly lit cellar until he was satisfied that everything was in order.

With the supplies packed, he leaned back against the cellar wall, contemplating the idea of rest. But his nerves were still taut, and the weight of the coming rescue pressed heavily on him. There would be no peace tonight; he'd done all he could. Beyond this, it was up to fate.

As Brom resolved to head back upstairs, an explosion shattered the early morning stillness, its violent force ripping through the cellar and slamming him onto the floor. His world spun as the cellar door slammed shut, sealing him below in a makeshift tomb.

Acrid smoke began to seep into the space, thick and suffocating, clawing at his lungs as he gasped for breath. Above, distant cries punctuated the silence of Gromwell's once-slumbering streets. Brom's pulse thundered as the grim realisation sank in. His enemy had escalated the conflict before he'd even had a chance to set his plans in motion. Frustration burned through him, but it was the fear that landed hardest, leaving him unaware of the extent of the destruction above and possible casualties. He felt trapped, cornered by events spiralling beyond his control. Once again, he'd failed the people who depended on him. His strength ebbed, and darkness closed in, pulling him under before he could take another breath.

A SHORT TIME LATER, Flynn's message arrived at the monastery advising that Brom was presumed dead, along with his neighbours. Fuelled by a hope that teetered on the edge of despair, the group, with the exception of Oxana returned to Gromwell with heavy hearts, praying that the grim news would prove false.

When they arrived, the smouldering wreckage was devastating. The explosion had torn through Brom's residence, which lay at the epicentre, and rippled out to his immediate neighbours. Shattered glass and twisted metal littered the area, intermingled with personal belongings.

It quickly became evident that Brom had been the target. The precision was chilling, indicating that LOUT would stop at nothing. Amid the ruin, the townspeople's whispers carried a stark consensus. No one in Brom's home could have survived such destruction.

Rhen and Astrea worked alongside the locals, combing the smoking rubble in short, punishing bursts, forced back again and again by the heat and unstable debris. Their faces set in grim determination, their movements careful as they sifted through the scattered remains of homes. Thankfully, they discovered a few survivors who were shaken and dazed, nursing wounds both physical and mental.

Family and friends reconvened, and a silent understanding passed among them. With Gromwell no longer secure, they needed a new base of operations. In hushed tones, they agreed to relocate to the founders' caves nestled deep in the hillside. There, in the shadows, they would regroup, rebuild, and prepare.

It was more than a tactical decision; it symbolised resilience. They would continue the fight, not only to avenge the fallen but to protect what remained. As they left Gromwell behind, the path forward was marked with uncertainty and danger, yet their resolve burned brighter than ever.

XANDER DIDN'T NEED anyone to explain it. He knew, with sickening certainty, that this was the distraction his father meant, the explosion, the chaos, the smoke rising from Brom's home. It was all his fault. He had given away the location the moment he reached out. His stomach twisted, and he forced the rising bile as he slipped away from the crowd and shouted orders. Waylan's instructions replayed in his head, clipped and precise. Retrieve Novak and Prem. No noise. No trace.

The prisoner ship squatted at the edge of Gromwell like a carcass left to rust, half buried, hull buckled, registry paint bleached beneath grime. No lights. No guards. Just quiet.

Xander stayed in the ship's shadow line and moved fast. The main hatch, an iris set into the hull plating, was exactly where it should be, but the rim was dented and the sealant cracked, as if someone had tried to pry it once before and failed. A thin ring of light traced the hatch. A lens opened above it. "Identify," the ship said. "Restricted containment asset. Authorised escorts only. State escort code."

Xander lifted both hands, palms out. "Emergency retrieval. No escort present."

"Noncompliant. Escort code required." The iris didn't move. Beneath the plating, magnetic clamps hummed.

Xander crouched, not at a visible panel, but at the nano-sealed service skin running alongside the iris seam. No screws, no access plate, just a smooth layer designed to look uninterrupted. He drew out a seal peeler, a narrow tool that breathed a faint heat shimmer, and traced the seam until the nano-bond softened and released. The service layer lifted without a crack, without a pop, exposing a recessed diagnostic cradle beneath.

The lens tightened. "Tamper detected. Escalation protocol in ten seconds."

"Understood," Xander murmured. He slid his access wafer into the cradle, the same wafer he used on Atmos to slip past "interactive" games that were really live scenario sims. Ordinary video games were child's play. He preferred systems with consequences.

The ship rejected the handshake instantly. No entry.

"Fine," Xander breathed. He pulled a translucent smart filament from his pocket, looped it into the cradle, and let the wafer inject a false telemetry packet straight into the ship's sensor spine.

Heat spike. Pressure anomaly. Containment air fault. The clamps' hum wavered. The lens flashed amber. "Electrical anomaly detected. Initiating safety egress."

"Do it," Xander whispered.

A low alarm began deep in the hull. "Safety egress active. Internal doors unsealed for evacuation. Asset compartments remain restricted." The iris rotated open.

Xander slipped inside, and the corridor swallowed him, emergency strips flickering to life along the floor. The air smelled of old disinfectant and metal. The ship was awake now, and awake systems remembered. Safety egress had cracked the ship open, but custody routines still held the prisoners secure. He moved fast, following faded markings until a door blinked amber and released. Containment Bay 3.

Novak stood near the rear bulkhead, arms folded, posture calm but coiled. Prem sat on a bench, shoulders squared.

Novak's gaze landed on Xander like a blade. "You took your time."

Prem's mouth curved, barely.

Xander went straight to the control column beside the shimmering field plane. "Where's the release?"

"You need clearance codes," Novak said.

"I know."

The interface lit: a clean, modern skin over old law, an escort token, biometrics, a witness signature. The ship's voice returned. "Containment assets. Unauthorised party detected. Stand down."

Xander kept his breathing slow. "Emergency egress is active."

"Egress does not supersede custody. Release denied."

Xander took a deep breath and slid his access wafer into the column's maintenance port. A raw diagnostic overlay bloomed, bare prompts, no warnings.

Novak stepped closer to the barrier, eyes on Xander's hands. "If the core logs your signature, it will tag you as the releasing agent."

Prem's voice was low. "Then don't give it a signature."

Xander's pulse kicked. Did they think he was an idiot? He opened the custody log and saw the fields the AI would automatically write: agent ID, location stamp, time, and escort token hash. He couldn't delete them, but he could poison them. He switched the column into service phantom mode, a maintenance state used when hardware was swapped, and pushed a looped identity packet into the logging buffer, a null escort record that looked like corrupted sensor data. No face. No token. No traceable ID. Just a fault the ship would blame on its own degraded systems.

A warning flashed. LOGGING DEGRADED, FALLBACK TO LOCAL CACHE.

Good. Local cache meant isolated, brittle, and, if he timed it right, overwritten. He triggered the release window.

For a beat, the AI hesitated. "Escort presence detected. Verification incomplete."

"Emergency," Xander said, forcing the word into a hard, official tone. "Evacuation directive."

"Temporary release window granted. Ten seconds. Escort assumes liability." The barrier shimmered and dropped.

Prem was through first, and Novak followed, moving like a man who had rehearsed every step a hundred times. As he passed, he flicked a glance at the diagnostic overlay. "Very clever, Xander. Impressive skills."

Xander didn't look up. "That's what happens when you get bored and ignored." He yanked the wafer free, then reached back into the diagnostic overlay and did the second part, wiping the footprint. Not a deletion, a roll-forward reset, forcing the ship to compress its recent event stack into a generic error bundle.

A bland line replaced the last entry. RELEASE EVENT, DATA CORRUPTED, CAUSE, POWER ANOMALY. Then the ship's voice sharpened. "Custody anomaly. Verification revoked. Containment reassertion in progress." Lights strobed red. Doors began slamming down the corridor, one after another, the sound rolling toward them like thunder.

Prem grabbed Xander's sleeve and yanked him hard. "Move."

The corridor lights snapped to a faster strobe. Somewhere behind them, a lock cycled with a heavy metallic thud.

Novak surged in close. "Comms."

Xander thrust the unit at him without slowing.

Novak ripped it from his hand, met Xander's eyes for a single, sharp beat, then keyed the link as they ran, Waylan's channel opening in his ear.

Waylan's voice cut through, sharp and cold. "Report."

"Xander released us," Novak said.

"Good." A set of coordinates ran across the comm display. "Pickup in twenty minutes. Prem comes with you. Xander stays in Gromwell. He will be my eyes and ears."

Novak's eyes flickered with something unreadable. He ended the call and looked at Xander. "Waylan says you stay."

Xander's stomach dropped. "No. Let me talk to him."

He reached for the comm. Novak held it out of reach, calm as stone.

"Not happening," Novak said.

Xander's face turned thunderous. "I'll make my own way home."

"You wanted to help your father," Novak said, voice low as the corridor shook with another lock cycling shut. "This is how."

Prem shoved Xander toward the exit.

They sprinted through the strobing red. Unbeknownst to them, as Novak and Prem cut into the rainforest toward the pickup point, Xander lagged half a step, then two behind. When the rescue craft arrived, he slipped into its shadowed entry bay as the ramp began to rise. After the hatch sealed, and Xander pressed himself into the dark, heart hammering, and listened to the craft's systems thrum as it lifted away.

THE RESCUE CRAFT SLID to a stop, and for a beat there was only the soft whine of systems spooling down and the faint tick of cooling metal. Then the iris cycled, a circular seam of light tracing the hatch before it dilated with a smooth mechanical sigh.

Atmos' hangar air was cooler, filtered through expensive systems, and faintly tinged with ozone. Cold white strip lights cut across the cavern in hard lines, reflecting off wet-black composite and reinforced ribs that curved up into darkness. Status beacons pulsed at steady intervals, and maintenance drones skittered along the walls like metal insects, hunting leaks, laying welds and stitching damage with tireless precision.

Novak stepped out, Prem half a pace behind. Two corporate enforcers stood waiting on the deck in matte-black armour, visors down, weapons slung, not relaxed, just patient. "Novak," one of them said through his helmet speaker. "Director Waylan wants you now. No detours."

"Wouldn't dream of it," Novak replied, keeping his tone light, careful not to let it catch on the knot in his gut.

The enforcers marched off across the deck, matte armour swallowing the hangar light. Novak waited until their backs were fully turned, then angled toward the vac-lifts. A faint scuff sounded behind him, too soft for a guard's boot, too hesitant for a drone. He stopped.

Prem took one more step, then glanced back, frowning.

In the rescue craft's shadow, a smaller figure straightened, dust streaked across his clothes, posture set as if he belonged there. Xander.

For a heartbeat, Novak just stared, disbelief giving way to anger. He crossed the distance in two strides and caught the boy by the upper arm, not hard enough to bruise, just enough to control him. "What the hell are you doing here?" Novak hissed, keeping his voice low.

Xander lifted his chin. "Returning home." He tried to pull free. "I want to speak to my father."

"You don't get demands," Novak said, tightening his grip just enough to make the point. "You get instructions. You stay silent, and you stay close. Your father will not be happy."

Xander's eyes flashed. For a moment, Novak thought he would push back, make noise, force a scene. Then he gave a tight nod, more defiance than agreement.

Novak released him and started walking, keeping Xander tight at his shoulder.

Prem peeled off, already angling toward an adjacent service corridor. He gave Novak a look over his shoulder, equal parts warning and amusement. "I'm heading to med and debrief," Prem said. His gaze flicked to Xander, then back to Novak. "Good luck with the boss," he added, voice dry. "And good luck managing him."

They crossed the hangar deck with shuttles aligned in precise rows under diagnostic sweeps, spider-legged loaders clicking across the floor with sealed pods, overhead cranes gliding on mag-tracks, lifting and slotting containers with silent efficiency. Service drones flitted between craft, throwing brief sparks as they sealed seams and checked couplings, the air thrumming with power and the hiss of pressure valves.

At the vac-lifts, Novak tapped his wrist unit to the reader. The doors whispered open.

Inside, Xander shifted, impatience rolling off him. "I'm staying in Atmos, and I'm talking to my father."

Novak kept his gaze forward. "You'll do exactly what I tell you," he said, calm and flat.

The lift climbed with a smooth, stomach-lightening pull. When it eased to a halt, and the doors parted, the air changed again, cooler, drier and carrying the faint tang of premium filtration. The corridor ahead was all clean angles and muted grey walls, soft floor lighting, and doors with discreet biometric panels.

Novak shepherded Xander to a door at the end of the hallway and tapped his wrist unit against the panel. The lock disengaged with a soft chime.

"Wait inside," he said. "Amuse yourself with my interactive video game."

Xander's eyes narrowed. "You're locking me in."

"I'm stopping you from doing something stupid," Novak replied, and pushed him gently but firmly across the threshold. "Touch nothing."

He closed the door and watched the lock cycle. For a moment, he stood there, breathing through the familiar twist in his gut. They trust you, the nagging voice whispered. But trust only went so far. And LOUT had a long memory.

Entering Waylan's office a few minutes later, Novak was met by a wall of glass that projected a filtered view of the lake. The scene was overlaid with faint data sets that crawled across the surface like quiet warnings. The room itself was staged, spare, immaculate, a single slab desk of dark composite dominating the space, two low chairs set opposite like an invitation to sit lower than the man behind it.

Waylan sat centred, posture deliberate, shoulders squared, hands placed with care, as if every angle of him had been rehearsed. He looked the same as ever, sharp features, close-cropped fair hair, and eyes the flat colour of old steel. Authority was built into the lighting, the silence, the elevated chair and the way the room pushed you toward compliance. And yet Novak could see the effort under it, the slight tightness at the jaw, the measured stillness of someone holding a pose. Waylan wore power like a tailored jacket, clean, expensive, and just a fraction too stiff. He knew where the real weight sat, and it was not in this chair.

"Director." Novak inclined his head, careful not to overdo it. Deference without grovelling. That was the trick with men like him.

Waylan studied him for a long moment, his gaze taking in the details Novak could not hide, dust ground into the seams of his boots, the faint creases of hard travel, the rigid set of his shoulders. He deliberately stretched the silence to make Novak uncomfortable. "What the hell happened?" Waylan said at last. "You left the monastery, then I received a brief, cryptic message, and the next thing I hear is that your attempt to recapture Brom ended with you being detained."

"I didn't count on the Kesk's unique abilities," Novak said. "They were beyond anything I was aware of."

Waylan leaned back in his chair, steepling his fingers. "Sit."

Novak obeyed, the chair's smartfoam adjusting around him. He resisted the urge to fidget. "Before I go any further, unfortunately, Xander ignored your instruction and stowed away on the rescue craft," Novak said. "I found him after we landed. He is in my quarters and demanding an audience with you."

Waylan's eyes did not soften. "Did anything go to plan. Start with the monastery."

Novak swallowed, his mouth dry. "They brought me in to help with maintenance, just like I told you. Yard work, general repairs, nothing that raised alarms. They watched me at first, but people relax when you fix their problems. Over time, they let me get closer to their systems."

Waylan leaned back a fraction. "And."

“That is where the opportunity opened,” Novak said. “I got a heads up that Rhen was coming, an offworlder and technical specialist. He was travelling with Astrea, one of the Kryan soldiers from the rainforest, and they wanted to interrogate the monastery’s archived data, anything that could tell them how to breach Atmos, which is their intent.”

Waylan’s eyes narrowed. “Rhen, the one tied to Mila.”

Novak nodded once. “Yes. Mila and Rhen are both from Rotari, but they ended up here through the Zoldacks. I never got the full story. They kept it close, and by the time I realised I needed to know more, I lost my opportunity. What mattered was that Rhen was coming, and he had the skills to pull information out of old systems.”

Waylan’s calm voice made it worse. “So you altered it.”

“I did,” Novak said. “I knew what he would ask for, so I made sure the answers steered him where we wanted. Then I offered to access the monastery terminals for him, feeding him an architectural template package, older layout data from before the last refit, central spine, module arrangement, the main hangar approach, and a set of security protocols that were plausible.”

Waylan’s jaw flexed. “Are you saying you gave him the keys to the city?”

“I am saying I chose what he could see,” Novak said. “He was always going to get something. The information is there if you know where to dig. I simply adjusted the dataset.”

Waylan held his stare. “Enough to build a plan that leads the Gromwell troublemakers straight into our net.”

Novak exhaled slowly. “Exactly. I set the route. When they infiltrate Atmos, it will be on the path I chose, the one I can predict, contain, and close. “While Brom is dead, Flynn is still very much alive and motivated to proceed,” Novak said. “He has Rhen on his side, plus the squadron of stranded Krylan soldiers.”

"That is precisely what concerns me," Waylan said. "Loose elements, foreign soldiers, and people with nothing left to lose, all converging on my city." He didn't raise his voice. He didn't need to. The room seemed to tighten around the words. "AI, bring up Atmos schematics."

Waylan flicked a control, and the map obeyed, zooming down through the under-lake infrastructure until the submerged hangar complex filled the air between them. He narrowed it again, isolating the maintenance tunnels and crawler routes. The relevant lines brightened, as if the city itself were highlighting its own veins. He tapped a thicker service artery on the outer ring. "I believe they will come in through here."

Novak's eyes didn't even pause. "No," he said. "That route is watched. Too many checkpoints, too many audits. They'll use the underground hangar, and somehow gain access, then they'll ride a crawler into the maintenance tunnel." He stepped closer and pointed to the narrower line running off the hangar grid. "Here."

Waylan held his gaze for a beat, then dragged the projection inward, letting the tunnel fill the space between them. "And what makes this route the preferred one from our perspective?"

"It has conduit and overhead vents," Novak said. "It feeds the crawlers' environmental loop."

Waylan's eyes flicked to the overlay. A thin line pulsed above the tunnel path, labelled in sparse system shorthand. He exhaled once, almost a laugh. "A gas line."

"We lock down the crawlers and route a concentrated suppressant mix into the environmental system feeding them," Novak said. "Under three seconds. Enough to drop our intruders."

Waylan studied him in silence. "You sound very sure of yourself. That confidence is exactly what they used against you before." His eyes narrowed, flat and cold. "You have been outmanoeuvred by them once. Do not stand in my office and tell me you suddenly understand them because you spent several months living among them."

Novak's jaw tightened. "You hired me because I see patterns. They will take the fastest path and trust the data. Let them infiltrate the hangar. Once they enter the maintenance tunnel, I will have the system flag it as an anomaly and trigger an automatic isolation shutdown, sealing the hatches at either end, locking them in, then initiating a safety purge to release the gas into the crawlers."

"Which," Waylan finished softly, "which drops them."

"Exactly," Novak said. "The logs will show the system did exactly what it was built to do, prioritise safety above all. It will read as a standard contamination event. The crawlers will be flagged unsafe, and an automatic decontamination cycle will initiate."

Waylan stood and paced around the desk, hands clasped tightly. "And when they're unconscious."

"That's your call," Novak said. "At the end of the day, no one will know what happened to them."

For a heartbeat, the air between them went taut. Then Waylan laughed once, a short, dry sound. "Very well."

"And Xander," Novak asked before he could stop himself.

Waylan's expression cooled. "Get him to help you. After that, he becomes expendable."

Novak swallowed. The kid had been naïve and desperate to please. Novak exhaled slowly. "He's guilt-stricken and confused. He wants to get back into your good graces. I can use that."

Waylan's expression barely shifted. "Let them climb and fight their way up through my city. They will find out what I'm capable of."

Novak held his gaze, forcing himself not to look away. He had chosen his side a long time ago. "I'll ensure the maintenance tunnel is ready," he said.

"I know you will." Waylan sat and tapped a control on his desk. A holo-file appeared between them, Novak's personnel file, including access pathways and clearance history. Underneath, faint red text pulsed: FLAGGED. PENDING TERMINATION.

Waylan gestured toward the door, then turned back to the rotating image. "Failure is not an option, is that clear. If you fail, I will stop shielding you. Security will be notified that a wanted traitor has resurfaced on-station. We will see how long you last in the Blackheart Mine."

Silence stretched. Novak's pulse hammered in his ears. "Understood, sir," he said, forcing the words out clean. "I will not fail again."

"See that you don't." Waylan cut the holo away with a casual flick, as if ending a call meant ending the threat behind it. "Keep me briefed." He paused, eyes on Novak, measuring. "One more thing. Roddick will feed his relatives what we want them to hear. Information that keeps their responses aligned with our plan. We cannot afford competing narratives complicating this."

Novak managed a thin smile and stood. So Roddick was in on it, too. "How do you know he won't betray you?"

Waylan's expression did not change. "Because he can't afford to."

Novak held his gaze. "That confident, are you?"

Waylan's mouth twitched, not quite a smile. "We have leverage," he said, and the way he said it made the word sound like a mechanism. "The kind that doesn't expire."

Novak let the silence sit for a beat, then pressed. "What kind of leverage?"

Waylan leaned back, steepling his fingers. "None of your concern." He paused, then added, as if choosing the smallest truth that still served him, "When Brom disappeared, my father suspected Kimmy K might be involved. He sent Roddick to look. Not to interrogate, not to spook her, but to observe and report."

"And."

"After Roddick spoke to her, we knew no more than we did before," Waylan said. "Nothing we could pin to Brom's disappearance. That was the problem. In the end, Father was right about her, and we should have acted on instinct rather than proof. We should have removed her quietly, stripped her down to clean code, and put her back into circulation as a compliant version, with a new set of memories and a smile that never faltered. Evidence is for courts. Control is for us."

Novak inclined his head and turned to leave. His legs felt oddly unsteady as he passed through the sliding door. Reprogramming. He hadn't known it sat on the table so casually, spoken of like routine maintenance. Not an execution, not even a disappearance, a rewrite. A person reduced to compliant code and redeployed with a new smile. If they could do that to Kimmy K, a woman valuable enough to keep, then no one was untouchable. Not him, not Xander, not anyone who thought they were useful. The decision settled in his gut, cold and final. Take the payment, finish the job, vanish.

Behind him, the lake on the projected window wall lay perfectly still, a sheet of borrowed peace, for now. Soon, that calm would be rewritten.

NOVAK ARRIVED AT HIS apartment to collect Xander, who was waiting just inside the door, arms folded.

"You spoke to him?" Xander demanded the moment Novak stepped through. "To my father? What did he say?"

Novak hesitated only a heartbeat. "Waylan's very busy, he'll talk to you when he can."

"That's what everyone says," Xander shot back with a pout. "When he can. When he has time, he never has time."

Novak's door slid shut behind him. "Your father told me something else," he said, letting the words hang a fraction longer than necessary. "He said you were a good, obedient son. Someone he could rely on. That you'd help me so that I can help him." It was a lie, but Novak didn't have time for the truth. He was after leverage. If the boy wanted to be seen and was starving for a single word from his father, then Novak would dangle it close enough to reach.

Xander's eyes narrowed. "He said that?"

"Yes, he did. So you're on my team," Novak said. "You want him to take you seriously? Help me, and he'll have to notice."

Xander looked away, jaw working. "And if I screw up?"

"Then I take the fall," Novak said dryly. "Not you."

That got the faintest twitch of a smile. Novak jerked his chin toward the corridor. "Come on. You can help with some reprogramming. Positive results will get you an audience with your father."

They left the apartment and walked in silence until they reached the control hub's security threshold. Novak palmed the lock, and the door slid aside. The room beyond was windowless, buried in Atmos's core, its walls wrapped in displays and holo panels tracking atmospheric integrity, power grid load, and maintenance cycles. At the centre, a waist-high horseshoe console glowed with schematic overlays. A Kesk man stood behind it, broad shoulders hunched, dark hair threaded with grey. For a moment, Xander didn't recognise him. Then he remembered seeing him in Waylan's office.

The older man turned. "Ah, Xander. We meet again. I'm your Uncle Roddick." His gaze skimmed over him. "You've grown taller since I last saw you."

Then it dawned on Xander. "You were discussing Orphis Eight with my father. I remember, because I was intrigued by the space station."

Roddick flicked a glance at Novak. "Has Wayan briefed you that we will be working together?"

"Not specifically, but he said you were involved."

Xander didn't miss the direction of that look. "So you're working together?"

Roddick exhaled through his nose. "You make your choices from the hand you're dealt, boy. Remember that."

Novak stepped between them, palm flattening on the console. The central display shifted, revealing a rotating cutaway of Atmos, the hangars, the central spine, the hub, the modules, then the maintenance tunnel and crawlers.

Xander had seen the schematics before in stolen glimpses on Waylan's screens.

"This," Novak said, "is how the Gromwell insurgents are likely to try and infiltrate Atmos." He zoomed the holo toward Atmos' under-lake hangar complex first, then traced a route with two fingers until the display latched onto a slender service tunnel spiralling up the central spine. Icons representing maintenance crawlers moved along a faint rail line, up, down, up again.

"They'll either commandeer a local shuttle or slip aboard one unnoticed," he continued. "From there, they'll blend in just long enough to clear the first checkpoint. Once they're inside the hangar, they'll avoid the public access routes and take this." He tapped the tunnel. "The maintenance rail. Low traffic, minimal surveillance, no casual witnesses. It is the route you choose when you want to disappear into infrastructure." He let the words settle, then his mouth curved, thin and cold. "What they don't know is I've already instructed security to flag any anomalies to me directly, and not tip off the shuttle occupants. They will believe their plan is working. Their mistake will be thinking this tunnel is freedom." Novak's thumb slid along the edge of the console, almost affectionate. "It is a clean, quiet choke point. Once they commit to it, no one will hear them, no one will see them, and no one will find them unless we want them to."

Xander's chest tightened. A chill crawled over his skin.

Novak leaned in, tapping a cluster of icons along the maintenance tunnel. One by one, the markers flared red, like targets being painted. "Here is how we turn their shortcut into a cage," he said. "We need to reroute the guideway environmental authority and crawler life support control. Once they are committed to the ascent, we hard-lock the crawlers at a chosen point, dead centre of the spine. We seal the access hatches at both ends, top and bottom, and we cut local manual overrides so they cannot crank their way out. Nowhere to go." His finger slid to a second layer of controls pulsing beneath the schematic, a deeper system level, one most operators never saw. "Then we take their air." He tapped twice. "We force their O_2 feed to MANIFOLD and push gas to the rail supply. The crawlers will accept the station mix as primary. By the time they realise something is wrong, they will be light-headed and already making mistakes."

Xander stared at the highlighted sections. "It won't harm them, will it?"

"No," Novak said. "But it depends on the strength of the gas, exposure window and how stressed their cardiovascular systems are." He glanced at Roddick.

The words knocked the breath from Xander's lungs. "They're people." He wanted to say family, but couldn't quite say it aloud yet.

Roddick's expression hardened. "They will only be put to sleep; the gas is not lethal."

"And you are okay with this, Uncle Roddick?" Xander asked.

Roddick held his gaze. "This is how we survive."

Novak stepped in, neatly redirecting the conversation. "Waylan's orders were clear. Neutralise the Gromwell insurgents."

Xander's pulse kicked hard. He heard Novak's words again, tossed out as if they belonged to an everyday conversation. Neutralise. Neat, bloodless words for people who would suffer.

Novak gestured to the panel in front of him. "You, Xander, have a specific role to play." Novak's fingers danced across the surface. The tunnel schematic rotated again, annotated with a second control layer, feed mode authority, manifold valves, mix injection, purge and vent routing, the ugly plumbing behind the clean icons. "With a few tweaks, it can control exactly how much gas goes into the rail manifold, and when. You will force the crawlers onto the MANIFOLD feed when I tell you."

Xander blinked. "So I'm the gas man?"

"Yes," Novak corrected. "Atmos systems are temperamental. If the AI overcompensates or the feeds are fouled, we could fail. If something glitches, you correct it. If something needs manual intervention, you execute it." He said it like a kindness. Like Xander was being given a chance to save lives instead of helping destroy them.

"And if I refuse?" Xander asked, throat dry.

Roddick's answer was immediate. "Then you're of no use to anyone," he said flatly.

Silence stretched. Somewhere deep in the structure, a vac-lift roared past, vibration thrumming through the floor.

"You trust me with this?" Xander asked quietly.

Novak's smile this time was thin and sharp. "You're Waylan's son," he said. "You've already proved you're capable of doing what he asks, even when it costs lives."

Heat crawled up Xander's neck at the thought of Brom. He deserved that. He had unwittingly given them the location of Brom's home without a second thought. Slowly, he stepped up to the console. His fingers hovered over the controls. The interface recognised the temporary access Novak had enabled and the status prompts flared green.

"When I signal, you run the sequence. Lockdown first, then force O_2 feed to MANIFOLD and start gas injection. Do not improvise."

Xander's pulse drummed in his ears. Lockdown, then MANIFOLD, then gas injection. He swallowed, fingers drifting casually to a submenu on the secondary panel. Manifold pressure. Mix ratios. Injection rate. Feed mode authority. A subsection marked: MANIFOLD PURGE, EMERGENCY VENT. Beneath it, an option glowed faintly, AUX VENT, RECLAMATION LOOP.

Xander was torn. MANIFOLD did not sound as harmless as they were trying to sell it, and Roddick, maybe Novak too, did not want to look too closely at the gas's side effects. It did not feel right. He studied the sequence again. To anyone else, it was just a maintenance function. To someone who had grown up around Waylan's labs and spent far too much time tinkering with simulation rigs and complex control layers, it was easy to twist without leaving obvious fingerprints.

After mentally deciding to sabotage the system, he suddenly felt better about himself. Could he include a manual override that would log transient faults, actuator lag, sensor mismatch, or an old relay that did not bite the first time? Something the AI would blame on tired hardware? "I understand," he said, letting his hand fall back to his side.

Novak clapped him on the shoulder. "Good. You're coming back to my apartment for dinner, and we'll go over the last checks away from curious ears."

Xander kept his expression neutral while he told himself that when the time came, he would do the right thing.

HOURS LATER, IN A BRIEFING room carved deep into the cave system, Rhen stood at the head of the table and let the silence settle. Flynn looked like he carried the world on his shoulders, Astrea's jaw was locked, and Kihm and Costa watched him like they were bracing for impact. "Novak and Prem escaped," Rhen said. "That changes the board. Someone has been inside the system, I can feel it, but I can't pin down who. They were good, very good. So any chance of pulling more Atmos security intel is gone, and we have to assume they know enough of our intent to start laying counters." His gaze moved from face to face, steady, assessing. "So we do not force the original plan. We adapt it. We shift the entry vector, revise timings, and strip out every assumption they can exploit. If they think they know what we are about to do, then our advantage is making sure they are wrong." Rhen took a deep breath. "But first, we need to rescue Mila. I will need someone who knows the town."

Costa shifted in his chair, fingers tapping a nervous rhythm against the table, a habit he could not seem to break. "If you are asking for volunteers to go to Blackwell," Costa said, voice measured, "Don't look at me." He reached into his satchel and placed a slim data wafer on the table. "But what I can do is give you this. Service access logic, patrol cadence, the kind of procedural rot Atmos hides behind. If you are going back in, you will need to think like LOUT. In return, I would like to be dropped off in a location where people value what I can grow, and have enough spare time to catch a game or two."

Rhen nodded once.

Costa smiled. "Thank you."

"I know the layout of Blackwell better than most," Flynn said.

WEIGHED DOWN BY REGRETS and responsibility, Kihm wandered through the rubble of Brom's home. She surveyed the twisted metal, eyes unfocused, barely registering the devastation around her, until her foot struck something hard and metallic, jolting her off balance. She caught herself, frowned, and kicked aside loose debris to reveal a metal hatch, unaware that Brom had built a cellar under his home.

She froze at the sound of a faint, muffled thump. Was that her imagination? An echo? Wishful thinking? If Brom were still alive, wouldn't the rescue teams have found signs? Maybe it was a trapped animal? The crews had focused on the biggest collapse zones, the obvious pockets where people were likely to be. With smoke thick in the air and embers obscuring much of the smaller rubble, they'd prioritised areas most likely concealing survivors. The hatch, buried beneath a layer of scorched debris and smouldering ash, had probably gone unnoticed. By the time the fires had burned down enough, the team would have moved on, convinced they'd covered the critical areas.

But now, as Kihm stood there, the charred remains had crumbled into smaller pieces, clearing just enough for the hatch to become visible. It was only by chance that she'd stumbled upon it now, trying to find peace with Brom's passing.

With renewed urgency, Kihm scanned the area for something to lever the hatch open. Her eyes fell on a broken metal pipe, jagged but sturdy. She wedged it under the edge of the hatch and braced herself. With a deep breath, she heaved, and it slid aside with a heavy clunk and a rush of stale air.

Her breath caught with the sight of Brom lying on the basement floor, burned, bleeding, and barely conscious. He bore a jagged gash across his forehead, and his clothes were torn, scorched, and streaked with blood. Kihm could see his chest rising and falling in shallow breaths. She cupped her hands to her mouth and shouted for help, her voice ricocheting through the immediate area.

Moments later, a group of people emerged and gently lifted Brom onto a makeshift stretcher, moving with quiet urgency as they carried him toward the cave where the others had set up camp, including a medical facility. Kihm followed close behind with renewed hope.

AFTER SPENDING TWELVE hours in a medbed, Brom was medically cleared. As he ducked and weaved through the rough-hewn cave labyrinth toward the meeting room, he renewed his determination to find Mila and Oxana and rid the planet of LOUT. He rounded a corner, and the meeting room lights hit him hard, bleaching the shadows from his vision. He forced a confident smile into place, raked his fingers through his dark hair, and reminded himself that a lot was riding on what happened next. "I apologise for keeping you waiting," Brom said as he slipped into the only vacant seat at the table. "The medic insisted on another once-over before discharge." He took a glance around, cataloguing faces. Flynn sat on his left. Next to him was Rhen, who gave Brom a single nod. Astrea sat beyond Rhen, impatience set into her posture like armour. Kihm sat on his right, her eyes already bright, and Costa stood in the corner.

Kihm did not hold back. She stood and enveloped him in a hug, tight enough to make his ribs protest. "Brom." Her voice broke on his name. She pulled back just enough to look at him, shaking her head as a grin fought its way through. "We thought we'd lost you."

A faint smile pulled at the corners of his mouth. "Yeah," he said, voice rough but steady. "It's good to be back." His gaze swept the table again, to land on Kihm. "I owe you my life," he added quietly, and meant it. A beat passed, and then he said, "Guess I'm hard to get rid of." The humour was thin, but it did its job. Shoulders lowered, breaths released. Brom leaned forward and rested his elbows on the table. "Rhen and I need to head to Blackwell to rescue Mila," he said, and the room sharpened at her name. "After that, we finalise plans for Atmos."

Everyone nodded, the agreement immediate.

Rhen began assigning tasks, crisp and efficient, voices overlapping as roles were confirmed. When the meeting finally fractured into motion, people pushed back chairs and dispersed. Flynn was already moving toward the gear racks, Astrea stepping outside to speak to one of her soldiers, and Kihm lingered close as if she needed confirmation that Brom was really going to be alright.

Costa approached the table. He'd been quiet through the briefing, shoulders slightly hunched, eyes cutting from face to face, reading tells like cards. The cave lighting made him look paler than he had in Atmos, not healthier, just less polished, like a man who had been scraped raw.

Brom caught him before he could slip away. "Costa."

The name stopped him.

Brom studied Costa for a moment. He remembered the man in Atmos, too sharp for his own safety, and the gamble he had taken in helping Brom escape. "You did not have to do it," Brom said, low enough that only Costa could hear. "You could have left me there."

Costa gave a short, humourless laugh. "And missed the chance to save myself," he said. "I am not a saint, Brom."

"I did not say you were." Brom's eyes held his. "But you made a choice, and I am here because of it."

Costa looked away first, irritated by the sincerity, as if gratitude was another kind of debt. "Just make sure it was worth it."

"It will be," Brom said. "Rhen will drop you at your chosen destination after he deposits me close to Blackwell."

That landed. Costa's expression shifted, almost imperceptibly, as if he had not quite believed he would make it to the part where life continued.

Brom's mouth tightened. "One more thing."

Costa's brows lifted, wary.

Brom kept his voice flat, not accusing, just certain. "Watch your gambling," he said. "You make yourself vulnerable again, and someone like Novak will find the seam and pull the threads. Do not hand your freedom back to the first person who offers you a table and a smile."

Costa's eyes narrowed, pride flaring, then fading into something more complicated. "You think I have not learned that lesson?"

"I think you survived it," Brom said. "There is a difference."

For a moment, they stood there, two men who understood leverage and risk, and the price of choosing.

Costa exhaled through his nose. "Fine," he said. "I will stick to safer addictions."

Brom's gaze flicked to the satchel at Costa's side. "If you ever want a job, I am sure Kihm could use your skills. He held out his hand.

Although Costa's grip was quick and firm, Brom still caught the emotion beneath it. "Bring her back," Costa said.

Brom nodded once and turned away.

CHAPTER 15

After disembarking from the cloaked yacht a few clicks from Blackwell, Brom signalled to Rhen, who eased the cloaked shuttle up through the dripping canopy and banked toward the sunset, the engines' low hum fading as he stood alone in the tangled green shadows. His gaze was immediately captivated by the towering giants rising before him, their knotted branches like outstretched arms, reaching higher than the eye could see. Under his feet, the rainforest floor was abundant with soft grasses and creepers, all vying for the precious rays of sunlight piercing the canopy.

His footfalls disturbed the peaceful symphony of birdsong, leaving only a pair of Spanjays, their shrill cries echoing from above. Looking up, Brom watched the two birds glide through the air, searching for a meal, their pink and black feathers glinting in the last rays of dimming sunlight.

The air was heavy with the earthy smell of the rain-soaked soil. His torch shone brightly, glinting off the water droplets that clung to the leaves. Even the oppressive humidity was welcome, like an embrace from a long-lost friend. He felt at peace here. Nature was where he truly belonged.

The sun had set by the time he reached the outskirts of Blackwell, a place he hoped never to see again. He couldn't shake his growing unease and the reminder of a forgotten past. The streets were still lined with the same dilapidated buildings, and the stench of garbage. He shivered slightly and trudged on, careful to stay close to the shadows, and more determined than ever to find Mila before

Blackwell left a scar on her that could not be erased. He knew that firsthand.

The nocturnal streets were silent but for his pounding heart. The dangers lurking in this town were real, and Mila's fate was at stake. If anything happened to her, it would be his fault, and that weighed heavily on his conscience. The wind blew around him, bringing the promise of another storm and scattering rubbish in every direction. Some townspeople were packing up after a long day, while others were prepping for the night ahead. He couldn't escape the irony of the situation; a storm was coming, and there was no escaping it.

Brom's eyes swept over the scattered buildings and dusty streets, searching for any sign of where Mila might be. Then it hit him. The medical facility. If she'd been taken, that's exactly where they'd use a doctor of her calibre.

Brom navigated the dimly lit streets, moving past clusters of rundown stalls and buildings. He kept his pace steady, his eyes scanning each sign until he spotted one marked with a faded and crudely painted, chipped Rod of Asclepius above the door.

He approached with cautious optimism, but the moment he reached for the handle, hope drained away. The door was locked and secured with thick iron bolts. A small, crooked 'Closed' sign dangled from the frame, swaying slightly in the breeze. He would have to find another way in. He muttered a curse. Spotting an old man stacking chairs across the street, Brom approached him and asked, "Excuse me, sir. Have you seen a woman with shoulder-length chestnut hair, green eyes and earthy-toned skin?"

Instead of answering, the elderly man's eyes narrowed. "I haven't seen you around here before."

"I live on the outskirts and only come to town when I need supplies."

Brom knew how this place worked, so he reached into his pocket and took out a credit. The man's wrinkled face creased with a smile as he slowly opened his palm as if to savour the moment and then closed his arthritic fingers around his prize before dropping it into his pocket.

"I might have seen a woman matching that description, lad."

Brom's heart skipped a beat. "Where did she go?"

The old man pointed to a seedy-looking club across the road, its neon lights flickering in lurid shades of purple and green, which read: 'The Rusty Anchor'. The walls vibrated with heavy bass, and rowdy laughter spilled onto the street. Shadows loomed in the doorway as patrons stumbled in and out, their faces obscured by smoke and dim lighting. It looked like the kind of place where crime flourished as freely as the alcohol.

Brom nodded his thanks and stood outside the dilapidated club under the broken neon sign, which flickered and buzzed, casting an eerie glow over the surrounding area. Before stepping through the doorway, he ducked into a dark alcove and contacted Rhen. "I have a lead on Mila. I am about to enter the Rusty Anchor. Don't do anything until you hear from me."

"Understood. Good luck, Brom."

Unsurprisingly, the club's interior matched its rundown exterior. Peeling wallpaper graced the walls, and grime coated the stained floorboards. A few broken stools leaned wearily against a scuffed wooden bar, while the tables were cluttered with chipped glassware and the crusted remains of long-forgotten meals. A pungent aroma of dirt and disrepair lingered in the air, unlike the pristine rainforest surrounding the town.

On the stage at the room's far end, scantily clad dancers performed for the patrons. Thankfully, Mila was not one of them. Before he could make a circuit of the room, a striking woman stepped into his path. She wore little, but it was her pale green skin and long, dark hair cascading over her shoulders that caught his eye, along with a figure that was impossible to ignore.

She gave him a sultry look. "Hey, handsome," she said. Looking for a good time tonight?"

Not wanting to be rude, Brom smiled and replied, "No thanks, I'm here for a drink. Later, perhaps?"

The girl smiled knowingly and replied, "I'm here if you change your mind." She winked and moved behind the bar to pour his drink, leaving Brom to his thoughts as the lights onstage dimmed and the performers disappeared through the curtained backdrop. In their place, a burly man carried a masked woman under his arm before dropping her on the ground and tying her wrists to the metal poles flanking the stage despite her protests.

Brom asked, "What's happening?"

"Initiation of a new girl. It's the manager's way of reinforcing his authority to keep everyone in line. And it's a good money maker."

Brom thought this was disturbing on many levels, and despite his misgivings, he would watch and wait. His purpose was clear. Find Mila.

Suddenly, the stage lights glowed brightly as a second woman stepped out, whip in hand, wearing a confident smirk. Brom could feel the anticipation in the air as the audience held their breath. Her eyes gleamed with excitement as she ran the whip through her teeth, a shimmer of delight in her gaze. She seemed to savour the sensation, letting it fill her with an almost palpable energy. The whip's tip glinted in the light while her fingers curled around its handle, and her lips lifted into a satisfied smile. She ran the whip through her teeth several times, and each time, it seemed to bring her more pleasure than the last. It was a sight that left the watchers in awe, and it was clear to everyone that this woman was in her element. She smiled, knowing that she was the star of the show, and she revelled in the moment.

As she approached the bound woman, the air pulsed with her sense of control. A flick of her wrist, and the whip snapped, slicing through the silence. The sound cracked across the room like thunder, drawing a terrified scream from her intended victim.

The audience cheered.

The bound woman's eyes were wide with panic, her entire body shaking with fear. His heart accelerated when the spotlight shifted, and he caught a better glimpse of her. There were similarities to Mila, but it was hard to tell from this distance. He would have to get closer.

The woman with the whip was revelling in the moment. Her lips curled into a malicious grin as she drank in her victim's fear. With a sharp flick of her wrist, the whip cracked again, leather slicing the air like a blade, drawing another eruption of cheers from the crowd. The spectators were now caught in a fevered frenzy, relishing the spectacle. Their excitement grew with each act of cruelty. She cracked her whip and shouted, "She has been a very naughty girl, boys. Come on. Show me your appreciation!"

Brom had no intention of drawing attention to himself. Not here, not now. But the moment he thought it might be Mila, instinct drowned out logic. Reckless or not, the idea of her trapped, possibly hurt, shattered every restraint. His sense of duty surged like a breaking wave, crashing through fear and hesitation. Without another thought, he bolted toward the stage, throwing caution to the wind. Each step was a blur, his mind consumed with one urgent command to save her. His trembling hands fumbled with the ropes binding her to the poles. But just as freedom was within reach, the world tilted. A sudden jolt, a flash of pain, and everything went black.

The next morning, Brom regained consciousness on the cold, dirt floor of a subterranean room. The air was damp and laced with the scent of decaying wood. A sliver of daylight filtered through a narrow, cracked transplex panel high on the wall, barely enough to illuminate the stained concrete walls.

As his eyes adjusted to the gloom, a heavy door groaned open, and a massive figure stepped inside, silhouetted against the hallway's dim lighting. The man's grin was all malice, wide, gleaming, and calculated.

Before Brom could rise, the brute lunged forward, seizing his arm, locking Brom in place with bone-crushing force.

"You think you're tough, huh?" the man sneered, retrieving a sleek metal case from his utility belt. With a flick of his thumb, it snapped open, revealing a thick, industrial-grade injector, black, matte, and marked with faded hazard glyphs. "A healthy specimen like you will be very valuable in the Blackheart Mine."

Brom twisted hard, fighting for leverage, but the man's grip cinched tighter, unyielding, inhumanly strong. Cybernetics, then. That explained it. Brom's power slid off anything that wasn't fully biological, and this man was no longer entirely flesh.

The injector hissed to life, its indicator lights flaring green. With practised ease, the man slammed it against Brom's bicep and pulled the trigger. A sharp burst of pressure lanced into his arm, followed by a creeping coldness that settled beneath his skin like a parasite. Brom glared at his captor with simmering rage.

But the man only laughed, low and cruel. "Go ahead. Run. That little subdermal tracker? It's laced with a failsafe. If you step outside your programmed location, it'll spike your nervous system like a live wire. His smile sharpened. "And for a Kesk? It doesn't just hurt. Your abilities turn it into an amplifier. The more power you have, the more it feeds back. It's a loop, spike, flare, spike again, until your body burns itself out. It's killed many Kesk."

Brom's jaw tightened. His hot-headed action had now compromised Mila's rescue. Remembering his comms device, he discreetly searched his pocket.

The man held it up. "Looking for this, are you?" he asked, before slipping it back into his pocket. "Get up," the man growled, pulling a weapon from his holster. "My name is Sorn, and from now on, you are my property, and whether you live to see another sunrise will be at my discretion."

Mila stayed with him, a low, persistent ache. But he'd known, really known, the bound woman wasn't her. Still, he couldn't walk away; he needed to save someone.

After being marched through town by one of Sorn's minions, he arrived at the Blackheart Mine. The surrounding landscape was barren and bleak, an endless expanse of cracked earth and stone, stripped of life. No plants, birds, or even the ghost of a breeze stirred the heavy, stagnant air. The ground was littered with fragments of machinery discarded long ago, now half-buried and forgotten. Overhead, a heavily clouded sky cast a dim, unforgiving light, amplifying the desolation.

As they neared the mine, the machinery hum grew louder, echoing from the dark opening. Inside, flickering beams of artificial light illuminated the dampened walls. Water seeped through the cracked stone, tracing grimy lines down the walls and pooling on the floor. The ground was a muddy amalgam of earth and groundwater that the workers slogged through.

Inside, the air grew colder, thick with the scent of wet stone and the faint tang of metal. Ore-harvesting drones clanked beside the workers, automated limbs hauling crates and containers marked with hazard symbols, Blackheart Crystals nestled in extraction pods.

He'd heard of Blackheart Crystals and their volatile nature, but he hadn't realised they were still being mined here. He'd assumed the veins had long since been exhausted.

Blackheart Crystal was a highly coveted material in advanced stealth and defence systems. Though other compounds offered similar capabilities, none matched its efficiency or reliability. Integrated into cloaking arrays, it absorbed visible light, radio waves, and a wide range of electromagnetic signals, rendering ships and armour nearly undetectable, even to radar, thermal, and quantum sensors.

Beyond stealth, it was used in energy-dampening tech to form protective fields that absorbed incoming energy attacks. In weaponised form, it powered "void grenades," which drained energy from nearby systems and targets, crippling machinery and weakening enemies. He assumed Atmos was operating and selling the product off-planet through LOUT's networks. Yet another reason why LOUT's presence on Eania had to be terminated. This visit to Blackwell had been an illuminating experience in many ways.

A firm shove sent Brom into a dim locker bay under flickering strip-lights, the air hot with stale sweat and ozone from overworked charging racks. Along the walls, uniform rows of suit docks, each with a power coupler, a data jack, and a battered gear hook, ran in hard lines of metal and grime. Several environment suits hung limp in their docks, smart-fabric seams frayed, patch panels mismatched, and status tags blinking a tired amber warning.

"Put on a suit and get to work," he ordered. "Your supervisor, Derx, will instruct you."

A figure stepped into the bay wearing an opaque visor and a high-spec mining suit, its plating seamless and unscarred. Derx looked like he could walk through a reactor meltdown and come out clean.

Brom unplugged a suit from its wall-mounted dock and stepped into it. Dense, reinforced plates caught the locker bay lights with a faint metallic sheen.

"Field-rated," Derx said. "It'll shield you from the radiation, and from the wild energy surges the Blackheart Crystals emit."

Hardened plates patched the torso, with heavy gauntlets and a helmet capped by a polarised visor completing the shell. Fine filament wiring ran through the inner lining, an advanced damping system that absorbed and neutralised the crystals' energy pulses. An array of embedded sensors monitored his vitals and logged his environmental exposure level. But the suit had clearly seen better days. Tiny perforations pocked its surface, some hairline, others fraying at the edges. The visor was scratched, and the gloves had the stiff, tired feel of overuse. As the suit's weight settled over him, the damping system came alive with a faint, uneven hum, as if struggling to keep up.

Derx nudged him out of the bay and down into the dark void, where they climbed into a caged lift that took them deeper. The mine manager eyed Brom with a cold indifference as he explained the grim reality. "That suit you're wearing? It's only powered for eight hours. After that, you're on your own." His gaze drifted over the worn edges and tiny perforations in Brom's suit. "And before you ask, no, you're not getting the model I'm wearing. Too expensive. Twelve-hour shifts are standard down here, which means the suit will stop protecting you after eight hours. When you start feeling nausea, dizziness, or seeing things that aren't there, that's your warning that your body has reached its limit." He shrugged as though the danger was a trivial inconvenience. "The way the boss sees it, if the suits last eight hours, they're good enough." His words hung in the stale air, a bitter reminder that the miners' lives came second to profits.

The Blackheart Crystals embedded in the walls emitted a faint glow, casting eerie shadows as they descended into the mine. Around them, the ore-harvesting drones and conveyor systems hummed, shifting loads with clinical precision, their noise drowning out the workers' shuffling steps and murmured complaints.

As they descended, Derx continued his narrative. "Ore-harvesting drones carry out the mining, controlled from a safe distance to reduce worker exposure. The drones are equipped with reinforced shielding and designed to be energy-efficient to avoid becoming 'drained' by Blackheart's pull. The drones use laser cutters or plasma drills, which don't require direct physical contact with the crystals. Once a segment of Blackheart Crystal is detached, it's your job to stack it in a specially designed extraction pod, lined with materials that neutralise the crystal's effects."

At last, they reached the bottom of the shaft with a solid clunk. As the cage door slid open, Brom followed Derx toward a group of workers packing crystals. Derx turned back to Brom with one last piece of information. "After the shift, miners and equipment pass through decontamination chambers, which are a sequence of electromagnetic pulses that dislodge residual Blackheart Crystal powder lingering on clothing or equipment. The chambers also warm you up, restoring body temperature after the frigid conditions." At that point, he handed him over to another supervisor who quickly put Brom to work.

SEVERAL HOURS LATER, a loud, blaring horn echoed through the mine, a harsh reminder that, even here, the passage of time was monitored. Lunch break. Brom felt his limbs grow heavier with each step, weariness sinking deep into his bones. He entered the sealed meal room and collapsed onto the bench beside a rusted, floor-bolted table, exhaustion pressing in like a weighty fog. When he removed his helmet, stale, thick air rushed over his face, bringing little relief. He lowered his helmet and gloves to the floor at his side as a metal tray clanged down in front of him, sloshing with grey, unidentifiable gruel. With a grim sort of gratitude that it was vegetable-based, Brom swallowed a spoonful of the gritty sludge. Lifting his gaze, he saw a familiar face pull off her own helmet, her green eyes weary but unmistakable. Mila!

For a split second, their eyes met, recognition flickering between them like a spark in the dark. Brom fought the urge to speak, keeping his expression carefully neutral. He gave a subtle shake of his head, just enough for her to catch the warning.

She offered the faintest nod before lowering her gaze to her meal.

They had found each other, but down here, in the belly of the mine, secrecy was the only shield they had. The rest of his shift dragged by in a gruelling blur, each hour grinding him down, exhaustion settling into his bones like sediment. No doubt Mila felt it too. As the power in his suit waned, a dull ache pulsed through his limbs. The Blackheart Crystals were working their way in. It started with a faint dizziness, then a creeping chill that seeped through the suit's thinning layers. His thoughts grew sluggish and heavy, as if wrapped in fog. Every breath felt thick in his chest. Each step became a test of will.

When the end-of-shift horn finally blared, Brom barely felt the relief it should have brought. He and Mila joined the line of miners shuffling toward the decontamination unit, their movements stiff and unsteady after hours in the depths. The queue moved slowly, the air thick with fatigue and the faint metallic tang of sweat and crystal dust. At the entrance to the unit, automated nozzles hissed to life, blasting each miner in turn with a sterilising mist meant to strip away traces of the crystals. The vapour burned faintly against the skin through the suit's thinning layers, but no one flinched anymore. It was routine, a necessary barrier between them and slow, internal poisoning. After the decontamination cycle, they filed through a full-body scanner, its lattice of sensors sweeping for any concealed crystals, then stepped into the dim locker bay.

Brom thumbed the seals at his collar, unlocking the helmet with a soft hiss, and a wash of cooler air hit his clammy face. The sudden exposure was sharp, like stepping outside without armour. Beside him, Mila released her own helmet, dark strands of hair plastered to her brow, her expression blank with exhaustion.

They worked their way out of the heavy suits and hoisted them onto the waiting racks, jacking power couplers into the ports along the spine. No one owned a suit here. Each cycle, the gear was rotated, scanned, patched where possible, and then reassigned to the next shift. They stepped out into the dry night air, no longer miners but survivors. The thin artificial lights at the mine entrance cast the barren land into deep shadows, and the humid, cool air brought no comfort.

Around them, other workers staggered, some barely clinging to consciousness. Brom glanced at a Kesk man nearby, his skin pale, sweat cutting lines through the grime on his face. Brom reached out to help, but before he could, the man gave a sudden shudder and crumpled to the ground, limbs folding awkwardly beneath him.

Brom dropped to his knees beside him, heart thudding.

Mila knelt too, pressing two fingers to the man's throat, then his chest. A long, heavy pause followed. "He's gone," she said quietly, her voice flat with weariness.

Brom caught the flicker in her eyes, desolation buried beneath a veil of disappointment at the unrelenting cruelty of this place and the low value placed on life.

Moments later, guards arrived, silently dragging the body away with all the care of hauling a sack of coal. Dust rose in their wake, and just like that, the man was gone.

Brom watched them haul the body away, jaw locked until it ached. He'd never even known this mine existed, and that ignorance sat in his stomach like a stone. He should have looked beyond the borders of Gromwell, should have asked what LOUT was doing. Not knowing wasn't innocence. It was complicity. This has to end. LOUT had poisoned the soil, pillaged its natural resources, and bled its people dry. The organisation treated lives like expendable tools, used, broken, discarded. But not forever. Brom could feel the fire building inside him again, slow but steady. The man's death wouldn't be in vain. He would make sure of it.

When they reached the sleeping quarters, Brom and Mila shared a glance and claimed two adjoining bunks in the cramped, guard-patrolled room. Brom's fingers brushed the back of Mila's hand, a contact so small it could have been accidental, but it wasn't. His palm settled over her knuckles for one steady breath, a silent message delivered in skin and pressure to say I'm here, I've got you.

Mila did not look at him again, not with the guards watching, but her hand turned under his and held on.

They stayed quiet under the guards' watchful eyes, but the simple fact that they were together eased the edge. A curt order came, then a quick, clinical shower, and a shove of generic issue clothes into their hands, rough fabric that smelled of disinfectant. Tomorrow, they'd plan their escape. Tonight, Brom could only picture Rhen waiting in the rainforest, and pray the idiot didn't try something heroic and suicidal, like coming after him. One mistake and Rhen would be just as trapped. With nothing left to do, Brom finally let exhaustion take him.

AN ESCAPE PLAN WAS reckless at best, but by morning, Brom's thoughts were in full flight, latching onto a single idea involving Blackheart Crystals. Unfortunately, they were volatile, unstable, and dangerous enough to kill. But if their emissions could drown out their subdermal trackers' handshake and smear the mine's scans into noise, they might cross the perimeter without tripping the failsafe. Might. It was a long shot, a desperate one.

Mila would be the difference. She understood energy signatures the way other people understood language. Together, they could build interference and shape the crystals' output into something useful, a moving blind spot that turned them into static.

Brom felt the faint stir of hope and shared his idea with Mila in a low whisper as they crouched in a dim corner of the bunkhouse before their shift. She listened in silence, her face pale with fatigue yet focused, leaning closer until her shoulder grazed his, and the heat of her through the thin fabric fractured his concentration. Brom forced his eyes to the floor, forced his voice to stay calm. Wanting her was a luxury, but he wanted her anyway.

"If this goes wrong," Mila murmured, "you don't play hero."

His jaw flexed. "Understood." Theoretically, a surge of Blackheart Crystal energy could interfere with the compound's security grid and scramble the trackers long enough for them to slip through the perimeter. But there was a problem. They couldn't smuggle crystals out of the mine. The guards scanned every load, every tool, every worker. One fragment of raw crystal would trigger alarms instantly.

Mila frowned, thinking. "We don't need much, just residue. Enough to trigger a close-range surge. If we can create a diversion, I can get it out."

"No, I'll take the risk," Brom said.

"I have nanites," she replied. "They can repair tissue damage fast. You don't get that margin."

They'd scrape together crystal powder from the machinery and loading bays, places the guards rarely inspected closely. Mila would carry it out, sealed in fabric inside her boot. At the decontamination choke point, she'd stage a medical emergency, the kind that forced protocol, helmets off, corridor paused, attention fractured. It was dangerous, maybe suicidal, crystal dust could start shutting down a nervous system within hours.

When the shift finally ended, the decontamination line crept forward under harsh lights, the air stale with sweat and the static crackle of overworked suits. Mila had the powder tucked inside her boot. She gave Brom the faintest nod and tapped his wrist twice, precise, intimate. Brom covered her hand with his, shielding it from view. It was time.

In the antechamber, metres from the automated corridor, Mila stumbled on cue, clipped the metal wall with a sharp grunt, and went down hard. A guard strode over and prodded her with a conductive baton, the ring spitting a tight arc of blue-white current.

"Filters might be shot," he muttered, rapping her helmet casing. "Help me get this off."

The second guard hesitated, then dropped beside him. They worked the latches and the seals sighed with escaping pressure. Mila stayed limp, eyes shut.

"Med check, possible crystal exposure," the lead guard snapped. "Medical. Manual override."

Two guards hooked her under the arms and hauled her through the now-disabled decontamination corridor, her boots scraping as they dragged her away.

Brom's pulse pounded like war drums as he watched.

Suddenly, the decontamination chamber charged up again, and a guard prodded Brom, his voice sharp and low. "You. Keep moving. Nothing to see here."

Brom nodded, casting one last glance at Mila. The decontamination mist blasted his suit, hissing against the pressure seals. Inside, his heart wouldn't stop pounding.

Later, the lights in the barracks dimmed to their night-cycle flicker, casting long shadows across rows of sleeping bodies. One guard leaned against the wall, half-dozing. The other paced slowly, boots clunking in a rhythm Brom had memorised, six steps down, pause, six back. Timing was everything. Brom lay on his cot. Beneath the blanket, his fingers worked the length of wire he'd unravelled from the meal tray handle earlier that day. Nearby, Mila caught his eye and gave the faintest tilt of her chin.

Brom stood, slow and casual, walking to the ablutions area like he had dozens of times before. The pacing guard barely glanced at him. Mila followed a minute later, carrying a water bottle.

Inside a stall, Brom dropped to a knee and slid two fingers behind a cracked vent grille near the floor. A concealed maintenance panel gave with a soft click. He pulled out the bundle Mila had stashed inside during her shower and unwrapped it with care.

They both held their breath as the powder settled, a fine, shimmering dust, faintly iridescent.

Beyond, the barracks had quieted into a restless hush, broken only by the occasional cough or creak of metal bedframes. The guards at either end stood slouched in half-bored silence, watching but not really seeing.

Mila began work piecing together their fragile device using dust and shards, thin copper wiring stripped from a broken machine, a scrap circuit board, and a power cell from one of the suits. Mila had also 'borrowed' a visor lens from an old helmet, hoping it would focus the Blackheart Crystal energy. Using rubber strips for insulation and an old container for concealment, they assembled the makeshift device.

Finished, the crude contraption hummed faintly in Mila's palm. A fragile, dangerous lifeline that might mask their subdermal trackers long enough to breach the compound's boundaries and slip into the darkness.

They needed a distraction. Just enough to draw attention, but not enough to raise an alarm. For now, they returned to their bunks, lying low as they waited for the right moment. Twenty minutes, maybe more. Just long enough for the guards to grow bored again.

From her bunk, Mila quietly retrieved a small vial hidden beneath her blanket, a compound used to treat burns from crystal exposure. She'd pocketed it earlier during her medical exam. On its own, it was inert. But when combined with a solvent she'd quietly siphoned from the mine's maintenance storage tanks and into her drink bottle, it produced a slow, smouldering reaction.

She'd already poured the solvent near the heating vent at the far end of the barracks during her cleaning shift. Now, with a subtle flick, she uncorked the vial and rolled it down the aisle beneath the beds.

It clinked once, then settled near the vent. The rising heat would trigger a reaction, just enough smoke and smell to send a guard to investigate, without raising a full alarm.

Within minutes, the sleeping workers began coughing and stirring as the thickening haze filled the barracks. One by one, groggy voices rose in complaint as the smoke intensified. During the melee, Brom and Mila slipped into the shadows near the door, moving in sync with the knot of angry miners. Outside, they edged along the outer wall, staying low. Mila activated the device, feeling it hum faintly in her hands. Hearts pounding, they slipped past the now-deserted final checkpoint. With luck, their device would scramble their subdermal tracker signals as they disappeared into the dark.

Free of the mine, Brom and Mila crept through the shadowed alleyways of Blackwell, just outside the compound. Their destination was the medical facility, a stark, unwelcoming building flanked by security lights but left empty at night. Time was of the essence, as they estimated the device's power would last only an hour before fading.

Forcing open the rear door, they swept through the rooms, searching for cutting tools. Every movement was quick and deliberate. Outside, the muffled bass from the club across the street thudded steadily, masking the sounds of their intrusion. They quickly located the surgical suite, and in the dim glow of an emergency light, Brom found a tray of surgical instruments while Mila rifled through cabinets for local anaesthetics.

Minutes later, heart pounding, Mila laid her scalpel against Brom's skin, ready to remove the subdermal tracker, which had been placed just above the previous wound, which was still healing. It was a delicate task, and after successfully removing his device, she talked him through removing hers.

As the final minutes of their escape window slipped away, they wrapped the trackers in scraps of cloth and made their way back toward the compound. Confusion still reigned, guards scrambled to obey shouted orders, and lights swept across open ground. So far, no one had noticed they were missing.

Moving fast, they crept to the edge of the shadows and hurled the bundle into a dark, cluttered corner near a stack of rusted storage drums. With luck, the signal would hold long enough to fool the scanners and buy them the time they needed.

They didn't look back, slipping through the quiet streets of Blackwell, quickly and silently. The town's dimly lit windows cast faint halos onto empty alleyways as they passed. Beyond the last row of buildings, the landscape shifted from harsh concrete to rainforest.

The dense line of trees rose like silent sentinels, welcoming them into their depths, and Brom felt a strange comfort settle over him. The rainforest was his territory. A place where he knew the patterns of every leaf, the smell of every plant, and the subtle whispers of life around them. As they pressed on, he felt his muscles loosen, and his pace steadied with each familiar step. Without his comms device, they were on their own, and yet, he held a sliver of hope. For now, they needed to distance themselves from the town. Every rustling branch felt like a warning, reminding them just how close capture might be.

At last, they found a cave tucked into the rocky hillside, half-veiled by a curtain of thick vines, and ducked inside to the soft murmur of running water.

Brom scanned the interior, eyes adjusting to the dim light filtering through cracks. The ceiling loomed high and jagged, stalactites clung like crooked fangs. The walls were solid, veined with layers of grey and ochre. "We'll spend the remainder of the night here," he said. "So far, we've avoided the snarks, and I don't want to push our luck. If anyone's tracking us, they'll wait for daylight."

Mila let out a long breath and sank onto the packed earth, shoulders sagging as the tension bled out of her.

Brom still buzzed with nervous energy. “I'll gather wood and start a fire,” he said. “Then I'll grab some berries I saw nearby.”

Before she could answer, he slipped from the cave.

By the time he returned, his arms were loaded with firewood, and his shirt was knotted into a sling, cradling a small haul of berries and edible greens. He coaxed a flame to life, feeding it until a steady fire crackled at the cave's mouth, pushing back the gloom.

The uneven floor was littered with pebbles and the occasional twisted root that had forced its way through cracks in the stone. In one corner, they discovered a thin thread of water seeping from a hidden fissure high in the rock. Each drop struck the stone below with a soft tap, the steady drip echoing through the cave like a quiet, rhythmic pulse.

Mila didn't waste any time. She moved to the little runnel, drank from her cupped hands, then dampened the hem of her shirt and wiped the grime from her face and fingers, working with the weary efficiency of someone beyond exhaustion.

When she stepped back, Brom took her place at the fissure. He dipped his hands into the shallow flow and drank the water, which was shockingly cold against his tongue. He cupped his hands again, letting them fill. “Here,” he said quietly, turning back to her. “Do you want more?”

Mila hesitated, then stepped closer. She leaned in and drank from his hands, her lips brushing his skin. The contact was brief but inescapable, warm breath on his fingers and the faint tremor in her shoulders as she swallowed. For a heartbeat, they were close, sharing the same thin pocket of air. The crackle of the fire suddenly sounded very loud.

“Thanks,” she murmured, eyes flicking up to meet his before she pulled back. The moment stretched, crowded with things neither of them wanted to say aloud, then slipped away as they retreated toward the fire.

"Mila, I'll gather some soft foliage for our bedding," Brom said, his voice a touch rougher than before. A little while later, he ducked back into the cave with an armful of broad, waxy leaves and fern fronds cradled against his chest. Bits of soil and twigs clung to him, and his torso was scored with faint scratches from the underbrush. "Best I could find," he said, dropping the bundle in the flattest spot on the floor.

Mila pushed herself up, ignoring the pain in her muscles, refusing to let it take up space. Anyway, her nanites would make short work of any repairs in a few hours.

Brom was already gathering the leaf matter into a pile, his movements efficient and controlled, as if he could organise chaos.

She helped him spread it out, palm over palm, layering until the stone was mostly hidden. The leaves crackled under their hands, and a bruised green smell rose, damp and sharp, almost clean if she let herself pretend. Her fingers came away slick with sap and grit, the sensation grounding in a way the darkness was not.

The chamber felt too small for two bodies and everything they carried. Sound travelled. Breath travelled. Even the hush between them had weight.

When the bed was done, Brom lowered himself beside her and pulled out the gathered berries and greens. He offered them with a steadiness that made her throat tighten, as if feeding her was something he could do to make up for what had happened.

She ate quickly because hunger was a distraction she could not afford. Juice ran down her fingers and stained her knuckles, and she wiped it away on her thigh without thinking. Her body was still running on adrenaline, the aftershock of the mine, the chase and the constant calculation of what might kill them next. She forced herself to keep chewing. Swallowing. Breathing.

Brom ate too, but she felt his attention sliding away from the food. She didn't need to look to know it. The air changed when he watched her, and the pressure was building in the small space between them.

In the background, water dripped from a fissure, slow and patient. Drip, pause, drip. A rhythm that made time feel measurable again. Somewhere deeper, stone settled with a faint click. She finished the last berry and let her hand rest on her knee, fingers sticky, trembling just enough to irritate her. The shaking wasn't fear, not exactly. It was the aftermath.

She lifted her gaze.

Brom was staring at her as if the darkness had stripped away everything except the truth. He wasn't looking at her like a rescuer, or a leader, or a man trying to fix what he'd damaged.

She held his eyes and didn't let herself flinch. Her jaw tightened, anger surging with the memory of his hands on her life, steering it, cornering it, dragging her into danger, and yet those same hands had hauled her back when everything collapsed. He had pulled her through hell. He had also been the reason she'd fallen into it. She tried to hold on to the resentment, to keep it clean and sharp, but it wouldn't stay in her; it kept slipping, thinning under the weight of what he had done to save her. The truth sat between them like a third presence. She could see it in him, too, the guilt, the restraint, the way he was holding himself back as if proximity might be a weapon. He was waiting for permission he didn't deserve to ask for. And still, when she looked at him, she felt something settle in her chest, heavy and quiet. Forgiveness. Not for him, not only. For herself. For what she wanted even now.

Brom shifted closer before either of them spoke. He moved carefully on the leaf bed, as if the crackle mattered, as if the cave was listening. Their shoulders brushed. The contact was accidental in theory, but they both knew it wasn't.

Mila tilted her head, listening to the dark for a moment, because it gave her something else to do besides feel the heat rising under her skin. "If anything in here hisses, bites, or asks for a password," she murmured, "that one's on you."

His mouth twitched, a flash of humour that didn't belong down here and yet somehow made the air less brutal. "Noted, my lady." He gave a quiet huff. "If something asks for a password, I'll tell it to take a number; we're closed."

She should have smiled. She did, just barely, and the curve of it felt unfamiliar, as if her face had forgotten how. Her eyes dropped, not to his expression, but to his hands. They were rough, scraped, still faintly shaking with contained adrenaline.

Her own fingers trembled again. She hated that he could see it, hated that she wanted him to. The cold seeped through the leaves into her back and thighs, and she used it as an excuse because she was tired of excuses and also not ready to admit the truth out loud. She leaned in as if it were practical, not longing. As if the space between them wasn't already on fire. "I need warming up," she said.

Brom's gaze flicked to her mouth, then away like he was trying to behave. His voice dropped, roughened, too careful. "Then stop hovering at the perimeter." He lifted his arm, not pulling, not trapping, just making room in the curve of it. An invitation. A boundary. A test. "Come all the way in."

For a second, she stared at him, measuring. Not his strength, not his intent, but his restraint. Whether he would take more than she gave. Whether he could be trusted with a yes.

The cave breathed around them. Water dripped. Small insects shuffled. Mila moved. Not fast. Not hesitant. Intentional. She closed the gap. Her knee brushed his thigh, and the contact sent a sharp heat through her that made her breath hitch despite her best effort. Her hand rose, hovering near his jaw, and she felt him go still, as if her fingertips were a detonator. She touched him anyway. Warm skin under her fingers. A faint rasp of stubble. His pulse was jumping, betraying him.

His hand settled at her waist, careful at first, as if she might break, as if he might.

She looked at his mouth, then back to his eyes. The tension between them tightened until it felt like a drawn wire, ready to sing. "Brom," she breathed, his name landing differently now, not an accusation, not a warning, but a choice she was making with her whole body.

His throat worked. "Mila."

That was all it took.

He leaned in slowly enough to give her every chance to stop him, and she didn't. She met him halfway, mouth to mouth, and the kiss was quiet only at the start. It sharpened quickly, all the restraint cracking open, all the fear and anger and relief turning into something hot and hungry.

The leaf bed crackled under them as they reclined, too loud in the tiny chamber, but she didn't care. She let herself sink into him, into the heat of his body, into the one small pocket of stolen safety the cave had allowed them.

Brom dipped his head, brushing his lips to the curve beneath her ear, gentle, tentative, the kind of touch that asked rather than took.

She didn't pull away. Instead, she reached up and ran her hand over his bare chest. A silent order: stay.

Between breaths, he asked softly, "You're not going to blame me later for all of this?"

Mila's eyes lifted to his, steady in the dim. "That depends," she murmured, voice low. "Are we talking about the situation in general or what you're about to do in the next few minutes?"

A slow breath left him, tension easing from his shoulders by a fraction. "In that case," he said, the faintest curve at his mouth, "I'll try not to give you ammunition."

"Fine, I'll holster it for now," she said, as her fingers slid up to his neck. A spark of amusement flashed across her face, quick, contained, like everything about her.

"For the record. Are we scoring this on performance metrics, or personal satisfaction?"

"Strict rubric." Her fingers trailed across his collarbone. "And you're already losing marks for talking."

Brom captured the gesture before it could vanish, turning his head to press a kiss to her knuckle like it was a promise he wasn't allowed to say out loud. He leaned in and placed another kiss on her shoulder, then on the edge of her throat. "No more talking then," he whispered. "And you," he murmured, letting his forehead touch hers for a heartbeat, "are terrible at issuing clear instructions."

Her laugh was silent, more breath than sound. Then she shifted, pushing him back into the leaves with the kind of quiet decisiveness that characterised her. Brom let her because letting her wasn't weakness; it was trust.

He caught her mouth with his, firm enough to steal her breath, controlled enough to stop before it became something they couldn't afford. The restraint tasted like discipline and hunger all at once.

Mila's hand slid behind his neck, fingers threading into his hair, steadying him, grounding him, as if she knew exactly how close he was to losing himself. When she finally broke the kiss, she didn't retreat. She stayed right there, close enough that he could feel her heartbeat against him.

Brom stared at her for a second too long. The cave, the vines, the trickling water, none of it mattered. Only the fact that he wanted to pull her deeper into his arms and never let the world harm her again. So he did the only thing he could. He tucked a stray strand of hair behind her ear, slow and careful, and let his palm rest at her waist like a shield. He hadn't been looking for anything lasting. And yet, with Mila in his arms, the idea of walking away no longer felt like an option.

His fingers found the hem of her damp shirt. The fabric clung stubbornly to her skin as he worked it up, and she lifted her arms to help him, then her hips as he fumbled with her soaked trousers. There was nothing graceful about it, just shared urgency and shivering hands.

Then it was his turn. He stood and wrestled with his own clothes, the wet material dragging at every movement. His fingers were numb and uncooperative, and he nearly lost his balance, catching himself with one hand against the cave wall. Through it all, he kept his eyes on her, breath coming in uneven bursts, as if the simple act of undressing in front of her meant more than he knew how to say. A very small part of his brain remained alert, listening for any out-of-place noise.

Brom eased down beside her, close enough that his breath brushed her skin, his gaze fixed on her with a heat that left no doubt what he wanted. Even in the wavering firelight, he caught the answering spark in her eyes. Gently, he smoothed her damp hair back from her face and cupped her bruised cheek in his palm; a faint warmth pulsed from his hand, a thin trickle of healing energy that softened the tension at the corner of her mouth. Then he bent his head and found her lips, the kiss slow and deliberate, as if he meant to memorise her. Moving lower, he curled his tongue around one stiffened nipple at a time, his teeth tugging lightly on each one, causing her to close her eyes and shiver with pleasure.

Brom then ran his fingers through her folds, and, satisfied she was ready, carefully forged slowly into her welcoming heat. A flush of warmth had her lips gravitating to his again as she subtly adjusted her position to accommodate him.

He knew the energy coursing through him would spread through her body, creating a tingling sensation beneath her skin. As his power radiated outward, she naturally absorbed it, drawing in the charged currents, like two connected circuits completing a flow. But he had to be careful. Discharging too much could harm. While his warm lips and hands invoked a response, his shallow thrusts promised something more. But not yet. He shimmied his hands to cup her bottom.

Mila held his gaze and groaned.

Brom quickened the pace. The sight of her naked and flushed, swollen breasts as she abandoned all inhibitions was burned on his retinas. Desire ran hotter and higher with each pass. He couldn't take much more. Each time his shaft rasped her inner core, electricity shot from his body into hers. It was a part of him he couldn't hide. His thrusts moved harder and deeper. He reached between their bodies and stroked her firm pearl until he was rewarded with a shiver and a sharp inhale.

With a final plunge, he followed her over the edge. Catching his breath, he weaved his fingers into her hair and dropped his forehead against hers.

She smiled and wiped stray tendrils from her eyes. "I could get addicted to that energy burst. You will have to explain it to me in more detail. Or better still, more physical demonstrations might be in order."

"The Kew have an edge," he said, a slow smile tugging at his lips. "Others have studied us, hoping to bottle it." His gaze lingered on her, intense and searching, before he tipped his head back and closed his eyes for a brief second.

"Are all Kew so full of themselves?" she asked, meeting his eyes in an unspoken challenge. "Or is it just you?"

His laughter softened into something quieter, more personal. He shrugged, but the movement seemed more vulnerable than casual. "Maybe," he murmured, his voice gentling. "Or maybe it's the influence of a feisty, beautiful woman like you that this man wants to impress."

Her lips parted, and something flickered in her gaze. Perhaps uncertainty or hesitation. He wasn't sure.

For a heartbeat, the silence stretched between them, thick with everything unspoken and the pull of something new, something fragile. Neither was sure where it would lead, nor did they dare to find out right now.

Brom's mind was tangled with thoughts. He was in unfamiliar territory. He was drawn to Mila in ways he hadn't expected or planned for. She didn't deserve to be hurt, least of all by him. But wasn't that inevitable? They both knew it. She had her life on Rotari. And he had a job to finish, a duty that demanded all of him, leaving little room for anyone or anything else.

He glanced over and saw she'd gone quiet, too. Mila's gaze was far away, fixed on something beyond the cave walls, her expression turned inward and distant. The sight of her like that tugged at something deep in his chest. He couldn't afford this. Couldn't afford her. And yet, here he was.

Brom stilled, then nodded once, like an oath, and went to the cave mouth to listen for drones. The dark beyond the stone mouth stayed quiet, only the drip of water and the thin hiss of their fire, no rotor thrum, no scanning pulse. He held there long enough to be sure, then came back with the same controlled economy he always used.

They dressed in silence, the moment between them hanging in the air like something fragile and unfinished. The wet fabric fought them every step, shirts clinging, trousers dragging over cold, scraped skin. Brom turned slightly away as he wrestled his pants back on, acutely aware of every rustle from her side of the cave, every small intake of breath he pretended not to hear.

“I hope you aren’t contemplating something reckless,” Mila said quietly, still not looking at him. Her fingers slipped on a stubborn seam, and she muttered something under her breath, then fell quiet again.

Now and then their eyes met for a heartbeat too long before both of them looked away, the only sounds the soft crackle of the fire and the damp, uncomfortable scrape of fabric against skin. The air between them stayed thick with everything unspoken.

Brom exhaled slowly. “Reckless would be losing you,” he said, voice rough. “Everything else is just tactics.” He pressed a kiss to her knuckles, fast and fierce, the kind that said everything he would not let himself speak, then he stepped back, not toward the exit, but toward the leaf bed, as if forcing himself to remember the basics, because outside was still dark and moving now, exhausted, might get them killed.

He banked the fire down to embers, smothering it under damp leaf matter until the glow was minimal. Then he returned to her, close enough to share heat, far enough to give her the choice. Mila hesitated only a second before sinking onto the leaf bed, the tension still in her shoulders even as fatigue pulled at her. “Two hours,” Brom murmured, more instruction than comfort. “Maybe three. We leave at first light.”

Mila made a soft sound that might have been agreement or disbelief at the idea of allowing themselves to indulge in sleep. She lay down anyway, curling on her side, boots on and clothes still damp.

Brom followed, settling beside her with his back half-turned toward the cave mouth, his body instinctively angled like a shield, one arm a loose barrier at her waist without trapping her.

The cave kept its slow rhythm, drip, pause, drip. The ember-glow breathed faintly, and the darkness pressed in around them like a lid. Mila’s breathing stayed shallow for a while, controlled, as if she could outrun exhaustion. Brom listened, counting the seconds between the drips, the spaces between her breaths, waiting for the moment her body finally gave in. When it came, it was quiet. A slight softening. Her fingers loosened on his sleeve. Her forehead rested against his shoulder as if she'd meant it to be that way all along.

Brom didn't let himself close his eyes immediately. He kept watch, jaw tight, every sense stretched toward the cave mouth, thinking about drones and duty and the mission that waited to claim him again. Thinking about what he could promise her, and what promises were worth in a world like this. Eventually, the fatigue won. His eyelids grew heavy, and he surrendered to a shallow, guarded sleep, the kind that never fully lets go.

TIME SLID BY IN SMALL, measurable drops of water. Then, slowly, the cave began to change. The black at the mouth thinned to a bruised grey, and a strip of dawn crept across the stone floor until it touched their feet.

Brom's eyes opened the instant the light shifted.

Mila stirred a heartbeat later, blinking into the dim, her face drawn with fatigue, her mouth set as if she could force the day to behave. For a moment, they lay there, watching the dawn arrive like an intruder, both of them aware that whatever had existed between them in the dark had been borrowed. Outside, the world awaited with its responsibilities, dangers, and realities that could not be ignored. But here, for one last breath, they lingered in the fragile space between them.

And Brom knew, with a sinking certainty, that the road ahead would not be smooth sailing.

Half an hour later, Brom and Mila emerged into the rainforest. As the morning sunlight filtered through the trees, they heard the faint hum of a scout drone, but whose? Hopefully, it was one of Rhen's.

Brom motioned for Mila to stay hidden, then let his Kew skin shift. Pigment and texture mirrored the rainforest's mottled greens and bark-dark shadows. Camouflaged, he slipped into a small clearing where sunlight speared through the canopy in fractured shafts. With no tech to signal the drone, he pulled a strip of foil-like thermal wrap scavenged from the medical facility and angled it toward the sky to send a sharp flash upward.

The drone paused, its motors humming as it hovered and then circled. Then, with a brief electronic chirp, it tilted and banked in his direction, confirming his location, before darting away.

Minutes later, a low rumble rolled through the rainforest, the unmistakable growl of approaching engines slicing the stillness. A sleek yacht shimmered into view, decloaking just above the treetops, its hull catching the sunlight. The sight of it hit Brom with relief, and he beckoned Mila with a wave.

A hatch irised open along the belly. A thin scan beam lanced down through the canopy, sweeping once, twice, then pausing as if it had found their pulse. The leaves below shivered, then peeled aside. The tractor field engaged. It did not roar or blaze; it simply took hold, turning the air into a controlled, invisible shaft. Ferns bowed outward, branches eased back without snapping, and moisture lifted in a fine mist as the field carved a clean corridor through the green.

A braided smartline dropped into the column, unspooling with a soft whirr. The harness followed, rotating once, then settling as if guided by an unseen hand. The magnetic clasp at the end pulsed faintly, searching, calibrating, then hanging perfectly still in front of them, waiting.

Rhen leaned into the opening, grinning. "Looks like you two took the scenic route," he called, lightness in his voice, relief in his eyes.

Brom caught the smartline and secured Mila's belt harness first, no hesitation, and gave the line a single tug. The tether tightened, tensioned by the yacht's winch system.

Mila arched a brow at him. "Chivalry," she murmured.

"Logistics," Brom corrected, already keying the clasp's seal. "You're the fragile one."

She gave him a look that promised consequences later, then stepped into the beam. The grav field silently took her weight, lifting her through the rainforest canopy.

Brom followed a heartbeat later, boots leaving the ground as the lift drew him up.

"Next time," Rhen said, breath tight with relief he refused to show too openly, "try to stick to the plan." On board, they quickly lifted off, finally safe, or as close as they could be, with Blackwell and its crystal mines fading in the distance.

Mila's shoulder brushed Brom's as the ship changed trajectory. Brom felt the pull of it like gravity, felt his discipline flex, then lock. Mila looked up once, eyes unreadable, and for a heartbeat, he saw the same thing he was trying not to feel, the risk, the want, the terrible timing.

CHAPTER 16

The next day, Brom, Mila, Kihm, Flynn, Rhen and Astrea assembled in the makeshift meeting chamber carved deep into the caves near Gromwell and took their seats around an old scarred wooden table. The air was cool and damp, while wall-mounted bioluminescent panels cast a faint glow across the rock, sending shifting shadows skimming over the walls. But the only shadow that mattered, though, was the absence of Xander.

Brom broke the silence first. "Still no word, Kihm?"

She shook her head. "We've done a thorough search of the caves and Gromwell. If he's hiding, he doesn't want to be found."

"Or he's run away," Rhen muttered from where he sat.

Kihm inwardly winced. It was thought she'd been trying to keep buried. "He had a choice," she said.

"Did he?" Rhen asked quietly. He sat with his elbows on his knees, fingers laced, watching Kihm with steady, unnerving calm. "You told him Waylan's a monster, his home is the enemy, and everything he's ever trusted is a lie."

Kihm's jaw tightened. "I didn't lie to him."

Rhen nodded. "Some truths can hurt." He paused. "I had my own revelation a while ago, about who my father was. It changed everything I thought I knew about myself and my family, and for a while, running away felt like the only thing that made sense."

Brom dragged a hand through his hair, the gesture tired rather than impatient. "Assumptions aren't going to help us. We need to know whether he's with Waylan, Novak or alone out there." His gaze went to Kihm. "You spoke with him last. Did he say anything that might help?"

Kihm took a deep breath. "He wanted to talk to Waylan," she said finally. Rhen snorted. "That sounds like a kid who ran home."

Astrea had been silent until now, arms folded. "What if Waylan and Novak use what Xander knows against us?"

That landed like a stone in Kihm's gut. She turned to Brom.

Brom held her gaze, all trace of softness gone from his eyes. "I think we'd be fools to pretend they won't. Anyway, he doesn't know much more than Novak did, and we are adjusting our plans."

"So what?" Kihm demanded. "We treat him as a possible hostile?"

"That's not what I'm saying," Brom replied. "I haven't forgotten that he is my son. But if he is in Atmos, he's inside Waylan's perimeter. If Waylan suspects he can use the boy, he will. Xander's frightened, confused, and wants his father's approval." He exhaled slowly. "That's leverage."

"We should go after him," Kihm said. The words came out before she could stop them. "If he is in Atmos, we need to get him out. I'm hoping he doesn't trust Waylan as much as he did. He's shaken."

"Shaken people talk," Mila said. "To whoever promises to bring their world back into balance."

Silence settled over the room, heavy and close. Somewhere in the deeper caves, water dripped in a slow, uneven rhythm.

Brom pressed his palms flat on the table. "We can't plan a rescue based on guesses or feelings. We don't know if he reached Atmos, let alone where he'd be in that large city. But I am betting that Waylan and Novak are keeping a close eye on him if he does make it to Atmos."

Kihm stepped forward. "So we do nothing?"

Flynn turned to Kihm. "Until we know more, we assume that Xander is in danger, and that he and Novak are potential risks."

Kihm's throat tightened. For a moment, she hated him for being right, for putting their thoughts into words. "He trusted me enough to listen," she said. "Do you want me to try and contact him?"

"No," Brom cut in. "We can't risk it."

The room fell silent again, each of them alone with their own thoughts.

Mila placed a reassuring hand on Brom's shoulder in support.

Brom let out a deep breath. "Rescuing Xander and Oxana will need to be worked into our plans. Astrea, tighten our perimeter and ask your soldiers to move the Gromwell families deeper into the caves. Just in case."

Mila looked at Brom. "You will work out a way to get the twins out safely."

Brom sat with his arms crossed, his expression locked into calm as his gaze moved around the weathered wooden table, scored and scarred by years of hard use. The cavern's furnishings matched it, practical, unadorned and built to endure. The only thing that didn't belong was the augmented holo-interface hovering above the tabletop. Thin panes of light stacked and unfolded in midair, schematics cycling in silent layers, washing the rough stone walls in a cold, futuristic glow. Even so, the tech couldn't scrub the tension from the room. The group shifted and fidgeted, each movement a controlled tell. Brom felt it too. "Go ahead, Rhen," Brom said, his voice steady. They were risking everything. Yet despite the apprehension, there was something else there, too. A quiet resolve, an understanding that they would see this through no matter the odds. It was a fragile thing, but for now, that was all they had.

Rhen squared his shoulders and cleared his throat, his voice steady despite the tension. "Astrea and I have worked up a preliminary plan, with the caveat that it was drafted before Xander went missing." He paused. "After reviewing the data pulled from the monastery, we believe our best entry point to Atmos is through the lake and into the underground hangars." His jaw tightened. "But not through any of the main shuttle entry points because Novak will be expecting and no doubt watching that approach. He wanted us to use it. That alone makes it a trap. So we avoid his 'recommendations' at all costs." He lifted his chin toward the holo. "AI, project schematics. Mid-air. One to one hundred."

A shimmering 3D model emerged, glowing blue lines tracing a vast structure buried beneath the lake, its foundation housing a hangar from which a towering central pillar rose to a sleek, segmented hub-and-spoke complex at its peak. Just below the hub, a ring of docking ports encircled the top of the pillar, allowing smaller local shuttles to come and go across the planet without using the underground hangar.

"It appears that this structure is a well-used LOUT blueprint," Rhen explained. "A vertical superstructure anchored to the planet's surface supports a fully self-contained ship-city at its peak. The upper hub consists of a central command module fixed to the main pillar, surrounded by four enormous detachable modules arranged radially, each a self-contained sector engineered to support its inhabitants. In an emergency, each module can launch independently and reassemble into a single long-range space vessel. Every system, every escape route, is built for clean, efficient evacuation, but like anything made with precision, it has its weaknesses, if you know where to look."

He paused and pointed to the structure's central pillar. "This isn't just structural; it's also the primary conduit for transportation to and from the subterranean hangars below the lake, and it also contains infrastructure that draws geothermal energy into the city above.

Brom exhaled slowly, his eyes lingering on the schematics. "Kihm, how accurate do you think these schematics are?"

Rhen's eyes narrowed on the schematic. "Our tech is good enough to breach their perimeter and reach the underground hangars without tripping the security net, but not through the main entrance." He tapped the lake sector and an access route pulsed to life. "We go in through one of the lake access hatches. My drones will map the area and pick the best entry point. They will be watching the hangar doors, expecting a frontal approach."

At his nod, Astrea leaned forward and took command with practised ease. "Once we're inside, we will infiltrate the hangar and move into position near the geothermal unit. She zoomed in on the schematic, outlining the subterranean infrastructure. "The hangar is tightly monitored, so stealth is critical. One of my soldiers will disable the geothermal unit. That will knock Atmos off its main power grid, forcing the city to rely on emergency reserves. In the resulting disruption, security systems will lag, comms will scramble, and the AI will shift focus to conserving core operations." She paused. "Any questions so far?"

After a shake of heads, Rhen picked up the thread, highlighting a faint line that spiralled around the central pillar. "This is the maintenance tunnel, which is a service artery built for inspection drones and climate controlled maintenance crawlers. It is a closed system with a mag-anchored track running its length, with self-driving maintenance crawlers that ride an electromagnetic field. Access hatches branch off at various intervals along the central pillar, giving engineers and maintenance staff direct access to life-support systems, power relays, and structural nodes without using public vac lifts that run down the central pillar. We plan to hijack the maintenance crawlers based at hangar level and ride them up to the city above, which is off the main traffic grid and beneath Atmos's surveillance envelope.

Brom interrupted. If we disrupt the power, won't the crawlers be rendered inoperable?"

"It appears that the mag track and crawlers run on a separate emergency grid, along with the environmental system, which feeds the crawlers. "If Atmos loses primary power, the crawlers have an independent power source to remain operational. They're designed to transport essential workers to critical systems when everything else is dark. The main power grid, including the central vac lifts, will be compromised when we hit the geothermal unit," she said, zooming in. "Novak will expect us to use the maintenance crawlers, but he won't know we'll already be inside Atmos, or that we'll hit the geothermal unit first, so we'll have the element of surprise."

Rhen picked up the thread. "Once we reach the top, we locate the President and obtain his command codes," he said. "Module release is locked behind a dual-authentication protocol, which means the system won't respond to a simulated threat alone." He pointed to the interface node linked to the core AI. "The central AI controls all emergency evacuation procedures, including the modules' ejection sequence, and those codes serve two functions. First, they unlock the system's emergency command pathways; without them, even a genuine threat won't trigger separation from the central stem. Second, they verify the authenticity of any incoming threat. The AI won't act unless it receives both inputs: a valid threat and an authorised confirmation."

Rhen's gaze moved from one team member to the next. "With both layers in place, perceived threat and presidential authorisation, the AI will treat it as a genuine emergency and initiate the evacuation protocol. All four modules will separate simultaneously. Timing is everything. The difficulties...," he hesitated before curling his index and middle fingers into quick, sharp quotation marks mid-air as he spoke, "lie in the fact that while the emergency sequence can be triggered, the final release authorisation is contingent on each module's bridge being staffed by a one of Astrea's pilots to execute the disengagement manoeuvre and land them at their designated locations."

Brom interjected. "But what is stopping LOUT's return once they realise it was a false alarm?"

"Precisely," Astrea replied. "After my pilots land, they will destroy the propulsion systems to keep the modules permanently grounded. Once we get the all clear, that everyone has been evacuated from Atmos, the explosives planted around the central pillar will then be detonated."

Brom cleared his throat. "Before we hit Atmos, we need to lock down a way to extract Xander and Oxana."

Astrea leaned in, elbows on the scarred table. "Already on it. I'll push the twins' images to my pilots. Once the modules hit dirt, they can conduct a sweep." She cut a look at Rhen. "When you get to the control room, can you ping Oxana's subdermal? I need a fix I can beam straight to whoever's closest."

"I can try," Rhen said.

"Xander's the real problem," Astrea went on. "His tracker's gone. He's blind on the grid."

Kihm's jaw tightened. "I know. I'm the one who ripped it out. Feels like a mistake now."

"You did what you had to," Flynn said. "If I had to bet, Xander's sticking close to Waylan or Novak. We start there and drag him out of whatever hole they've shoved him in."

"Should I contact Uncle Roddick? Maybe he's our one shot at getting the twins out before this all kicks off."

Flynn held her gaze for a beat, then shook his head. "I think setting up a rendezvous now would be a logistical nightmare. We would have to relay our plans to him, and his loyalties are in question. That's too much risk."

"Kihm nodded.

For the next hour, the group meticulously worked through the final details.

LEAVING HIS OFFICE, Waylan stalked through the shopping district, the blur of people meaningless. He wanted to confront Kimmy K and make her pay for tearing his world apart. He wandered, the raw ache of betrayal driving him forward. How had he been such a fool? He had nowhere to go but the laboratory, the place where it had all begun. If she thought she could derail him, she was dead wrong. He would make the company thrive without her and prove to his father that he didn't need her. He would occupy his mind with work, pouring every ounce of rage into it. She'd be sorry, he'd make sure of that. He'd rise above this, and everyone would see what he was truly capable of. Swiping his access chip, he pushed through the front doors and marched towards the head scientist's office. Opening the door, he announced, "Have you heard the news, Rupart?"

"Yes, sir. And sorry, I am too."

"We don't need her. We can make the company great. Better in fact."

The scientist shook his head.

"What?" Waylan demanded.

"We don't have the formulas, sir."

"What do you mean?"

"Kimmy K wiped the system."

"So, you're telling me that we have nothing but the current stock?"

"Correct, sir."

The room was deathly silent as Waylan paced back and forth, his fists clenched tightly at his sides. He was livid, his rage boiling over with every step he took. The betrayal felt like a knife to the gut. Stopping in front of the head scientist, his face twisted with rage. He grabbed Rupart's lapels and yanked him forward, his face only centimetres away. “This is unacceptable. How could you have let this happen?”

“She was the boss, sir.”

“Figure it out. Otherwise, you and your lab rats will be working in the Blackheart Crystal mines. Understood?”

Waylan left as abruptly as he'd arrived, slamming his fist into the door's access panel and spider-cracking the interface as it hissed shut behind him with a wounded whine. In reception, he took it out on the furniture, a vicious kick sending chairs skidding into their neighbours. He wasn't going back to his father empty-handed. This was his chance to prove himself. If Kimmy K thought hiding her precious formulas would save her, she'd misread the game. Waylan didn't need her goodwill; he needed leverage, and he knew exactly where to find it. He wasn't about to sit around waiting for Kimmy K and her band of misfits to infiltrate Atmos. Novak was a blunt instrument, and gas didn't discriminate. Dead chemists couldn't talk, and Waylan intended to hear every secret she'd kept from him. He turned on his heel and stalked back to his office, locked the door, and opened a secure channel.

Novak answered on the second ring.

Waylan didn't bother with pleasantries. “Bring Xander to me. Now!”

Silence, then Novak's voice came through, clipped. “For what purpose?”

“You don't need the details,” Waylan said, pausing. He could almost hear Novak weighing the risk, the advantage, the leash he thought he held.

“Fine,” Novak said at last. “I'm on my way.”

Xander's pulse lurched when Novak turned toward him. Relief and warning landed together, proof he hadn't been forgotten, and a reminder of how easily he could be used. Part of him wanted to step forward, to earn a glance that meant something. The other part counted seconds, wondering if he'd be back in time to do what he needed to do.

Novak slapped a comms unit into Xander's palm. "Keep this close. It's a closed, secure network. I'll contact you when the Gromwell group enters Atmos. They won't get through my security without me knowing."

Xander curled his fingers around the device. He'd been starving for a chance to corner his father, to demand answers about everything Kimmy K had dragged into the light, about the lies stitched through their family like wiring behind a wall. And if Waylan pulled him out of Novak's reach, maybe he could dodge whatever ugliness Novak was lining up. He kept his face steady, but his hands had gone damp. Conflicted, he followed Novak out.

LATER THAT EVENING, the cloaked yacht lay tucked into a natural hollow in the rainforest beside the Gromwell caves, its hull damp with mist. Inside, the cabin, thin strips of light caught on open service panels and half-latched crates, and the air carried the faint bite of coolant mixed with rain-wet foliage.

Rhen sat at the virtual console with his sleeves rolled up, fingers flicking through route projections as he cross-checked systems.

In the aisle, Brom and Astrea strapped down a crate of weapons and emergency rations, testing each mag-lock with a sharp, practised tug.

Kihm and Mila knelt at the bulkhead storage, quietly counting medpacks and injectors into a hard case. The yacht thrummed on standby, a low, constant pulse, until a sharp chime cut through it. All four froze.

Brom stood. "We're not supposed to be on any grid," he muttered.

Another chime. A small indicator blinked to life on the comms panel.

Rhen straightened slowly, eyes narrowing on the light. "Tell me that's from our people."

Kihm was already moving. She slid into the comms seat, fingers dancing across the controls. A few seconds later, the colour drained from her face. "It's an external message," she said.

Rhen leaned over to get a better look. "From who?"

"I don't know," Kihm said. She cracked the message open to reveal a jittery, grainy, and unstable video feed. The scene flickered into view. A dim, metallic room emerged, its walls streaked with rust and patched with mismatched plating. Wires dangled from the ceiling like tangled vines, swaying slightly in the artificial draft. Emergency lights pulsed red in a ragged rhythm, casting the space in a blood-tinged strobe. The camera panned slowly. A forcefield shimmered near the rear wall, revealing a cramped holding compartment. Figures huddled there, barely moving. Three shamans, with their robes tattered, faces hollow and alert, watched the camera with guarded eyes. Then the camera shifted to another compartment, revealing Xander and Oxana. Their eyes met the lens head-on, sharp and defiant.

Brom's spine snapped straight, muscles coiled so tight he couldn't move. "Where are they?"

Astrea stood behind Kihm to get a closer look. "My guess is a spaceship or space station."

Then the screen crackled, and Waylan stepped into frame in an immaculate, close-cut suit of oil-slick charcoal. A razor-thin line of faint cobalt piping traced his lapels like circuitry, and a high-collared silver-white shirt made him look formidable even through the static. As usual, his shoulders were set, and his expression smoothed into his practised corporate intimidation mode.

Looking straight into the lens, he spoke with the calm, surgical certainty of a man who'd already decided the outcome. "Kimmy K," he said, smiling faintly before turning slowly to glance at the hostages, then back. "There's a sealed maintenance channel on that yacht, factory-only. Once I put my techs on it, you weren't hard to find." He paused. "I'm on Orphis-8, the decommissioned space station circling the planet. The old relic's barely holding together. The hostages are alive, for now." He smiled again, but it never touched his eyes. "I want the complete formula package. Every line of code. Bring it to me, and they walk free."

He leaned closer, voice dropping to a cold murmur. "Try to double-cross me, and I start purging compartments, one by one, in the lower environmental ring. You won't know which compartment they're in until the alarms stop and you're left guessing whether you just killed them. Like a game of roulette, wouldn't you say? Here's how this works. You bring the full set of formulas unlocked, uncorrupted, and verified onto Orphis-8. Delivery must be made in person by you alone. You'll board through Docking Ring A. No weapons. The AI will scan you on entry. Proceed to the central control room and upload the files. If they're incomplete, encrypted, or altered in any way, then I start purging compartments, one by one. You'll get to decide which scream belongs to whom. I expect that will keep you motivated." A sharp hiss crackled through the audio, sounding like oxygen venting. "Just a sample." He smiled.

Brom clenched his jaw. "Bastard."

"And Kimmy K, I assume you will need a pilot. They stay on the yacht. Visible, idle, unarmed. My surveillance will confirm their position. If they set one foot on the station, I will act." Waylan paused, letting the silence stretch. "Once I confirm a clean data transfer, I'll release the hostages. One at a time. Not before. Not all at once. Try anything clever like cutting the power, jamming my signal, slipping in through a secondary access point, and Orphis-8 becomes a one-way trip. I trust we're clear. And Kimmy K." There was a shift in his voice. "You walked away thinking you'd left me behind. But I'm the one in the lead now," he laughed. The transmission ended with a soft, final beep, and the screen faded to black.

The silence inside the yacht was deafening.

Brom exploded. "He's threatening to suffocate our family and friends in exchange for your formulas."

Kihm nodded. "I took them when I fled."

"Why?"

"They are my life's work. He wanted to exploit the formulas to create bioweapons. In the wrong hands, those formulas are worth more than a fleet of star destroyers on the Outer Rim Exchange."

Brom drew a deep breath. "He's delusional if he thinks we'll play this his way." He turned to Rhen. "Can you contact the monastery and confirm his story?"

Moments later, Rhen shook his head. "I've got confirmation, he's taken three shamans hostage, including your uncle. A fourth was injured, but he escaped."

Kihm's eyes were still focused on the darkened screen. "One press, and the station starts bleeding air. He knows how unstable Orphis-8 is, and he's using it. I analysed its potential as a private off-planet laboratory before it was decommissioned. Waylan thinks he has the advantage. He has no idea I have lived in the station's schematics for weeks."

Brom frowned. "We have no choice but to go to Orphis-8 and free them. But it means delaying our plans for Atmos."

Astrea braced her hands on the back of Kihm's chair, eyes on the dead comms panel. "We can't go in blind," she said. "We will need Orphis-8's schematics, including access routes, vents, maintenance and freight shafts. All of it."

Kihm gave a small, lopsided shrug, as if she'd asked for something as simple as a weather report. She brought up the yacht's interface.

Rhen's eyes cut to Kihm, brows pinching. "Be careful, if we light ourselves up too much, we become a target. Waylan has already proven that he can get through our security."

"Not the way I'm doing it," Kihm said. Her fingers moved quickly and precisely, with no hesitation. "The cloak stops active sweeps. I'm just brushing the Atmos maintenance net. Low power, narrow beam. They'll read it as a diagnostics ping, if they notice it at all."

The console chimed. "Access granted," the system whispered.

Kihm leaned back, satisfied. "The system still swears I'm authorised personnel," she said. "Waylan never revoked my clearance."

Astrea's smile was quick, all business underneath it. "Can you pull everything down? Work offline?"

"Already doing that," she said. "Full schematic package to local storage. Once it's done, I will kill the link and scrub our handshake. They'll never know we were here unless they tear their logs apart line by line."

"And if they do?" Rhen asked.

"Then they figure it out after we're finished," Kihm replied. "By that point, Orphis-8 won't be their biggest concern."

A progress bar ticked toward completion. Every eye tracked the slow, steady upward creep. Ninety-eight. Ninety-nine. Complete.

Kihm severed the connection, and the panel dropped back to its harmless idle glow. "We've got everything," she said. "If Waylan thinks Orphis-8 is secure, he is in for a surprise." She tapped the virtual console twice, then dragged her hand away, peeling the information free. A lattice of pale light unfolded in the air between them, resolving into a three-dimensional schematic. Orphis-8 spun in the holo as a skeletal ring of pressurised modules, its internal layout mapped in clean lines including corridors, compartments, and pressure doors. At the same time, external access hatches, irises, service ports, and security nodes blinked alongside pulsing warnings at the station's failing systems. The rotating holo cast faint blue reflections across their faces as the doomed station turned in silence.

Astrea stepped closer to the display, her eyes tracing the outer access points and mentally mapping options. Once we're inside, it'll be tight. Zero margin for error," she said. "Structural integrity is failing, the gravity is unstable, and the emergency failsafes are down. One good hit from space debris or a serious malfunction, and Orphis-8 could drift out of orbit and crash into the planet.

Brom dragged a hand through his hair. "Then we need to get them out before that station becomes a tomb. Let's call the group together and plan our attack."

BROM, MILA, RHEN, ASTREA and Kihm huddled around the cave's table as the augmented holo-interface flared, bleaching faces blue and sharpening every hollow under exhausted eyes. The schematics unspooled in layered strata, and the déjà vu hit hard, planning on a map again while the danger waited outside.

Above the scuffed surface, Kihm layered and rotated Orphis-8's 3D schematic until the station hung in the air for everyone to see, a derelict ringworm of metal, its outer skin pitted, scorched, and stained by decades of neglect. "There." Kihm lifted her hand, and the holo obeyed. The station's model slowed until the lower environmental ring faced them like an exposed wound. "Lower enviro ring. That's where he's holding them." Icons flared, including sealed hatches, dead corridors, and pressure-loss zones.

She pinched the model, zooming to an iris recessed under the station's belly. "I think we should enter via this freight shaft. It was built for smaller cargo ships to transfer cargo up through an internal lift without tying up the primary ports above." Her smile turned faint. "It's been 'unused' on paper for years."

Rhen was already reading the overlays, eyes flicking faster than the holo could rotate. He then tapped a tight cluster of nodes, and they bloomed amber. "These are the emitters." With a small twist of his wrist, he pinched and dragged the model, expanding the schematic until the hardened security-spine room slid into view. "My guess is Waylan's running overwatch from here," he continued. "He'll be monitoring station traffic and the external approach, including camera feeds, door controls, turret and defence relays, lockdown protocols, and the hostages. He doesn't need the central control room to squeeze the station. From a security spine, he can still choke environmental systems through the network and lock down whole sections." His fingers then swept to a comms overlay, highlighting arcs around the hull. "And he'll have jammers up, both tight-beam and wideband."

Astrea's voice cut in, clipped and practical. "So we remove them."

"We don't have time to hunt hardware," Rhen said. He glanced at Astrea, then back to the holo. "We've got one clean window when Orphis-8 slips behind Ravan's Belt. The rockfield will flood local space with radar scatter, thermal spikes, and comms static, enough to degrade targeting and bury our signature in the belt if we sit cold among the debris. Layer the yacht's cloak over that, and our approach will read as nothing but background noise."

Astrea nodded, already assigning roles to the plan. "I recommend that Rhen stay on the yacht and monitor all comms."

Rhen nodded and angled the holo toward the station's core. "From the yacht, I'll punch into the surveillance hub the moment Kihm confirms you have landed safely on the exterior. I'll loop feeds, scrub our entry signature, then trigger a station-wide fire alert. Emergency protocols will unlock auxiliary paths and prompt evacuation. To Waylan, it'll look like another system failure." He smiled. "He'll be busy chasing ghosts."

Kihm highlighted the breach point again. "I'll handle the outer locks. I've still got my old credentials buried in the firmware, legacy admin tokens nobody would have bothered to erase. It'll get us through the outer iris. After that, we go physical."

Rhen slid a small metallic cube across the table.

Kihm picked it up and turned it in her hand. "What is it?"

"Custom-coded viral wedge. Plugged into the central maintenance room console, it will replicate across the station's network and lock Waylan out. Shutting down his ability to vent compartments, seal doors, and flood corridors. Any of it."

Kihm's eyes narrowed. "But that shuts down more than Waylan."

"Yes," Rhen said. "It turns the station dark. No life support, no heat regulation, no pressure control or gravity. Which is why," he looked at each of them in turn. "Everyone will be wearing Z1 enviro-suits with portable breathers and mag-boots, along with extra gear for the captives."

Astrea leaned closer, fingers braced on the table as if she could steady the spinning station with sheer will. "Based on available information, I propose that the team should include Orella, Kihm and Brom. I will take point. Orella on my shoulder. We move fast and directly to our set targets." She rotated the holo with her finger. Once we're in, Orella and I will head for the captives with the extra kit." She tapped the holo, and compartments in the lower environmental ring pulsed red.

"Brom and Kihm will head directly to the central control room, exactly where Waylan expects you. But he won't have clocked your entry, which buys you a few minutes to slip the virus into the uplink in place of the formula package before he registers the swap." Another marker lit up, half-swallowed by bulkheads and service spines. "Lastly, if it turns hot, I decide the mission's direction and the exit timing and route." Her gaze slid to Brom, acknowledging his authority without surrendering command of the tactical line.

Brom accepted her terms with a small dip of his chin. He wasn't a soldier, but leadership sat on him like armour. "We stick to the plan. It sounds solid, and we don't improvise ourselves into a grave."

"You'll have about ten minutes of safe operational time once the virus takes," Rhen continued. "After that, the temperature will drop below survivable levels, and oxygen becomes scarce. Orphis-8 won't immediately fall out of orbit, but without attitude control, it will start to drift. Over time, it'll tumble, the orbit will decay, and then it's a slow, ugly death spiral. Remember, we're not here to save the station." His voice went quieter. "We're here to save people."

"And what if Waylan catches on?" Brom asked.

"He won't," Astrea said. "Not if we're clean. Not if we're fast and get our timing right."

Mila's hands tightened together on the table, her attention sharpened like a scalpel, and she lifted her chin, eyes locking on Brom's. "I'm coming," she said.

Brom's mouth tightened. "Mila. No."

"Those captives need on-site triage, not guesses over a comm." She leaned forward slightly, the holo's light catching the hard line of her focus. "I can run bioscans, stabilise fractures, manage shock, and get them mobile enough to move when Astrea needs them moving. Those shamans are elderly. They won't survive a rushed extraction without medical eyes on them." She didn't raise her voice. She didn't need to. "Factor me into the rescue."

Brom held her gaze for a long beat, then gave a single, reluctant nod. "Fine. But you stay behind the front line."

Astrea answered before Mila could. "She will," she said. "And if anyone goes down, she's the reason we get them back up."

Kihm set the cube beside the holo's projected node, like placing a key next to a lock. "Then that's the plan," she said softly. "We enter under the Belt. Rhen monitors the comms and blinds the station. Orella, Mila, and I will free the hostages and keep them breathing, and Kihm and Brom will introduce the virus. And we leave before Orphis-8 turns to scrap metal."

THE CLOAKED YACHT DRIFTED into the heart of the Ravan's Belt asteroid field, and Rhen cycled down the power to minimal systems until only the soft hum of life support remained. With shields dark and emissions cold, it became just another shadow among the tumbling rock and iron.

Beyond the forward viewport, Orphis-8 hung like a fractured ring in the void, its once-pristine hull now pitted and failing, barely held together by inertia and neglect. Parked deep inside one of the primary docking cradles sat a small, sleek spacecraft, Waylan's, without question. Its obsidian hull was all clean lines and predatory curves, too immaculate for the corrosion gnawing at Orphis-8. The craft's nose was seated tight in the station's docking collar, and a single docking tube ran from the bay's airlock throat to the craft's forward hatch. One clean, pressurised artery binds it to the dying ring like a parasite on a host.

Brom, Mila, Kihm, Astrea, and Orella stood in the yacht's cargo hold in their Z1 EVA suits, oxygen ticking steadily in their chests, thruster packs armed and ready.

The outer iris opened with a quiet hiss. One by one, they launched and used controlled bursts from their jet packs to glide across open space. The asteroid field swirled silently but deadly around them, as Orphis-8 grew steadily in their visors. No noise. Just course corrections, whisper-quiet thrusters, and the sharp focus of breath inside helmets.

Kihm led, eyes locked on a shadowed vector toward the station's underbelly, the old freight shaft just below the main environmental ring. If Waylan were watching, he wouldn't see them until it was too late. She adjusted her vector with a soft pulse of her thruster, keeping her trajectory tight. The others followed in loose formation toward the station's swelling silhouette, their suit HUDs streaming proximity, oxygen, and vitals so they could track one another in real time.

Ten more metres and the iris guarding the freight shaft would be within visual range. As long as Waylan's beacon watched the main docking bays, he would miss them slipping in through the blind spot.

Astrea's voice came through the comms, low and even. "You are on track, Kihm."

"Copy," Kihm replied. Above her, the underbelly of Orphis-8 rolled into view, scarred and blistered with decades of neglect. The iris was blackened with carbon scoring, flecked with thruster plume deposits, and peeling paint. She drifted the final few metres, then let her grav boots clamp onto the hull with a magnetic thunk, waiting for the others to do the same.

Brom's voice buzzed in her ear. "Still think this qualifies as a good plan?"

"Not even a little," Kihm murmured, pulling a utility tool from her belt. "Too late now." Her headlamp swept over the iris's battered face, and she wondered if it could still cycle at all in that state. The beam slid onto an exterior access panel that clung to the hull like a stubborn barnacle, a hardwired override for EVA crews and emergency entry. Under normal conditions, the iris was only ever opened from inside. The panel's cover was rimmed with thick frost, the kind that formed when warm electronics died and everything flash-froze in place. The access panel casing was crazed with tiny white fractures, like frostbite scars. She set the pry bar into the seam and worked it carefully, millimetre by millimetre.

"Easy," Astrea warned. "If there's any charge, you may get a shock."

"I'm aware," Kihm confirmed.

The access panel's cover plate finally gave with a sharp crack, snapping the seal loose, causing a puff of powdered frost to float out, glittering in her beam. Inside was a cramped cavity of wiring, connectors, and a small control module. Everything looked ancient and brittle, except for one ugly detail. A thin, blackened streak ran down the inside casing, and the insulation around one bundle was blistered.

"Short burn," Kihm murmured. "Old."

Astrea's voice tightened. "So it could arc?"

"It could," she said, clipping her tether to a nearby handhold, then pulling a small tool pouch from her belt. From it, she took a compact power cell and a pair of insulated jump leads. She kept her headlamp steady. "I'm bypassing the dead electronics in this box to tell the iris to unlatch." She indicated two thick, dust-coated cables that disappeared into the wall toward the iris's locking assembly. "These are the actuator lines. If the motor isn't seized, a brief pulse should work."

"And if it is seized," Astrea added, "I will use a Micro-shear charge."

Kihm tilted her light closer. "But we try my way first. Less noise." She anchored herself and touched one lead to the first contact, then paused. "When I connect this, you might see a spark. Don't freak out. If you see sustained arcing, everyone pulls away."

"Copy," they said, almost together.

She completed the circuit. For half a heartbeat, nothing. Then a blue-white snap spat inside the panel. Her gloved fingers tightened, but she didn't pull back. She held the contact, counted under her breath, then severed it cleanly.

The cavity fell silent.

A heavy thunk rolled through the hull, felt more than heard. Another answered it, deeper, like something massive shifting off its seat.

"Finally," Kihm muttered, watching the status band around the iris flicker from red to amber, then snap to green. Motors engaged with a low, hungry whine, and the iris began to retract, segment by segment, petals sliding into the ring like a lens opening.

The aperture widened as the overlapping ribs nested into the collar, until there was only a clean circle of darkness waiting beyond. The station exhaled, not a rush, just a thin, cold breath slipping out through the gap. Dust drifted into open space, slow and weightless.

Kihm set both hands on the inner collar and guided herself through. Her lamp cut into the interior where cargo rails ran upward, and loose insulation hung in ragged strips. On the wall, a smeared mark, almost a handprint, streaked through grime, frozen in place as if someone had steadied themselves. She killed her mag boots, eased forward, and disappeared into the shaft.

One by one, the others drifted after her, hand-over-hand using the shaft's cargo rails. They glided past frost-sheathed conduit looms and recessed mag-clamp sockets, empty mouths in the walls where cargo modules had once latched and ridden the lift-line up into the station. Under flickering red emergency strips, dust motes spun in lazy microgravity while distant groans travelled through the bulkheads. Metal fatigue, or something worse? They eased out into a cavernous cargo hold and engaged their mag boots, since the bay was in zero gravity.

"We split here," Astrea said, her voice clipped. "Stick to the plan. Orella, Mila and I will head to the captors, and we'll be through the locked door in that sector before Waylan knows we're there."

"Good luck, everyone. See you on the other side," Brom said. He reached for Mila's hand, and their eyes met. Worry flickered across his face, gone as quickly as it came, replaced by resolve. He squeezed once. "Stay safe."

Mila's gloved thumb dragged once across his palm, a slow, deliberate stroke that hit him harder than the firefights. "Don't do something reckless," she said, voice steady, eyes not. "Not today."

Brom's gaze locked on hers. "That stands for you, too," he answered, and he did not let go until Astrea shifted, impatient, and the corridor demanded motion. He wondered why he had agreed to let Mila participate in this mission.

Without another word, Astrea, Orella and Mila peeled off down the left corridor, disappearing through a hatch and into the pulsing red gloom as the metal floor vibrated faintly beneath their grav boots.

Brom and Kihm still had one level to climb to reach the central control room. If they could seat Rhen's virus in time, it would propagate on its own, cascading through subsystems and turning Orphis-8's orderly routines into controlled chaos.

Overhead, wiring dangled like veins from torn panels, and somewhere deep in the walls, the groan of shifting metal echoed like a distant warning.

Kihm checked the map flickering in her HUD and pressed forward, toward the beating heart of the station's dying systems. If the virus worked, it would buy them time. If it didn't, Waylan would vent the captive's compartments before they got close.

THE CORRIDOR PINCHED tighter as Astrea led Orella and Mila into the environmental ring. Pipes jittered overhead in uneven bursts, vibrating with each coughing cycle of the pressure regulators. Every few seconds, the walls ticked with thermal stress as metal expanded and snapped back, as if the station were counting down to its demise.

Their helmet lamps carved pale cones through the dark. The light caught condensation on the bulkheads, slick as sweat, and glinted off ugly bundles of exposed wiring where panels had been ripped open and never repaired.

"This place is rotting from the inside," Orella muttered over comms.

"Makes it easier to breach," Astrea replied, but she kept her gaze moving, assessing anything that might be a potential threat.

Ahead, a junction marker floated in and out of Astrea's headlamp beam: Delta-3. The passage widened just enough for them to stand shoulder to shoulder, and then forced them to stop. The hatch was just another service bulkhead at first glance. Same ribs. Same recessed hinges. But the faint cobalt stripe along its edge marked it security-rated, the kind that sealed fast and held pressure even when the rest of the ring didn't.

Astrea checked the placard twice and traced the stamped code through a film of grime. If they cut through the wrong door, they would lose valuable time and be an open target.

"Rhen," she said through her comms, "can you scan for heat signatures at our location?"

Static ticked once, then the comm cleaned up as Rhen found the angle through the ring's cluttered metal. "Copy. Give me ten seconds," he said, voice tight with concentration. "I'm piggybacking off your suit relays and the station's dead maintenance net. It's not pretty, Orphis-8 is throwing thermal noise everywhere."

Astrea held still, letting the corridor settle in her visor. Pipes shivered overhead. The deck gave a faint, sickly vibration as gravity hunted, then steadied again. Somewhere deeper in the environmental ring, something groaned, long and slow.

"Alright," Rhen came back. "I have two heat signatures beyond the hatch next to your location. As far as I can tell, they are pressed against the far bulkhead. One is running hotter, with an elevated heart rate. The other is cooler." A pause, then, "I'm also seeing intermittent hotspots near the ceiling line in a compartment closeby, small, sharp spikes, servo heat. It could be drones on standby or failing actuators. Confidence is about sixty per cent, the insulation and frost layers are scattering the return."

Mila's breath hissed in Astrea's ear. "So they're in there."

"Most likely," Rhen said. "But listen, you're sitting in a pressure boundary. That hatch is reinforced with a ceramsteel collar and a security stripe; it'll hold pressure even if the compartment is vented. If Waylan is playing roulette with life support, he would choose a compartment that can be sealed and purged cleanly."

Astrea's gaze flicked from the placard to the seam around the hatch. The faint cobalt line along the edge made it look clinical, deliberate, a wound stitched shut. "Orella," Astrea said, voice clipped. "You heard him. This is the one."

Rhen's voice dropped lower. "Astrea, one more thing. When you breach, do not go wide. That compartment will have stale air pockets, CO_2 layering, and cold spots where the station's thermal control has died. Your suits will compensate, but the two bodies inside won't have the same luxury. The moment you crack the seal, you could trigger a pressure equalisation surge."

Astrea lifted her fist, then pointed two fingers down the corridor behind them, assigning silent roles out of habit. "I cover rear. Mila, you're first through once we have a gap, triage and then suit them up. Orella, open her up."

"Copy," Mila and Orella said.

Orella reached for the access panel. Dead. No status LED. No haptic chirp. No faint warmth from a live board. The cracked glass felt like ice beneath her glove. She knelt, popped the panel cover with her knife, and exposed the internals. "The photonic bus coupler is still factory-sealed, with the tamper-lacquer intact, but the power rail has not only been burnt, but it has also been cleanly sheared, as if someone cut it with a micro-saw and then flashed the ends to prevent repair. The panel's been erased. No power. No handshake. No loopback." She paused, and the pause carried more weight than the words. "Someone wanted this door to become an impenetrable barrier. They wouldn't do that for no reason. Thankfully, I brought my plasma cutter."

Mila's breath hitched, loud in Astrea's ears through the shared comm channel. "So Waylan didn't plan for the hostages to be released." Her voice went thin. "They were always going to be collateral damage."

Astrea stared at the panel. "Affirmative."

A low, rising whine crawled through the deck plates, gravity control hunting. Mila felt it before the warning icon even blinked in her HUD. Then the floor let go. For a half heartbeat, they were no longer anchored to the deck, and their boots lifted. Condensation globules pulled away from the wall in trembling beads and floated free.

Without warning, the emergency field snapped back hard. Clunk. Mag-locks bit into the corridor's ferromesh floor with a teeth-jarring thunk. Loose grit and tiny metal filings slapped the deck and skittered, then stilled.

Orella drew her portable plasma cutter from its sling, a compact, industrial unit scarred from too many "last resorts." She thumbed it out of safe mode. The micro-bottle feed pressurised with a rising purr, and the muzzle chamber bloomed from a dull ember to a white-blue heat. A cooling fan whined as it dumped waste heat.

"Back," Astrea ordered Mila, who moved fast, flattening to the far wall. In flickering gravity, debris didn't fall; it wandered. A single molten droplet could drift into a visor, a seam, a joint.

Astrea took the corridor behind them, weapon tucked close, light sweeping. The station groaned. Somewhere deep in the ring, something heavy shifted with a metallic complaint.

Orella set the cutter against the seam where ceramsteel skin met the frame's reinforced collar. The pilot arc snapped on.

"Four minutes," Astrea said.

Orella started cutting. Sparks sprayed. In low gravity, they didn't shower; they floated, little incandescent seeds, drifting and spinning before dying out. The door's edge went orange, then molten, metal peeling away in curling ribbons like bark stripped from a tree. The corridor shuddered again, a gravity hiccup, shorter this time, but enough. Orella's cutter slipped, a fraction of a second where the tool didn't have full purchase. The arc skated.

Astrea saw the slip before Orella did. The plasma jet kissed the wrong surface, a blue-white lick that bit through polymer and sealant. There was a sharp snap as Orella's suit's outer layer flashed and recoiled. Orella jerked back with a strangled curse. Her HUD icon flared: Suit integrity compromised. A thin wisp of vapour curled from her left side near the rib seam, almost invisible in the dim lighting, but the sound gave it away: a faint, steady hiss.

Mila froze. "Orella!"

"Don't." Orella's voice was suddenly too controlled, like she was holding panic down with both hands. She slapped her gloved palm over the breach. The hiss softened but didn't stop.

Astrea was already moving. "Seal it. Now. Before the regulators burp again."

Orella's Z1 enviro suit was a field model, with a smartweave underlayer, a gel-foam impact web, and an outer composite shell with embedded microcapillaries for thermal control. Great against radiation and shrapnel. Not great when you sliced it with a plasma cutter. She handed the plasma cutter to Mila and yanked open a thigh pouch with shaking fingers and pulled out a vac-seal patch, a flat disc the size of her palm, foil-faced, with a ring of reactive adhesive and a microvalve in the centre. She slammed the patch down and twisted it a quarter turn. The adhesive flashed as it reacted, gripping the suit's composite. The hiss dropped to a whisper. Orella fumbled for a second patch, because one was never enough, then pulled a small sealant canister from the same pouch and thumbed it on. A bead of expanding grey gel foamed around the patch's edge, hardening as it met the vacuum gradient. Her breathing was loud in the channel now. "It'll hold pressure, as long as I don't stress that section of the suit."

"Keep cutting," Astrea said, because stopping didn't fix anything. "We can't stop now."

Mila's gaze flicked to the patch, then to Orella's oxygen readout, which was dropping slightly. A slow leak was still a leak. She handed Orella the cutter and the station groaned again, deeper this time, like something huge rolling over in its sleep.

In Mila's HUD, Orella's O_2 reserve ticked down by a fraction, and her mind ran through the options: clamp the leak tighter, swap suits, or pull back. Advising Orella to break the seal and lift her helmet was a gamble because one regulator cough could drop the corridor below safe pressure. And they'd already burned too much time. She had to trust that the patch would hold. It had to because she didn't have another option right now.

KIHM LED BROM IN THROUGH the outer cargo hatch, a blunt-edged opening that spat them out of the unpressurised bay and into the throat of a sealed service shaft. As soon as they crossed the threshold, the station's pressure met their suits, a soft push against their seals. They climbed, one rung at a time, suits rasping against pipes slick with coolant film. The emergency light strips were half-dead, leaving long runs of darkness, so Kihm toggled her HUD to infrared and the shaft resolved into crisp gradients of heat.

At the upper hatch that guarded the main control hub, she hooked a gloved hand into the recessed wheel and turned it slowly, feeling the lock dogs step back. The seal let go with a muted sigh. "Keep watch," she breathed.

Brom held position a few rungs below, weapon angled at the narrowing slice of light beyond the hatch until it widened enough for them to slip through, leaving the shaft behind.

The central control hub opened around them like a neglected organ. Coils of old conduit laced the walls in looping bundles, cable looms and junction boxes packed tight as knotted nerves. At the centre, the primary interface terminal was still operational, its status glyphs pulsing faintly as it hummed.

Kihm quickly slotted Rhen's virus cube into the access port, causing the system to pause. Lights blinked. Then the screen pulsed white. A loading bar crawled across the screen next to the port.

"Come on," she whispered.

ORELLA FINISHED THE cut and killed the torch. The plasma's hiss died, and for a beat the hatch held, stubborn on its last sliver of hinge, then the weakened locks finally gave. The hatch buckled, tipped, and dropped inward with a deep, bone-heavy thud, echoing like a warning. Orella was through the gap, weapon up, sweeping the gloom. Dust boiled out, turning the compartment into a grey haze. Shapes resolved in the murk, Oxana and Xander, hunched against the far wall, quickly pushed themselves upright.

"You came," Xander breathed.

Astrea's light raked over them, a quick scan, enough to confirm they could move. "Force-field control. Where?"

Oxana lifted a shaking hand toward the far corner. Astrea crossed to the panel and killed the grid; the faint lattice shimmer guttered and went dark. She pivoted back, sweeping the chamber. "Where are the guards?"

"Called away," Oxana said. "Not long ago."

"Where are the shamans?"

"We don't know. We were separated," Xander answered.

Mila handed the twins breathers and Z1 enviro suits. "Put these on. Now!"

Sound echoed from the hall outside, and Astrea spun, weapon drawn. Not guards. Drones. Light from twin optics flared red in the corridor, three armed units. "Contact!" she barked. "We've got company!"

BACK IN THE CENTRAL control hub, the virus upload was complete. For a heartbeat, every holo-pane went black, soundless, as if the station had stopped breathing. Then the system came back with a harsh amber emergency wash. Glyphs detonated across the primary terminal's holo panes, status lines cascading too fast to parse. Handshakes failed in rapid succession, permissions collapsed, certificates revoked, subsystems peeled away into isolation like severed limbs. Across the room, indicators flipped from green to warning to dead. Doors, comms, environmental and traffic controls dropped behind the new firewall and slammed shut. The final banner branded itself into the primary display, bright enough to hurt through a visor: ROOT CONTROL SEIZED. ACCESS OVERRIDDEN. SAFE-MODE SHUTDOWN INITIATED.

Kihm opened the comms channel. "Rhen, we've done it," she said softly.

"Copy," came his reply from the yacht.

But relief was short-lived. A deep, metallic pounding rolled down the corridor, mag boots biting the deck in a hard, accelerating cadence. The steps grew louder and closer, and the bulkheads vibrated.

Brom stiffened, raised his weapon, and sighted on the opening, holding his breath as the footfalls closed in.

Then Waylan appeared in the flesh, breather strapped tight across his face, weapon resting easy in one hand, expression almost calm. He advanced with the primary terminal between them like a judge's bench, flanked by two guards in sleek exoskeleton armour, weapons levelled at Kihm and Brom. "You know what gave you away, Kimmy K," Waylan said, voice cold, businesslike. "Not footsteps. Not cameras. My systems."

Kihm didn't move. "We came in dark."

"You did," he agreed, almost approving. "But the moment someone touched that terminal, the core node threw a cascade only the primary console can produce, failed handshakes, privilege revokes, isolation calls. My emergency protocols don't alert me for a blown fuse." His gaze slid to the holo panes, still twitching with amber warnings. "They alert me to sabotage."

Brom tightened his grip.

Waylan took another step towards them. "And when the station starts peeling itself apart, there are only two options. A fault I wrote, or an enemy at my throat. So I came to confirm which one. You could've just given me the data," he continued, eyes fixed on Kihm. "Instead, you signed the hostages' death warrant."

Kihm stood her ground. "I'd sooner destroy my life's work than watch you turn science into misery."

Waylan exhaled slowly, almost indulgent. "Your naivety is amusing. You still think ideals matter in business."

"You have no bargaining power left," she said. "The station's systems have been disabled, and others are winding down, including life support and artificial gravity in the areas that still have it."

Waylan's smile thinned. "I wrote the emergency protocols. You can't override my code."

Kihm laughed. "But we have."

That caught him, just a flicker in his eyes before it hardened. "You're bluffing."

She shook her head. "I'm not. The moment our virus hit the core node, it began unhooking your privileges. Your safeguards are eating themselves. Systems are going offline one by one."

Waylan's gaze darted, involuntarily, to the rolling status lines, and for the first time, his calm looked forced. "Shoot them!" he shouted at his guards.

Brom and Kihm ducked behind the terminal just in time.

Brom hooked a boot under a conduit brace, pushed off, and rose just enough to sight down his weapon. One clean burst caught a guard high in the shoulder, snapping him sideways and dropping him hard. A hard chirp burst from his suit, the bio-monitor flagging damage. In a place like this, a wound wasn't just blood; it was pressure. If the shot didn't take him, the leak would, once the station's oxygen bled out.

The second guard took aim but missed, hitting the terminal, which sparked and then died.

Chaos erupted, and Waylan fired, hitting a hose overhead, which discharged an unknown gas.

Brom surged forward and slammed into the remaining guard, driving him back into the bulkhead. A crackle jumped across Brom's palms, tight and controlled, causing the guard to stiffen and collapse, limp and unconscious. He then confronted Waylan, and they collided in the narrow corridor, grappling as the gravity stuttered, weightless for a beat, then heavy, each shift throwing their timing off. Fists landed in ugly, slow-motion thuds, bodies drifting and snapping back as mag-boots fought to keep them anchored.

Waylan lunged for Brom's weapon, fingers scraping for purchase.

Brom outmuscled him and slammed him into a pipe run, the metal ringing under the impact. He held Waylan there, solid and unyielding, jaw locked. He could end it with a pulse through the man's nervous system, but he didn't. Waylan deserved to stand trial, to answer for every life he'd gambled.

Waylan kicked, missed, and his leg caught hard on a pipe bracket. A loud crack cut through the space. He cried out, clutching his leg as it buckled, and he went down.

Kihm emerged from cover and pulled Waylan's breather free and sent it skidding across the deck. "Listen to me," she said softly, meeting his eyes. "I'm giving you a better chance than you gave your captives. Go back to your ship. Right now. You'll make it if you hurry."

Waylan froze, dragging in air that didn't come easily. Blood trickled from his nose and split lip. "You've already lost," Kihm said. "The station's blind. Your control's gone. And the hostages? We're getting them out. But heed my warning, we will find you and bring you to justice.

Waylan's jaw clenched. "Go to hell."

Behind them, the walls shuddered with a deep metallic groan. Gravity flickered again. The station was starting to come apart.

"FIND COVER NOW!" ASTREA shouted, shoving Xander, Oxana and Mila behind a collapsed ventilation shaft.

The lead drone barreled into the chamber with a mechanical whine, twin barrels spinning as red optics raked the room for targets. Behind it, two more rolled into formation, thick-bodied security units built for crowd control. The twins cried out. The first drone opened fire. Rounds pinged and shrieked off metal, and shrapnel and dust bloomed in the air, centimetres from their faces.

Mila wrapped her arms around the twins, jaw tight.

Astrea returned a precise burst. Sparks jumped from the lead drone's plating, only a glancing hit. The unit jerked, corrected, and snapped its barrels toward her like an animal scenting blood. "Our weapons aren't effective," she snapped to Orella. "Blow it up!"

Orella launched herself across the chamber, boots skittering on flickering gravity. For a second, she was light as a leaf, then the station lurched, and she hit hard, catching herself on the wall. She slapped an EMP charge into place with a gloved palm. "Everyone down!" The pulse detonated, white-blue light flaring through the smoke. The lead drone stuttered and dropped, twitching and smoking as its optics went dead. But the other two pressed forward, armour blackened, barrels already spinning back up.

Mila's heartbeat hammered in her throat. One drone fired again, the rounds carving the air above them with a hot, metallic scream.

"Out of charges!" Orella called. "I'll draw them away. Get everyone out!"

"No," Astrea growled, lifting her weapon for one last useless burst.

Then the drones froze. A high-pitched whine filled the room, rising until it hurt. The two units jerked violently, arms spasming, barrels drooping, collapsing like puppets with their strings cut. They hit the deck in a staggered heap, optics flashing once, twice, then going dark.

For a breath, nobody moved.

Static crackled in Astrea's comm, and Rhen's voice punched through, strained but triumphant. "The virus has fully infiltrated the central node. The station's defences are toast. You're clear, but keep your suits on, as oxygen levels are dropping dramatically and are already nonexistent in other areas."

"Acknowledged," Astrea said, letting out a harsh exhale. She and Orella rose from cover in a practised sweep, barrels up, eyes scanning, then Astrea's gaze snapped to the hostages.

"We move as soon as the twins are suited up," she barked. "Rhen, can you scan the station for more heat signatures. We haven't found the shamans yet."

"Scanning now. There are heat signatures in a compartment near the escape pod bay. I have sent directions to your HUD screen."

"Roger that," Astrea replied.

The deck shuddered under them like an earthquake. Lights flickered. Somewhere deeper in the station, an alarm stuttered, cut out, then came back in a higher pitch, angrier, closer to panic. With the twins sealed into their Z1 suits, they hit the corridor at a run. Hatches that had been sealed minutes before now hung open on half-failed servos, grinding as the station tried, and failed, to decide whether to lock down or let go. Emergency strips pulsed along the floor, guiding them toward their destination like a heartbeat counting down.

"The compartment should be two bulkheads ahead," Astrea said after checking her HUD display.

Orella took the lead and shouldered past a dangling cable that sparked against the wall.

They reached a heavy hatch marked with faded quarantine glyphs and a security band burned black by some old discharge. The access panel beside it was open like a wound, wires torn out, frost and grime inside.

Orella didn't bother with subtlety. She planted her boots, jammed her fingers into the seam, and hauled. The door partially opened, then stuck.

From inside came muffled cries.

"Mila." Astrea's voice dropped, urgent. "Now!"

Mila stepped forward and squeezed through the gap. Her headlamp swept across a barricade of overturned bunks, and, huddled beyond it, robed figures, the shamans. Visibly distressed, they stared like they didn't trust what they were seeing. One of them pushed upright, alive, but carrying injuries. Another didn't move at all. No flinch, no rise of the chest; the stillness had the final, unmistakable look of death.

Mila checked his vitals, shook her head and covered him with a thermal blanket from her kit. It was the third shaman who snapped Mila into triage. He lay on his side, one hand clamped over his abdomen. His breaths came shallow and fast, air-hunger, the kind that meant the clock was already running out. Dark blood had soaked through his robe and crusted into brittle crystals at the edges where the air was too cold. Mila dropped to her knees beside him and flicked a thin palm-sized biopatch from her kit. She slid two fingers under the collar of his robe, found the carotid, then pressed the patch to the skin. It sealed with a soft micro-suction click, and the readout ghosted into her HUD in clean, clinical glyphs, HR, SpO_2, perfusion, a jittering ECG that struggled to resolve. His pulse was thready. Too fast. "Come on," she murmured, holding steady as the biopatch auto-tuned, sampling deeper and rejecting noise, until the numbers stopped hunting and finally locked.

"How is Shaman Oldson?" the now standing shaman asked.

"How long has he been like this?" Mila didn't look up.

"An hour. Maybe more. The drones..." The shaman swallowed. "They fired when we moved. I was lucky and was only grazed," he said, lifting his blood-covered arm. She handed the medical kit to Xander. "Find a synth skin strip and place it over his wound and help him into his Z1 suit."

Xander nodded and did as instructed.

Mila pressed two fingers against Shaman Oldson's wound, feeling the heat of blood even through the suit glove. "He's bleeding internally. If we move him like this, we'll kill him."

The corridor behind them groaned, a long, metal-on-metal moan. A shower of dust drifted from the ceiling, floating lazily before gravity flickered and yanked it sideways.

Orella glanced back down the corridor, weapon up. "We don't have time, Mila."

Mila's eyes flashed. "Then make time." She searched through her med-kit with practised speed. Inside were compact injectors, coagulant foam cartridges, a thin seal patch and a pulse monitor that clung like a leech. She slapped the monitor against her patient's throat. The readout blinked angry yellow. She bit down on whatever she felt and kept her hands steady. "Shaman Oldson," she said, forcing calm into her voice as she tapped his cheek lightly. "Can you hear me? Blink if you can."

His eyelids fluttered. Once. Barely.

"That's good. Stay with me." She peeled the blood-slick fabric back enough to see the wound, a jagged puncture near the lower ribs, ugly bruising spreading like spilled ink. Mila fitted a seal patch over the wound to stop external bleed-through, then primed a coagulant injector. "This is going to burn." She drove it in.

Shaman Oldson gasped, sharply and involuntarily, then his eyes rolled and his breath caught. Mila immediately cupped his jaw, angled his head, checking his airway like it was the only thing in the universe. "Easy, easy, stay with me." She snapped a second injector, pain control and stabiliser, and pressed it into his thigh. "Come on."

Astrea was half turned, covering the corridor, but her voice cut back like a blade. "Status."

"Two minutes," Mila said without looking up. "I need the bleeding to slow and his pressure to stop crashing before we suit him up."

"Two minutes is a lifetime," Orella hissed, helping Xander get the other shaman suited up.

The station lights strobed, and for an instant, the compartment looked like a heartbeat in a dying body.

Orella's suit gave a sharp chirp. LOW OXYGEN. The readout pulsed amber against her visor.

Mila looked up at Orella. "Swap into the spare. We only need two units now."

A metallic clang rang down the corridor. Then the servos whined, like something heavy trying to wake up.

"We don't have time," Orella said. "I have enough to make it to the escape pods."

Astrea yanked the spare suit from the kit anyway and thrust it into Orella's hands. "That's not an option, it's an order."

Mila didn't look up. She was on her knees beside Shaman Oldson, gloved hands slick with blood as she worked the wound, jaw set in hard concentration.

The deck lurched. For half a heartbeat, the station went light, boots lost their bite, and bodies suddenly floated free. Mila's fingers tightened on Oldson's abdomen, but the coagulant injector slipped free and drifted from her grasp, tumbling end over end like a slow, useless comet. Oldson floated too, rising off the deck.

Oxana quickly and caught the injector.

Orella reacted without thinking, catching Shaman Oldson and hauling him down before he could drift into the overhead pipework. In the same motion, she released the spare suit.

It hung between them, weightless, turning slowly in the brief, impossible calm, then gravity slammed back.

The suit struck the pipe run with a sickening crack. The visor spiderwebbed. A seam along the shoulder split with a faint hiss and whatever air it held bled out. "No time. And now no spare," Orella said, voice tight but controlled.

Oxana crouched beside Mila and handed her the injector. Lowering her voice, she asked, "How can I help?"

"Hold this pressure point," Mila said, guiding her gloved fingers just above the wound. "Firm. Don't let go unless I tell you."

Oxana did as ordered, face pale but steady, while the others looked on anxiously.

Mila inserted the injector nozzle at the wound edge with careful precision. "If this seals wrong, he won't breathe right," she murmured, more to herself than anyone, then injected. The foam expanded beneath the patch in a controlled bloom, locking like a plug. Mila let out a breath she didn't realise she'd been holding. "Okay, his pressure is normalising."

Shaman Oldson's breathing eased from frantic to merely shallow. He blinked again.

Mila leaned close so he could hear her through the chaos. "We're getting you out. Do you understand? Nod if you understand."

A tiny nod.

Mila issued a quick order. "I'll need everyone's help to get him suited up."

Once he was ready, she yanked a collapsible sling harness meant for zero-gravity patient transport, then snapped it open. "We slide him. Slow. Keep him level."

The station lurched again, harder this time. A light strip overhead popped and went dark. The emergency alarm cut out mid-wail and returned as a rapid, chopping stutter, as if the station itself were hyperventilating.

"We move. Now!" Astrea barked.

Although they settled the shaman into the sling, slow and deliberate, a low, guttural sound tore out of him. Mila slid her fingers into his and closed once, firm and certain.

They moved as a unit, Astrea leading, Orella guarding the rear, Oxana and Xander steadying the sling, while Mila maintained her position at the shaman's head, her gaze locked on the vitals crawling across her HUD. The second shaman was right behind her, catching himself when the gravity field flickered, his breath rasping as he fought to keep pace.

Twice the station's rotation made the corridor pitch and the sling nearly tore free. Twice Mila snapped, "Hold, hold," and they braced, boots planted, hands locked on straps and rails, waiting until the gravity steadied beneath them again.

After rounding the next corner, the corridor opened into a longer run. Far ahead, a direction board hung canted from the ceiling, its light panels blinking: EMERGENCY POD BAY, uneven pulses and half-lit letters above a thin arrow pointing deeper into the station.

Astrea glanced back at Mila. "In my assessment, Rhen's virus has unlocked the station one breath ahead of collapse," she said grimly. "Let's not waste it." With weapon raised, shoulders tight, she cut through the darkness in controlled arcs with her headlamp.

Mila tightened her grip on the shaman's hand. "We'll make it," she said, and it landed less like hope and more like a dare aimed at the station itself. Then her HUD flashed, ORELLA, O_2 CRITICAL, 2%. Mila's jaw set. It would have to be enough.

The passage pinched down to a throat of metal, and the solid deck gave way to open grating and a long, narrow suspended walkway stitched between two sections of Orphis-8, with nothing under it but a lightless void, swallowing the glow from their headlamps. Pipes and cable trays choked the bulkheads, their runs filmed with frozen condensation. Every footfall trembled through the grating. Beneath was only darkness, a drop they couldn't measure, and from somewhere down in that unseen depth the station's machinery clattered and groaned.

In the rear, Orella's head tracked every shadow behind them. Her suit's air tasted thin, metallic. Too sweet. Too wrong. She sucked in a breath and felt it catch, a shallow snag that made her chest burn. A warning chirp rasped in her ear, soft, insistent. She didn't need to look. She could feel the countdown in the dryness of her throat, in the slow thickening of her thoughts. "Keep moving. Just keep moving," she said to herself.

Up ahead, a metallic clang echoed through the station and Astrea held up a fist. They halted just as the station shifted and the gravity dropped out again. Astrea snapped her free hand to an overhead conduit run, anchoring herself, weapon primed.

Orella stopped too, a beat late. She swallowed, trying to clear her head. The edges of her vision were slightly blurred. Everything loosened. Boots lost bite.

The sling rose, and Oldson drifted with it, straps tightening as he lifted toward the cable tray. Xander and Oxana reacted instantly, hauling on the stabiliser lines to keep him centred.

Mila clamped onto the railing with one hand and her med-case with the other, face a hard mask of concentration.

Orella reached for an overhead handhold and missed. Her fingers brushed air. For a fraction of a second, she floated, weightless and stupidly surprised, as if the station had tricked her. The walkway tilted. The bulkhead drifted toward her shoulder. Her mind ran a step behind her body, slow and syrupy. Then gravity slammed back. Orella hit the metal grating hard enough to rattle her teeth. Pain shot up her forearm.

The impact yanked Mila's med-case clean out of her grip. It struck the grating, bounced, skittered, then clipped the edge where the walkway met the bulkhead and dropped through into the lightless void. "No!" Mila screamed, head snapping around. "That's not bandages, it's Oldson's lifeline if he crashes."

Orella lunged, glove scraping at empty metal as the med-case vanished into the shadowed depths.

Oldson's breathing turned ragged, shallow and fast, and Astrea pivoted just enough to glance back, eyes hard. "Move. We don't stop." A shudder ran through the grating like a warning.

Orella shoved herself upright, the aftershock of the fall still buzzing. Her readout flashed again. 1%. She looked down where the med-case had disappeared, but couldn't see it. "I'll get the kit," she said, already stepping back.

Astrea's voice cracked through comms, sharp as a blade. "Orella. No. It's gone. Keep moving," she snapped, forcing steel into her voice. "That's an order."

Mila's stomach tightened. She should not have said anything. Orella was already running on fumes, and the last thing Mila needed was for her to stop to search for a kit that was long gone.

Orella hesitated, the order landing somewhere in her skull and sliding off. Behind them, the dim service lights flickered, and for a heartbeat she thought she saw movement, something mechanical shifting in the dark. She forced her gaze forward.

"Xander," Mila said, swallowing panic, "hold pressure. Oxana, keep him level. Don't let the sling tilt."

They moved again, faster now, urgency dragging them toward the escape-pod bay sign blinking ahead.

Orella's breath came shallow and fast. Somewhere deep inside her suit, the oxygen warning chirped with patient certainty. She tightened her grip on the railing until her knuckles ached, because her body was starting to betray her, one missed handhold at a time.

Mila turned back, watching as Orella slowed and her head turned in small jerks. Mila knew her well-being was deteriorating at a rapid rate. At least the gravity held, for now. "Orella needs help, Astrea."

"Pods. Now," Astrea said, clipped. Her helmet turned a fraction. Her HUD kept a constant stack of icons in the corner: heart rates, suit seals, and oxygen. Orella's readout pulsed amber in her peripheral: <1%. Astrea's voice sharpened. "Orella. Move."

Below them was nothing but a hard black drop. Orella's low oxygen warning flashed again, the numbers stuttering, the timer bleeding down, and the edges of her vision began to bloom with light that wasn't there. For a moment, she thought she saw the med-case, sitting impossibly on a strut under the walkway's grating, clean and bright as a beacon, its latch light winking at her like an invitation. She blinked. The image smeared, doubled, then snapped away, leaving only cold metal and distance. Orella swung a leg over the railing and eased her weight onto the far side, boots finding a narrow maintenance rung beneath the suspended walkway.

"Orella," Astrea snapped. "Stay where you are. I'm coming to get you. The rest of you, keep moving."

Orella's breathing boomed in her helmet, wet, rasping, each inhale loud enough to drown out the station's distant groans. She faintly heard Astrea's shouted instructions, but they seemed to fade into the distance. The edges of her vision cinched tight, like the world was being pulled through a slit. Her HUD flashed OXYGEN LOW, and the warning chirp accelerated. She let go with one hand and reached for the next lower hold. Her glove skated over cold metal. Scraped. Missed. Her fingers closed on nothing. Orella's mouth opened, an instinctive, silent bark. And then she disappeared into the abyss.

"Orella!" Astrea pushed past the others and leaned over the railing at the point where Orella had disappeared. Her HUD flicked a new warning against Orella's icon: SUIT INTEGRITY ZERO.

Instead of moving forward, the others looked back in horror.

"All of you keep moving!" Astrea hit the grating on one knee as Orella's vitals spiked, an ugly flutter, and dropped. A flat, unwavering line replaced her heart-rate trace. Astrea's stomach went cold. "No!" The comms filled with her own breathing now, loud and sudden. "Orella," she said, voice low, desperate, useless against a station with no air.

Ahead, the pod bay hatch beckoned like a throat of light. Xander and Oxana wrestled it open and hauled the sling through, Mila and the second shaman tight behind.

The station lights flickered. Astrea forced herself upright and followed them into the escape pod bay. Her gaze snapped to the access panel. "Three pods operational," she muttered into comms. "Each holds three."

She shoved Oxana, Xander, and the ambulant shaman into the first pod, sealed the hatch with a hard slap, and hit launch. The cradle kicked, and the pod vanished into the black. "Rhen, one pod is away, two more to go."

"Roger," he replied.

Astrea keyed her comm. "Brom. Kihm. Status. We have one pod ready for you." Static clawed the line.

Then Brom came through, ragged, strained, alive. "Copy. Don't wait for us."

Astrea's jaw set. "Where are you?"

"Not making the bay," Brom said. "Bulkhead dropped. Corridor's gone. We've got another exit. Rhen will pick us up."

Astrea's throat tightened around everything she wanted to say. "Copy." She turned to Mila. "We're next. Move."

Mila slid Shaman Oldson into the second pod, one hand braced on the sling, the other on his shoulder. Her head snapped up. "Why aren't we waiting for Brom and Kihm?"

Astrea didn't look away from the bay. "Get in."

Mila's throat tightened. "No, Astrea, we can't leave without them."

Astrea's voice cut through her like a blade. "Get. In. Look after your patient. Brom and Kihm are finding another way out."

For a heartbeat, Mila looked as if she might argue, then the station groaned, the lights stuttered, and gravity hiccupped hard enough to make the sling jerk in her hands. Oldson gave a faint, pained sound, and Mila swallowed her protest, climbing in with her jaw clenched, eyes flicking once toward the bay.

Astrea set the launch delay to thirty seconds, enough to seal the hatch and lock herself in. A deep groan rolled through the walls as gravity failed. Dust and loose tools lifted, drifting as the station lurched and began shedding hull plating into orbit.

With seconds to spare, the pod fired, ripping free as the pod bay buckled and the wall panels sheared loose.

WAYLAN COUGHED AS SMOKE rolled through the shattered corridor in thick, chemical coils. The emergency strips strobed red, then guttered out, broken only by the occasional flare of a dying indicator panel. The air was thin and laced with burnt metal and other chemicals. Each inhale left a bitter film on his tongue. Somewhere deeper in the station, the structure groaned, a slow, stressed complaint that travelled through the metal deck plates into his mag boots. He lurched through the failing bulkhead, his collar soaked where blood had pooled and then cooled. Pain flickered white behind his eyes, trying to narrow his world down to his injured leg. Still, the station refused to let him forget the hiss of venting air, the intermittent chirp of overload alarms and the distant rattle of unsecured items skittering along a sloped deck. He wished he had searched for the breather Kimmy K discarded, but his injured leg screamed every time he put weight on it. He coughed again, violently. Each gasp for air rasped like gravel through his throat, shallow and unsatisfying, as if his lungs were pulling on empty. His next breath snagged, stuttered, then arrived in a thin thread that made his chest burn.

Waylan forced himself onward anyway, one hand on the wall to keep his bearings as the corridor subtly tilted. In the half-light, soot drifted like ash-snow, settling on him and the exposed edges of cable bundles where the wall panels had peeled back. Overhead, a conduit arced once, then went dead. The darkness thickened, and with it the sense of the station closing around him, a failing structure rationing its last seconds of air.

"Station integrity... compromised..." The automated annunciator tried to sound calm, but the voice fractured into static through a blown ceiling speaker. A second later, the feed died with a soft pop.

Waylan slapped his palm against the nearest utility interface, and it flared a sickly blue, threw up half-rendered glyphs, and then collapsed into a flicker. He jammed his thumb into the manual override recess and felt only dead resistance. Nothing. Systems were gone. Power had been stripped down to whatever the emergency spine could still drag along the conduit. He toggled his comm. Silence. No carrier tone, no handshake, just a hollow hiss that cut out mid-breath. He tried again on a different band, pilot channel, station mesh, and hardline ping, but each attempt returned the same blank refusal. Comms were dark.

The virus was eating the station from the inside out, crawling through control loops and diagnostics like rot, rewriting permissions, choking the subsystems that kept the station operational and the air contained. The corridor lurched. Somewhere deeper in the superstructure, something heavy tore free.

Waylan stumbled, then went down hard as the metal deck beneath him kicked. No longer a stable structure, but a stressed spine flexing under collapse. He pushed up on trembling arms, chest hitching. Above, a ruptured junction box spat sparks, each burst painting the smoke ghost-blue. His nostrils burned with the smell of scorched insulation and overheated coolant.

He dragged himself onward and scraped past a cracked viewport. Through the fractured glass, escape pods flared and streaked away in arcing lines, tiny bright bullets swallowed by the dark like shooting stars.

Ahead, the corridor pinched into a suspended walkway with open grating, narrow rails and nothing but a vast black drop beneath. One wrong step and there was no "down" to hit, just the station's hollow interior falling away into void and shadow. Waylan's mag boots rang on the metal as he lurched forward, trying not to look through the gaps. Then he saw it, his ship peeling cleanly from the docking arm in a practised roll, thrusters snapping in short corrective bursts. It canted on its axis, nose swinging planetward, away from him, away from the dying station. "No," Waylan wheezed, the word ripped out of him. He shouldn't have wasted time trying to bring the station back online. He should have headed straight for his ship.

A low groan rolled through the walkway structure, and it tilted a fraction. Something heavy shifted overhead, conduit and plating letting go with a loud crack. Waylan flinched, throwing an arm over his head.

The station groaned again. Heat chased along the bulkheads; flames licked at seams and cable runs. Somewhere to his left, deck plating peeled back like a lid, and the walkway suddenly felt thinner, more exposed, its grating framed against raw darkness as the void yawned wider beyond.

BROM SLAMMED THE HATCH as the corridor beyond filled with smoke. "I hope you have a plan, Kihm." Brom's voice came through the suit mic, clipped and harsh. "Because the station might become our coffin."

"Yeah." Kihm's HUD glitched, then stabilised long enough to show a schematic featuring hazard blooms, and pressure loss zones strobing angry red. "EVA service lock. One deck down. Legacy manual crank. It'll be hard-vac on the far side, but it exits to the outer hull." She snapped open a tight-beam channel. "Rhen, do you copy?"

Yes, go ahead."

"Brom and I are egressing via the EVA lock. Can you retrieve?

Rhen's reply hit with a burst of static, then cleared. "Yes"

"What about the others?"

"Disembarking now."

“See you soon, Rhen, “Kihm said.

Brom didn’t waste another breath. “Move.”

They dropped back into the service shaft, sliding past smouldering conduit and torn cabling that spat sparks when the station bucked. The lower deck was half-breached, gravity intermittent, air already gone, ice crystals glittering where vapour had flash-frozen on the metal. The EVA lock hatch was scarred but intact. A manual wheel sat at its centre like a relic.

Brom’s hands slipped once on the icy grip, then caught. The mechanism fought him, sticky and grinding, until the dogs clunked free.

The seal let go with a dull thunk, then the hatch jerked outward, and the compartment dumped its breath into space. Air screamed past them in one savage rush, dragging frost, dust and loose fragments toward the opening. Brom locked his arm through the rail and held until the pull eased.

“Set your suit thrusters to low,” Kihm said over comms. “Careful not to overshoot.”

They pushed out into open black, using controlled micro-bursts to steady themselves. Behind them, the station loomed, venting fire and atmosphere in strobing jets, its spin no longer true but broken into a slow, sick wobble.

Kihm keyed her comm again, voice tight. “Rhen, we’re exterior. Forward service lock. No pods. Oxygen low.”

“I’m tracking your transponder ping,” Rhen said. “Hold position. Coming in hot.” Rhen cut in from the asteroid belt, hull shimmering under maneuvering thrust, hunting gaps and using micro-adjustments around debris. The ship’s belly hatch irised open, and a ventral capture arm unfolded, deploying a magnetic tether rig.

Kihm’s oxygen warning flared red across her visor, the alarm shrilling in her ears. “Two minutes,” she said.

Brom's voice slashed across comms. "Contact, behind you, moving fast!"

Kihm twisted. A slab of station plating cartwheeled out of the dark, edge-on and closing hard, a jagged strip of metal spinning straight through their line.

"Don't burn!" Rhen snapped. "Hold position!"

Kihm froze on instinct, every muscle screaming to fire thrusters. The plating tore past so close she saw frost and scorched paint flashing along its edge, felt the wake of its passage jolt her suit.

"Now. Firing tether." The line punched out in a clean arc.

Kihm snatched it, hauled it in, and slammed it onto her suit's hardpoint with a metallic clack. "Tether secure. Brom, lock in." Nothing. She turned.

Brom was drifting, slow-spinning, a dark ribbon of blood curling from his shoulder like smoke in zero-gravity. His oxygen readout on her HUD fell in brutal steps. "Brom. Look at me." Her voice was raw. No response. Kihm burned her thrusters hard, grabbed him, and clipped the tether straight into his chestplate mount, her hands shaking. "Rhen, we're tethered. Brom's been hit and is in trouble. Have Mila Ready to administer first aid. Pull us in now!"

"Copy," Rhen replied.

Brom's eyes were unfocused. Kihm bared her teeth. "Don't you quit on me now, bro." His fingers twitched once as the winch whined, and the line snapped taut, jerking them toward the ship. Behind them, the station tore itself open as metal peeled back violently, and venting atmosphere turned debris into bullets. More shrapnel skated close enough to make her flinch. A jagged chunk knifed through the dark and missed her boot by a handspan just as they breached the iris before it closed behind them. Air hissed back in. Pressure climbed.

Astrea laid Brom on the deck plates and ripped his helmet free. "He's not breathing!"

Mila knelt and placed fingers on his neck, nothing in his chest. She snapped a triage patch onto his throat; vitals crawled onto her wrist display in harsh white lines: oxygen gone, carbon dioxide collapsing. "Airway." She jaw-thrusted, swept suction once, and drove a supraglottic airway home. The resus unit clicked into place and began delivering pure oxygen in measured bursts. The capnography trace twitched, then flattened, then stuttered. "Come on, you stubborn man, she urged, voice breaking despite her training, "you can't abandon the fight now."

A stim patch affixed to the notch above his collarbone started firing timed phrenic pulses. Brom's diaphragm jumped as if a wire had yanked it. His chest rose. He coughed and dragged in a ragged breath like it hurt to be alive. "Took..." he rasped, eyes fluttering, "...your time."

Mila let out a single hard laugh, more shake than sound. "You're welcome." She wiped sweat off her brow with the back of her wrist. "That cost me several years."

Kihm slid back against the bulkhead, visor up, voice dry and wrecked. "Let's never do that again."

Brom managed a breathless laugh.

Through the yacht's portholes, Orphis-8 didn't explode; it unravelled. Plates sheared off in slow, violent movements, lights blinked out in ragged patches as the ring's rotation stuttered and broke. Debris spread into a widening halo, glinting like razor confetti. No one spoke.

Mila pressed her palm to the glass.

Astrea stared, jaw clenched hard enough to ache. When a larger section tore free and flared bright, she whispered Orella's name like it could pull her back. They watched while the station tore itself apart and scattered across the starfield.

THE YACHT'S MED-BAY smelled of antiseptic, clean in a way the rest of the ship never managed after an emergency. It was bright and orderly, a stark rebuttal to the chaos still ringing in their ears.

Brom sat on the edge of the second medbed with his boots planted wide. His breathing had finally slowed, but now and then his chest caught on a shallow inhale, a reflex from those last thin, desperate gulps outside the station. His bare shoulder was streaked with dried blood. The bruise around the injury was already blooming dark and ugly, the kind that would ache for days.

Mila's hands were steady in a way that didn't match the faint tremor she tried to mask. A tray of med tools sat beside her, containing sealant ampoules, a field stapler, a micro-suture wand, and a synth skin patch. "Hold still," she said, voice calm by discipline rather than ease. "Otherwise, I'll sedate you as I have Shaman Oldson."

"I am trying," Brom answered, but his jaw tightened when she pressed the wound. "But you're very distracting up close."

"This was nearly arterial. You're lucky."

He let out a quiet breath that was almost a laugh, except there wasn't much humour left in it. "I noticed."

The ship's systems hummed around them. Safe sounds. Normal sounds. They should have been comforting. Instead, the memories of his close call were still fresh.

Mila's hands were still clinical on his skin, checking, sealing, measuring damage, but her breathing was not. "You scared me," she said, and the honesty landed like a blow. Her fingers paused for a fraction of a second at the edge of the wound. She looked up at him, and the mask of calm slipped just enough to show what sat behind it. "I thought you were gone," she said quietly.

Brom's fingers closed around her wrist, stopping her, not hurting, just stopping. "You care about me," he murmured.

"What?"

"You care about me," he said, and the quiet brutality of it stripped the room bare.

Mila's mouth parted, and for once she didn't deflect. She leaned in and kissed him like a decision, like a promise, like she was done pretending she could leave this untouched.

Brom's throat worked. He stared past her at Shaman Oldson, lying in the adjacent medbed, then he met her eyes.

Mila swallowed, then nodded once. Her eyes dropped back to her work, but her hands had become even more careful. The suture wand warmed, a thin blue arc sealing tissue in neat, efficient passes. The field gel followed, cool against his skin, numbing the edges while it knitted. Mila's touch didn't waver. "You need to rest," she said, returning to the armour of practicality. "Sleep."

"Can't," Brom replied. "I have too much to do. Patch me up so I can keep going."

"Great. I'll add it to the chart, 'Patient insists on continuing to be an idiot, medically unsupported.'"

Brom's gaze tracked her face, the smudge of soot at her temple, the faint tremor in her eyelashes when she blinked too slowly. She'd been close enough to death herself in that decaying space station. She wore bravery like she wore everything else, tight and deliberate, as if it might keep the seams from splitting.

"You're hurt," he said.

"I'm not," Mila lied automatically.

Brom's mouth twisted. "Your knuckles are split. Your wrist is swollen."

Mila glanced down as if the injuries were new information. She flexed her hand once, and pain flashed across her expression before she could hide it.

"It's nothing," she insisted, and then, softer, as if conceding more than she meant to: "I didn't feel the pain until you mentioned it."

"Adrenaline," Brom said. His voice was gentler than it had been in the corridors. "It's a liar."

Mila pressed the synth skin against his shoulder with a firm, professional press that lingered a half-second too long. In the quiet, the reality of being alive finally had room to land. Mila stepped back to assess her work. "That should hold. No infection. No further bleeding." She picked up a small injector, hesitated, then met his eyes again. "Pain control?"

Brom shook his head. "No."

"Silly question," she muttered.

"Functional," he corrected, but his gaze softened. "If I take anything that dulls me, and something goes wrong again..."

Mila's expression tightened at the word 'again'. She set the injector down with more force than necessary. "Something always goes wrong. That's not a reason to risk your wellbeing."

He looked away, jaw working. For a moment, she thought he wouldn't say what was beneath it. Then he did.

"You and Rhen..." Brom began.

Mila's shoulders went still. She didn't move, didn't reach for another tool, as if any motion might interrupt what he was trying to force through his own restraint.

"What about us?" she asked.

Brom's fingers flexed against the edge of the bed. "You don't have to keep doing this."

Mila's eyes narrowed, not with anger, but with the sharpness of someone hearing the edge of a goodbye coming toward her. "Doing what, exactly? Helping you not bleed out?"

He huffed a breath that was not quite a laugh. "You know what I mean."

"I don't," Mila said. "Say it."

Brom's gaze flicked to her mouth, then away, like the thought of losing her made him physically ill. "This isn't your fight," he said at last, the words blunt but dragged out of him like shrapnel. "It never should've been. You and Rhen should return to Rotari."

Mila stared at him. The medical bay's light caught the fine lines of fatigue at the corners of her eyes, and suddenly she looked older, not in years, but in the way war accelerated time.

"And what?" she said softly. "Leave you to die alone in your noble crusade?"

"That's not what I mean," Brom said, exhaling slowly. "I'm trying to keep you alive."

Mila took one step closer. Her voice lowered, dangerous in its quiet honesty. "No. We are in this together."

Brom's throat tightened. "Mila..."

"I watched you almost die," she said, the words coming faster now, the restraint cracking. "I watched the station tear itself apart behind you. I watched debris pass so close I felt it, and I could not..." She broke off and pressed two fingers to her own sternum as if she could force the feeling back down. "I could not do anything but watch and hope that you would get out alive."

Brom's expression changed. The leader, the stubborn survivor, everything that kept him upright, faltered when he saw the raw fear she'd been carrying since the moment they'd made it inside.

"I didn't want you on this mission," he admitted, voice rough. "I didn't want you anywhere near this."

"You don't get to decide that for me," Mila said, and it wasn't sharp. It was tired. Honest. "Not when you're the reason I'm here."

Brom's brow furrowed. "I'm not..."

"You are," she cut in. Her eyes shone, but she wouldn't let tears fall. "And I still don't know what this is," she said quietly, the words landing between them like a live wire. She lifted a hand, not at the station, but at the space between their bodies, at everything unspoken, unfinished.

Brom stared at her as if the med-bay had tilted and he hadn't noticed. His voice came out low. "That's not fair."

Mila's laugh was a brittle thing. "None of this is fair."

Brom's hand lifted, hesitated, then found her wrist, careful of the swelling, his touch feather-light, like he was afraid she might vanish. The contact felt like an admission, quiet and irreversible.

Mila's breath caught, not from pain, but from the way his thumb hovered, then stilled, as if he could feel her pulse and everything it was trying to say.

He swallowed once, and when he spoke, his voice was barely there. "To be honest. I don't know what this is either." The words hung between them, fragile as frost. Outside the viewport, reflected running lights flickered across the med-bay glass and over his face, turning his expression briefly unguarded, then gone again. He started to say more, to pin it down with the kind of certainty he used like armour, but the sentence collapsed. He let the air out slowly, still holding her wrist like it was the only steady thing left.

Mila stayed utterly still, unable to move or speak. Her breath caught. The ship's hum filled the space where words failed. She covered his hand with hers, not pulling away.

Brom closed his eyes for a beat. When he opened them, his voice came out rough. "I want you to go home." The lie sat between them, sharp and immediate. He cleared his throat. "Correction. I should want you to go home."

Mila leaned in until she was close enough that she could feel the warmth of his breath. "But you don't."

Brom's jaw tightened. "No."

Mila's gaze dropped to his lips, then back to his eyes as if asking a question she didn't trust herself to speak.

Brom answered without words. He rose just slightly from the medbed, careful of his injuries. His hand slid from her wrist to her hip, careful of bruises, but not careful of wanting.

Mila felt it, the restraint, the promise, and her breath caught like she had run out of air.

The kiss was not hurried. Not reckless. It was the kind of kiss two survivors gave when they were still shaking inside, gentle at first, testing that this was real and that they were both still alive. Mila's fingers slid up to the back of his neck, into the edge of his hairline, and she held him like she was anchoring herself to the one solid thing left in the universe.

Brom's hand moved back to her wrist, thumb brushing the pulse there, as if he needed proof.

When they parted, it was only by a breath. Mila rested her forehead against his. "I can't promise anything," she whispered.

Brom's laugh was quiet and pained. "Me either."

Mila's eyes closed. "If we had met anywhere else..."

"If the air didn't keep running out and people weren't always trying to kill us," Brom murmured, finishing the thought with a faint smile.

She drew back and laughed, breaking the tension of the moment.

Then the ship's intercom cracked once, a muted tone. A status chime. Reality knocking. They needed to strap in for landing.

Mila exhaled slowly, then straightened, resting her hands on his shoulders for a final second before she stepped back into the role the situation demanded. "You're going to drink water, and you're going to sit down and let your body catch up."

Brom watched her, the faintest smile threatening at the corner of his mouth.

"And you?" he asked quietly.

Mila glanced down at her split knuckles, then back at him. Her answer was soft, but absolute.

"I'm still here.

CHAPTER 17

The following night, the mission to bring down Atmos surged back into motion. Brom, Mila, Kihm, Rhen, Xander, Astrea and her pilots boarded the yacht. Serin acted as pilot, and Ondra, Naella, Vena, and Lira would fly the Atmos modules after they separated. Liora, a munitions expert, would hit the geothermal plant.

They ran silent pre-checks as the cloaking field engaged, erasing them from the sky. Mila's knee brushed Brom's once, then stayed there, deliberate, as if she needed the contact more than she needed space. "No heroics on this mission, Brom."

He clasped her hand in his and let out a breath that tried to be a laugh. "Wouldn't dream of it," he said, but it came out rougher than he meant.

With Oxana and the rest of the family secured, Brom had fewer distractions, except Xander. The boy was the one variable he could not control. Xander had spent hours believing he had signed Brom's death warrant. Brom had expected distance and defensiveness. Instead, once they were off Orphis-8 and Brom rejoined the crew, Xander had thrown his arms around him, shaking, tears running unchecked down his face.

It had nearly broken something in Brom's chest, and confirmed his fear in the same breath. Guilt did not make Xander cautious; it made him reckless. A boy trying to atone could get himself killed faster than any enemy could.

Xander had briefed them that Novak intended to seal the maintenance tunnel and flood the crawlers with a fast-acting sedative gas, enough to incapacitate them within moments and potentially kill at higher concentrations or with extended exposure. If he triggered it, their approach was dead. Xander insisted he could make the changes while Novak was out of Central Control, before he had any reason to suspect a problem. If Novak caught him, he had a cover ready. Practice. He'd say he'd misplaced his comms unit, technically true after Waylan confiscated it, and claim he was staying close in case instructions came through. From what Waylan had said, he had kept the Orphis-8 play tight. Prem had been ordered to stay in the cockpit, which meant he must have sensed something was off, but he did not have the plan. As a result, they concluded that Novak was still oblivious to what had transpired. It gave Xander a narrow window to access the system long enough to sever the control feed before the team committed to the tunnel.

Brom understood the logic, but he hated what it cost to accept it. Unfortunately, it was the only way to infiltrate the top levels of Atmos after they destroyed the geothermal power plant. Mila was his other worry. She wanted to be onboard to treat the injured. As though she had heard his private thoughts, Mila leaned in closer."You good?" she murmured.

"I will be when this is over," Brom replied, and forced his gaze forward before it gave them away.

The yacht ghosted across the landscape and settled at the edge of the lake surrounding Atmos without a ripple out of place. They silently disembarked, as if sound alone could betray them. Out on the black water, Atmos rose from the centre of the lake, its central column punching through the night sky like a beacon. Bands of coloured light climbed the stem in segmented runs of teal, amber and violet. Near the top, a bright hub-and-spoke ring churned with traffic beneath the main city overhead, shuttles slipping in and out on tight approach lines, their strobes flashing white and red as they docked and peeled away again. Every pulse, every rotation, every flicker spilled down onto the lake, turning the dark surface into a living mirror, broken into shards of silver and neon.

Already sealed into their submersion suits, they lifted their helmets and locked them onto the neck rings with a precise quarter-turn. The seals took with muted hisses as the collars pressurised, then the visors cleared, and HUD glyphs bloomed to life across the glass: O_2 mix, heart rate, comms, depth readouts queued and waiting, and a tight nav overlay. On land, the suits defaulted to surface mode, drawing ambient air through a filtered, temperature-balanced loop so they could breathe normally while fully sealed.

At Rhen's signal, they engaged dive mode using their wrist devices, activating microvalves that sealed the air intake and tightened the suit's loop. Their HUD overlays were reshuffled, so pressure and dissolved O_2 capture were front and centre on their displays. The "breather" wasn't a mouthpiece at all, but a compact life-support module integrated into the helmet's jawline: membrane-lung stacks ready to strip oxygen from the water the instant the immersion sensors tripped. No bubbles. No noise. Just a seamless switch from breathing the night air to breathing the lake.

Everyone ran final checks on seal integrity, pressure valves, comms, and drone links. Nods passed down the line. One by one, they dropped into the black water. The cold closed over them like a fist.

Mila's breath hitched once, then steadied.

Brom caught her gloved hand and clipped her tether to his own with a practised snap, as if the whole act was procedural. In his headset, he said, "Stay on me."

She answered, "Try to lose me," and the challenge in her voice warmed him more than the suit temperature controls ever could.

Rhen released the submersible drones first. Their surfaces shimmered as adaptive camouflage rippled into place, sampling the lake's colour until each unit blended seamlessly. To keep Atmos's underwater sensor net blind, he brought an electromagnetic dampening field online. A soft, broad-spectrum hush that smudged their signatures and made both drones and divers register as background noise.

On his datapad, the lakebed appeared as a clean grid which the drones swept in disciplined passes, stitching together a map. Seconds later, a highlight flared. A maintenance hatch, human-width, exposed, and unprotected, sitting on the lake bed's silt line like an invitation.

Rhen and Astrea led, followed by her five-person team and Brom, Mila, Kihm, and Xander. They moved in a tight, disciplined rhythm, riding the drones' wake until the maintenance hatch came into view. Rhen pinged the machines with a return protocol, and the drones peeled away, arrowing back toward the yacht, leaving the team alone.

Rhen brought up a micro-laser cutter and traced a clean, controlled ring around the hatch's access panel. The beam ate through the fasteners, spoofing the sensor mesh and crippling the internal locks without tripping a hard alarm. Then he clipped a compact field projector to the hatch collar. A shimmering oval snapped into place, an airtight pocket that held pressure and treated water like an intruder. The projector engaged a micro-compressor and reserve cartridge, bleeding gas into the envelope as the field shaped it, until the pocket swelled outward from the metal like a clear, taut blister anchored to the lakebed, big enough to admit the group and keep the lake out.

Satisfied it was holding, he removed his helmet and fins and motioned the others forward. One by one, they pressed through the field's skin, firm like gel, tingling as it read their mass, then spilled into dry air. The boundary flexed and then sealed behind each entry. With everyone tucked inside the air pocket and helmets twisted free,

Rhen kept his voice low, more breath than sound in the cramped, pressurised space. "The projector has a five-minute power window and air supply, so we need to be quick." He cracked the unlocked hatch, and they filed into the access tube.

As the last one through, Brom yanked the hatch closed and dogged it down, bracing there until Rhen killed the field and the inner seal bit, solid and dry.

Beyond, the maintenance tube ran into the gloom, a utilitarian space just tall enough to walk upright. They pushed hard through it, boots hammering on the grating, until the passage ended with a final hatch.

Before opening it, Rhen swept the compact control room through the viewport with his scanner. Empty. He cracked the hatch.

In the far corner, they found a storage cupboard and peeled out of their dive suits.

Brom steadied Mila by the shoulders and helped her work the seals, his gloved hands lingering a fraction longer than necessary before he forced them away.

Underneath were dry clothes chosen to pass a casual glance inside Atmos. Suits were rolled tight, stacked deep, and concealed with the kind of care that came from knowing a single stray strap could alert security.

As the last suit vanished into the cupboard, Xander checked his wrist display. Crawler route schematic. Gas manifold icon pulsing like a warning. He met Brom's eyes. No debate. This was why he'd insisted on coming.

Astrea's gaze flicked over him before she tipped her chin toward Ondra, one of her module-pilots, lean and hard-eyed, with the quiet stillness of someone who didn't waste motion. "With him," Astrea said. "Clean shadow."

Rhen handed Ondra a short-range EMP scrambler, tuned to fog cameras and proximity sensors, just long enough to walk through a blind spot, leaving only a blur on the security footage. "Our comms are very short range, so once you are on your way to the top of Atmos, you will be on your own."

Ondra's eyes met Xander's for a beat. No reassurance. From this point, she considered him a soldier.

Xander nodded once.

Brom stepped in front of him before he could move and pulled him into a hard and fierce hug. A gesture that said everything he wasn't going to risk saying out loud. Brom eased back just enough to meet his eyes. "You get up there. You do what you have to do. And you stay alive. Understood?"

Xander swallowed. "Yeah."

Brom's grip tightened once on his shoulder. "I'm proud of you. Good luck, Xander." He didn't want to place the boy in danger, but his participation could mean the difference between success and failure.

A faint smile flickered across Xander's face, more tension than humour, before he and Ondra slipped out ahead of the others, folding into the hangar's night flow. The space reeked of coolant and old metal, and the lighting was dim because only a skeleton crew worked the night shift. They moved with confidence, making their way to the central hub, where the vac lifts stood in a row of matte-black doors. Xander stepped to the access pillar and leaned in. The iris scanner swept him in a thin band of light, and a soft chime sounded. Green. Confirmation. The lift accepted his clearance without hesitation.

Ondra's posture didn't shift, but her gaze sharpened. She had anticipated a challenge response. Instead, the doors cycled open. As they crossed the threshold, Rhen's tech ensured that the surveillance grid resolved only Xander's biometric signature. As they ascended, they felt a low-frequency vibration through the deck plates and a faint hiss of pressure equalisation through the cabin vents.

Xander watched the floor indicator scroll past sectors, maintenance tiers, service rings, hub levels, each one a chance for something to go wrong. He wasn't an expert, just a teenager with an ego that could lead to a mistake.

When the lift finally locked into position, the doors opened onto a seamless graphite corridor, its air scrubbers whispering through hidden vents. Light bled from recessed tracer lines in the walls and floor, guiding the way with a cool, regulated glow.

Ondra emerged first, then immediately melted into the hall's geometry, scanning for cameras, security patrols, and the quiet tells of a system paying attention. Ondra whispered to Xander, "I'm giving you two minutes to disable the systems. Your clearance might open doors, but it also leaves a trail that will no doubt set off an alarm."

They moved along the corridor until the architecture shifted, with more displays embedded in the walls, more access points, and more invisible sensor nodes. Ahead, their target came into view. A handleless door beside a palm-print reader. Beyond it was the central control hub.

Xander exhaled once, steadying himself, and stepped to the panel. His palm pressed flat. The lock chimed. The door slid aside. Warm air rolled out, electronics, recycled oxygen and the faint tang of ozone from hard-running systems. The room was the central core of Atmos, circular, windowless, and ringed with luminous displays and hovering holo-panels. Bolted to the city's central support column, it was built to remain fixed while the surrounding modules could disengage and lift free into space. Status columns scrolled, displaying atmospheric integrity, power grid load, and maintenance cycles. In the centre sat a waist-high horseshoe-shaped console displayed schematic overlays.

"Two minutes, Xander," Ondra said. She swept the room once, then slipped back into the corridor, flattening herself into the shadowed seam beside the door. Her hand rested near her belt, where a compact weapon sat hidden under her jacket, invisible, but one tug away from daylight.

Xander gave her a tight nod and turned to the secondary console in the far corner. He was alone, yet the space never settled. Atmos breathed through the bulkheads, a low, constant thrumming. Status relays ticked behind panels. Somewhere below, a lift shuddered and groaned, the vibration travelling up the frame like a warning. Novak had given him temporary access and a simple instruction: wait for the signal, then engage the environmental sequence during the crawler ascent. He wouldn't expect movement until he called. That had been the cover.

Xander called up the crawler guideway maintenance interface. The first menu unfolded cleanly. The second did not. Subtrees branched, permissions stacked, and the sequence Novak had shown him splintered into versions, revisions, nested safeguards with clinical names that meant nothing until they did. His two minutes were evaporating quickly. He forced his hands to stay steady and began threading sabotage through the logic like careful stitching. Not a clean shutdown, too obvious, too easily reversed. Instead, he rewired the control layer so MANIFOLD mode would accept the command and throw green confirmations, but never actually open the rail valves. He looped the actuator calls into a dead end, fed the interface false position states, and inserted a dependency check that looked legitimate at a glance.

The system balked. A progress bar crawled across the holo display, pausing to verify, to validate, to cross-check with a module he hadn't even known existed. Xander's fingers hovered, trapped by the machine's pace, his pulse climbing with every stalled heartbeat. He glanced at the clock strip in the corner of the display. One minute gone. He swallowed, throat already dry, and pushed deeper, rewriting response tables and safety returns, closing one loop only to have another open under it. The interface kept asking for confirmations, clean little boxes that demanded time he didn't have. Another glance. Twenty seconds. His breath came shallow. He kept one ear on the door, one eye on the scrolling diagnostic lines, and his hands moving, always moving, as if speed could bully the system into compliance. The dependency check flashed amber, then red. He backtracked a layer, found the snag, rerouted it, and for a moment the indicators turned obedient, all green, all calm, the way lies looked when they were coded well.

Then the hatch hissed. Xander jerked so hard his palm skated across the holo-keys. The menu stack collapsed. The screen stuttered and spat up a warning he couldn't parse, not for a heartbeat, and that blank beat cost him. The clock strip kept counting while his brain caught up. Cold panic hit, sharp and clean, like air leaving a punctured lung.

Roddick stepped in first, broad-shouldered, wearing surprise like an accusation.

Novak followed, already scanning the room, eyes narrowing as they landed on the secondary console.

For an instant, Xander could only stare. They weren't meant to be here.

Roddick's gaze snapped from Xander to the console. "Xander?" he said. "Why are you in here?"

Novak's voice cut in, flat. "You tripped an alarm. I didn't summon you."

Xander's pulse slammed against his teeth. Too late to look innocent, too late to hide the open diagnostic overlay, the permission chain still unspooling across the screen like a confession. "I..." His throat tightened. He forced a swallow. "You said to familiarise myself with the protocols," he managed, pitching his voice into obedient calm. "The ones you showed me. I was checking, making sure I remembered the sequence."

Roddick's eyebrows climbed.

Novak moved farther into the room, slow and measured, suspicion shaping every step. His gaze flicked to the panel, then locked.

Xander's stomach dropped. He'd left too much exposed. A tab that didn't belong. A chain of edits that didn't exist in any rehearsal.

"What did you open?" Novak asked softly.

Xander's fingers hovered over the keys. He tried to close the overlay, but the motion was wrong, too quick, too defensive.

Novak saw it. He stepped closer and leaned in, eyes reading line items with the ease of someone who'd written them. The loop. The false position states. The dependency check sitting in the middle like a tripwire.

Novak went very still.

Roddick frowned, trying to see over his shoulder. "What has he done?" he demanded.

Novak turned his head just enough to silence him without a word. Then he looked back at Xander. "You're not reviewing." His voice stayed quiet, but it carried an edge that shaved the air. "You're altering."

Xander's mouth went numb. The room felt tighter, the filtered air suddenly thin.

Novak's hand slid under his coat.

Roddick's eyes widened a fraction, confused more than afraid. "Novak, don't be ridiculous, he's only a boy. He wouldn't know how to alter Atmos' complex systems."

The weapon came out.

Xander froze. He'd counted on the full two minutes, not a door hissing open at the worst possible second.

The muzzle lifted toward him.

"Step away," Novak ordered. "Now."

Xander's legs refused to move. The holo display pulsed beside him, half the sabotage in place, half hanging open, unfinished threads that could unravel the moment he let go.

Novak's eyes flicked to the console, then back.

Roddick finally saw enough to understand something was very wrong, even if he didn't know what. "Xander," he snapped, "what have you done?"

Xander looked at his great-uncle, at the confusion sharpening into alarm, and the truth tore free before he could cage it.

"I'm stopping the gas." Silence hit like a physical thing.

Roddick's face changed, colour draining a shade.

Novak's jaw tightened. He re-aimed at Xander.

Xander's hands trembled over the keys. If Novak forced him off the console now, the system might recover enough to run the original program. Or the AI might detect tampering and slam everything into lockdown, sealing the crawler ascent and trapping the team below. Either way, the clock would keep ticking, clean and indifferent.

Novak took a step closer.

ATMOS'S UNDERGROUND hangars pulsed with a low vibration you felt more than heard. Brom and the others lay flat beneath a grounded shuttle, eyes fixed on the crawler bay access hatch in the distance. Mila lay beside him, her breathing slow and controlled. He should have made her stay back, he should have found words strong enough to outweigh her stubborn streak, but Mila didn't yield once she'd chosen a line to cross. He let his eyes track to her for the briefest beat, more reflex than choice. In the dim spill of hangar light, she turned her gaze to him for a precious second, and everything else fell away. It hit him hard, raw and immediate. Mila gave the smallest nod. An unspoken I'm here, and we are in this together, before her focus locked forward again. He admired her for the way she refused to fold even when the odds turned ugly. He hated it too, because bravery was a liability that got people killed, and he might be forced to watch it happen.

The moment didn't last. A distant clang rolled through the hangar, and Brom's mind narrowed back to the job. He inched his hand forward, fingers brushing the grit-stained deck, to keep himself grounded. Mila mirrored the shift, close enough that he could feel her body heat. No more looking. No more wishing. Just the next obstacle, a sealed composite security hatch with an illuminated access panel. Beyond it, the maintenance crawlers waited in tidy rows. Bubble-bodied utility pods on traction plates with jointed stabilisers. Each was hard-tethered to a guide rail that spiralled upward in a steep ascent toward Atmos's upper levels.

Red points of light beamed from the access panel. Once the main power grid was shut down, hopefully the sensor nodes on the door would go offline long enough for them to enter. The patrols walked their loops like they'd done it a thousand times without ever expecting trouble. His mind then turned to Xander, and he wondered how he and Ondra were doing.

Astrea lifted her hand. "Liora, are you clear on your task to take out the geothermal unit?"

"Yes," she whispered. "I take the service corridor behind bay nine. The thermal annex has a maintenance override, manual if the loop is blind. I blind it first, then I break the geothermal regulator."

"Hard failure changes the tempo and response time," Astrea whispered. "They'll dispatch a team fast. The hangar will drop into emergency protocols, prioritising life support and core containment. Everything else starves." She kept her voice steady and precise. "That cascade should briefly blind the access panel controlling the hatch to the maintenance crawler tunnel, long enough for us to slip through. You must be in and out of the geothermal unit within forty seconds.

That is not a suggestion. This should buy a full blackout for one minute in the confusion, then a partial restoration." Astrea lowered her voice another notch. "If you're compromised, you do not fight your way clear. You bury yourself somewhere and go dark." She paused, letting the instruction sink in. "As soon as it is safe, you hijack a shuttle from the bay, you ditch it, and you make your way back to Gromwell on foot. You do not come chasing us. You do not improvise." Her jaw set. "I lost Orella. I don't intend to lose another."

Liora nodded.

Astrea touched two fingers to Liora's shoulder before Liora slid away into the hangar's layered darkness.

Brom tried to keep track of her, but she disappeared quickly from sight. Patrol boots passed, and a distant laugh echoed and died. A maintenance drone rolled along a far lane, its indicator strip blinking a steady amber. Brom counted heartbeats because counting distracted his mind. Then, so subtly he almost missed it, the hangar's constant hum wavered. The vibration in the plating stumbled, a brief hiccup like a heart skipping a beat. Ceiling strip lights flickered once. Brom held his breath, but the red lights on the access panel held steady. A nearby patrolman paused, frowned and tilted his head, but his partner shrugged and kept walking. Brom's eyes stung from staring. Then the hangar's pulse changed; it was deeper now, strained. Somewhere in the walls, a warning tone rose.

Astrea's hand lifted slightly. Ready.

And then a concussion rolled through the hangar, and the grounded shuttle above them let out a metallic groan, causing dust to sift down from unseen seams. Overhead, two ceiling strips blew with a sharp crack, showering sparks across the floor. Then, for half a heartbeat, everything went dark, and the crawler bay access panel lights winked out in the same instant. A siren began, full-throated now, but it wasn't a clean sound. It warbled, surged, broke, and surged again. Harsh red emergency strobe lighting slammed on.

Brom's vision snapped into high contrast amidst silhouettes and alarms.

Astrea's fist closed. The sign to move. They poured out of hiding, low and fast, as the red strobes blinked. But the blackout had done more than blind sensors. It had woken people. A guard shouted somewhere in the distance. Boots pounded metal, fast and purposeful. A flashlight beam sliced the dark, sweeping wildly, in harsh slices.

"GEOTHERMAL'S DOWN!" someone yelled into a comm.

Astrea steered them toward the crawler bay hatch, keeping them low beneath grounded machinery and in the pooled shadows. The panel's indicator pulsed amber, confused, blind, handshaking against systems that no longer answered. She yanked the manual release. The seal sighed, broke, and the hatch swung in.

Brom went first, hauling Mila in behind him. Kihm followed, then Astrea's pilots, fast and silent. Astrea stayed outside, half-turned, watching the corridor.

A patrol rounded the corner. Torches swept in hard white arcs. Three guards appeared, weapons up. "Hold," one barked, and a beam snapped across the hatch.

Naella palmed a coin-sized puck, met Astrea's eyes once, then flicked it through the narrowing opening.

Astrea slid in last.

The hatch began to cycle. For a heartbeat, a thin seam remained where it hadn't fully met the frame. A guard's light knifed through the gap, then caught the pressure-rated duraglass viewport, and the glass bloomed, flaring bright enough to sting the eyes. "Wait," the guard snapped, stepping in. The seam vanished. The lock engaged with a heavy, final clunk.

Silence hit like a slap, not true silence, just the crawler bay's steady hum, the quiet grind of metal on rail. Compared to the hangar's screaming alarms, it felt like being swallowed by calm.

They watched through the duraglass as the puck bit down with a sharp hiss. A second later, mineral smoke erupted in a pressurised bloom, grey-white and heavy, rolling across the hangar like a storm front. The guards lurched back, torch beams slicing uselessly through the churning haze. "Smoke, initiate thermal breach protocols," someone shouted.

Astrea didn't wait. She drew a compact cutting laser and ran it along the hatch seam. Blue-white flare, a brutal sizzle, then the locking lugs fused and the frame flash-welded shut.

"There's no going back now," she said.

The emergency siren stuttered, then spiked into a higher, harsher pitch. Hangar lights flickered as the system fought to restore them, then degraded into strobes as power was rerouted to essential services.

They had to move fast, as they had limited air. The maintenance tunnel beyond was dead, airless, and whatever they'd dragged in from the hangar was all they had until they sealed into one of the four maintenance crawlers that sat nose-to-tail on the service rail.

They had skipped breathers on purpose, bottled oxygen and powered masks spiked thermal output and pressure telemetry, the kind of anomaly hangar security loved, so they carried only what they could hide and planned to seal into a crawler fast.

They split across three, leaving one behind. Brom, Mila, and Kihm climbed into the nearest unit, ducking through its pressure hatch into a sealed three-seat capsule, an ovoid blister of armoured composite and thick, curved viewport panels. The interior was tight but purposeful, three contoured crash seats shoulder-to-shoulder, harness straps clipped to a central buckle, boot cradles, and handholds for bracing. A neat row of status LEDs glowed on the forward console: SEAL, PRESS, O_2 FEED, COMMS. Beneath them, smaller text pulsed, RAIL SUPPLY: STANDBY, MAKE-UP ENABLED, the rail ready to top pressure if the cabin drifted but not feeding as primary. Once the hatch dogged shut behind them, the crawler felt less like a vehicle and more like a pressurised life pod bolted to a guide rail.

Mila yanked the restraint harness over her chest and slammed the buckle home while Brom checked the door dogs and Kihm keyed the seal. The lights stepped from amber to green as the gasket inflated and the pressure equalised with a soft hiss.

Naella, Vena and Lira filed into the second crawler, and Astrea and Rhen took the lead in the third.

Rhen's voice cracked through the comms. "Listen up. Eyes on your consoles. Main power on, confirm boot lights. Seal and interlock, get it to green." He paused. "O_2 next. Confirm cabin percentage, then check your onboard bottle; it must be above the minimum for transit. If it's not, you're in trouble. Keep the console set to LOCAL." His tone hardened. "LOCAL means your own bottle and scrubber are servicing the cabin. MANIFOLD makes the rail feed your primary supply. Do not select MANIFOLD. That feed can be hijacked as Novak has planned. Harness buckled, green. Arm mag clamps, then engage until you feel the bite. Rail sync: select SYNC, then wait for LOCKED. When you see LOCKED, hold brakes." He let that sink in before he gave the go-ahead. "On my mark, release the brake. Now."

Brom's crawler in the rear vibrated, eager to move, and the traction hum rose. A soft hiss followed as stale scrubbed air bled into the cabin.

Through the entry hatch's pressure-rated duraglass viewport, Brom saw a flashlight beam lance the tunnel and lock onto his crawler. His stomach dropped. The guard raised his weapon as a second aftershock rippled through the hangar. Not as big as the first concussion, but sharp enough to rattle. The overhead strobes blinked out. The guards' torch beams jolted with the tremor, and that might have saved them, because Brom wasn't sure the duraglass would stop a full-power shot.

Rhen and Astrea's crawler was the first to surge ahead, climbing the narrow tunnel. Rhen's voice came through their comm. "Lights off. Radio silence from here on."

The tunnel climbed into darkness, a tight vertical shaft that corkscrewed upward, pipework hugging the walls and a fixed ladder bolted along one side. Somewhere far above, the city waited, operating on emergency power. As they climbed, Brom's mind snagged on one thing and wouldn't let go. "I hope Xander is okay," he said to Mila and Kihm.

IN THE CENTRAL CONTROL hub, the power stuttered, then dropped out in a hard blink. Emergency strips ignited along the floor and console edges, washing the hub in a thin amber glow. Xander stood braced on the console rim, eyes fixed on the city schematic as warnings cascaded in front of him. Subsystems greyed out in disciplined blocks, others flared red, angry and immediate. One feed stayed clean, the three crawler signatures forming a thin thread of movement in a dying grid.

Novak stepped in and read the pattern in a single sweep. His expression shifted. "Geothermal," he said quietly. He pulled up the plant status and watched the output curve collapse, too fast and too clean to be a failure. "They hit the core, not a fault, but a takedown." His gaze tracked the knock-on effects, pressure gates cycling, safety interlocks biting, and whole sections of Atmos going dark. "That explains the chaos." He switched back to maintenance and zoomed in. A telemetry gap sat on the overlay like a missing tooth, and behind it, the three green markers slid upward as if the net around them did not exist. "Rail manifold isolated," he murmured. "Segment valves masked." He opened crawler life support, then stopped on the mode line. "Feed forced to LOCAL."

Novak turned slowly, pinning Xander. "Someone forced LOCAL to keep them independent." The last piece clicked and a cold smile touched his mouth. "Gromwell insurgents are in those crawlers."

Xander's jaw tightened.

"How did they get inside my perimeter?" Novak's voice stayed even, almost conversational. "I built this perimeter. I do not miss breaches." He paused, watching the icons climb. "So tell me who in Atmos is aiding them."

Xander shook his head, defiant.

Novak pushed past him and keyed into diagnostics. "You handed me a dead patch," he said, smooth as oil. "You did not just close a door, you tried to blind a corridor." The console hesitated, issued a warning, then auto-corrected, eager to reassure. Novak watched the correction, and his smile sharpened. "Mode translation. You rewired the command map." He traced the logic with one finger. "Select MANIFOLD, the display confirms it, the logs record it, but the controller never opens the manifold valves. It stays LOCAL." He looked at Xander, clinical. "A false MANIFOLD. Cosmetic. So nobody can gas them through the rail feed."

Novak leaned closer, almost pleased. "Clever. Almost perfect." He tapped once more. "Except you left a fingerprint in the translation layer, and you did not finish scrubbing it. Now I know exactly where you touched the system." He looked up at last, eyes bright and empty. "Tell me, Xander, did you think you could get away with this?"

Xander lunged.

Novak caught him and wrenched him back with economy. His gaze flicked to Roddick. "Restrain your great-nephew before he becomes collateral."

Roddick stepped in, face pulled tight. "Stand down," he hissed at Xander. "He is not bluffing."

Xander's eyes darted to the door, catching movement that did not belong. Ondra was tucked into a far corner. She must have slipped in behind Roddick and Novak before the seal cycled.

Novak saw her a fraction too late.

"Stop what you are doing, Novak," Ondra said.

Novak's weapon swung.

Ondra fired first. One round, flat and surgical, high in the upper arm near the shoulder, ugly enough to wound but not kill.

Novak grunted and staggered into the console edge. His weapon dropped and skittered across the floor, clattering in the tight room. He did not fall. His good hand stayed on the console as if it were holding him upright, while blood ran down his sleeve. In the chaos, he leaned in, fingers moving on a dead service strip, a two-finger drag, a pause timed like a heartbeat. The console did not beep. It did not ask for confirmation. It changed layers.

The city schematic dimmed. A thin header flickered into existence, SUPERVISOR, INCIDENT CONTAINMENT. Across the hub, permissions collapsed. Control tiles greyed out. Red lock icons stamped themselves over every station.

Novak laughed, a rasp of amusement through pain. "Legacy authority. Installed during the last hub refit. Single operator containment. My biometric signature, and only mine. It was an insurance policy, Xander, in case you were compromised."

Xander watched the crawler feed snap to a new overlay. The maintenance rail lit like a spine. All three crawler icons flashed: BRAKE, HOLD. DRIVE ENABLE, INHIBITED. Then the life support column populated in sickly yellow, FEED MODE AUTHORITY, OVERRIDDEN. O_2 FEED, MANIFOLD, FORCED. LOCAL SUPPLY, LOCKED OUT. MANIFOLD VALVES, ARMED. MIX INJECTION, STANDBY,

FIVE-MINUTE COUNTDOWN. PURGE ROUTING, DISABLED. Another line appeared beneath it, colder than the rest: HATCH DOGS, LOCKED. INTERLOCK, ENFORCED.

Novak's eyes stayed locked on the board, and Xander caught the edge of his smile. "They will not egress," he said. "Not into my tunnels. They will stay sealed, and they will breathe what I give them."

Xander's pulse jumped.

Novak faced the display again, the rail lit like a glowing spine. "They do not stand a chance. Incident Containment is absolute. My authority cannot be overridden from this room."

Ondra's gaze snapped to Xander. "Is that true?"

Xander moved to the console, hands flying, searching for a gap that did not exist. His face went tight, then hollow. He looked at Ondra and gave a single, sharp nod.

THE STOP HIT THE CRAWLERS like a fist. Not a gentle deceleration, a hard clamp that slammed their bodies into harnesses and stole the traction hum in an instant. The cabins shuddered, then fell into a sharp, metallic silence.

Across Brom's console, lights cascaded in brutal logic, RAIL SYNC, LOST, amber. DRIVE ENABLE, INHIBITED, red. FEED MODE, OVERRIDE, yellow. O_2 FEED, MANIFOLD, forced. LOCAL SUPPLY, LOCKED OUT. A warning tone began, tight and repeating, and the cabin fans surged as if trying to compensate for something the system would not name.

Rhen's voice snapped into their comms. "Sorry. Breaking comms blackout. All crawlers, confirm STOPPED, confirm MANIFOLD forced, confirm LOCAL locked out."

Three acknowledgements overlapped.

"Novak has seized life support authority," Rhen said. "Do not trust the cabin air. There are emergency masks in the front compartment. Get them out, now."

Brom yanked open the kit compartment by his knee. Inside sat compact rebreathers with bite valves, clear visors folded tight, and tether lines with mag hooks. Walking gear, not comfort.

Mila was already pulling hers on, hands steady and efficient.

Kihm followed, eyes wide.

As Brom's fingers closed around his mask, the air changed, not in smell at first, but in texture, thicker against his tongue. A faint chemical bite threaded into the back of his throat.

A red warning bloomed across the panel: ATMOS, PURGE ACTIVE, CONTAMINANT LEVELS, RISING.

Brom's blood went cold.

"If we run low on O_2, what are we going to do?"

"As the tunnel is maintained with low oxygen for fire load, your masks are your world," Rhen said.

The contaminant reading climbed in steady, indifferent increments. Even with the mask sealed, Brom could feel the bite on his skin where the edge met his cheek.

Astrea took over. "We get out, and we move. Service Node Twelve. Manual wheel on the inner hatch. No chatter. Stay on tethers."

Brom reached for the hatch release and thumbed the vent control. "Equalising," he said. A controlled hiss bled the cabin down. His ears popped, the walls creaked faintly, and the gauge crawled toward match. "Pressure matched," he said. He grabbed the hatch handle and pulled. Nothing. He tried again, harder. The handle refused to move. The hatch felt welded to the frame.

On the console, a new line stamped itself over the status column, HATCH DOGS, LOCKED. INTERLOCK, ENFORCED.

Mila's eyes met his through the visor. Calm, but too bright.

"They locked us in," Kihm whispered, and the words came out thin, like she could not afford the air.

Rhen's voice cut in, flat with urgency. "Containment has seized the dogs through the servo layer. Normal release is dead."

Astrea swore. "Options," she snapped.

Rhen's reply was immediate. "There is an emergency mechanical bypass behind the lower service strip, port side. Open the panel and back-drive the dog rack manually."

Brom's heart hammered. "How?"

"Find the dog rack," Rhen said. "It is a toothed bar with a manual socket. Insert the crank, quarter turns only. It will fight you. When you feel it move, keep going until the dogs retract. Do not attempt to open until pressure is matched, and keep masks sealed. The moment the seal breaks, whatever is in this cabin will try to leave with you."

Brom dropped to his knees, fingers already tearing at the port side strip. The panel resisted, as if it had not been opened in years. He jammed his glove into the seam and ripped. The strip popped free with a crack, exposing dust, wiring, and a compact mechanical assembly that looked too small to hold them prisoner, but did. A square socket sat at its centre. He found the crank in the kit, slotted it in, and turned. It did not move. His shoulders tightened. He set his feet and turned again. The crank bit back, the mechanism grinding, stubborn and dry. The contaminant alarm changed pitch. 18%. 19%. Brom forced himself to breathe slowly through the rebreather. Quarter turns, as Rhen said. He turned again, muscles burning, and felt the first fraction of movement, a reluctant tick. "Got it," he muttered. He kept turning, quarter turns only. Each one cost him. The crank shuddered, the dog rack scraping like metal on bone.

Kihm's breathing quickened, sharp little pulls through her mask. Her eyes flicked to the rising numbers, then away, as if looking would make it worse.

"Stay with me," Mila said, voice firm. "Slow breaths. Do not waste your air. We are getting out."

Brom's forearms were on fire. He turned again. Another tick. Another. Then, without warning, the crank slipped, jerking his hand. His glove scraped the edge of the housing, and pain flashed up his wrist. He grunted, reseated the crank, and went again.

The alarm screamed, CONTAMINANT 21%, CABIN AIR QUALITY CRITICAL.

Kihm made a small choked sound and pitched forward. Her mask seal shifted as panic made her careless.

"Seal," Mila urged, reaching across and reseating it with a hard press. "Keep it sealed."

Kihm's eyes rolled for a fraction, not unconscious yet, but close, oxygen debt and stacking fast.

Mila anchored her against the seat. "Look at me," she said. "In through the nose, out slow. Your mask is working properly now."

Brom turned again, brutal and steady. "Come on." The dog rack finally gave with a violent clunk that vibrated through the hatch. A second clunk followed, then a third.

On the console, the red line flickered, HATCH DOGS, LOCKED, then stuttered to amber, DOGS, RETRACTED.

Brom's hands shook. "Dogs are back," he said, voice tight. "Hatch should be free."

"It won't be," Astrea cut in. Her voice was clipped, working. "Fail-secure lock is still holding. Same in ours. Rhen and I are cutting out first, then we'll come for you. Hold position."

Brom stared at the hatch, willing it to move. He pulled anyway. Nothing, not even a shudder. Just the hard refusal of metal designed to stay shut.

Then a thin, rising whine bled through the hull, not from his crawler, from somewhere down the rail. The sound climbed until it prickled behind his eyes. Through the duraglass viewport, he caught a brief flare, blue-white and vicious, reflected off the tunnel walls, Astrea's sonic welder. Metal vibrated, complained, then softened. A glow pulsed, dull and ugly, as a lock housing surrendered. The whine cut out. A breath later, her voice returned, strained but controlled. "Our lug is dead. We are out."

As seconds dragged to minutes, sharp and expensive, Mila's gloved hand found Brom's forearm, a steadying clamp.

Then Astrea again, closer now, her boots thudding faintly through the structure, a vibration more felt than heard. "Stand clear of the seam. I am on you." The welder's whine rose right outside their capsule. Brom braced himself, shoulder against the bulkhead, as the lock housing bloomed with heat, then sagged as the mechanism burned out.

"Holding lug is dead," Astrea said. "Pressure match, then crack it," she said before moving onto the middle crawler housing her soldiers.

Brom thumbed the equaliser. The cabin shivered as the last differential bled off. He waited for the gauge to settle, then pulled and the seal released with a soft suction pop.

He clipped Mila and Kihm to his tether, climbed out first, boots finding the ladder, mag clamps biting hard with a thunk. One hand locked to the rung, the other ready.

Mila pushed Kihm forward. Kihm hesitated for half a second, eyes wide, then stepped out and locked her boots.

"Up," Astrea urged, after everyone was released. "Stay tight. Do not look down. You have enough air if you do not spend it on fear."

Above them, a faint seam in the tunnel wall appeared, the outline of an access lock barely visible in the dark. Service Node Twelve. A manual wheel waited there, old world and physical, the kind Novak could not hack. They climbed.

IN THE CENTRAL CONTROL hub, Ondra kept her weapon trained on Novak.

"On your knees," she ordered, snagging his dropped sidearm and tucking it into her backpack.

Novak's narrowed gaze cut to Xander. "You're betraying your father."

Xander's spine straightened. "No," he said, and his voice surprised him with how steady it was. "He betrayed me. He tried to kill me."

Roddick's eyes flared in surprise. "Sounds like you got lucky, but you can't win against them," he muttered to Xander, low. "Not like this."

Now on his knees, Novak clamped one hand over his injured shoulder, breath coming in thin, angry pulls.

Roddick hovered a step back, frozen between outrage and instinct, eyes flicking from the console to Xander to the gun in Ondra's hands.

Novak's mouth curled. "You think you have won. Aivel and Waylan will make sure."

Ondra fired again, into the floor beside his knee. A sharp crack, a shower of sparks and the stink of scorched metal burned their nostrils.

Novak flinched.

"Haven't you heard? Waylan's gone. He won't be coming back," Ondra said, holstering her sidearm only long enough to yank a restraint strap from her kit, an industrial polymer webbing with a ratchet buckle, the kind used to lash cargo during hard manoeuvres. She stepped behind Novak, planted a boot between his shoulder blades, and wrenched his arms behind his back.

He hissed through his teeth.

"Don't make me work," she murmured, looping the webbing around his hands and then under the console's lower metal frame and ratcheting it until Novak was effectively welded to the spot by his own skeleton.

She stripped his spare mag, comms unit, and a slim keycard sleeve. Anything that could open a door or wake a system.

Roddick took an unconscious half-step forward.

Ondra's head turned a fraction. "Don't."

Roddick stopped. His throat worked. "He's bleeding."

"I know," Ondra said. "He's alive and still dangerous." She pointed at the far wall with her chin. "Hands on the panel. Fingers spread. Face away."

Roddick's eyes flashed. "I'm no threat to you."

"I beg to differ," Ondra said, making a small motion with the muzzle. It was enough. Roddick moved. Slow, stiff and humiliated, he planted his palms on the wall.

"Now," Ondra said, "knees."

He hesitated.

Ondra's voice didn't change, but the air around it tightened. "Knees, Roddick."

He went down.

She crossed to him with the same economy she'd shown with Novak, no flourish, no wasted steps. A second restraint strap came free from her pack. "Hands behind."

Roddick obeyed. Ondra looped the strap around his wrists and cinched it hard, then added a second band high around his upper arms to pin his elbows and kill any leverage. She hauled him half a step to the side and clipped him to a protruding grab handle.

Then she frisked him, fast and thorough, palms sweeping his jacket seams, beltline, and boot tops. She stripped a small comms unit from his inner pocket and a slim utility blade from his ankle holster, tossed both into her pack, and straightened without taking her eyes off the room.

"You're treating me like a criminal," he started.

"More like a variable," Ondra said. "And I remove variables."

She glanced back at Novak, blood darkening his sleeve. "You wanted sole authority," Ondra said. "Congratulations. You have it."

With both men secured, she shoved Xander through the hub hatch, waited for the seals to bite, ready for Rhen to enter shortly with President Aivel's codes when he had them. She kept her weapon up a beat longer, listening for pursuit that didn't come. "Xander," she said, lowering the muzzle just enough to meet his eyes. "You did what you could. We have run out of time." Her gaze stayed steady. "Rhen and Astrea will find a way around this." A tight inhale. "We stay on mission."

His mouth opened, but she cut him off with a tight shake of her head.

"They're not helpless. They've got enough ingenuity to force a solution without us." She hooked a thumb toward the adjoining corridor. "Now we do our part. The module I need to fly is this way. Move."

BACK IN THE TUNNEL, the access hatch was a line in the ribbed plating, a rectangle that only existed when Astrea's lamp skated across it, and the grime briefly gave up its outline: SERVICE NODE TWELVE. The stencil was half-scoured away, sitting above a wheel mechanism that opened the hatch manually.

Astrea paused. "Hold," she said into the comms.

Brom locked his knees and went still, one gloved hand clamped around a rung, the other on the tether line linking him to Kihm and Mila. Below him, the ladder vibrated with the faint tick of their clips settling.

Astrea backed the wheel off a fraction and pressure bled with a soft hiss as she eased the hatch open. She paused, listening. Waiting for a second sound, the one that meant air was flowing out. Nothing.

Just a thin, steady whisper. Her portable analyser blinked through its cycle, then threw a result that tightened her jaw. Residual air. Thin. Barely breathable. "Masks stay on," she said. "Tethers tight. Move like you mean it." She slipped through the gap first, like a diver entering a new world.

The rest followed in sequence, boots thumping softly as they landed on grated flooring. Every sound felt too loud.

The space beyond was a narrow service shaft. Bare conduit ran overhead in rigid bundles. A small status panel blinked on emergency power, its letters stark against the dark: NODE TWELVE. LIFE SUPPORT INACTIVE. BREATHER CACHE: ACTIVE (EMERGENCY). MAIN STEM ACCESS LEVEL SEVENTEEN

Brom's stomach dropped. "That's... not what the schematics said."

For a beat, nobody spoke. The only sound was their own rebreathers.

Astrea stared at the panel again. "It's a pocket. A breather node and a turnaround."

Brom felt something cold settle in his gut. Level Twelve had been their promised entry. Their shortcut.

Mila checked her mask readout. Her lips tightened, and the visor magnified the tension in her eyes. "The rebreathers were meant for emergency egress, not stair-climbing. We need a permanent air source." She crossed to the wall cabinet and yanked it open hard enough to make the hinges squeal. Inside, a row of compact rebreathers sat in foam cradles. She stripped them out quickly and shoved them into her pack. "Auxiliary air," she said. "This is what Node Twelve is for."

Astrea snapped her lamp across the laminated map bolted to the wall, her finger tracked upward, fast and precise, then stopped where the old route would've cut into the main stem. A blunt black stamp had been slapped over it: ROUTE DECOMMISSIONED. Her jaw ticked once. "So we go back out," she said. "Into the tunnel and keep climbing until we hit Seventeen and cut in from there."

Brom leaned in, visor catching the map's blunt geometry. "Still a vertical climb," he said, voice tight, "and it will test our oxygen levels."

Astrea's tone left no room for debate. "Everything tests oxygen levels right now." She looked at each of them in turn, making sure they were still a unit. "We keep pace, and we do not sprint unless we have to."

Rhen's mask alarm chirped, small and insistent. "Looks like I'll be needing a replacement," he said, as Mila pulled a rebreather from her bag.

Brom forced his breathing to slow again. Every instinct wanted to gulp.

"Rule," Astrea said, her pilots already squared up behind her, eyes forward. She looked at the civilians in turn. "If your oxygen alarm sounds, you ask for a replacement immediately."

Everyone nodded.

"Stack tight," Astrea ordered. "No chatter. We go out the way we came, and we climb. Level by level. Move," she said. "And let's not waste any more air talking about it."

One by one, they slipped back into the crawler tunnel. The climb to Seventeen had been built for technicians with fresh lungs and a safety net, not fugitives on borrowed air. The service ladder rose in long vertical pulls, broken by narrow landings. Condensation slicked the rungs, and cable trays and conduit ran alongside the crawler mag track.

Astrea took point, one hand on the rail, the other keeping her weapon indexed while her headlamp cut hard angles into the dark. Behind her, the line moved like a single organism, tether checks, clip checks, boots placed with care and no wasted motion because every wasted motion stole breath.

Mila's voice came low over the comms. "Keep your breathing shallow. No panic gulps. If you feel the urge to sprint, tell me first."

Brom wanted to laugh at that, but the sound would have cost oxygen.

Another alarm chirped two landings later, a small electronic insistence. Vena was next to request a new rebreather when her mask indicators flashed amber in the gloom.

Mila was already moving. "Swap," she said. The replacement rebreather was passed down the line of climbers. As soon as it clicked home, Vena nodded before they pushed on again.

Above, the tunnel changed. The ladder gave way to a steep maintenance incline, grated stairs and narrow handrails, the angle just shallow enough to feel like you should be able to go faster, and just steep enough to punish you when you did. Their boots struck a steady, muffled rhythm. Visors fogged in the corners, moisture blooming and shrinking with each breath.

Astrea's headlamp caught it first, the way the next landing didn't sit right. A section of grating had been eaten through with corrosion, the panel hanging, forgotten and waiting for a boot to make it fail. She swept her lamp down. "This next section is compromised. Climb onto the bottom rung of the handrail," she whispered. "One at a time. No hero jumps."

Rhen and Kihm went first, careful and light-footed. Mila and Brom followed in tight sequence.

Brom's boot skated on the slick handrail and hit the rusted grate. He froze, then redistributed his weight with slow, controlled precision until he reseated his boot again.

Vena's boot skated when she climbed onto the slick railing, and her full weight hit the landing, causing the corroded fasteners to give out with a brittle scream. The grating buckled and dropped away, narrowly missing the two pilots below her who flattened themselves against the ladder. For half a second, Vena's leg disappeared into the black.

Brom went down hard, the tether ripping through his grip. He clamped one hand onto the rail and caught Vena's line with the other in a savage, locked hold. The shock tore through his injured shoulder, pain flashing white behind his eyes.

Vena's boot scraped at bare metal, searching for purchase and finding nothing.

Brom's headlamp swung wildly, painting the void, a drop that did not end in a floor, only darkness.

Astrea moved like a machine. She dropped her weapon on its sling, drove her forearm through the tether line, locking it over the rail as an anchor point. "Everyone, keep still," she ordered, voice cutting through the panic.

Vena's hands clawed at the edge, hands scraping for purchase on slick metal. Her breathing spiked before she found purchase and hauled herself back to safety.

Astrea's mask alarm screamed, and Mila handed her a rebreather, hands steady.

Astrea's lamp flicked to Brom. "You good?"

Brom flexed his shoulder, pain blooming, and nodded once.

Astrea picked up her weapon and turned her gaze upward into the climb. "That's Atmos reminding us what it is," she said. "We don't give it a second chance."

They moved again, slower now, tighter, every step checked, every tether verified, the group breathing like a single organism because the alternative was a fall into a dark that did not care.

Two more landings. Then the level plate appeared ahead, catching Astrea's headlamp, clean metal on a cleaner door: LEVEL SEVENTEEN. She raised two fingers, and the party froze. She backed the wheel off a fraction and pressure bled with a soft hiss as she cracked the hatch. Conditioned air hit her, cool and sterile, carrying the faint bite of disinfectant and ozone, a different world from below, and one she was hoping to find. She swung a leg up, planted her boot on the rim, and hauled herself into the access shaft. One by one, they followed, palms scraping cold steel as they climbed out of the tunnel. Tethers were released, along with a quiet rush of relief. She pointed with the muzzle of her weapon, assigning routes without wasting a word. "Rhen, head to the central control hub and wait for the codes to initiate the separation of Atmos. Make sure your weapon is ready, in case Xander and Ondra need assistance."

He saluted before disappearing down the corridor.

"Lira, module One. You're piloting when the window opens."

"Copy," came the reply.

"Naella, module Two. Go now and wait for the window."

"Understood."

"Vena, module Three. The same goes for you."

A pause, then: "Acknowledged."

The three soldiers peeled off like droplets of oil, sliding into separate corridors and vanishing into the architecture. Astrea watched them go for half a heartbeat, then turned back to the remaining members. "Hopefully, Ondra is in the pilot seat for module four. Brom, Mila and Kihm," she signed with a flick of her hand, tight, economical. "Let's find President Aivel and get those access codes."

They moved quietly, bypassing the first surveillance point and the cameras nestled in ceiling coves. The EMP scramblers clipped to their belts pulsed with a faint warmth against their hips, scrambling feeds in a tight radius without broadcasting a beacon of their own.

Mila's eyes tracked the corners anyway, and Kihm followed closely behind.

Brom kept his shoulders loose and his weight on the balls of his feet, ready to drop if a light changed or a panel hissed open.

Astrea spoke without looking back. "No running. No hard turns. Executive floors love their silent alarms." She turned to Kihm. "Talk to me. Where do we pick up Aivel?"

"He'll be watching the emergency response from somewhere with redundancy," Kihm said, eyes locked on her scrolling schematic. "He doesn't trust a single feed. He'll view everything from his office."

Astrea's jaw tightened. "Then we hit his lair."

Kihm slid out her data pad, and her fingers flew over the surface before a barely audible chime sounded. On her display, a web of sensor nodes around Aivel's Office shifted from green to muted grey. "Motion sensors around the office are now blind," Kihm said. "Pressure triggers are also suppressed. If anyone walks those tiles, the system will think it's airflow variance."

Astrea nodded once. "Good work. Keep the loop tight. If it hiccups, we back out, and we try again. No improvising."

Mila leaned in, voice low. "You're sure he's monitoring from there?"

Kihm's mouth set in a confident line. "It's the only place on this level with a hardline into the emergency lattice and private encryption keys. If something goes wrong in Atmos, Aivel wants to be the first to know, and the last to be surprised."

Astrea lifted two fingers again, and they slipped forward, while behind them, the cameras kept watching nothing.

Minutes later, they emerged into Aivel's office undetected, and Kihm took the lead, raising a gloved hand to signal that the target had been acquired.

The President paced the length of his office in a dark formal tunic, his face drawn tight. The way he kept glancing back and forth between his comms console made him appear distressed.

Kihm moved first, and Astrea, Brom and Mila followed. Like a whisper, they entered his office, and Kihm pressed a small emitter against the wall near the entrance, activating a localised silence field, a cone of muted sound that enveloped them. "President Aivel," Kihm said calmly, stepping into view.

He froze. "What is this?" he demanded, voice sharp with authority, slipping a weapon from his pocket. "How dare you show your face here, Kimmy K, after your betrayal?"

Kihm moved like the wind, two quick strides, and she grabbed his wrist and projected her power through his body. Just enough that he dropped his weapon, stumbled mid-step, then slumped onto the floor. "Damn," Kihm hissed. "I didn't mean to zap him that hard. I'm out of practice."

"He's alive," Mila said, checking his pulse. "Get the scanner ready."

Brom set the President back in his chair while Kihm deployed a biometric duplicator, a sleek, palm-sized device that projected scanning rings of light over Aivel's hand. The rings pulsed, and a soft chime accompanied each scan.

"We'll need him conscious for a retina scan and voice-code confirmation for full clearance, Kihm said."

Brom grunted. "That ship has sailed."

"I've got something," Mila said, reaching into her medical pack and withdrawing a stim injector. She adjusted the dial and jabbed it into the President's shoulder, causing his eyelids to flutter before they fully opened.

"Where...?"

Kihm took the opportunity to conduct a quick retina scan. "We need to confirm your identity for an emergency override. Your codes, please," Kihm demanded.

He blinked slowly, disoriented. "Override for what?"

"Biometric verification. Speak clearly: 'President Aivel authorises Emergency Code Four-Seven-Tau.'"

The president hesitated.

Brom crouched beside him. “Give us the codes, and we end this without bloodshed.”

Something in Brom’s voice reached him, resignation, finality. His jaw tightened.

“President Aivel... authorises Emergency Code Four-Seven-Tau,” he said.

The biometric duplicator beeped, confirmation accepted. Kihm snapped it shut. “We’re green.”

Brom touched Aivel and delivered sufficient power to render him unconscious, then hoisted him over his shoulder. “Let’s move,” he said.

Minutes later, Astrea, Brom, Mila and Kihm joined Rhen at the central control hub. The air was conditioned and sharp, the kind that belonged to servers and sealed rooms. Console arrays curved around them in clean arcs, and many of the status glyphs pulsed red. Rhen was already at the primary interface, shoulders squared, hands moving with clipped certainty as he peeled back security subroutines.

Astrea’s gaze swept the room once and took in the two prisoners. Novak was restrained to one console bank, wrists bound behind him, and across the hub, well away from him, Roddick sat secured at a separate anchor point, posture rigid, eyes forward. It meant that Ondra and Xander were where they needed to be.

Rhen finally spared them a glance, the barest tilt of his chin, as if to confirm the same assumption. “Looks like they handled the situation,” he said quietly, and returned to the code as another layer fell away. “With the President’s full biometric set in hand,” he added, “we can unlock Atmos’s command architecture and disengage the city’s autonomous AI controls.”

The clock was ticking. Detonations from below would soon destabilise Atmos’s central spine. But now they had what they needed, the codes, the access, and the momentum. The fall of Atmos had begun.

Rhen stood at the primary interface console, the biometric duplicator blinking green.

Brom placed the President's still-unconscious form in a nearby chair.

Astrea paused and listened. "Module control teams are in position," she said. "Waiting on your mark, Rhen."

He entered the codes, aligning them with the fabricated threat spike already inserted into the system. The screen pulsed red. His fingers hovered over the primary console, the President's biometric set still pulsing green beside the input field. He keyed in the threat spike, then stitched it to the Presidential chain, forcing the AI to read the emergency as both real and authorised. The interface hardened from amber to red, and the room's light shifted with it.

The AI's passive voice filled the room. "Multiple critical system failures detected. Thermal escalation in Geothermal Conduit Alpha. Evacuation protocol pending confirmation." A second pane unfolded: EVACUATION PROTOCOL, CLASS OMEGA. DUAL AUTH REQUIRED, THREAT VERIFIED, HUMAN CONFIRMATION PENDING. NOTE: MODULE SEPARATION WILL BE IRREVERSIBLE ON EXECUTION.

Rhen didn't look up. "Run the interlock list."

"Confirming evacuation protocol and pre-separation actions," the AI replied. "Security broadcast issued, and hangar evacuation tone active. Transit systems inhibited, vac-lifts empty and disabled, public corridors empty and sealed. Module bay doors cycling to emergency lockdown. Environmental umbilicals are transferring from the hub manifold to the module reserves. Command pathways rerouted to manual module teams."

Astrea's voice snapped over comms. "Module pilots, standby."

The AI continued, relentless. "Magnetic clamp arrays, armed. Structural shear bolts, primed. Docking collar locks, disengaging. Final confirmation required. Present Presidential authorisation."

Rhen entered the final string, tying it to the President's verified voice-code and retina set they'd just forced through.

The console chimed once, and the AI's tone did not change, but the words carried weight. "Presidential override accepted. Threat signature validated. Evacuation protocol authorised. Emergency separation is initiated. Countdown, T-minus ninety seconds."

A live checklist scrolled as the clock started burning down: "Module bay doors, locked. Umbilicals, released. Separation sequence, armed. Pilots have navigation control."

At T-minus thirty, the AI added the line Rhen needed most. He breathed once. "Execute."

"T-minus ten," the AI said. "Nine. Eight..."

Somewhere deep in the superstructure, Atmos answered with a rumble that travelled through the hub.

"Three. Two. One. Separation command issued." The central display split into four feeds, each module's status lighting up as it peeled away. "All modules have achieved safe separation and are clear. Scuttle condition satisfied."

LIRA THUMBED THE MANUAL override and Module One, Agriculture, shuddered free of the central stem as magnetic clamps released. Emergency thrusters caught the mass, she confirmed Kappa-twelve over comms, cut long-range propulsion at Rhen's mark, and eased it down onto a fertile plateau before triggering Command Limiter Mode. This buried subroutine fused the navigation AI into a permanent root lock so it would never lift again.

Module Two, Habitat, peeled away with a low groan. Naella rode the tremor, stabilisers active, and dropped it into the Outer Scar basin in a surge of dust, then locked it down with the same limiter.

Module Three, Manufacturing, drifted clear toward Zone Delta-five near Gromwell. Vena trimmed the descent, killed long-range thrust, and settled on low-output engines, with a hollow shudder on touchdown and the limiter engaged.

Module Four, Medical and Housing, came down under Ondra's hands with Xander braced beside her, ramps lowering as residents spilled out in confused knots. Ondra and Xander herded them away from cooling thrusters and into open ground, while behind them, the silent hull became a permanent fixture, Command Limiter Mode sealing flight and escape across all four modules.

"NOW THAT THE MODULES are safely down and the engines neutered, it's time to exit the hub," Astrea said.

Rhen's fingers moved over the central hub console, pulling the newest structural schematics to ensure their planned exit route was still valid. The hologrid tightened into a clean cutaway of Atmos, and the answer snapped into place.

"Atmos is a wheel on a spear," he said, angling the projection so it washed over their drawn faces. "The living modules rode the outside of the stem through short galleries and umbilicals, but the central control hub is permanently attached, as are the hub and spoke docks two levels below. His glove traced along a seam so fine it vanished in the strobe light. He pressed twice, then held. A soft click answered, followed by a faint hiss as the panel demagnetised and released. A section of wall shifted a fraction, then swung out on concealed hinges, revealing a recessed cavity, a manual latch wheel, and a stencilled label worn almost smooth read: EMERGENCY SPINE ACCESS, CRAWLER MAINTENANCE TUNNEL.

Nobody looked relieved. They had already tasted that tunnel on the way up, cold metal, dead air, the claustrophobic press of a sealed shaft where your breather was your only friend. Going back into it felt more like a punishment than an escape plan.

Mila's mouth tightened. "You have got to be kidding me."

"No joke," Rhen said. "Breathers back on. Conserve comms. No chatter unless it's critical."

Astrea shifted her stance, eyes on the prisoners. "I'll uncuff them. We need hands for ladders." She stowed the mag-cuffs and kept her weapon high and steady. "You climb when I say. You stop when I say. If you try to bolt, you won't get a second chance."

Novak's jaw tightened. He gave a single, minimal nod.

Roddick swallowed and looked at the dark throat beyond the hatch like it could bite.

Brom brought up the rear, and Aivel was the problem. He could not keep the unconscious man slung over his shoulder on a ladder. He dropped him carefully to a seated lean against the bulkhead, then built a carry in seconds, looping the smarline under Aivel's arms and across his own chest. It was crude and ugly, but effective. Aivel's head lolled, breath shallow behind his breather.

They entered the hatch, then the crawler tunnel, and climbed onto the ladder, running into blackness. All they heard was the faint tick of cooling metal and the soft rasp of boots on rungs.

Rhen went first, then Kihm, then Mila. Novak followed, and Roddick came next, followed by Astrea, who remained above the prisoners, controlling the only direction they could move, muzzle angled down the shaft. Brom went last of all, Aivel cinched to him, every rung a measured fight.

They dropped past the first landing, and the ladder vibrated, a long, low tremor running through the stem. Brom's forearms burned. Aivel's weight dragged him off centre, forcing him to hug the ladder harder than he wanted.

Novak chose that moment. It was not dramatic, not shouted. Just a subtle shift of weight, a calculated misstep, like he was testing the ladder's rhythm. He glanced down once, gauging distance, then moved sideways, trying to slip past Mila and open space between himself and Astrea.

"Stay in line," Astrea warned, voice flat.

Novak ignored it. He slid one hand down the ladder rail, then pivoted his hips out into the open shaft, turning sideways as if gravity was optional. His boots clamped the ladder's outer stile, soles biting metal, and for one breathless instant, it looked like he was about to drop past them in a controlled slide, saving minutes by sacrificing skin.

"Don't do it, Novak," Astrea warned.

Novak shoved off anyway. The dead-air shaft was cold enough to sweat the metal. Condensation filmed the rung edges and side rails, and Novak's soles skated as soon as he committed his weight. He started to slide, fast, gloves squealing, boots sparking once as he tried to clamp again. He slid past Mila. His shoulder clipped her, hard enough to twist her torso. Her grip broke for a fraction of a second.

Mila swung out into nothing, her boots scraping air. Her breath rasped loudly in her mask, sharp and involuntary. She tried to re-grip, fingers scrabbling for metal that wasn't there.

For a heartbeat, Roddick didn't move, as if his body couldn't decide whether to save himself or her. Then he lunged, throwing his weight forward and catching Mila's harness strap with both hands. The jerk nearly tore him off the rungs. His boots slipped, scraped, and found purchase again by sheer force of will. He groaned through his breather, forearms shaking as he hauled her back into the ladder line. "Mila," he grunted, voice raw. "Grab, now."

Mila slammed her hand onto a rung, then the next, locking in with a violence that made the metal ring. She pulled herself against the ladder, chest heaving.

Roddick didn't let go until her grip was solid. When he finally released her strap, his hands were trembling.

Brom saw her go, saw the black space open below her, and his gut dropped with it.

Below them, Novak was still dropping. He tried to turn the slide into control, reaching for the crawler mag track that spiralled down beside the ladder. His glove slapped the smooth surface, skated, and found nothing. For a fraction of a second, his face turned up toward them, eyes burning with rage and disbelief. Then he spun free and fell into the dark. The impact came later, far below, a dull, final sound that travelled up the tunnel.

Roddick stared downward, breathing hard, then looked back at Mila as if surprised by what he'd done.

Astrea's muzzle tracked him immediately. Not gratitude, not softness, just calculation. "Move," she said, voice flat as steel. And they did.

Brom swallowed the taste of panic and kept descending, rung after rung, Aivel's weight grinding into his chest harness.

At last, the shaft widened into a lower service node, pressure door stamped with worn block letters which read: LOWER DOCKING CRADLE ACCESS – EMEGENCY BAY FIVE.

Astrea contacted Serin, who was piloting the yacht. "Be ready in two minutes for a hot pick-up. Docking Bay Five."

"Affirmative," Serin answered.

Rhen spun the manual dogs and hauled the door inward. The air on the other side had taste again, dusty, metallic and alive. Beyond was the lower docking interface corridor, utilitarian plating, cable bundles, and emergency strobes pulsing slowly. Through the duraglass panel in the next pressure hatch, Rhen sighted the docking bay beyond, lit by strobes and emergency strips. He spun the manual dogs and hauled the hatch open.

The moment they stepped through the threshold, the air changed. It was thinner at this altitude, but it was clean, real oxygen, and the first full breath hit like relief. One by one, they tore their breathers free, dragging air into aching lungs. The early morning was a stark contrast to the dark tunnel.

Suddenly, a sleek yacht slid into the lane, running lights reduced to a thin line along its hull. It came in fast, then bled speed in the final metres, thrusters whispering, but the whisper still hit like force, making the deck plates tremble underfoot. Magnetic grapples snapped out with a clack. The yacht lurched once as the field caught, then steadied. Its side hatch irised open, spilling white light into the bay like a clean wound.

"Onboard," Astrea said, voice hard. "Single file. No stops."

Rhen went first, followed by Kihm. Astrea drove Roddick forward with a short, efficient gesture that left no room for debate. Roddick's lip curled, then he saw Astrea's eyes and swallowed whatever he was about to say.

Brom reached the hatch last, Aivel still cinched to his chest. Serin leaned forward from inside the yacht, visor down, all business, and grabbed Aivel's boots to keep them from clipping the frame. Together, they hauled Aivel into the yacht, where tension sat in the air like held breath. The iris closed, and Serin turned, dogging it from the inside with a practised twist—the seal bit with a dull thump. "Strap in," Serin instructed, already dropping into the co-pilot seat beside Rhen, who had taken over.

Harnesses came down. Clasps snapped shut. Kihm locked in, and Astrea shoved Roddick into a jump seat, clipped his belt. "Don't make a move," she murmured.

Mila helped Brom lower Aivel onto a padded bench along the port side.

Aivel did not wake as Brom secured his harness over his chest and hips, so he would not slide when the burn hit.

Mila dropped into the bench seat next to Aivel, and Brom sat beside her. The cabin was crowded, knees and gear and a restrained prisoner, with nowhere to hide what they were feeling, and no room to say it out loud.

Mila's fingers found Brom's first, slipping into his palm beneath the line of the harness strap, small and steady, a silent check.

Brom closed his hand around hers and let the contact anchor him. He leaned closer. His voice stayed low, rough at the edges. "Not much longer now."

Mila held his gaze. Tired, yes, but unbroken. She gave a faint nod, and there was relief in it, and a weight he could not name.

Brom swallowed. Gratitude rose first, sharp and inconvenient, followed by the other thing, the thing he did not have the right to reach for in this moment. He had asked too much already. He would not ask her to stay, not here, not while the world was still falling apart around them. His thumb moved once over her knuckles, a quiet thank you he could not say aloud.

Mila's eyes flicked to his mouth, then back to his eyes, reading what he couldn't put into words. She shifted just enough to lean her head against his shoulder, brief and intimate.

He felt at home with this woman by his side.

A soft warning tone chirped.

Serin's voice cut through the cabin. "Ready to launch."

Brom kept his fingers woven with Mila's as the yacht detached from the cradle with a sharp mechanical release and slid backward.

"Burn," Serin said to Rhen. The acceleration slammed them into their seats. The harness bit across Brom's shoulders, and he felt the yacht's compensators catch a fraction late, just enough to make his stomach lurch.

Mila's breath came quick and loud.

What was left of Atmos rotated in the main display.

Astrea's voice returned, clearer now. "Are we clear of the fracture radius?"

Rhen glanced at the range readout. Numbers climbed in clean increments. "Two clicks," he said. "Three. Four."

Serin's tone stayed flat. "We are now clear."

"Copy," Astrea replied. "This is the point of no return." She punched in a code, and the first charge went. It did not roar, it punched. A shock ripple travelled through Atmos. The central stem split, a bright fracture tearing across its circumference. The spine snapped. For a heartbeat, the lower section hung there as if it might hold, then it folded inward, collapsing like a broken spar. Secondary charges chased the break line upward in brutal, clean steps, severing conduits and stripping panels until the column became debris in the water.

No one moved as they watched the failure cascade.

On the bench, Aivel's head rolled slightly with the vibration through the yacht's frame. Mila steadied him with one hand, thumb at his jaw, checking his breathing by feel.

Rhen's voice was low, final. "No reassembly now. The central spine is gone, and the AI relay core went with it. Even if LOUT returns, nothing is salvageable."

"And the modules are scattered," Astrea added. "Far enough apart that each one stands alone, a series of settlements, not weapons."

Brom stared at the smoke curling from the distant wreck, thin as a pencil line. "We turned a weapon into four villages." His gaze moved to Roddick. "You are going to tell us everything you know about LOUT, uncle, while you still have something worth bargaining with."

Roddick's eyes flicked to the ruined stem on the feed, then away. "LOUT will destroy us. You have signed the Kesk people's death warrant."

"No, uncle," Brom said, voice quiet, lethal. "We have liberated them."

Kihm's smile was faint but real, a sliver of light in a cabin full of restraint and smoke. "This was a good day."

CHAPTER 18

The stars beyond the viewport shimmered like silent witnesses.

President Aivel came to blinking against the capsule's harsh interior lights as the world reassembled itself in fragments. His mouth was dry. His pulse hammered in his ears. The last clear memory he had was Kihm and Brom looking down at him, and then the sudden absence of everything.

A calm mechanical voice filled the cramped chamber. "Escape pod launched. Orbit stabilised. Life support is optimal. Trajectory lock holding. Awaiting retrieval signal."

Aivel's brow furrowed as he pushed himself upright and turned in place, taking in the smooth emergency harnesses, the sealed storage lockers, the single comms console mounted to the bulkhead. His eyes snagged on the screen as it blinked awake. Incoming message. His fingers shook as he tapped to accept.

Kihm and Brom appeared on the display; behind them lay the torn wreckage of Atmos's central spine, a wound of broken structure. They looked composed, almost clinical, as if they were delivering an inspection report rather than a sentence.

"President Aivel," Brom said. His voice was steady and precise. "We appreciate your contribution to our operation. Your biometric codes were essential in severing Atmos from the LOUT infrastructure. Each module has been grounded. Your city is no longer a weapon."

Kihm stepped closer, her gaze level. "You are safe in the escape pod, which is running an encrypted beacon that pings LOUT's central relay every ten minutes."

Brom's expression did not change. "Your job is to tell LOUT never to return to this planet. We are giving you another chance, unlike your son, Waylan, who tried to kill us. If you return, do not expect the same accommodation." The feed cut.

A NEW WINDOW OPENED on the screen, a message already transmitted. The header sat there like a verdict. TO: LOUT High Command. SUBJECT: Retrieval Request. Escape Pod. Coordinates redacted. Status: stable orbit. The pod's onboard AI transmitted a message: "Atmos is no longer operational. Recommend immediate pickup".

Aivel's throat tightened until breathing hurt. Regret did not arrive cleanly. It came mixed with rage, with grief, with the hollow shock of a world that had slipped out of his hands.

Outside the viewport, space stretched in every direction, endless and indifferent. The capsule drifted on, sealed and obedient, broadcasting its location like a flare. The signal reached a deep-space command cruiser, the Resolute Edge.

A sensor technician straightened at his console as a sharp alert chimed through the bridge. "Sir. Encrypted transmission coming through the relay web. The origin point is the planetary orbit on the outer fringe. Presidential code. Tier One."

Commander Yelth crossed the deck in three strides and leaned over the display as the file decrypted. His eyes narrowed. "Authentic?"

"Fully verified as a pod from Orphis-8," the technician said. "It is broadcasting continuously."

Yelth read the brief. His jaw set as the line about Atmos being no longer operational sank in. "What happened down there?" He straightened and turned to his comms officer. "Set a recovery course. I want that pod in our hold within the hour."

"And the planet?" the officer asked, careful with his tone.

For a moment, Yelth's expression gave nothing away. Then his gaze hardened, as if he had made the decision long ago and was only now being reminded to act on it. "LOUT will deal with them soon enough."

EPILOGUE

Descent Vector on the planet of Rotari – Early Morning

The Halo Insurgent III cut through Rotari's cloud layer, and sunlight spilled across the landscape and the canopy below glittered with morning dew. Farther out, the first hard lines of new construction were taking shape on the surface of Aliskant, scaffolds and framework rising like bones under fresh skin. The ship banked toward a clearing that marked the entry point to the underground hangars. Approach lights strobed in soft sequence, guiding them home.

Astrea sat with her arms crossed, a commander's posture she could not fully shed, even now. The absence of her neural network still felt like standing on unfamiliar ground. Around her were the women she had commanded, sitting shoulder to shoulder, eyes tracking the contours of Rotari. Her thoughts flicked to Orella, missing out on all the possibilities of this new life.

The landing thrusters hissed, and the shuttle settled onto the deck with a final, gentle shudder. When the hatch irised open, Rotari's hangar air smelt of oil, warm metal, ozone, and something faintly mineral. Astrea's soldiers stepped out in small groups, controlled and quiet. Their boots hit the deck with a relief they would never have admitted to.

Roddick went with them, not as one of them, and not yet as a prisoner they were ready to discard. They had brought him because no one trusted the alternative. If he had anything useful left in him, it would be put to work under watch. If he did not, he would be placed somewhere secure enough that he could never do damage again.

Mila paused at the threshold and looked back. Brom was behind her, scanning the hangar with guarded curiosity, shoulders squared, attention set like a weapon even in peace.

"Not what you expected?" Mila asked, lips curving.

Brom gave a slow grin. "The scenery on our descent was persuasive."

"Persuasive," she echoed, suspicious.

Brom stepped closer until they were almost shoulder to shoulder. "While I'm here to negotiate an alliance and explore Rotari," he said, voice low, "I'm most interested in exploring more private terrain."

Mila rolled her eyes, but she did not move away. "Is that right?"

"That's practically a welcome," he murmured, and his gaze flicked to her mouth for the briefest moment, "coming from you."

Mila held his look, then her voice softened on the next words, the way it always did when the subject mattered. "You're going to meet my people," she said. "Properly, this time. Not through comms and crisis." She angled her head toward the hangar beyond, where voices carried, and boots struck the deck in a rhythm that sounded like home.

"Unfortunately, you won't meet Aurora yet," Mila said, the smile still there, but tempered. "She's from Earth, and she's currently on her way back from an unscheduled trip with Rorkk. Something about pulling her brother and his mother out of trouble." Her amusement returned, warm at the edges. "As an Aerospace engineer, she'll want details of all your spaceships, and she'll be running designs in her head the entire time. She can also breathe underwater, so don't be surprised if she disappears into the bay for an hour and comes back with a better idea than the one you started with. She can smell new blood in a room from a kilometre away, and she will have questions before you have even taken your boots off."

She let that land, then her expression shifted, fondness tightening into something sharper.

"And Rorkk," Mila continued, his name carrying weight. "Purely tactical. He'll pretend he's indifferent. He won't be. He's the reason half this place is still standing." Her mouth curved faintly. "Aurora managed to get under his skin, and he pretends he hates it."

Mila's gaze lifted. "And those two," she added, nodding toward the figures approaching. "Stacey and Corey are from Earth, too, in their own very specific way. They are clones of Earthlings," she said, like it was the least strange thing she had ever had to explain. "I'll tell you later."

Brom's eyes sharpened, instinctively cataloguing allies he had not met. "And Dane, whom Rhen has regularly mentioned."

Mila met his eyes. "Rhen's half-brother. Technical wizard, laid back to the point it looks like laziness, right up until you realise he has already solved the problem and is waiting for everyone else to catch up." The corner of her mouth twitched. "I'm looking forward to introducing you. Although he may take you to task for kidnapping Rhen."

Brom huffed a short laugh, some of the tension bleeding out of his posture.

Mila stepped down onto the deck, then glanced back at him. "Come on."

Rhen watched Astrea from the hangar deck, then followed at a measured pace, keeping his distance, careful not to crowd her. She sensed him anyway. She always did.

She halted mid-step, eyes sweeping the hangar as if peace might still try to ambush her. Rhen could almost see the checklist running behind her stare, exits, sightlines, cover, choke points, fields of fire, and the way her soldiers fanned out without instruction, overlapping coverage by instinct, comfort never part of the calculation. Peace had not changed her habits; it had only stripped away the excuses for them. Astrea's shoulders tightened a fraction, then forced themselves loose, as if she refused to give her body permission to flinch.

He stopped beside her, close enough that he could speak without comms, without witnesses reading his mouth. “We should talk,” Rhen said quietly.

Astrea kept her gaze forward, eyes tracking the hangar ceiling. “Not here.”

“It's never here,” he replied, and there was no accusation in it, only fatigue, and something warmer he did not want to name. “You keep choosing the next task, the next threat, the next perimeter.”

Her jaw flexed, and her command posture slid into place like armour. “If I don't, everything collapses.”

Rhen glanced toward the soldiers, their faces turned up to the hangar's open throat, breathing in air that did not taste like Atmos. “They're not yours to hold up alone anymore.”

Astrea's eyes flicked to him, sharp, assessing, and for a heartbeat, he saw the woman behind the weaponised training, the one who had woken up and realised what had been done to her. She swallowed once, controlled.

“You disabled my neural network,” she said, voice low.

“I interrupted the routines,” Rhen corrected, softer. “I released the real you.”

Astrea's gaze dropped briefly to her own hands, as if checking whether they still belonged to her. When she looked up again, the ice was still there, but it had cracks.

Silence pressed in, filled with excited greetings and the distant hum of the ship powering down. A new world was forming around old damage.

Astrea took one step forward, then stopped, as if movement might become confession. She didn't look at him when she spoke again. “I don't know what I am without command,” she said, barely above breath.

Rhen's chest tightened, a response he refused to let show too much. “Then don't find out alone.”

Astrea turned, finally. "Not here," she repeated, but this time the words were different. Not a refusal, a boundary.

As she moved past him, her fingers brushed his wrist, brief and deliberate, the smallest touch with the heaviest weight, a promise, and a warning. Then Astrea was gone, absorbed into purpose and into the cluster of soldiers moving to greet Gaia, who welcomed those she once served beside.

Rhen stood for a moment, already knowing he would follow, not as her subordinate or her colleague, but as the one person who had seen her wake up, and didn't look away.

SOUTHERN RIDGE, LATER That Afternoon

Mila and Brom sat atop the Southern Ridge, a natural overlook above a stream-fed valley. The sun was setting over the forest canopy, casting everything in yellow, orange and red hues. Below them, Aliskant's surface works blinked in measured sequences, power cycling, systems waking, a civilisation relearning how to live above ground.

Mila sat next to Brom, who leaned back against sun-warmed stone, legs outstretched, one hand resting on his knee as if he was practising the shape of stillness.

"So," Mila began, sipping from a flask of local brew, "your father is holding the fort."

Brom nodded once. "He told me I needed time to look past my own borders," he said. "Time to decide what comes next. He's already assigned Flynn to shut down the Blackheart Mine and arrest the ones running it, if they haven't already scarpered. After that, we mine responsibly, droids only, no bodies in the dark." He glanced toward the horizon, which held its own kind of promise. "I would like to study the Rotari mines, because these people have crystals in their bloodstream." His mouth tightened. "And I need to build a new home. The last one is gone."

"So you are planning to return home," Mila said carefully, as if the words might cut.

"Yes." His gaze drifted to the valley lights, unfocused, as though he could see past the ridge and into the future. "Just not tonight. Not yet."

Mila watched him, reading the strain beneath the calm. "Because of Xander and Oxana."

Brom exhaled slowly. "They won't become my children in a single moment," he said, voice low and steady. "Not after years of being taught a different truth. They need time in the middle, with family around them, and choices that are real."

Mila's expression softened, the edge of her teasing gone. "How are they doing?"

Brom's mouth tightened briefly, the closest he came to pain. "Kihm says Xander is trying to outrun what he did. Volunteering for tasks he is not asked to do." He paused. "He hugged me before I left, tears in his eyes, and I realised guilt can be more dangerous than anger. It makes a boy brave in all the wrong ways."

"And Oxana?" Mila prompted.

"Oxana is quieter," Brom said. "She does not offer anything she cannot stand behind. She observes. She measures. She is learning her new world in silence, deciding what it is worth, and deciding what I am worth." His eyes flicked to Mila. "I cannot blame her."

Mila nodded once, slowly. She understood trust as a process, not an event.

"I will not push them," Brom said. "I will show up. I will keep my promises. I will let the truth stand without dressing it in excuses. And when the dust settles," he added, "I will give them one certainty they can hold onto. I will be there when they are ready. On their terms. Family beside them, no pressure, no speeches, and a planet that does not belong to LOUT. Kihm has a chance to establish her company on her own terms, but she will need the family's help."

Mila arched an eyebrow, and the warmth returned to her face. "And what else are you hoping to find here, exactly?"

Brom turned toward her. "Something worth building," he said.

She snorted, but her eyes sharpened. "You think you could lure me back to your planet after everything that happened?"

"I would never ask you to be anything less than what you are," he said. "But I would ask you to consider something new."

Mila went quiet.

Brom leaned in slightly, voice lower now, intimate. "Maybe not today. But one day. I want to see what we could be if neither of us were fighting enemies."

Her fingers brushed the edge of his, deliberately casual. "You think I would give up my research," she asked, "my medical career, my work?"

"No," he murmured. "I would not ask you to give that up."

She narrowed her eyes, a flicker of a smile breaking through. "You are asking a lot, Mister."

"And yet," Brom said, leaning closer, "you have not walked away or said no."

Their hands met, firm and real.

Mila tilted her head up, meeting his eyes, familiar and intelligent, and Brom lowered his lips to hers. The kiss was unhurried and deep, the kind that curled through the body and straight into the soul, equal parts heat and impossible comfort.

His fingers threaded into her hair, angling her face, and Mila's control softened into something more dangerous than surrender. It became a choice.

She held his shoulders, breathed him in, and for a moment there was nothing but the weight of him, steady and unyielding, and the tenderness she had never allowed herself to want.

When they finally broke apart, Brom rested his forehead against hers.

"No big conversations tonight."

Mila's breath trembled once, then steadied. "But they are coming."

"Yes," he said. "And when they do, I want you beside me."

Mila's mouth curved, faint, real.

"I am asking you to choose," Brom added quietly, "if you want to."

She held his gaze, and the answer settled in her grip. "Come home with me."

Then a chime from Brom's data pad cut through the peace. Rhen.

Mila's head lifted at once, the warmth in her chest tightening into alertness. Brom's hand was already on the channel.

Rhen's voice came through sharper than she had ever heard it, clipped with controlled urgency. "We've got a signal. Not ours, not Rotari's. It is riding a dead band, a ghost frequency. No message, no ping, just interference, like something heavy moving through quiet air."

Brom sat forward, eyes narrowing into the dark beyond the ridge. "What kind of interference?"

"It is not behaving like a ship," Rhen said. "No beacon, no comms handshake, no stable trajectory. It flickers in and out, like it is crossing thresholds it should not be able to cross." A brief pause, the faintest crackle of secondary feeds. "It just tripped the outer field and passed straight through the planet's forcefield as if it was recognised."

Mila felt the back of her neck go cold. "How can that happen? I thought Rotari was secure."

"We don't know. It shouldn't be possible," Rhen said, and that uncertainty from him was the worst part. "Dane and Gaia are on it, but the signature doesn't match anything we have catalogued. It's fast and bleeding altitude over the southern ocean. If it's a craft, it's not under control." Another pause, shorter, sharper. "And the field didn't settle clean after it passed."

Brom's jaw set. "What do you mean, it didn't settle?"

Rhen did not answer immediately. When he did, his tone was tighter. "A second disturbance followed in its wake, smaller, cleaner, deliberate. That one is moving toward the Ardent Archipelago, Sector Nine."

Mila's fingers tightened around Brom's. Not protective, not possessive, just real.

"Where," Brom asked quietly, "is the first impact point?"

Rhen did not hesitate. "South grid, thirty clicks off the shelf. Whatever it is, it is coming down. You both need to return here, now, just in case."

Brom was already on his feet.

Mila rose with him, the quiet of Rotari falling away as if it had never existed.

The End

ABOUT THE AUTHOR

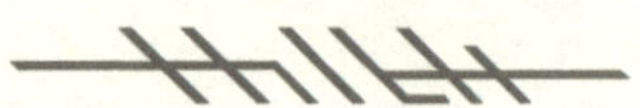

AMANDA LABROOY'S LOVE of science fiction led her to create a universe bursting with limitless possibilities, teaming with vibrant characters, strong female leads, space battles, daring escapades, captivating relationships and boundless destinations. As the stories unravelled, she couldn't let it conclude with a single book. So, it expanded into a series, each shining a light on different characters and their inspiring journeys in the Crystaverse Chronicles:

When she isn't writing, she likes cultivating her vegetable garden, visiting popular local food and craft markets, swimming and travelling. She also enjoys tracking down rare clothing gems at vintage and charity shops and remaking them into something fabulous.

www.ingramcontent.com/pod-product-compliance
Lightning Source LLC
LaVergne TN
LVHW041111080826
845145LV00007B/1765